Stephen McCranie's

SPACE BOY

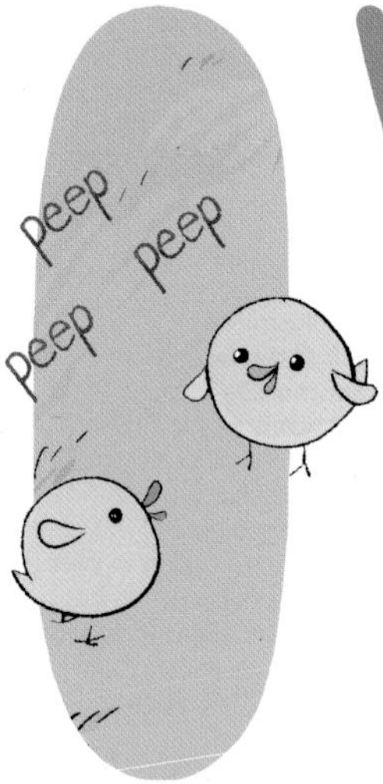
peep
peep
peep

VOLUME 3

Written and illustrated by
STEPHEN McCRANIE

DARK HORSE BOOKS

President and Publisher **Mike Richardson**

Editor **Shantel LaRocque**

Assistant Editor **Brett Israel**

Designer **Cindy Cacerez-Sprague**

Digital Art Technician **Allyson Haller**

STEPHEN MCCRANIE'S SPACE BOY VOLUME 3

Space Boy™ © 2019 Stephen McCranie. All rights reserved. Dark Horse Books® and the Dark Horse logo are registered trademarks of Dark Horse Comics, Inc. All rights reserved. No portion of this publication may be reproduced or transmitted, in any form or by any means, without the express written permission of Dark Horse Comics, Inc. Names, characters, places, and incidents featured in this publication either are the product of the author's imagination or are used fictitiously. Any resemblance to actual persons (living or dead), events, institutions, or locales, without satiric intent, is coincidental.

This book collects *Space Boy* episodes 33–48, previously published online at WebToons.com.

Library of Congress Cataloging-in-Publication Data

Names: McCranie, Stephen, 1987- writer, illustrator.
Title: Space Boy / written and illustrated by Stephen McCranie.
Other titles: At head of title: Stephen McCranie's
Description: First edition. | Milwaukie, OR : Dark Horse Books, 2018- | v. 1: "This book collects Space Boy episodes 1-16 previously published online at WebToons.com." | v. 2: "This book collects Space Boy episodes 17-32, previously published online at WebToons.com." | v. 3: "This book collects Space Boy episodes 33-48, previously published online at WebToons.com." | Summary: Amy lives on a colony in deep space, but when her father loses his job the family moves back to Earth, where she has to adapt to heavier gravity, a new school, and a strange boy with no flavor.
Identifiers: LCCN 2017053602| ISBN 9781506706481 (v. 1) | ISBN 9781506706801 (v. 2) | ISBN 9781506708423 (v. 3)
Subjects: LCSH: Graphic novels. | CYAC: Graphic novels. | Science fiction. | Moving, Household--Fiction. | Self-perception--Fiction. | Friendship--Fiction.
Classification: LCC PZ7.7.M42 Sp 2018 | DDC 741.5/973--dc23
LC record available at https://lccn.loc.gov/2017053602

Published by Dark Horse Books
A division of Dark Horse Comics, Inc.
10956 SE Main Street | Milwaukie, OR 97222
StephenMcCranie.com | DarkHorse.com

To find a comics shop in your area, visit comicshoplocator.com

First edition: February 2019
ISBN 978-1-50670-842-3
10 9 8 7 6 5 4 3 2 1
Printed in China

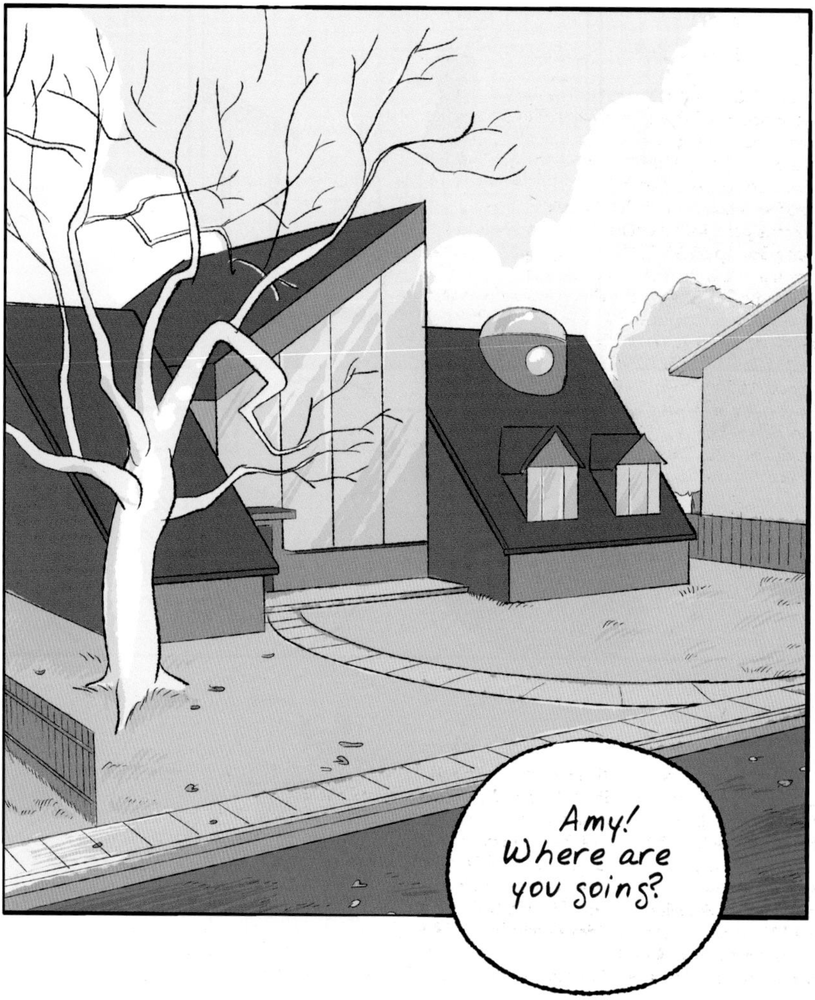
Amy! Where are you going?

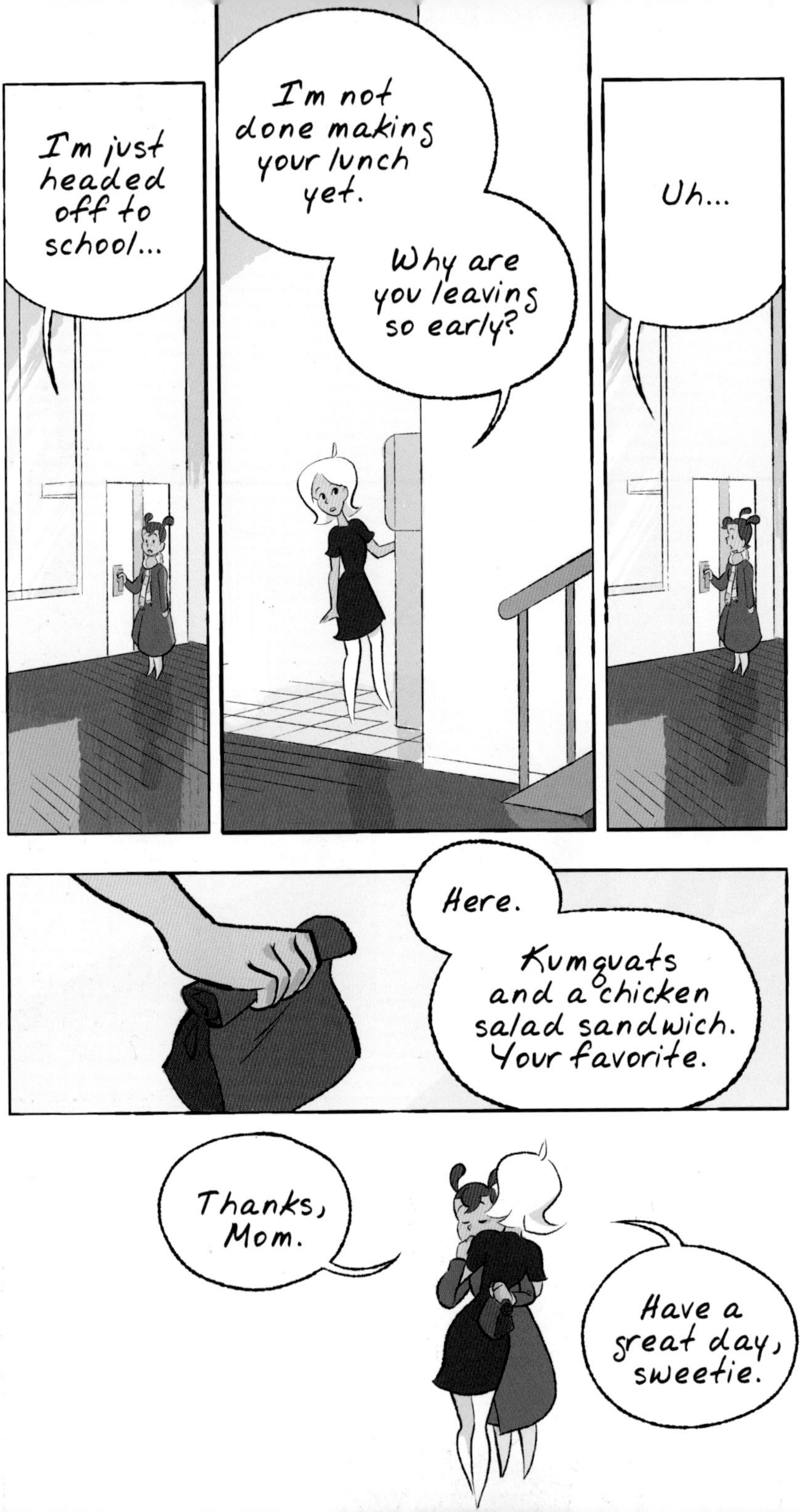
I'm just headed off to school...
I'm not done making your lunch yet.
Why are you leaving so early?
Uh...
Here.
Kumquats and a chicken salad sandwich. Your favorite.
Thanks, Mom.
Have a great day, sweetie.

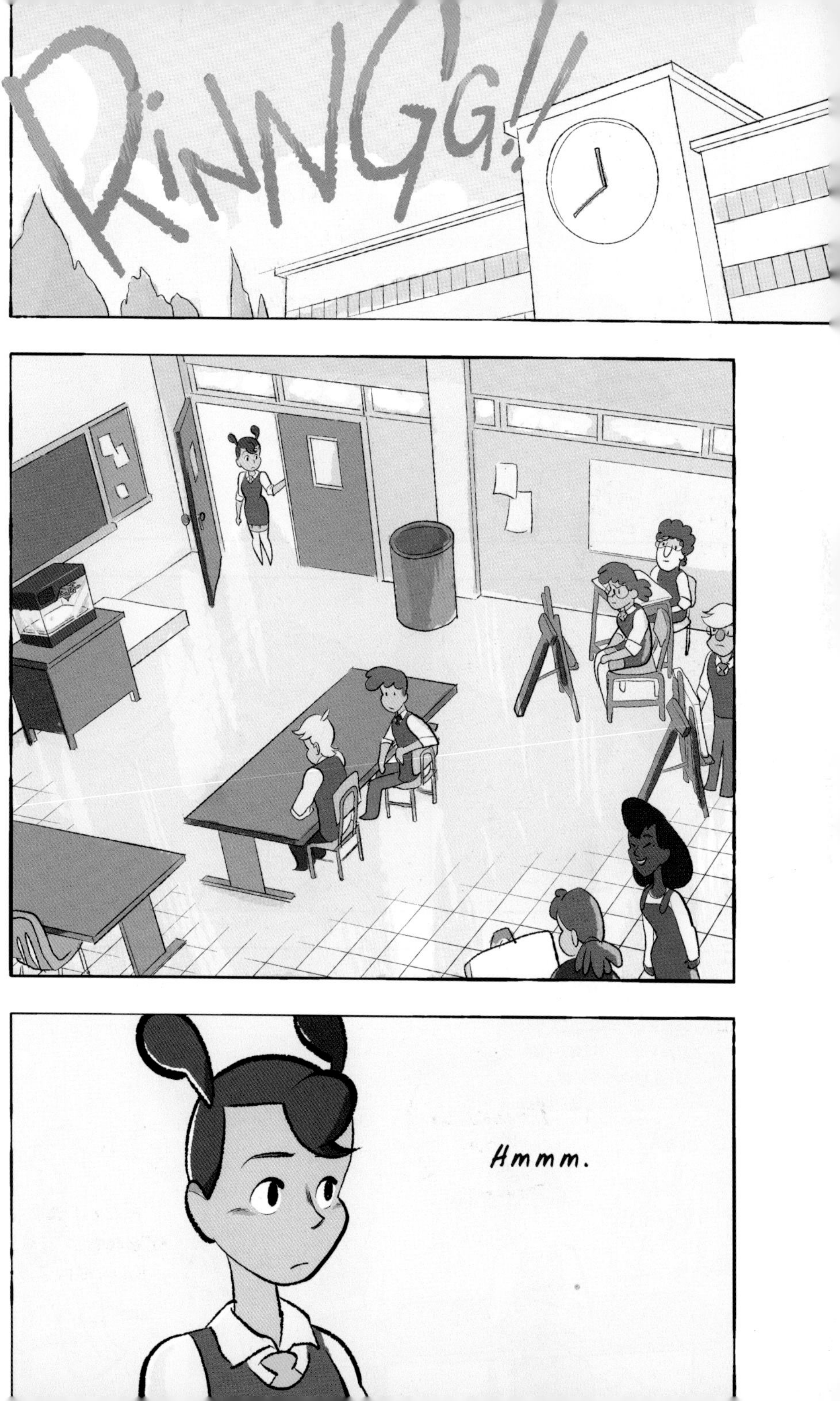
RiNNGG!!
Hmmm.

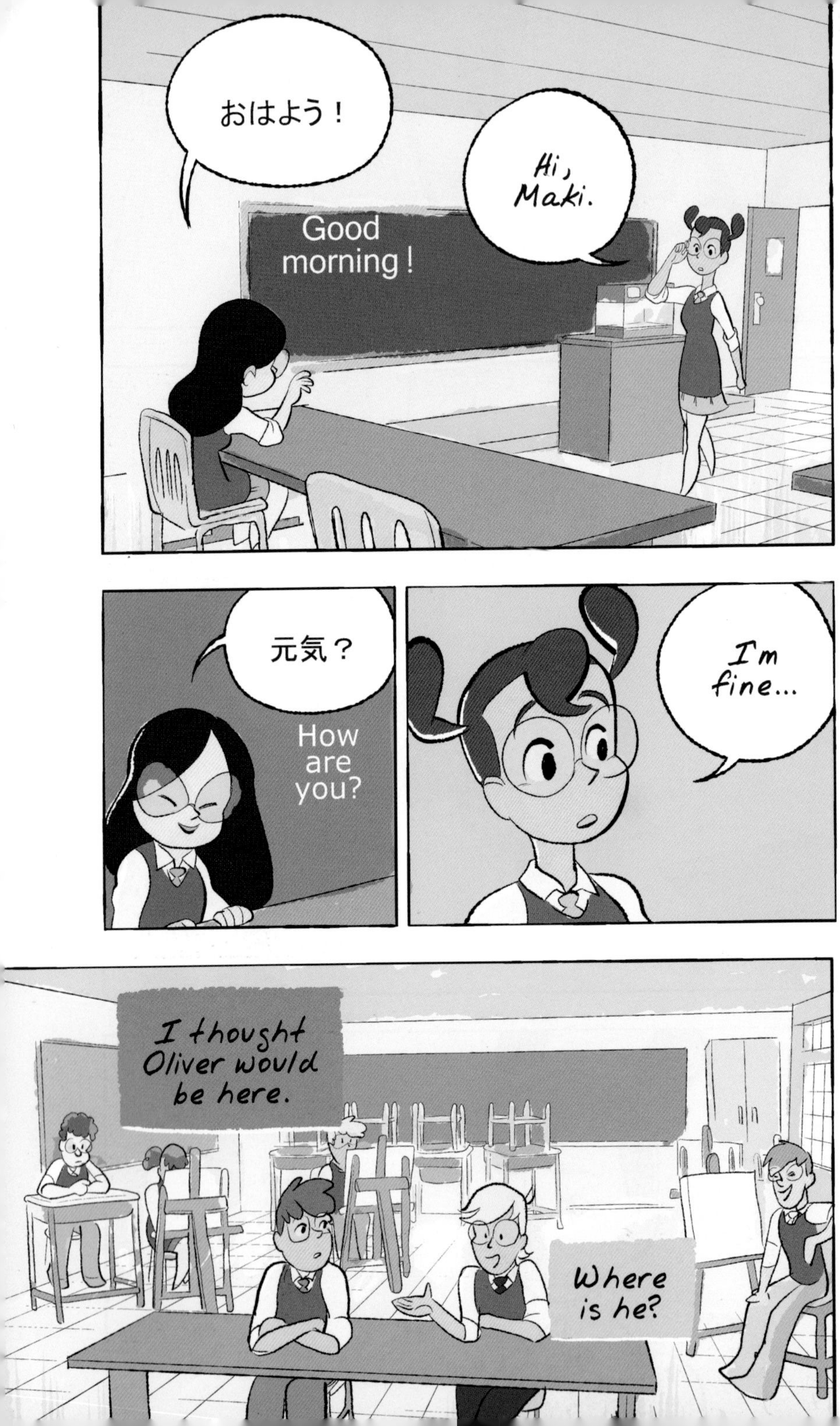
おはよう！
Good morning!
Hi, Maki.
元気？
How are you?
I'm fine...
I thought Oliver would be here.
Where is he?

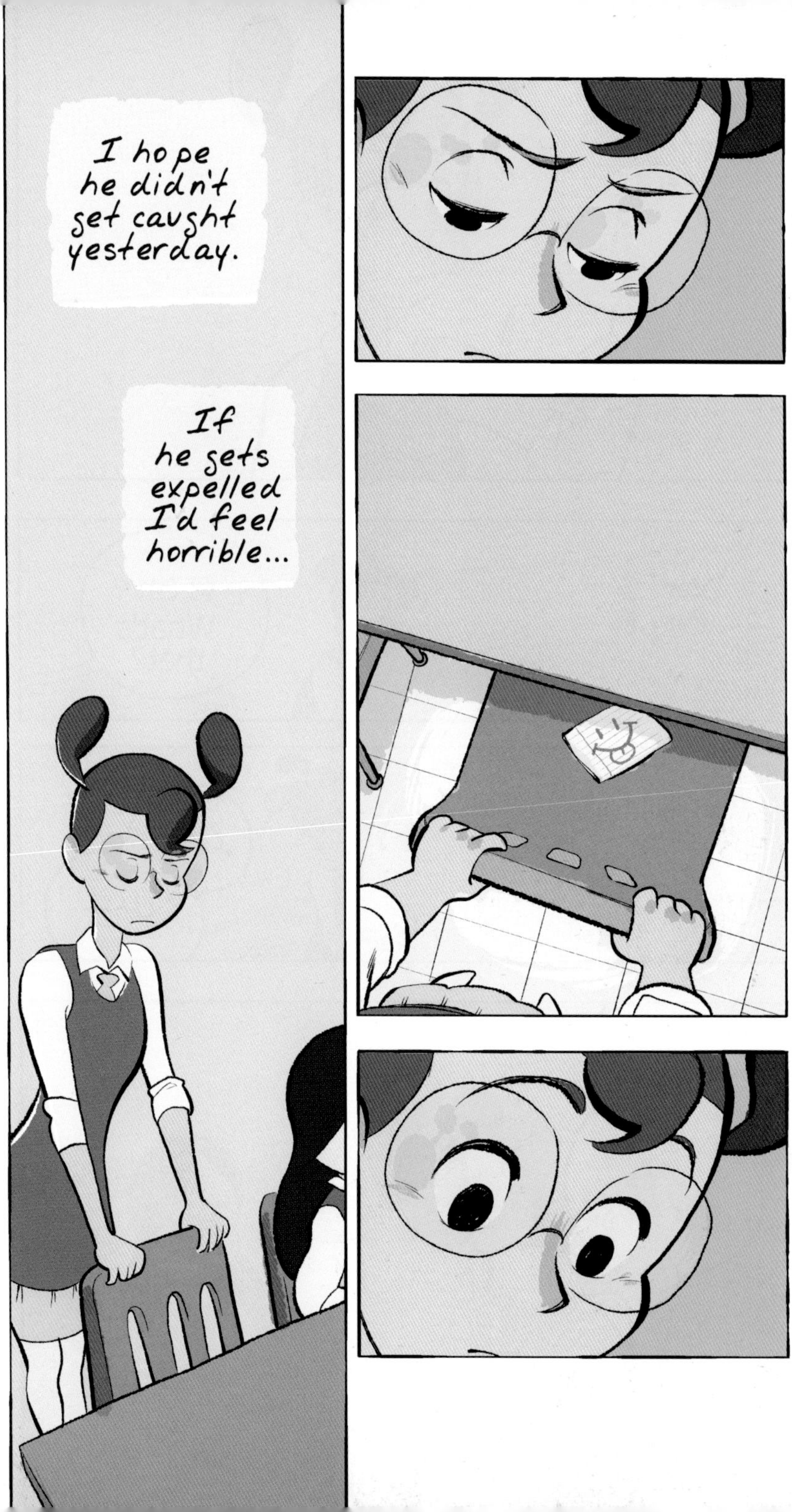
I hope he didn't get caught yesterday.
If he gets expelled I'd feel horrible...

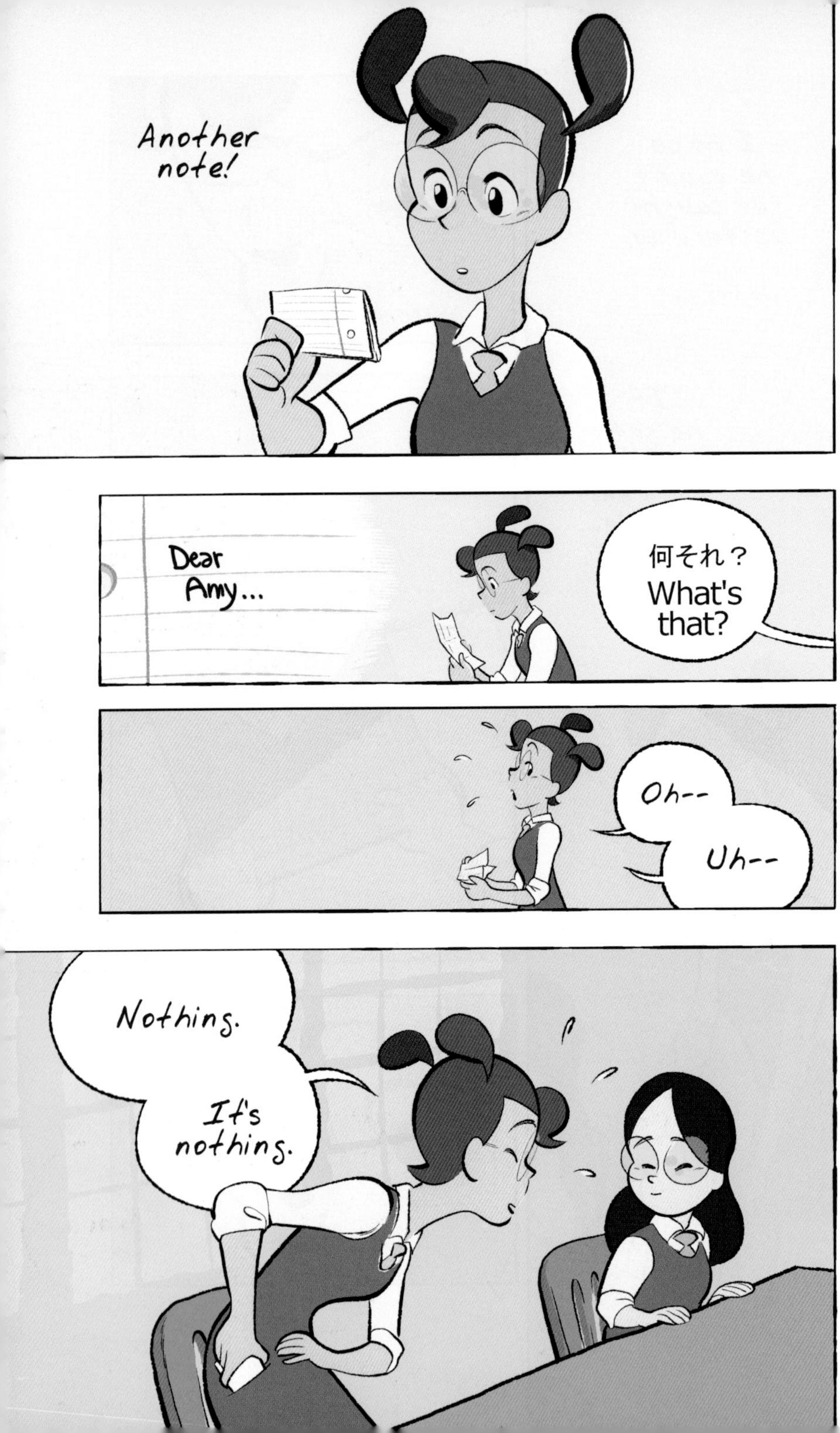
Another note!
Dear Amy...
何それ？
What's that?
Oh--
Uh--
Nothing.
It's nothing.

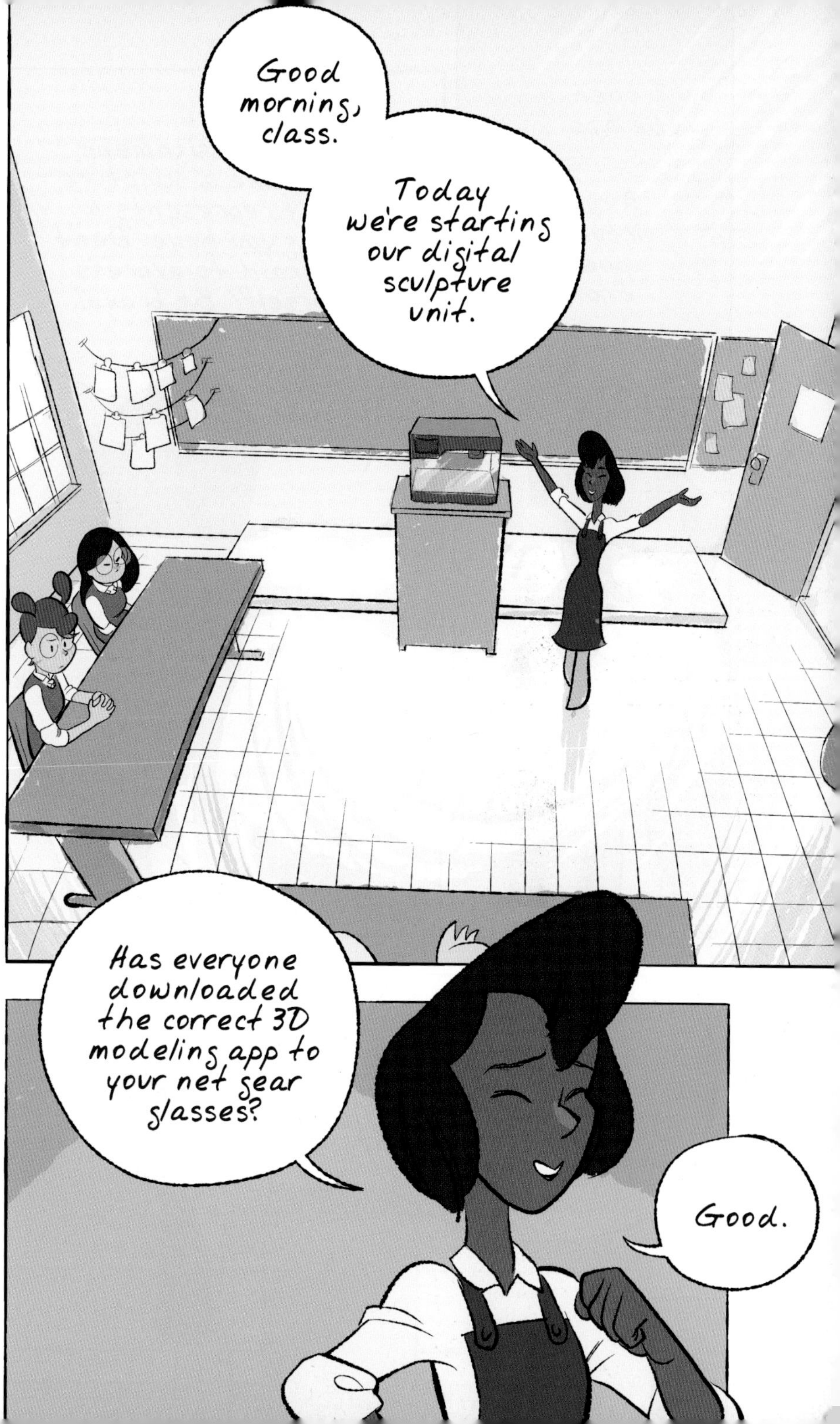
Good morning, class.
Today we're starting our digital sculpture unit.
Has everyone downloaded the correct 3D modeling app to your net gear glasses?
Good.

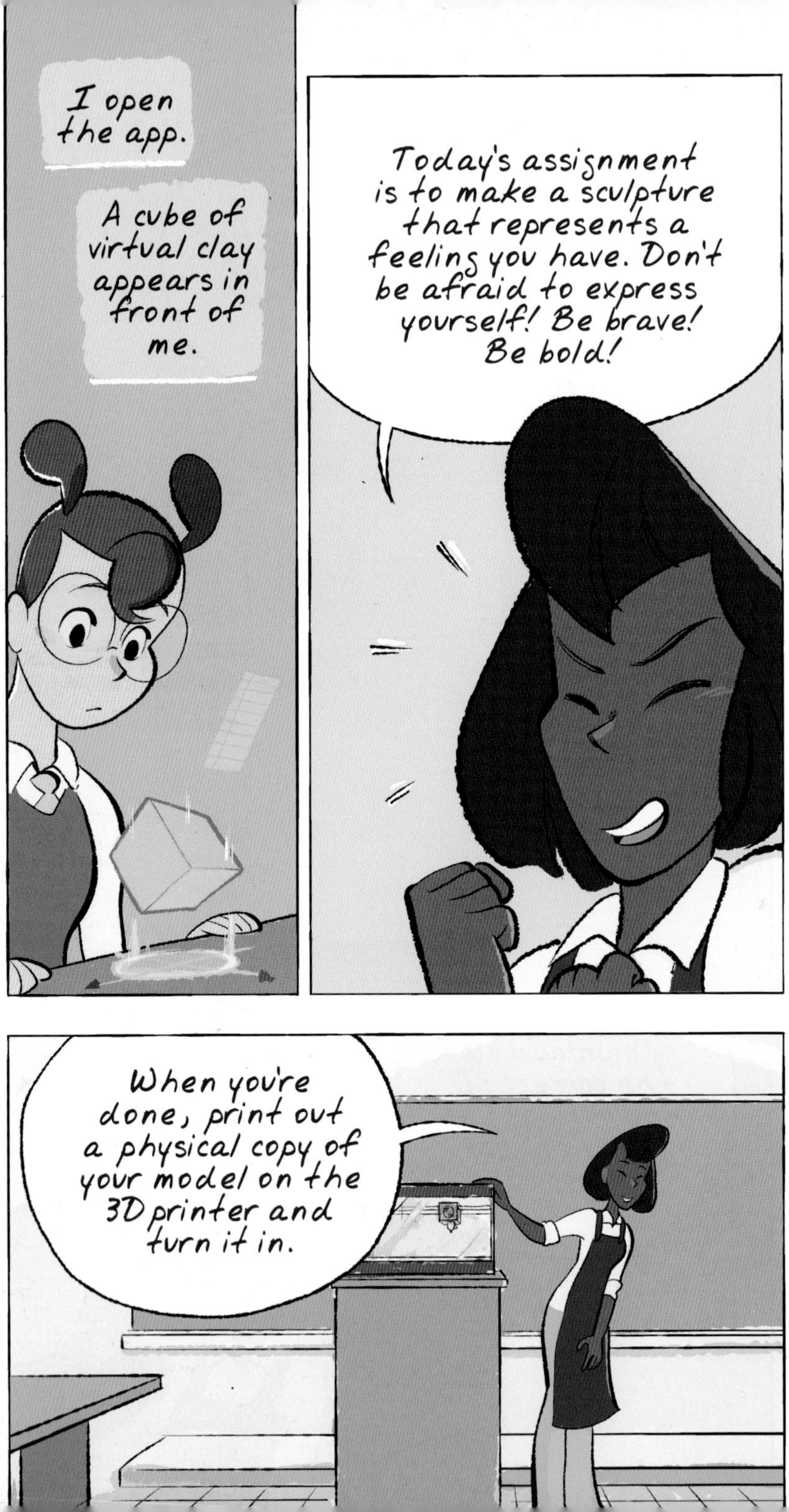
I open the app.
A cube of virtual clay appears in front of me.
Today's assignment is to make a sculpture that represents a feeling you have. Don't be afraid to express yourself! Be brave! Be bold!
When you're done, print out a physical copy of your model on the 3D printer and turn it in.

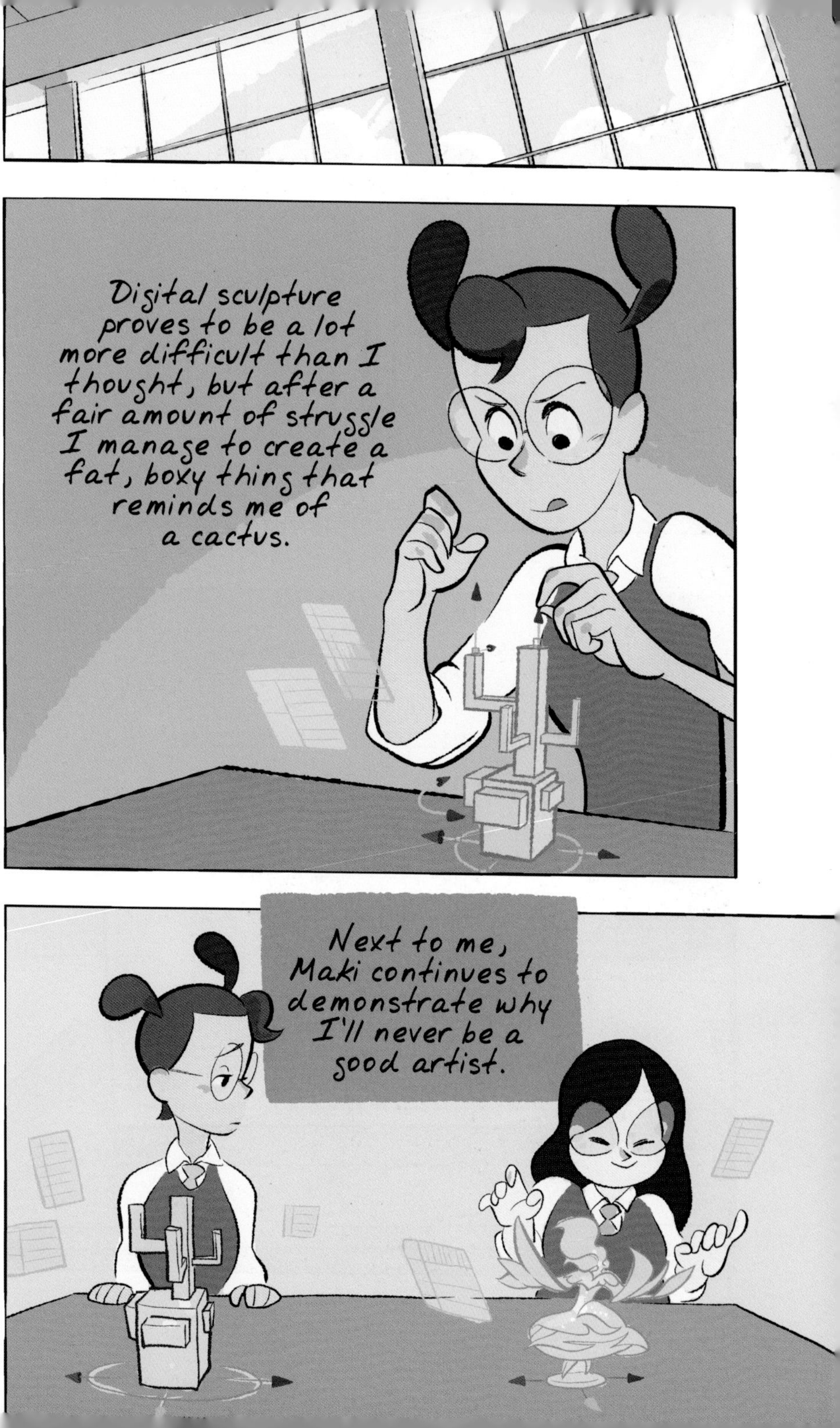
Digital sculpture proves to be a lot more difficult than I thought, but after a fair amount of struggle I manage to create a fat, boxy thing that reminds me of a cactus.
Next to me, Maki continues to demonstrate why I'll never be a good artist.

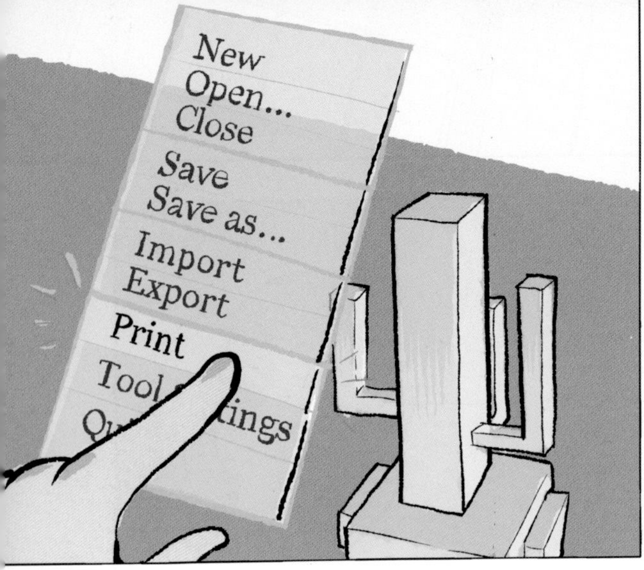
New
Open...
Close
Save
Save as...
Import
Export
Print

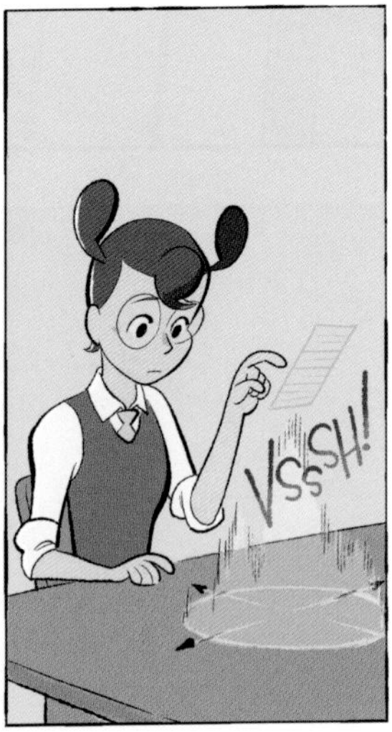
VSSSH!

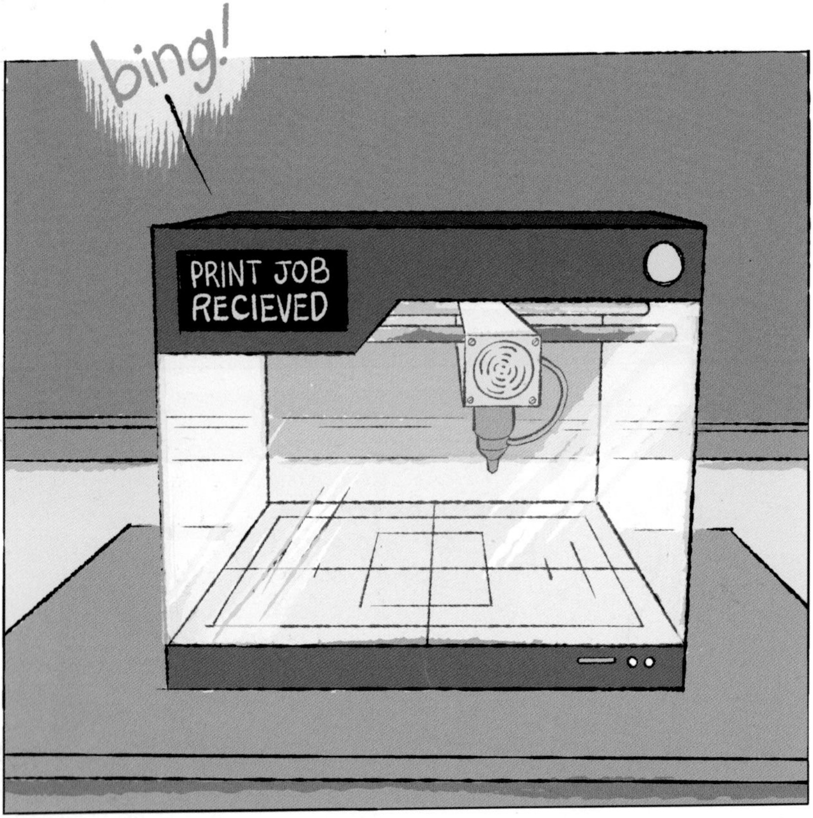
bing!
PRINT JOB RECIEVED

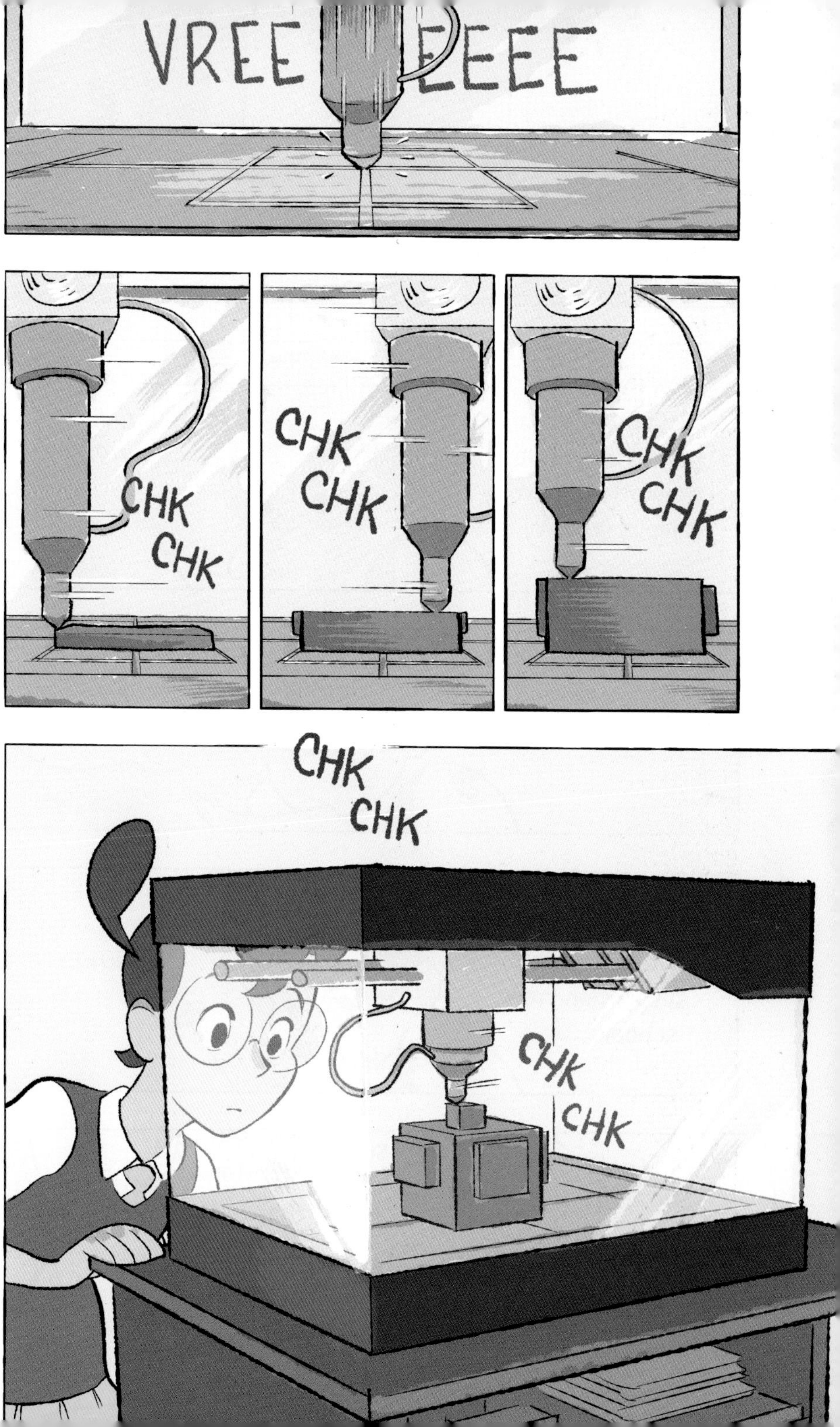
VREE EEEE
CHK
CHK
CHK
CHK
CHK
CHK
CHK
CHK
CHK
CHK

Dear Amy,
Yesterday after we parted ways I was promptly caught by campus security.

Oh no!

Don't worry. I wasn't expelled.

Phew!

I did however get a three day suspension from school.

Aww...

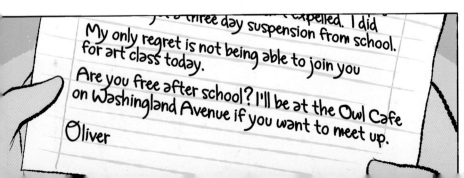

...three day suspension from school. I did

My only regret is not being able to join you for art class today.

Are you free after school? I'll be at the Owl Cafe on Washingland Avenue if you want to meet up.

Oliver

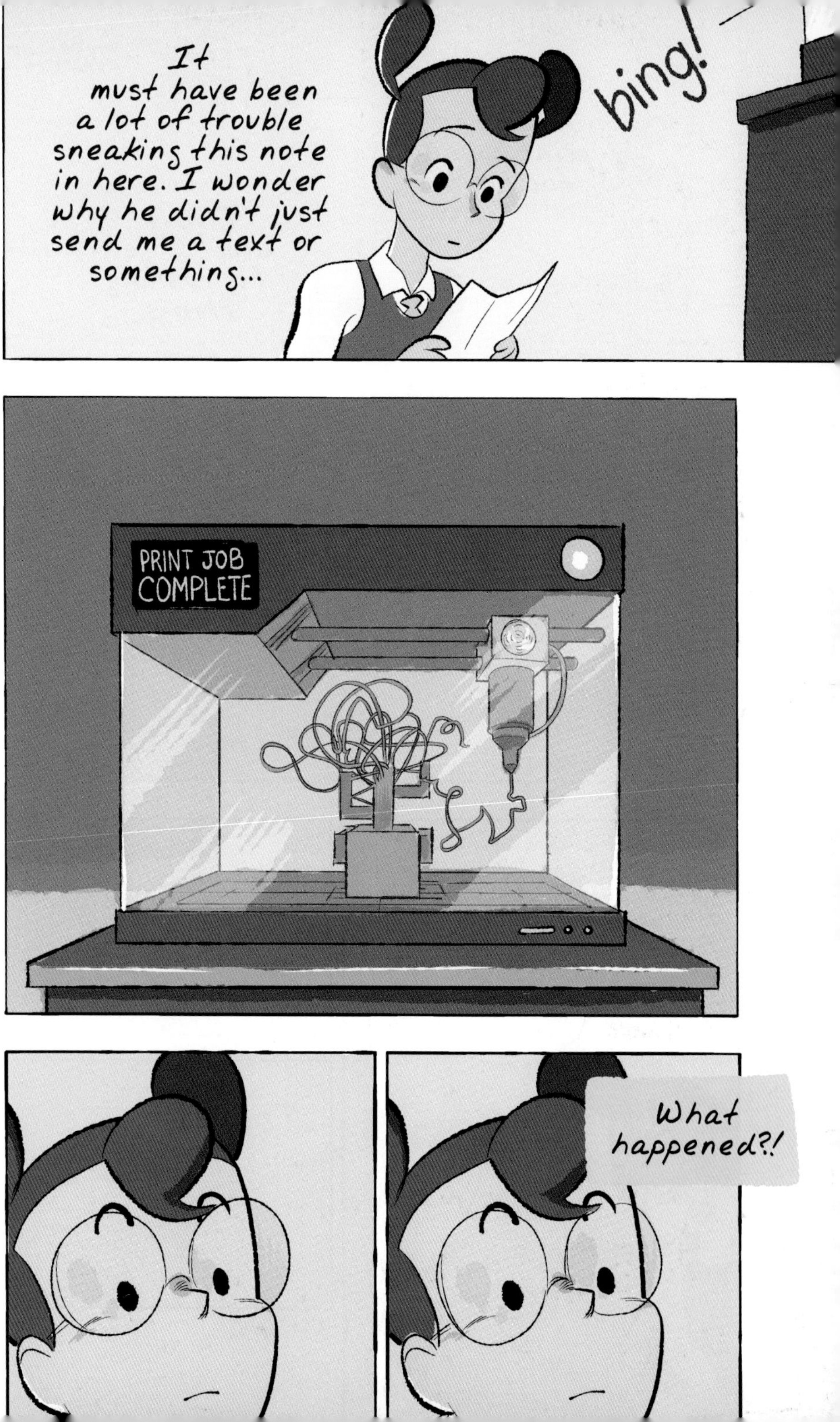
It must have been a lot of trouble sneaking this note in here. I wonder why he didn't just send me a text or something...
bing!
PRINT JOB COMPLETE
What happened?!

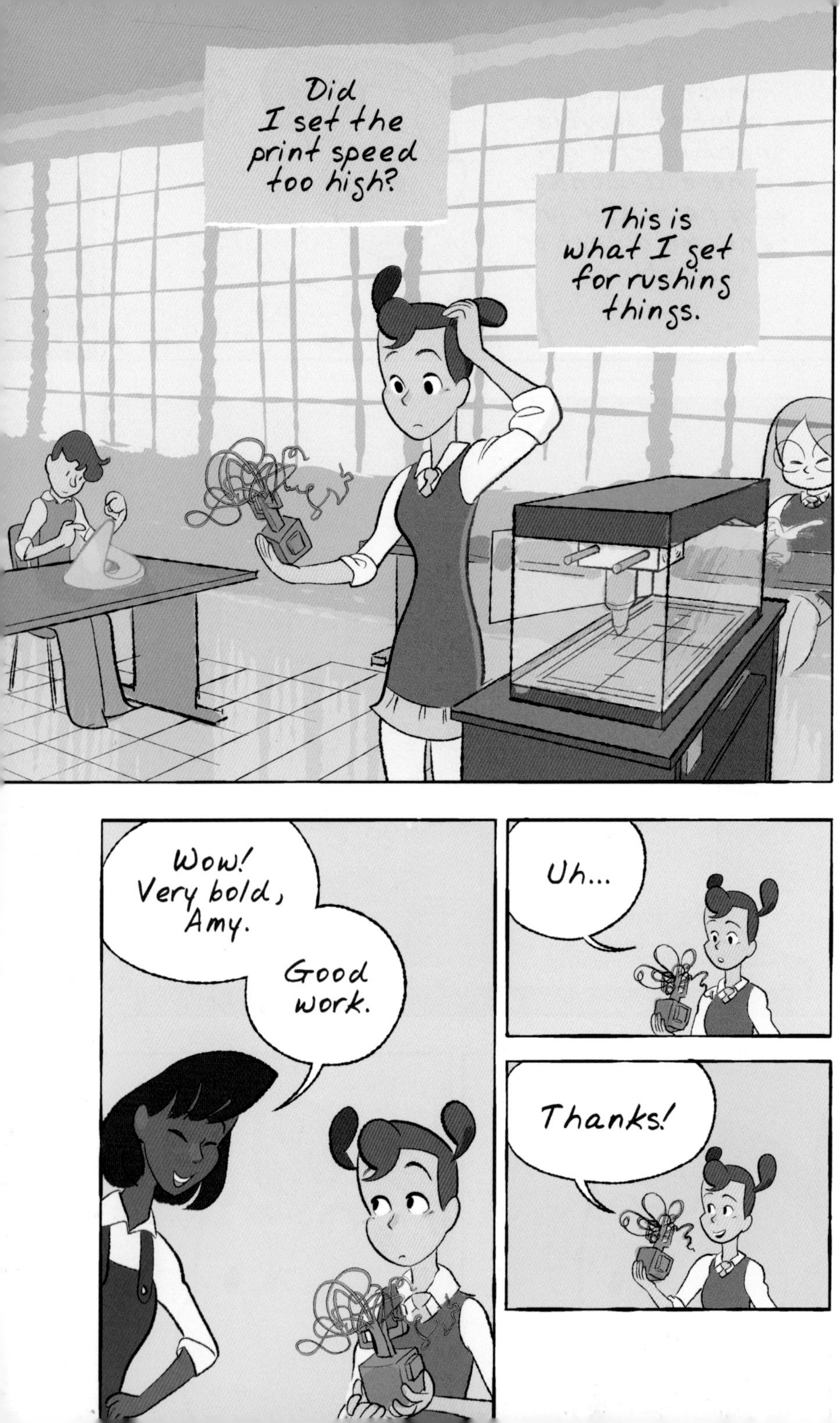
Did I set the print speed too high?
This is what I set for rushing things.
Wow! Very bold, Amy.
Good work.
Uh...
Thanks!

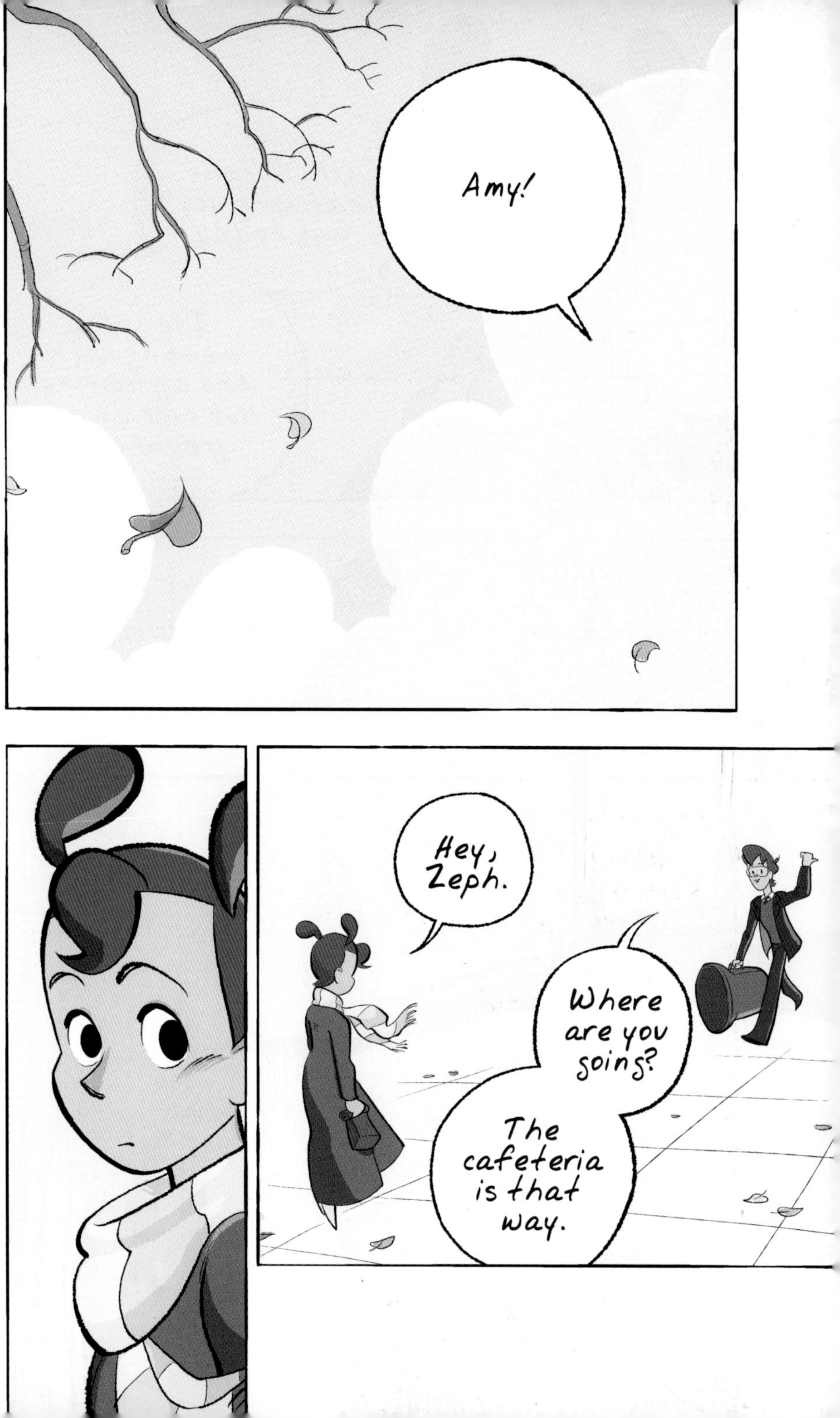
Amy!
Hey, Zeph.
Where are you going?
The cafeteria is that way.

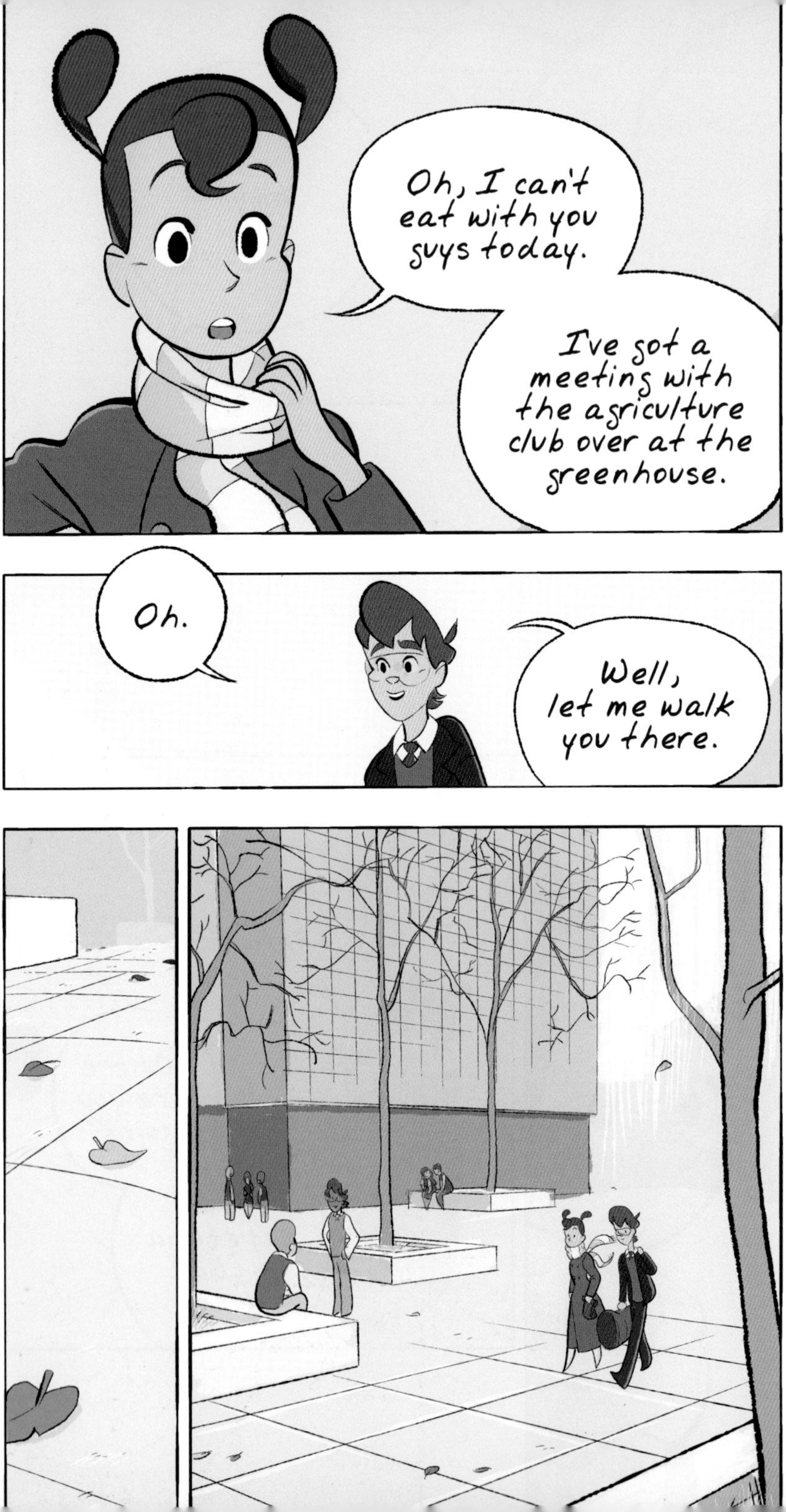
Oh, I can't eat with you guys today.
I've got a meeting with the agriculture club over at the greenhouse.
Oh.
Well, let me walk you there.

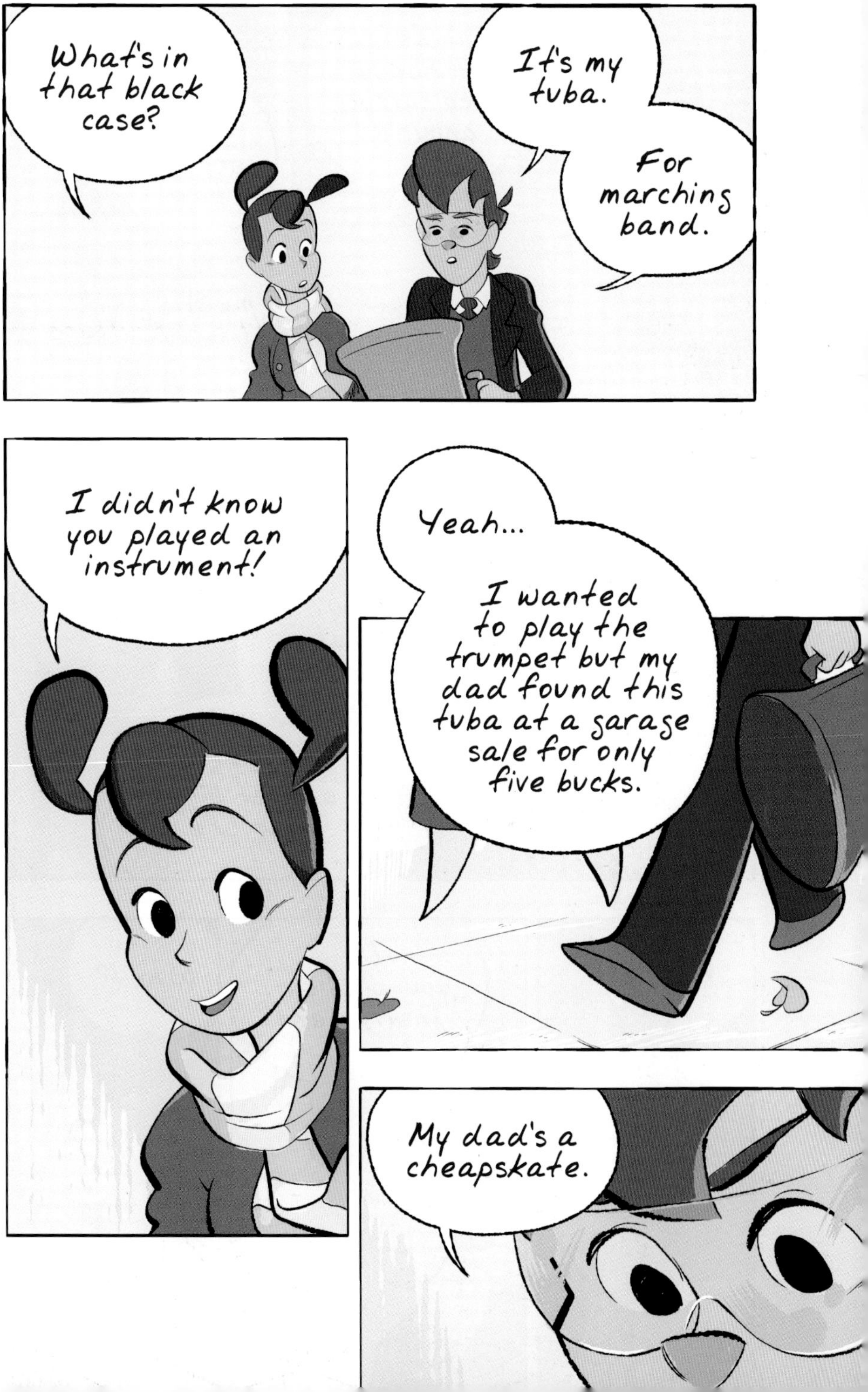
What's in that black case?
It's my tuba.
For marching band.
I didn't know you played an instrument!
Yeah...
I wanted to play the trumpet but my dad found this tuba at a garage sale for only five bucks.
My dad's a cheapskate.

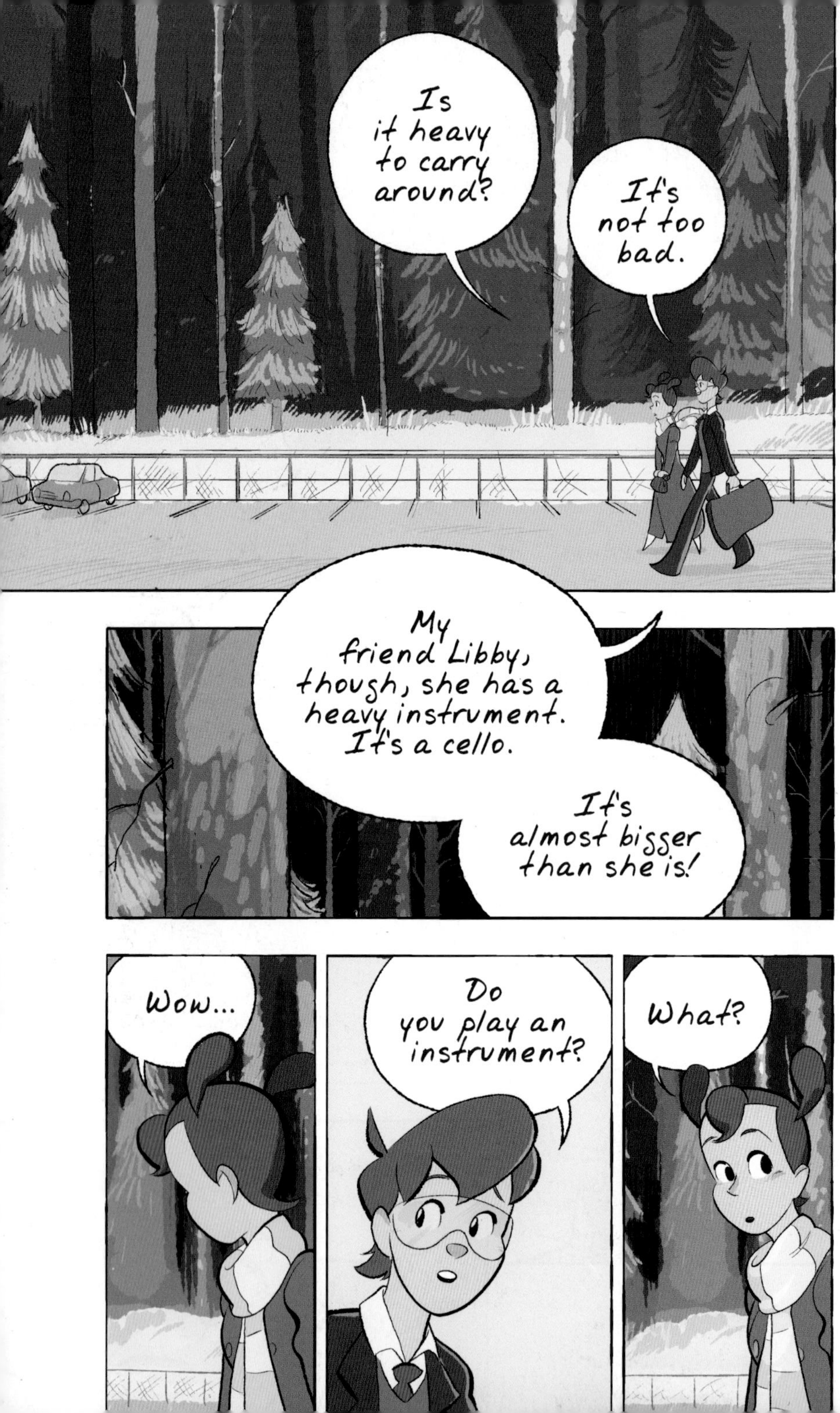
Is it heavy to carry around?
It's not too bad.
My friend Libby, though, she has a heavy instrument. It's a cello.
It's almost bigger than she is!
Wow...
Do you play an instrument?
What?

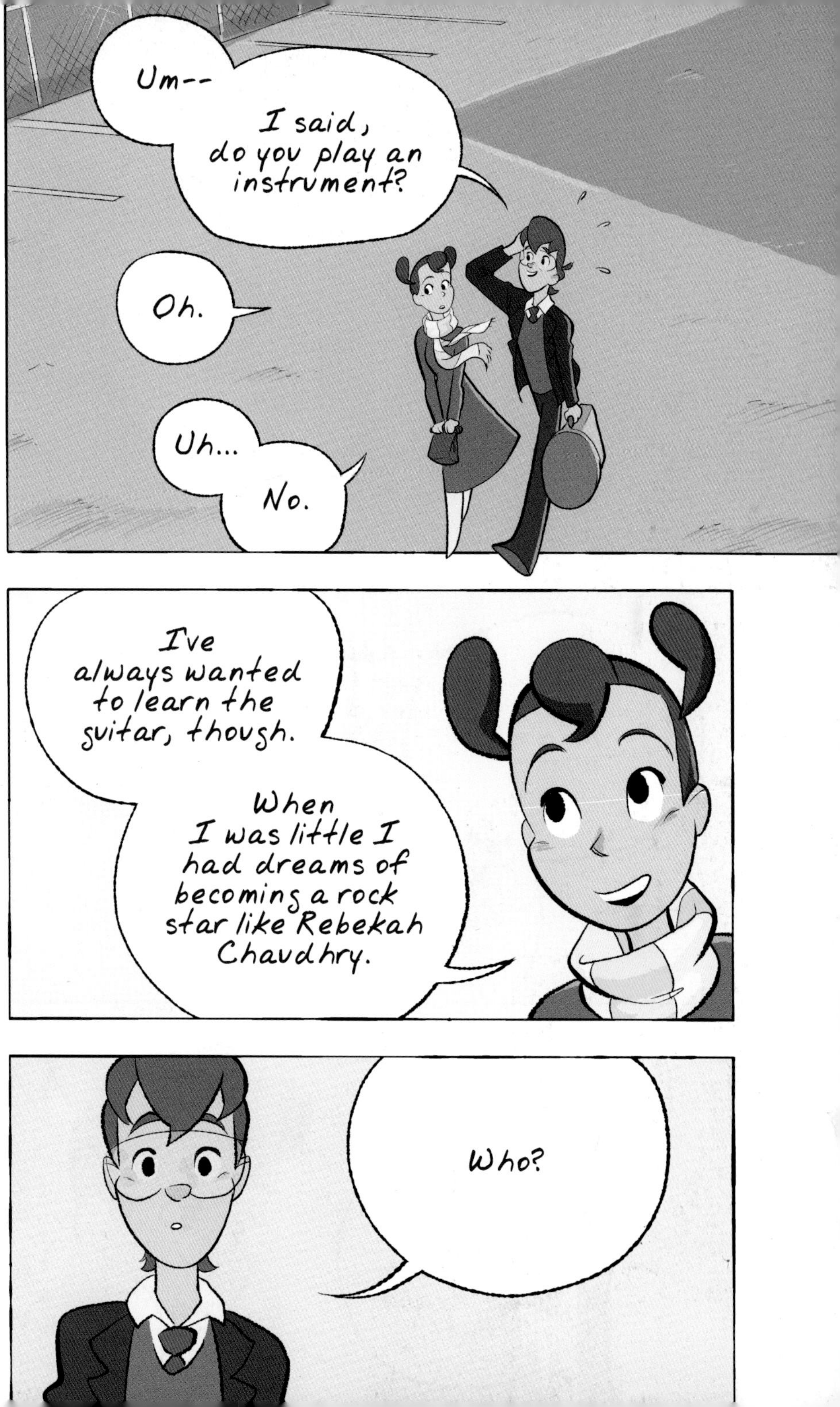
Um--
I said, do you play an instrument?
Oh.
Uh... No.
I've always wanted to learn the guitar, though.
When I was little I had dreams of becoming a rock star like Rebekah Chaudhry.
Who?

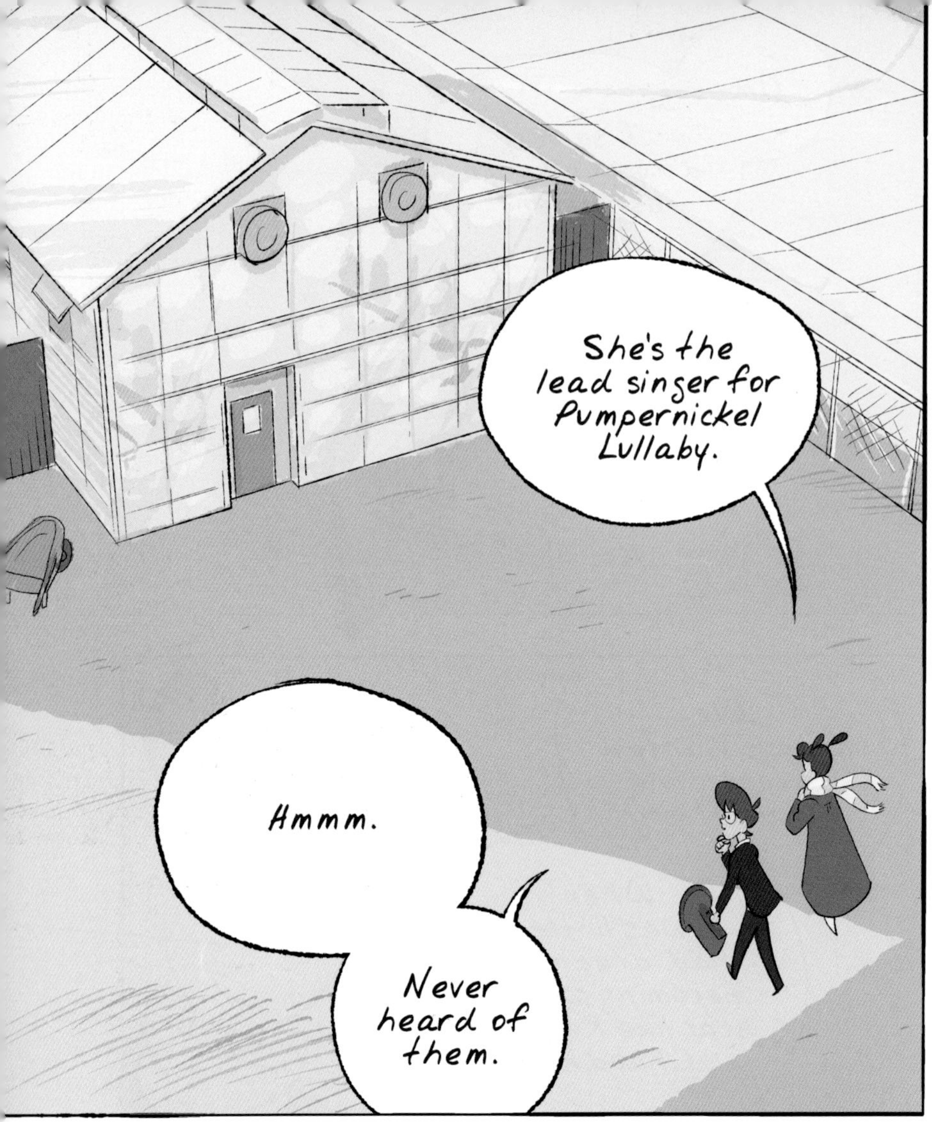
She's the lead singer for Pumpernickel Lullaby.
Hmmm.
Never heard of them.

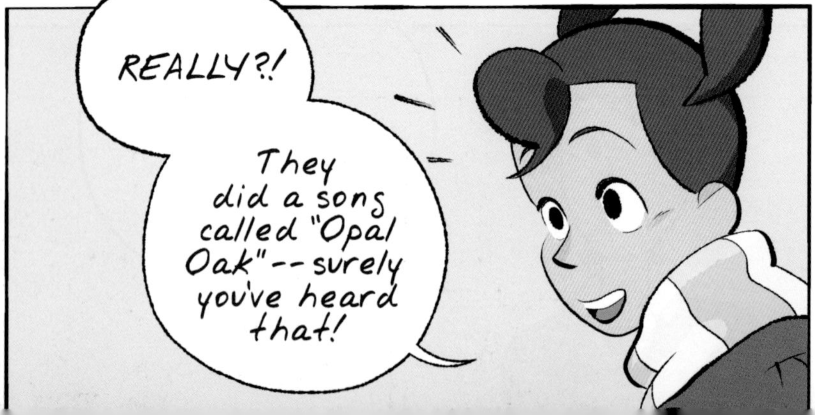
REALLY?!
They did a song called "Opal Oak"--surely you've heard that!

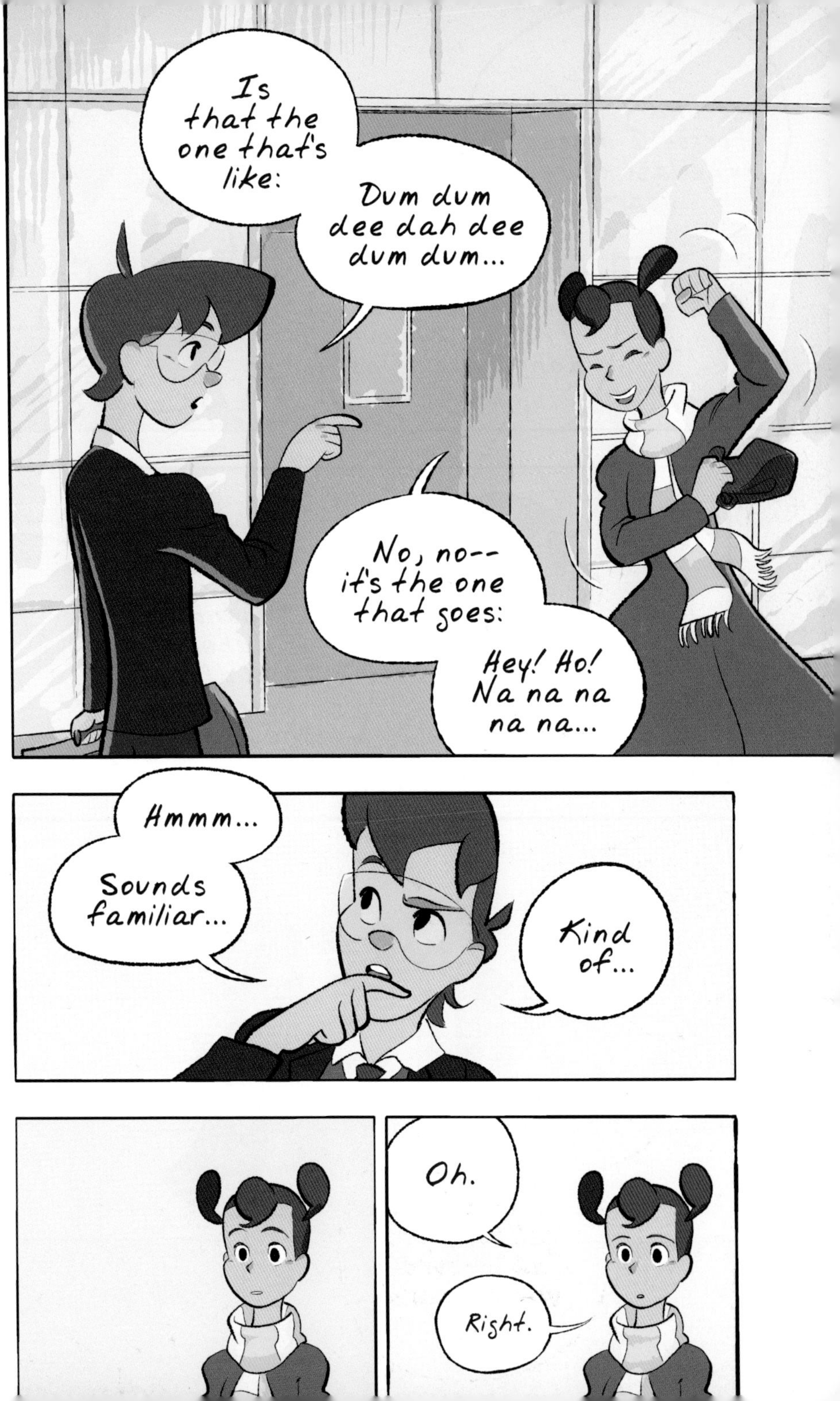
Is that the one that's like:
Dum dum dee dah dee dum dum...
No, no-- it's the one that goes:
Hey! Ho! Na na na na na...
Hmmm...
Sounds familiar...
Kind of...
Oh.
Right.

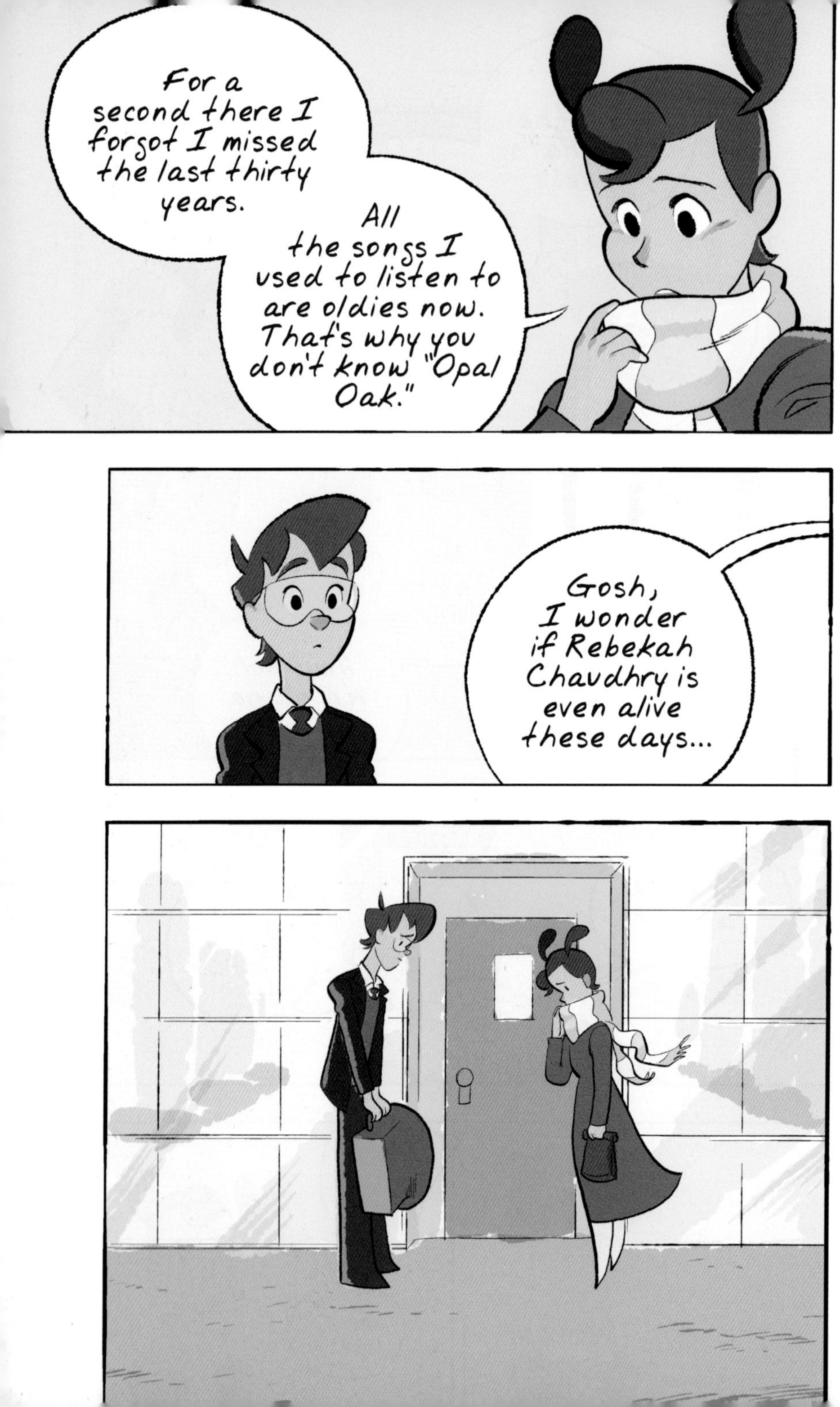
For a second there I forgot I missed the last thirty years.
All the songs I used to listen to are oldies now. That's why you don't know "Opal Oak."
Gosh, I wonder if Rebekah Chaudhry is even alive these days...

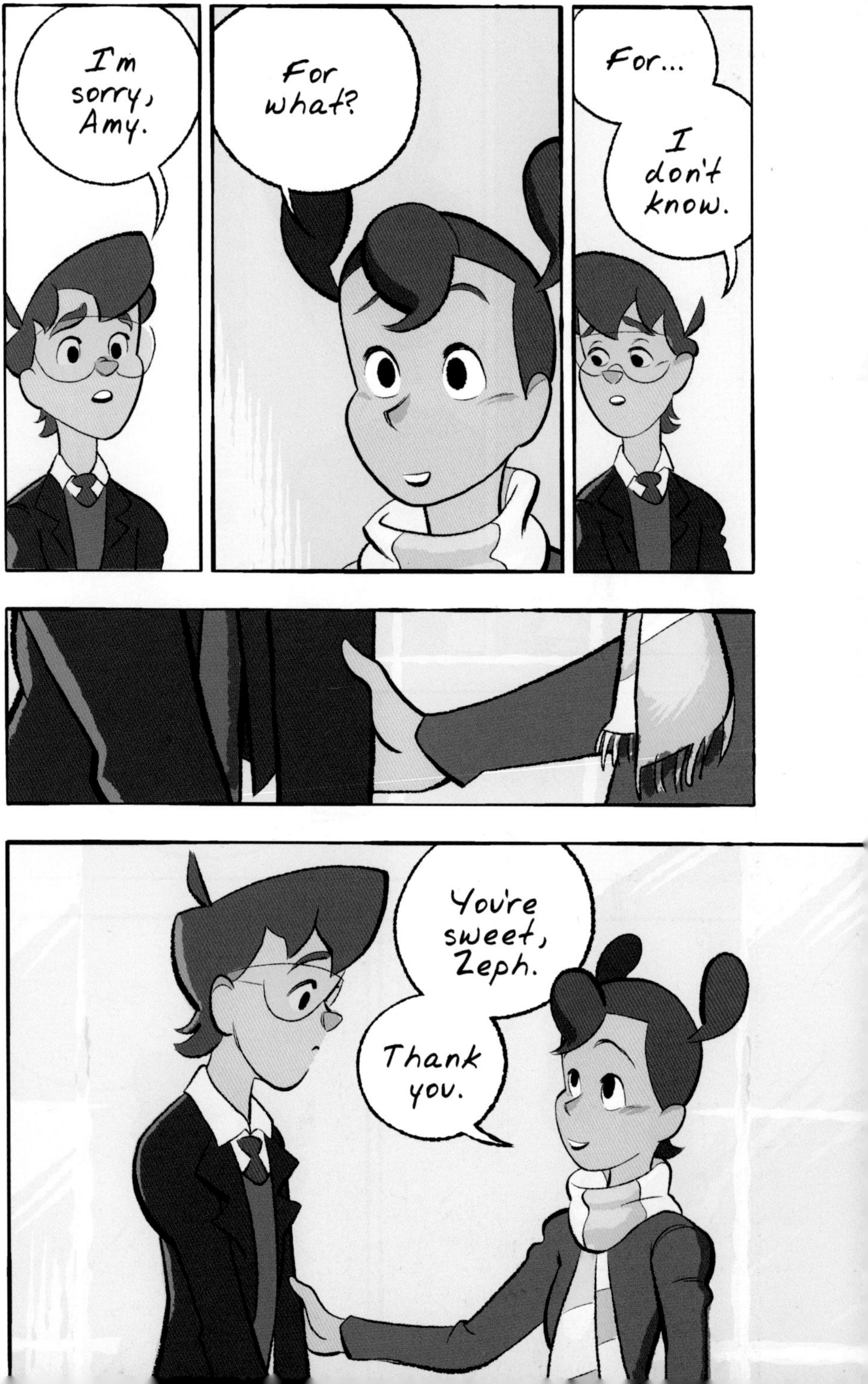

I'm sorry, Amy.
For what?
For...
I don't know.
You're sweet, Zeph.
Thank you.

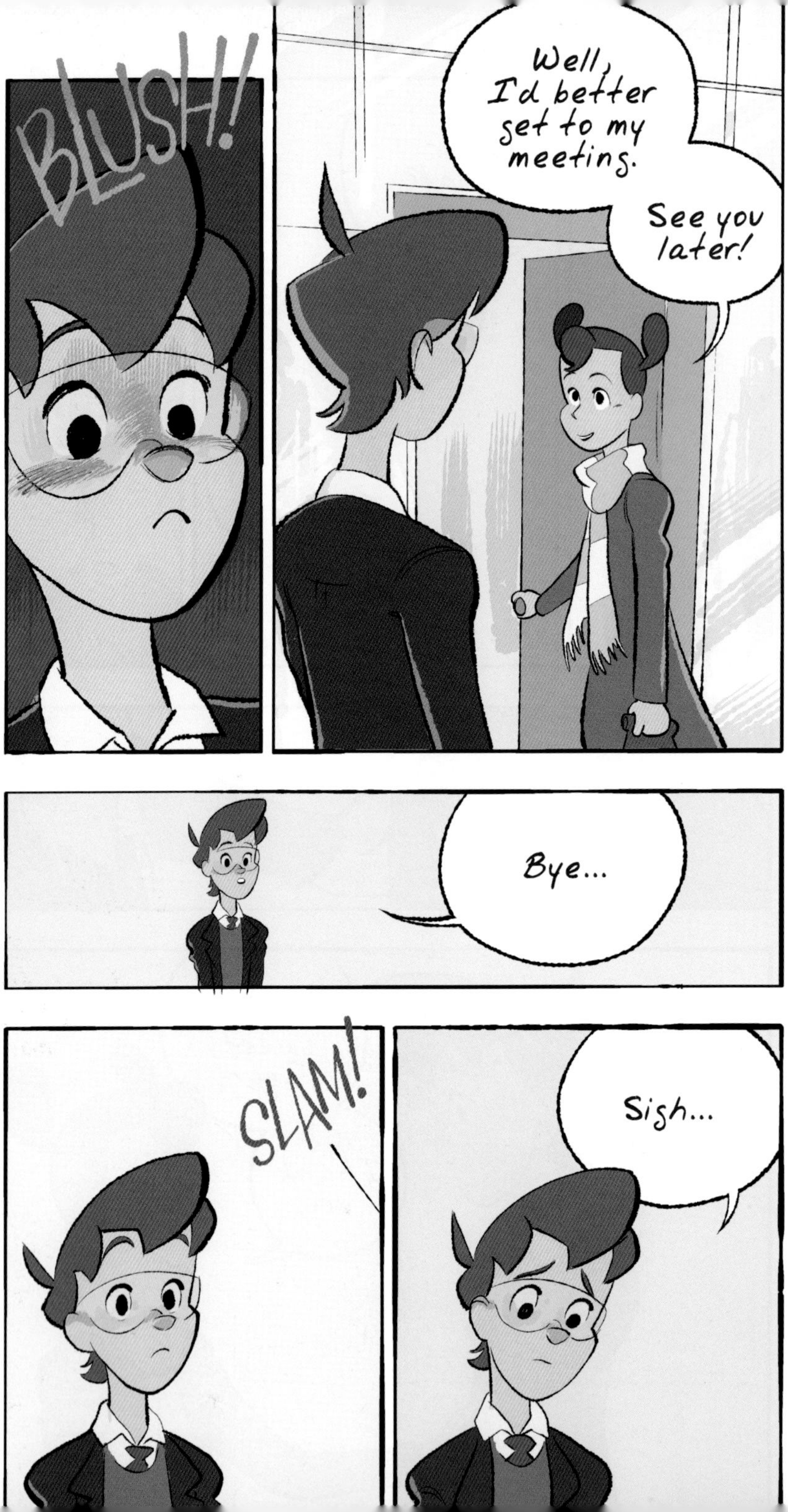
BLUSH!
Well, I'd better get to my meeting.
See you later!
Bye...
SLAM!
Sigh...

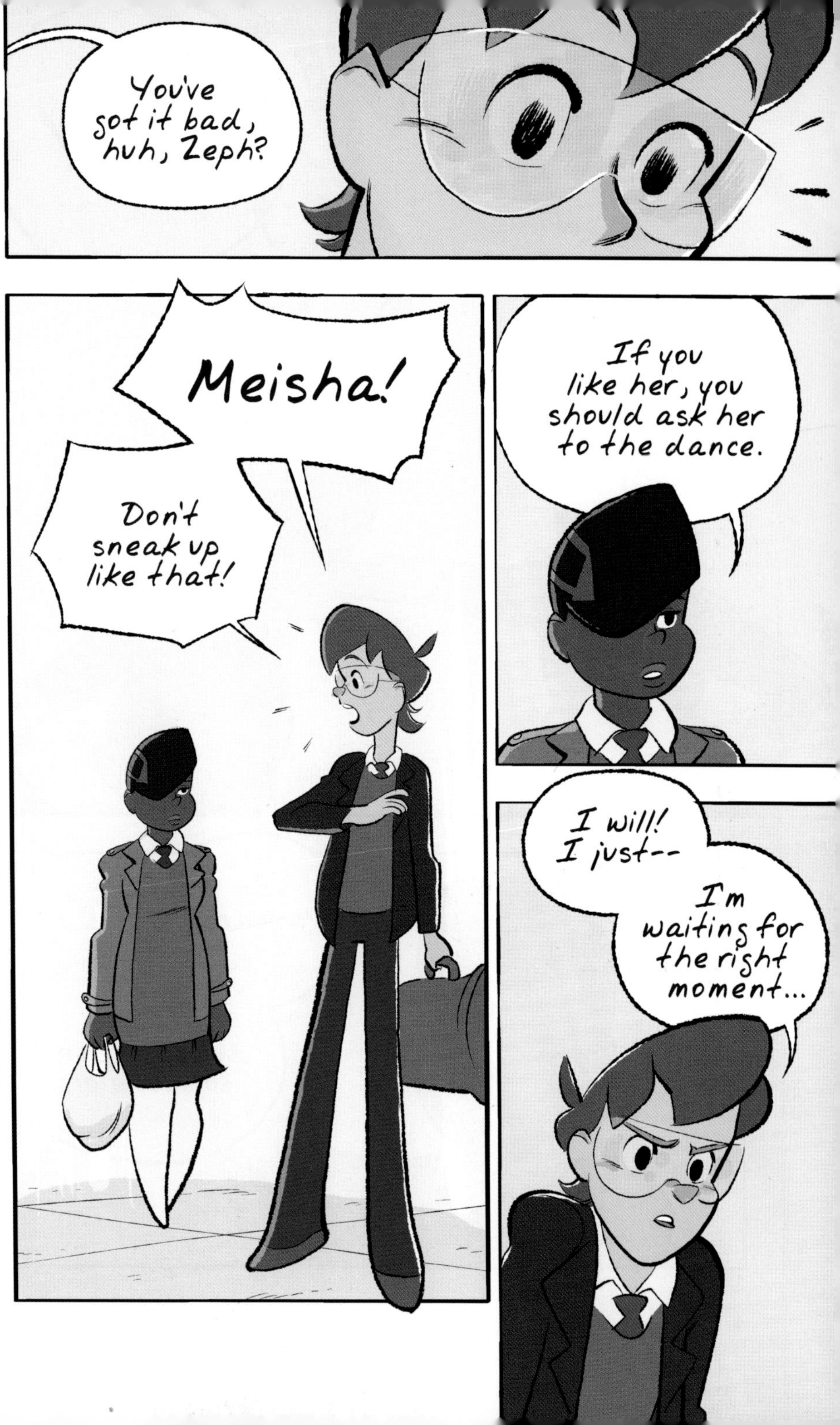
You've got it bad, huh, Zeph?
Meisha!
Don't sneak up like that!
If you like her, you should ask her to the dance.
I will! I just--
I'm waiting for the right moment...

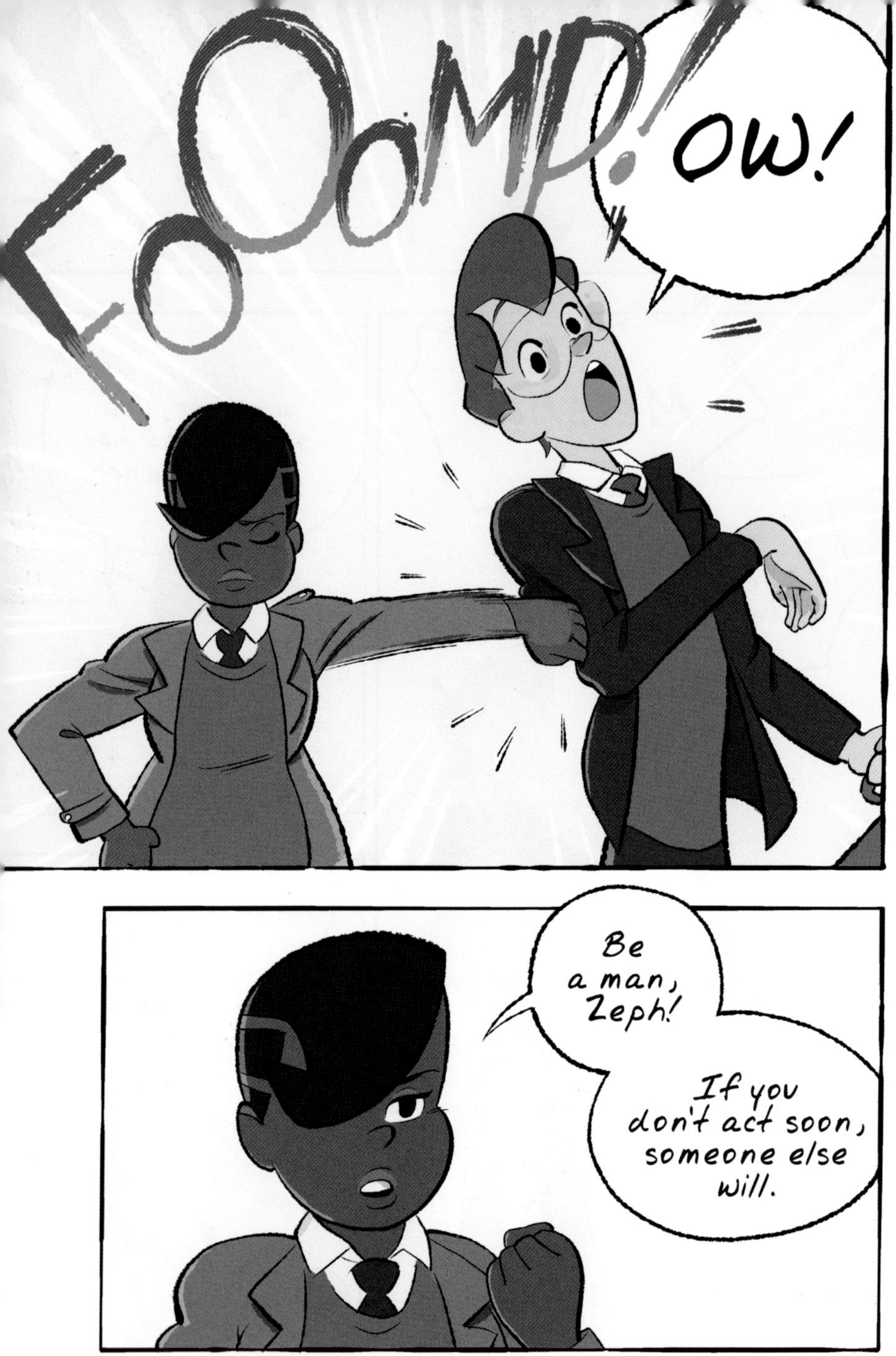
FOOOMP!
OW!
Be a man, Zeph!
If you don't act soon, someone else will.

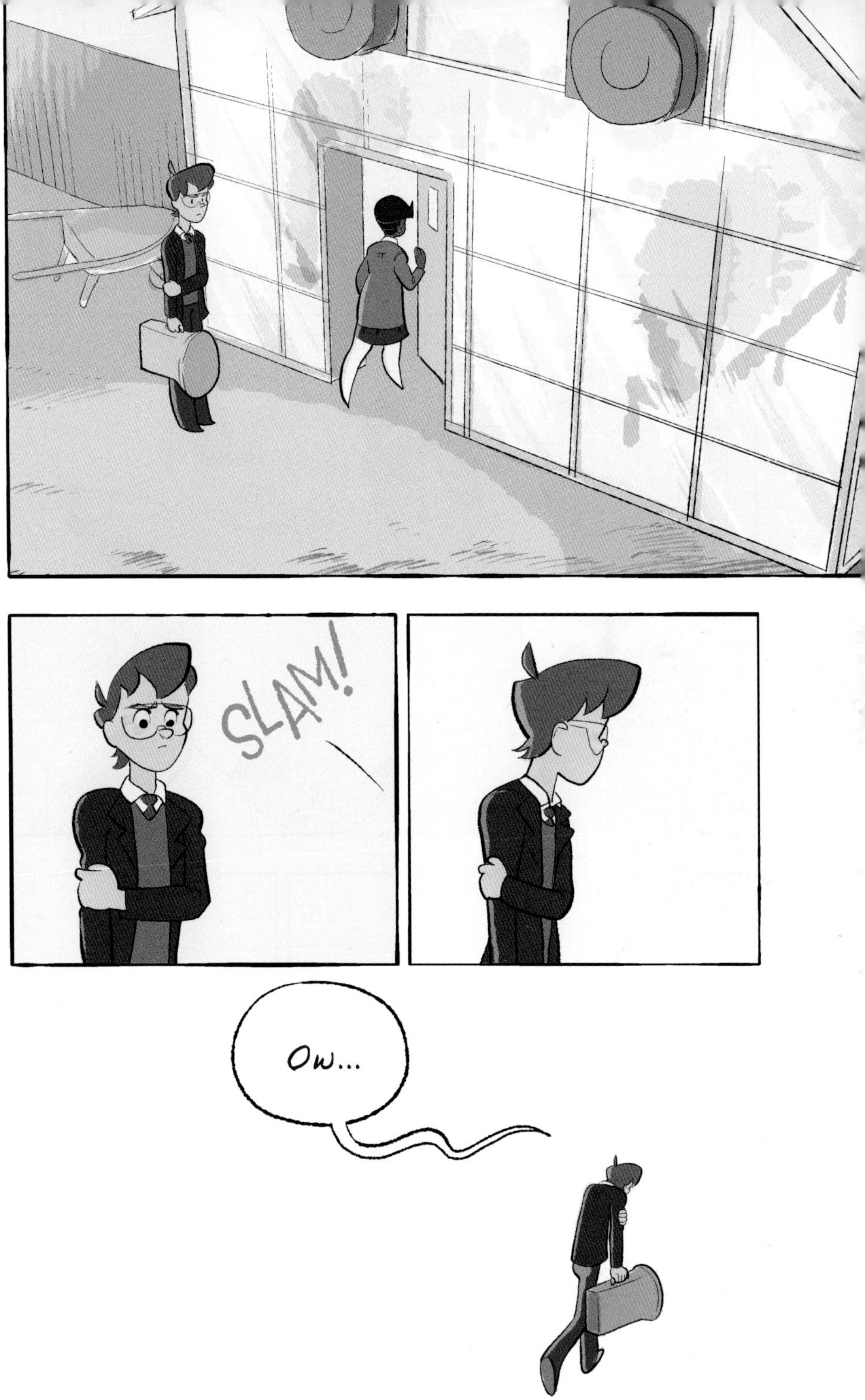
SLAM!
Ow...

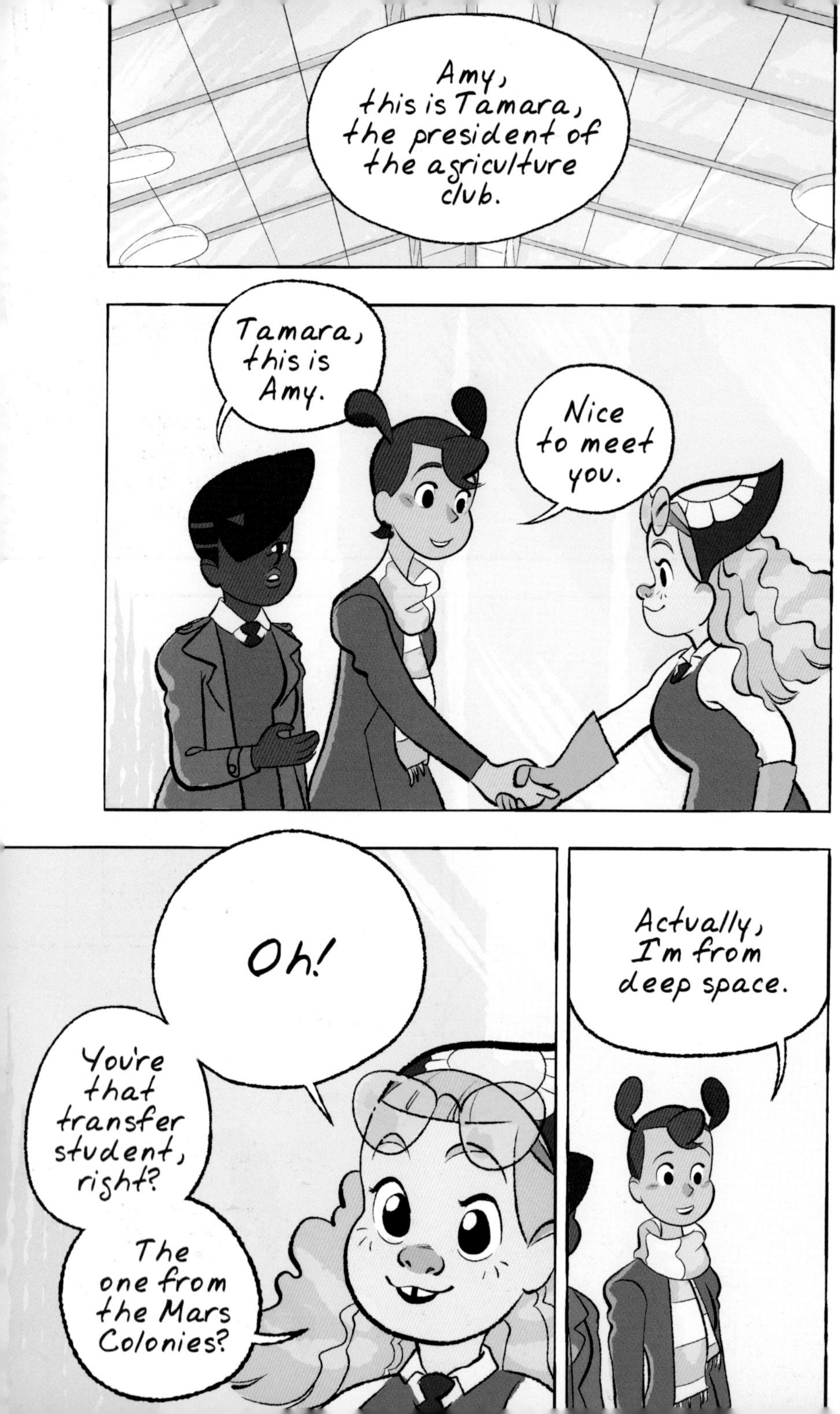
Amy, this is Tamara, the president of the agriculture club.
Tamara, this is Amy.
Nice to meet you.
Oh!
You're that transfer student, right?
The one from the Mars Colonies?
Actually, I'm from deep space.

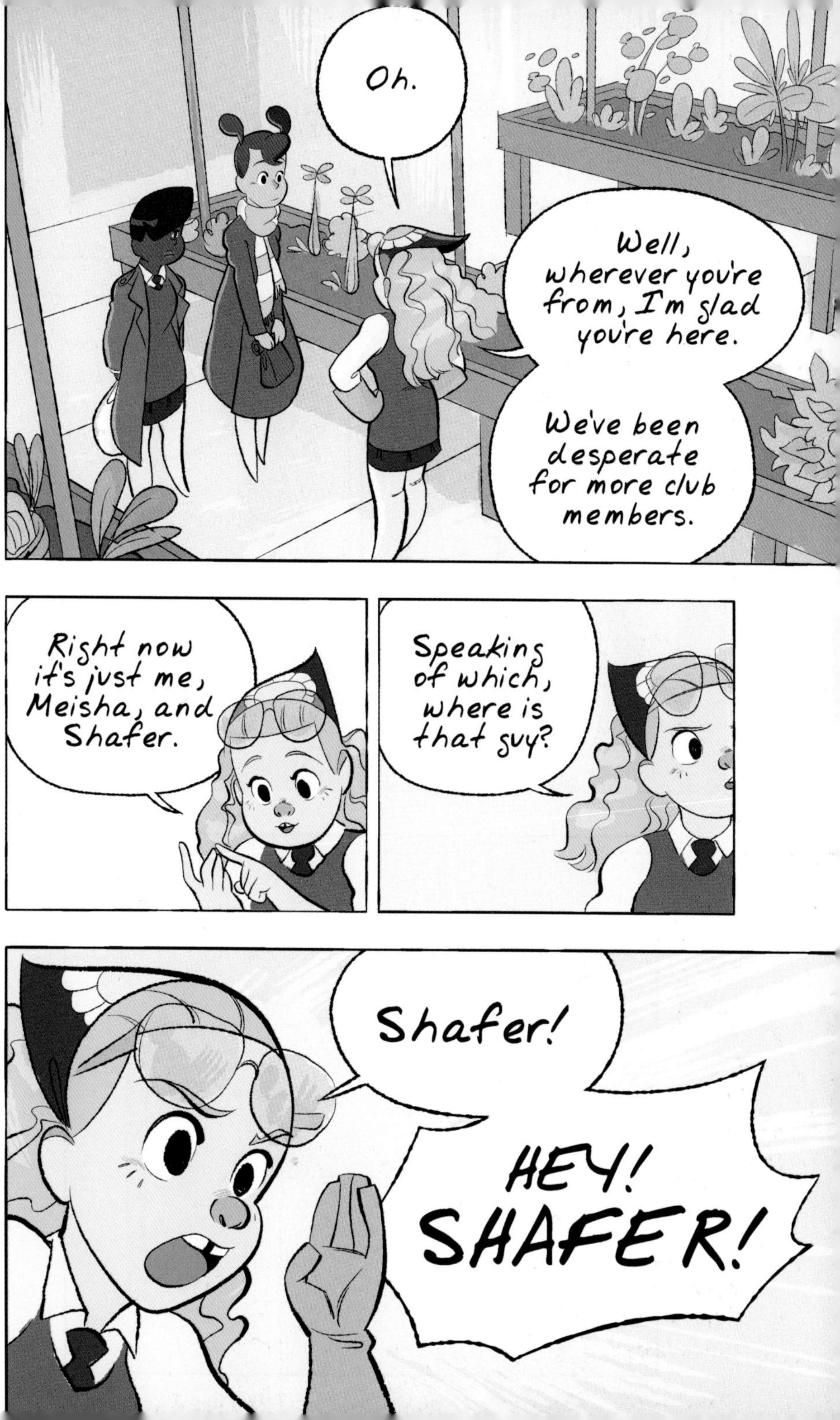
Oh.
Well, wherever you're from, I'm glad you're here.
We've been desperate for more club members.
Right now it's just me, Meisha, and Shafer.
Speaking of which, where is that guy?
Shafer!
HEY! SHAFER!

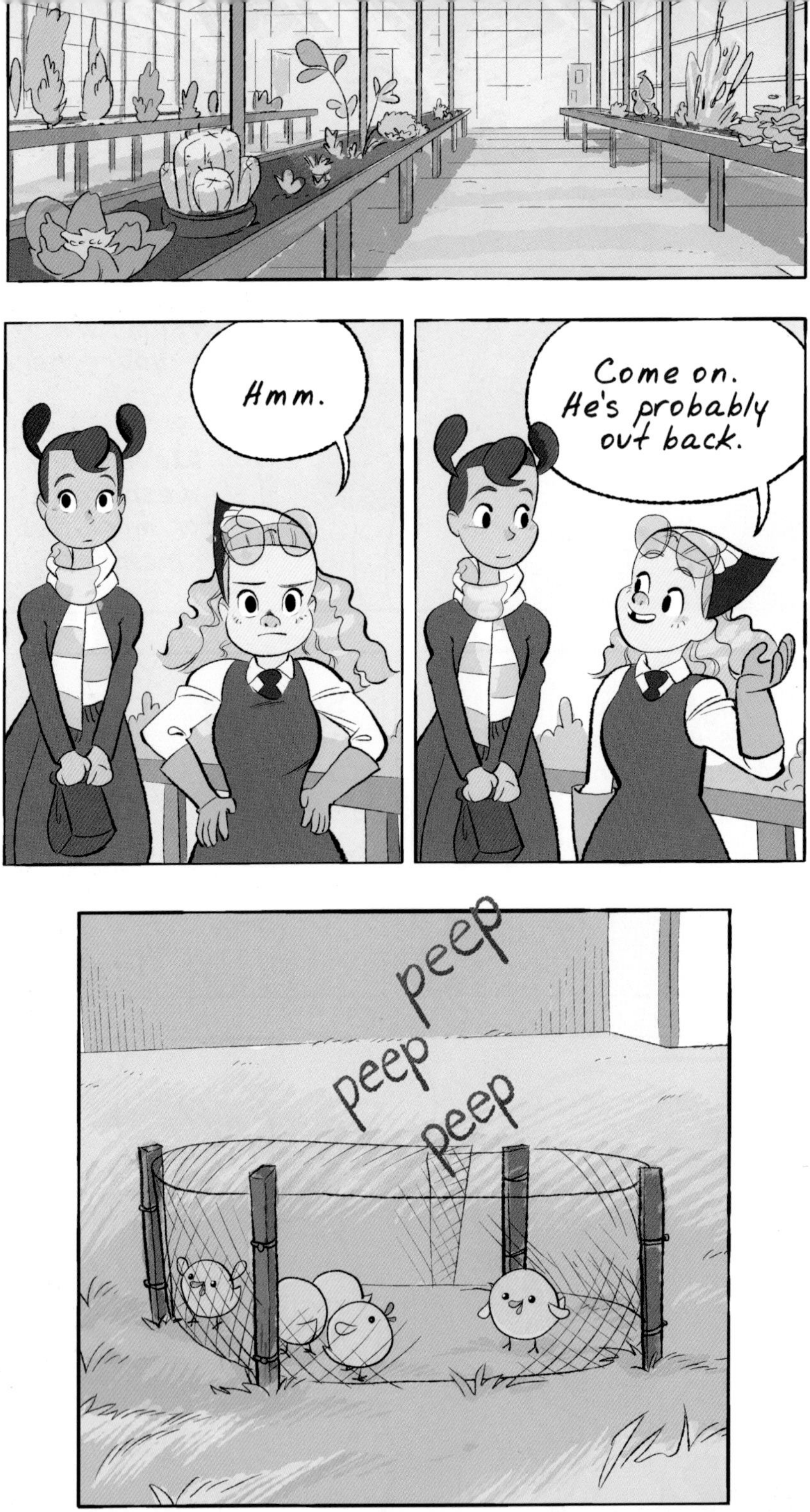
Hmm.
Come on. He's probably out back.
peep
peep
peep

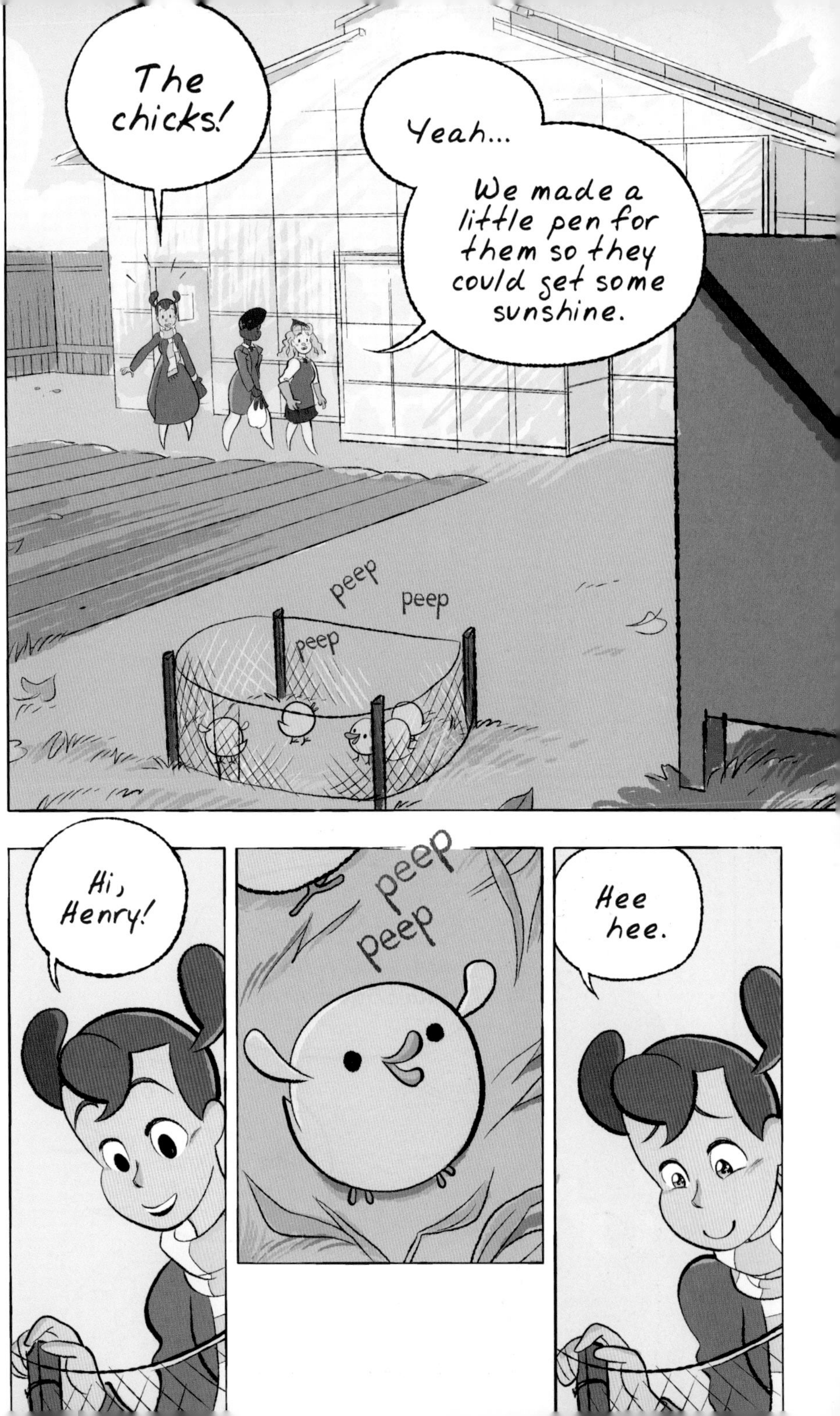
The chicks!
Yeah...
We made a little pen for them so they could get some sunshine.
peep
peep
peep
Hi, Henry!
peep
peep
Hee hee.

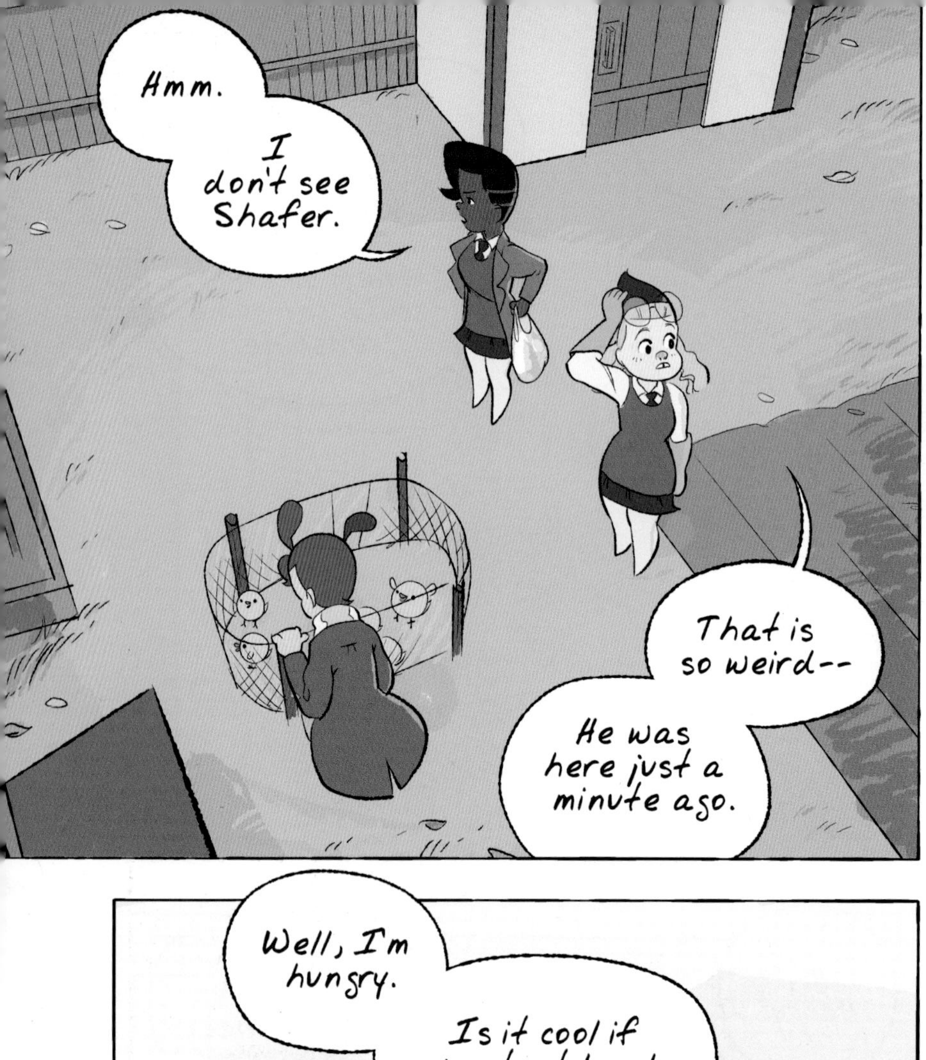
Hmm.
I don't see Shafer.
That is so weird--
He was here just a minute ago.

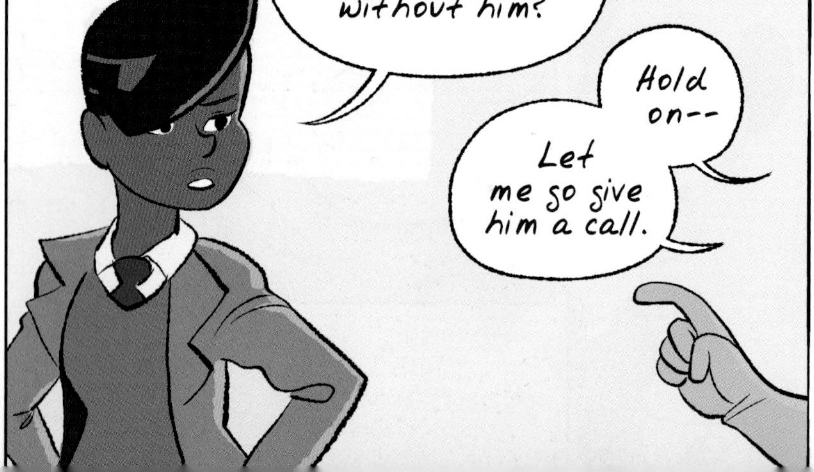
Well, I'm hungry.
Is it cool if we start lunch without him?
Hold on--
Let me go give him a call.

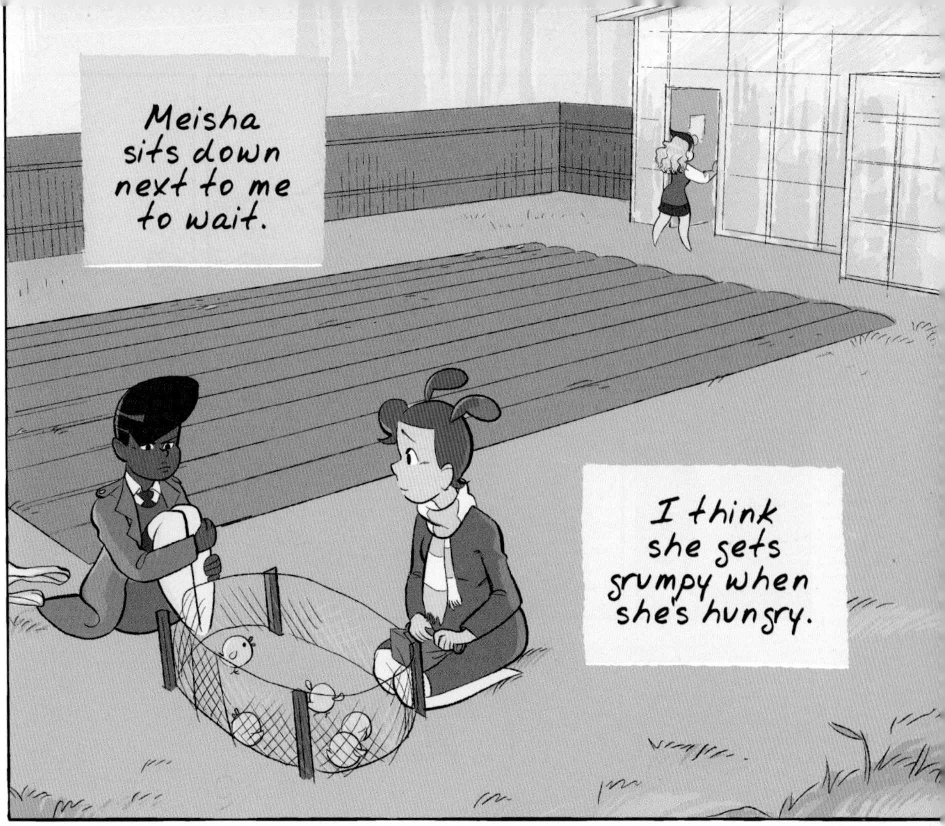
Meisha sits down next to me to wait.
I think she gets grumpy when she's hungry.

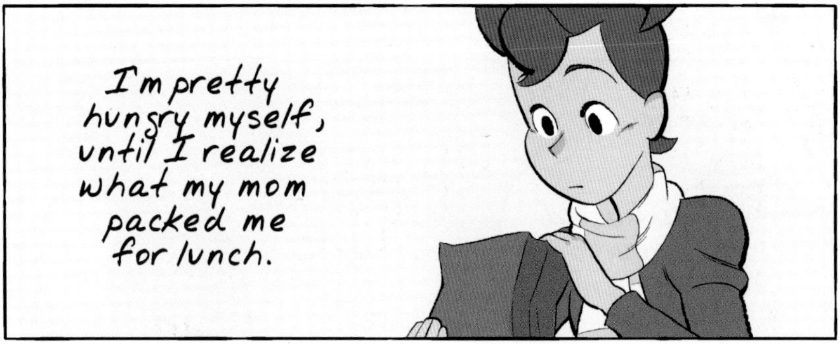
I'm pretty hungry myself, until I realize what my mom packed me for lunch.

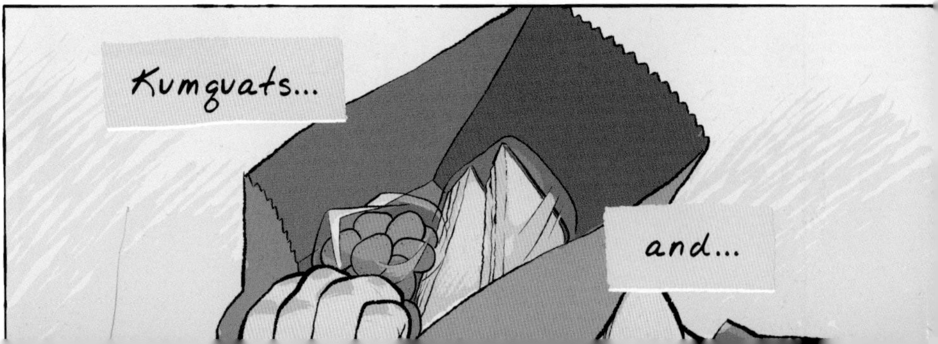
Kumquats...
and...

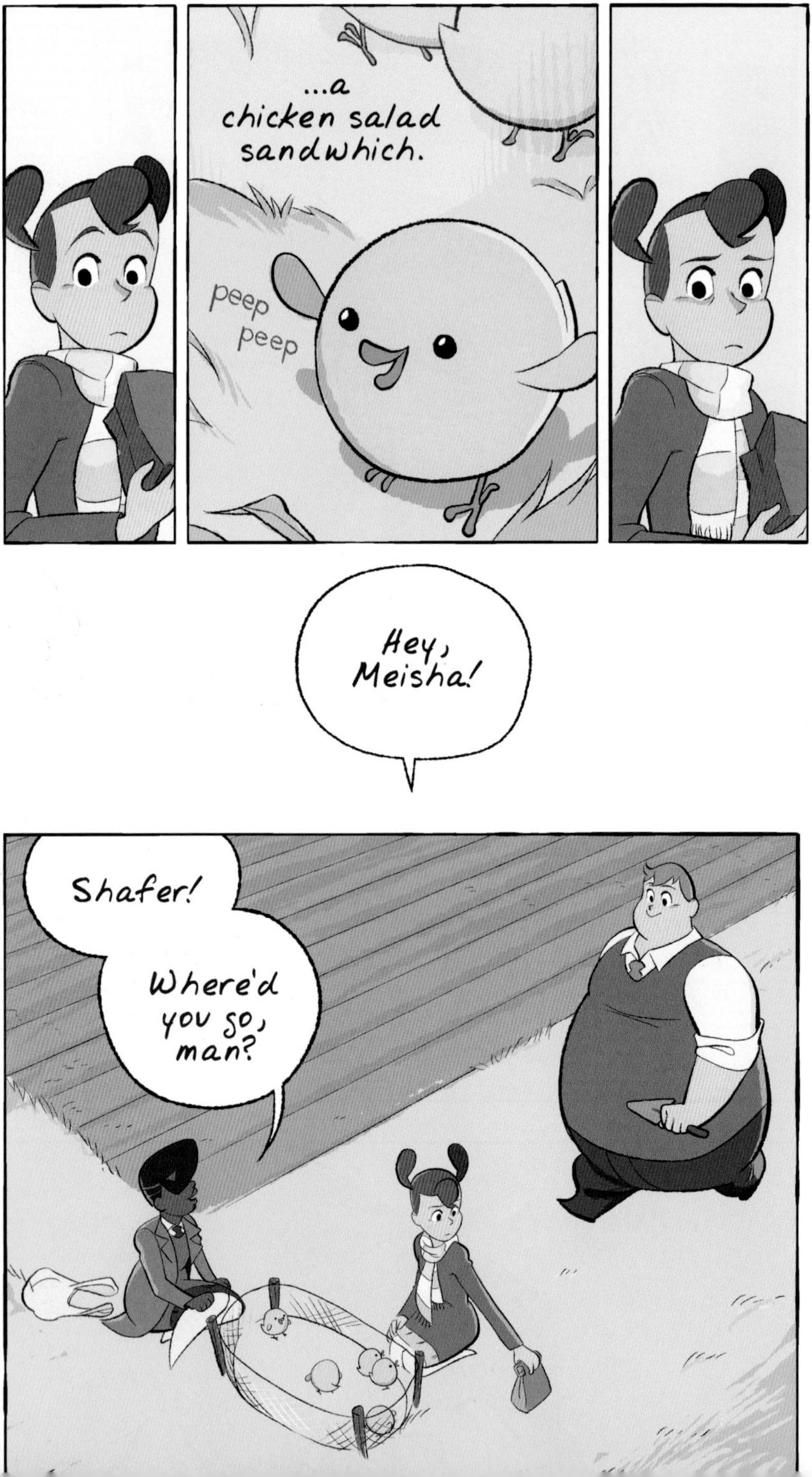
...a chicken salad sandwhich.
peep peep
Hey, Meisha!
Shafer!
Where'd you go, man?

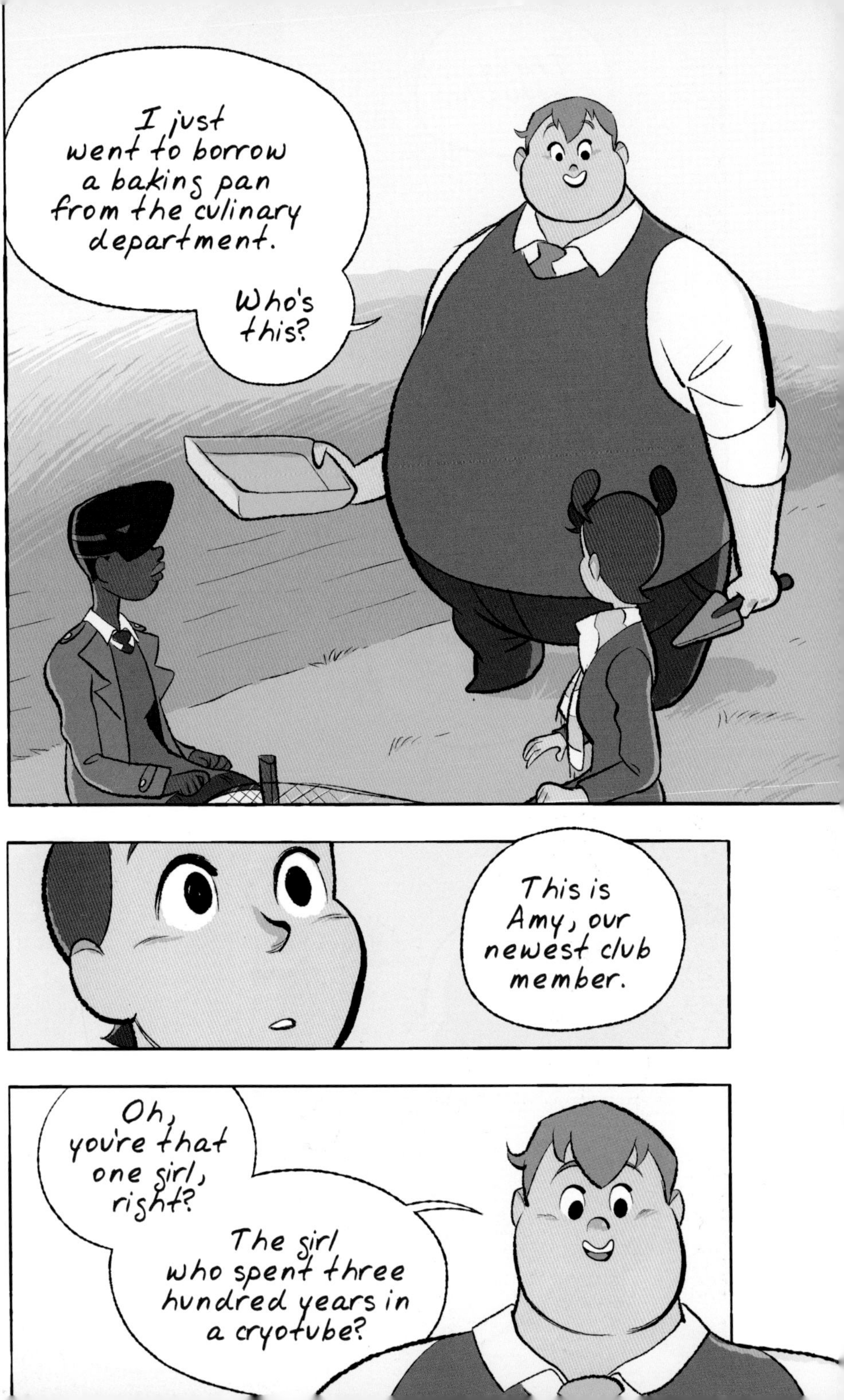
I just went to borrow a baking pan from the culinary department.
Who's this?
This is Amy, our newest club member.
Oh, you're that one girl, right?
The girl who spent three hundred years in a cryotube?

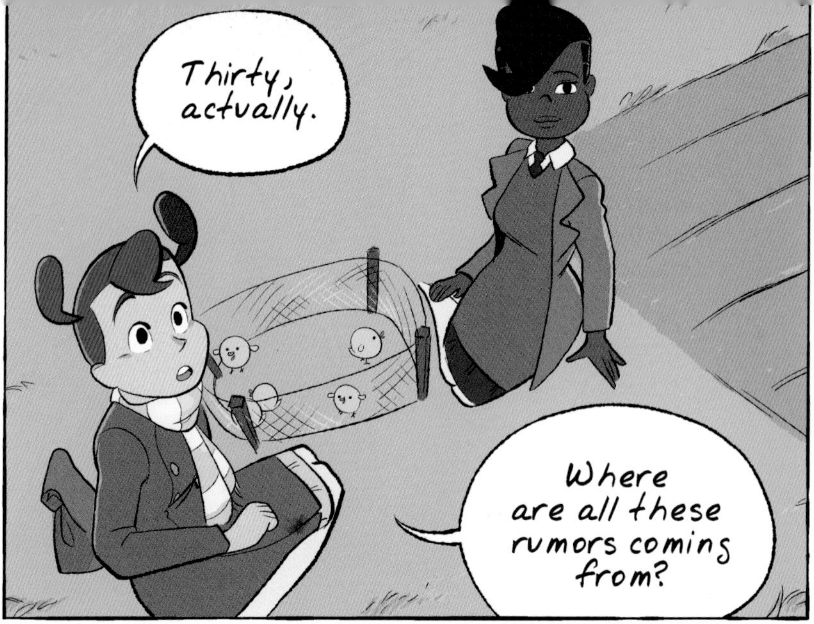
Thirty, actually.
Where are all these rumors coming from?

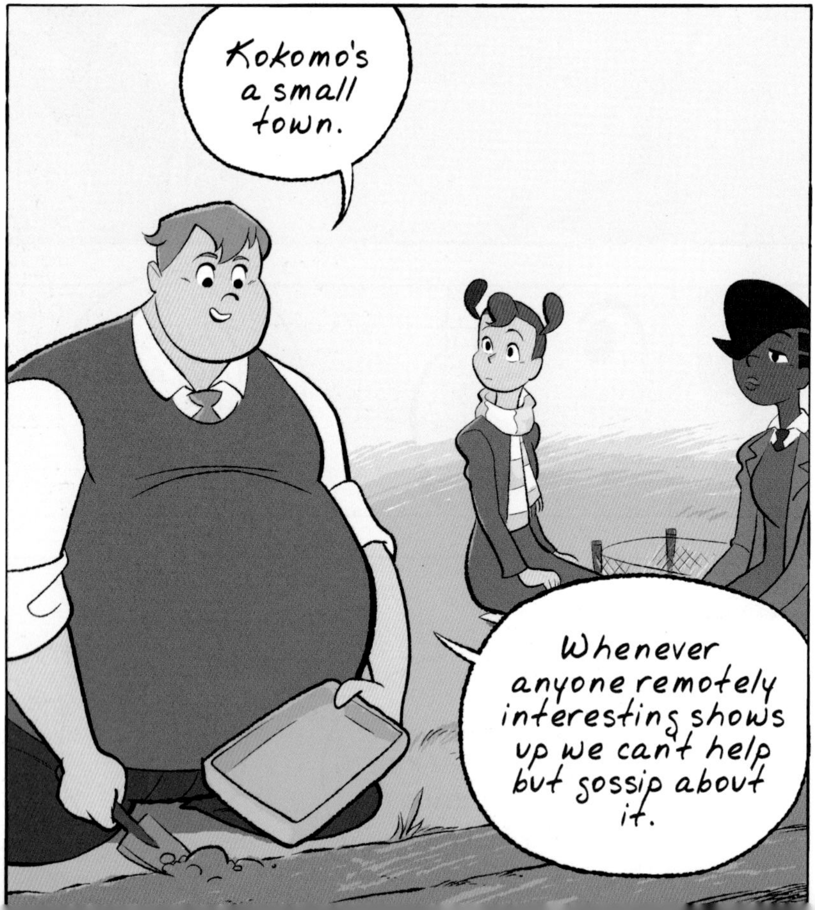
Kokomo's a small town.
Whenever anyone remotely interesting shows up we can't help but gossip about it.

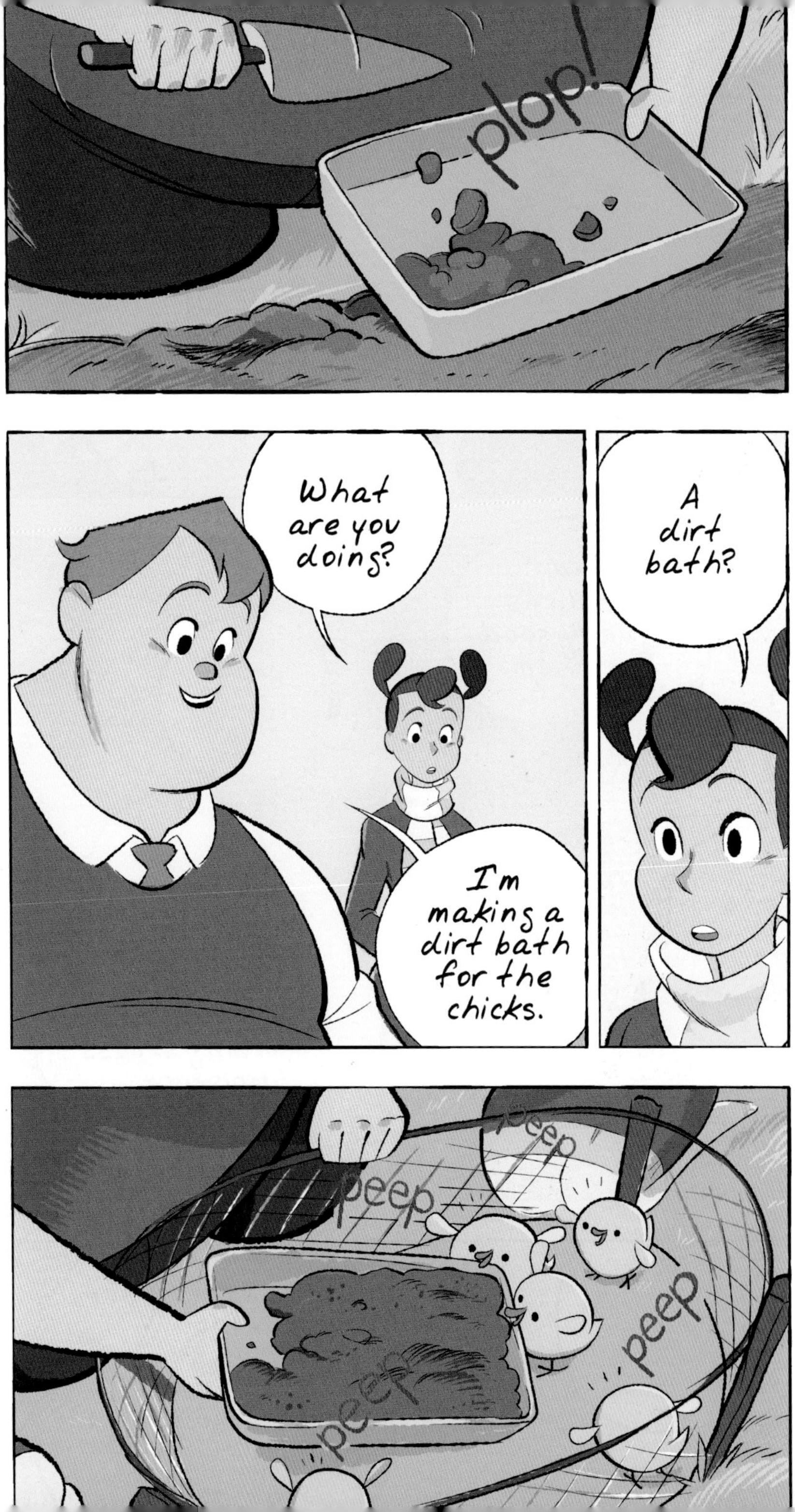
plop!
What are you doing?
I'm making a dirt bath for the chicks.
A dirt bath?
peep
peep
peep
peep

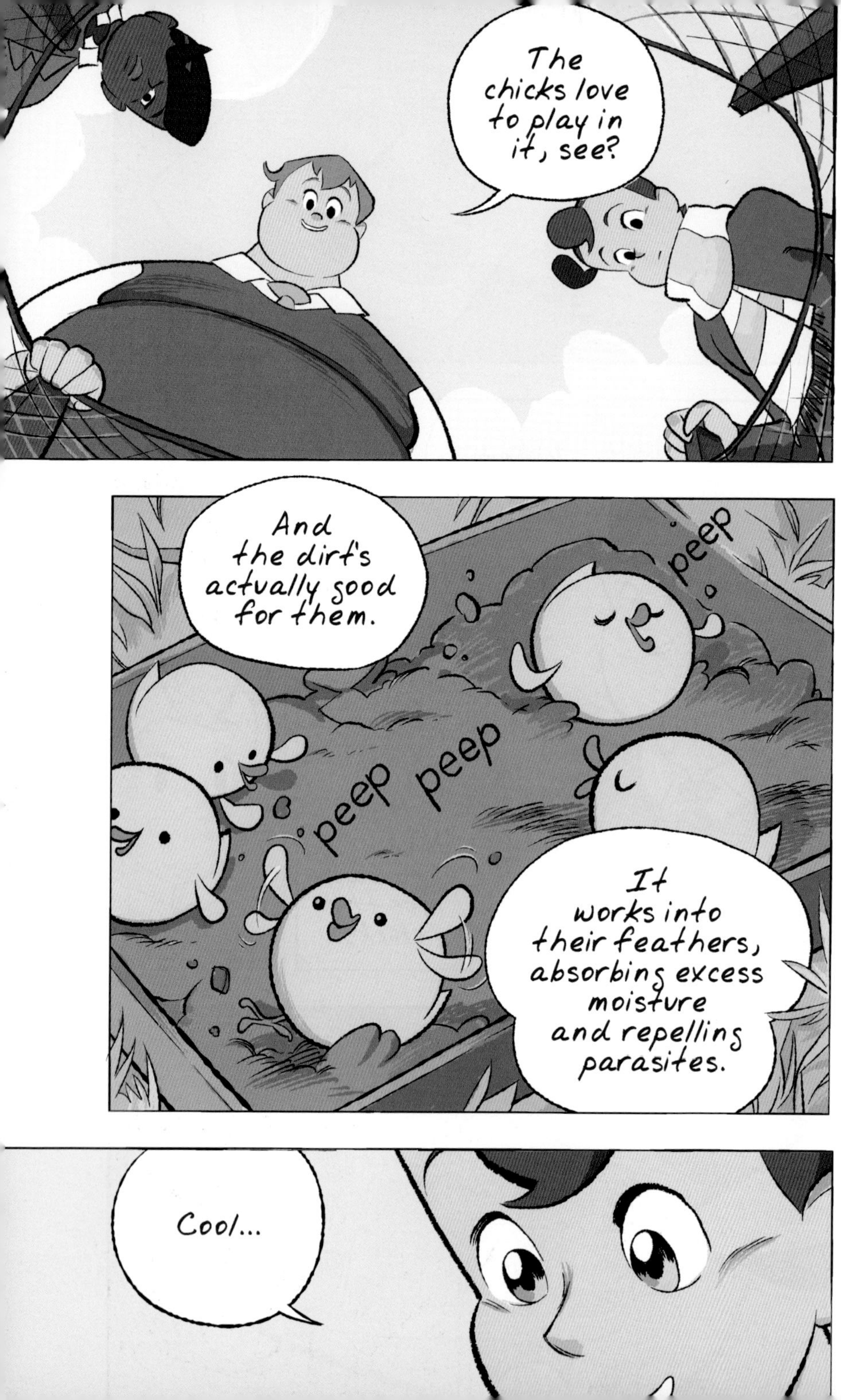
The chicks love to play in it, see?
And the dirt's actually good for them.
peep
peep peep
It works into their feathers, absorbing excess moisture and repelling parasites.
Cool...

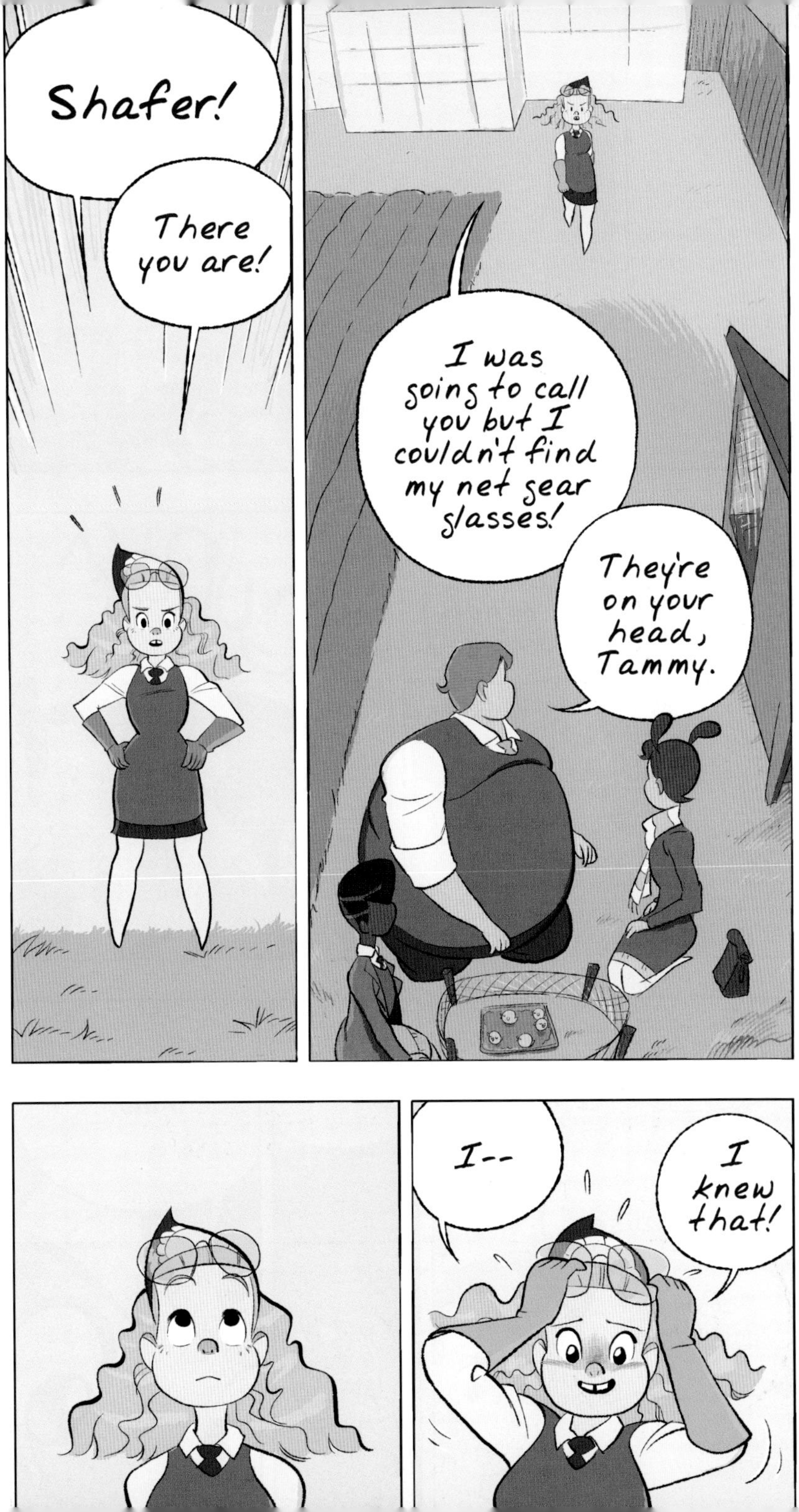
Shafer!
There you are!
I was going to call you but I couldn't find my net gear glasses!
They're on your head, Tammy.
I--
I knew that!

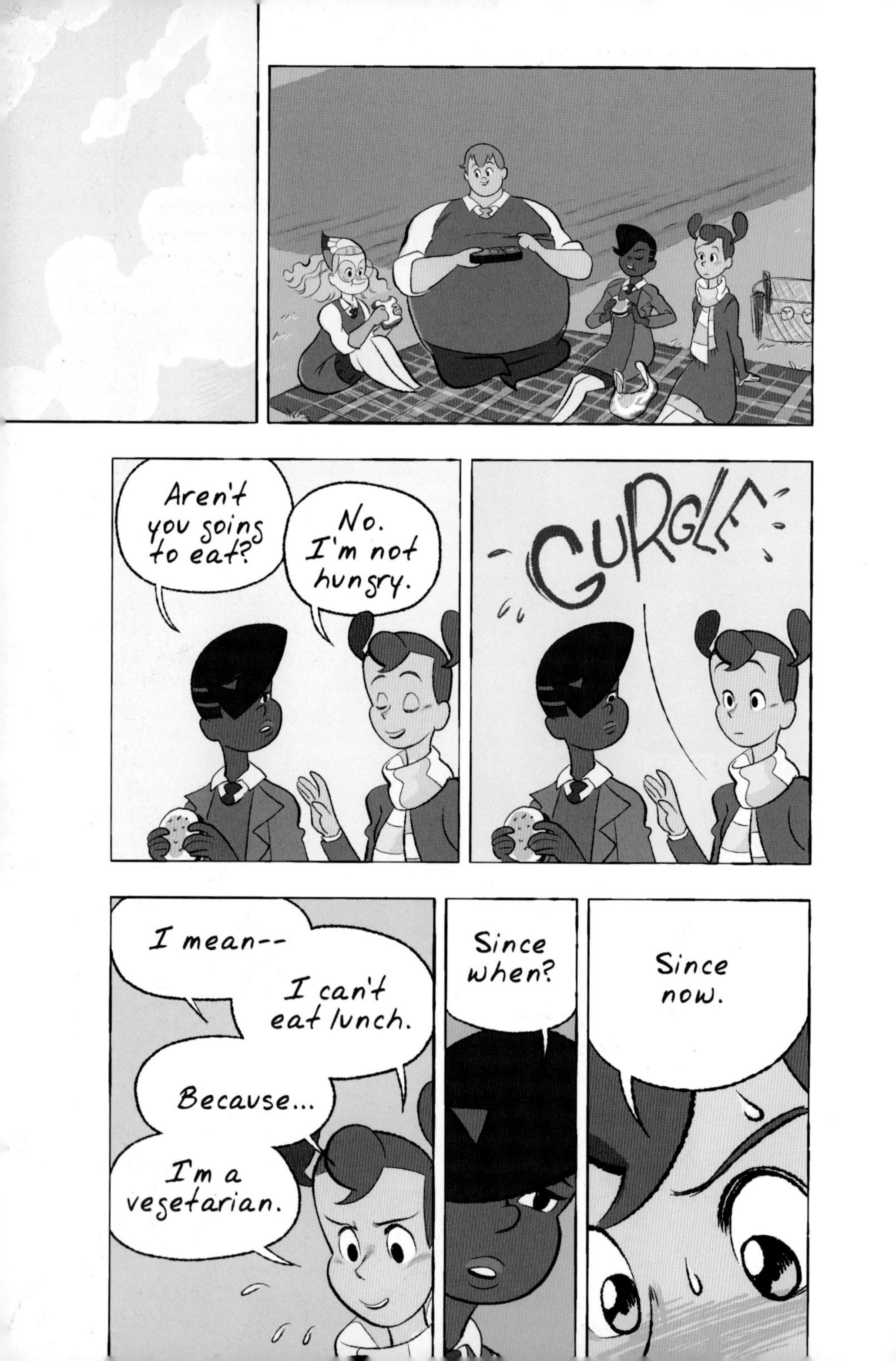
Aren't you going to eat?
No. I'm not hungry.
GURGLE
I mean--
I can't eat lunch.
Because...
I'm a vegetarian.
Since when?
Since now.

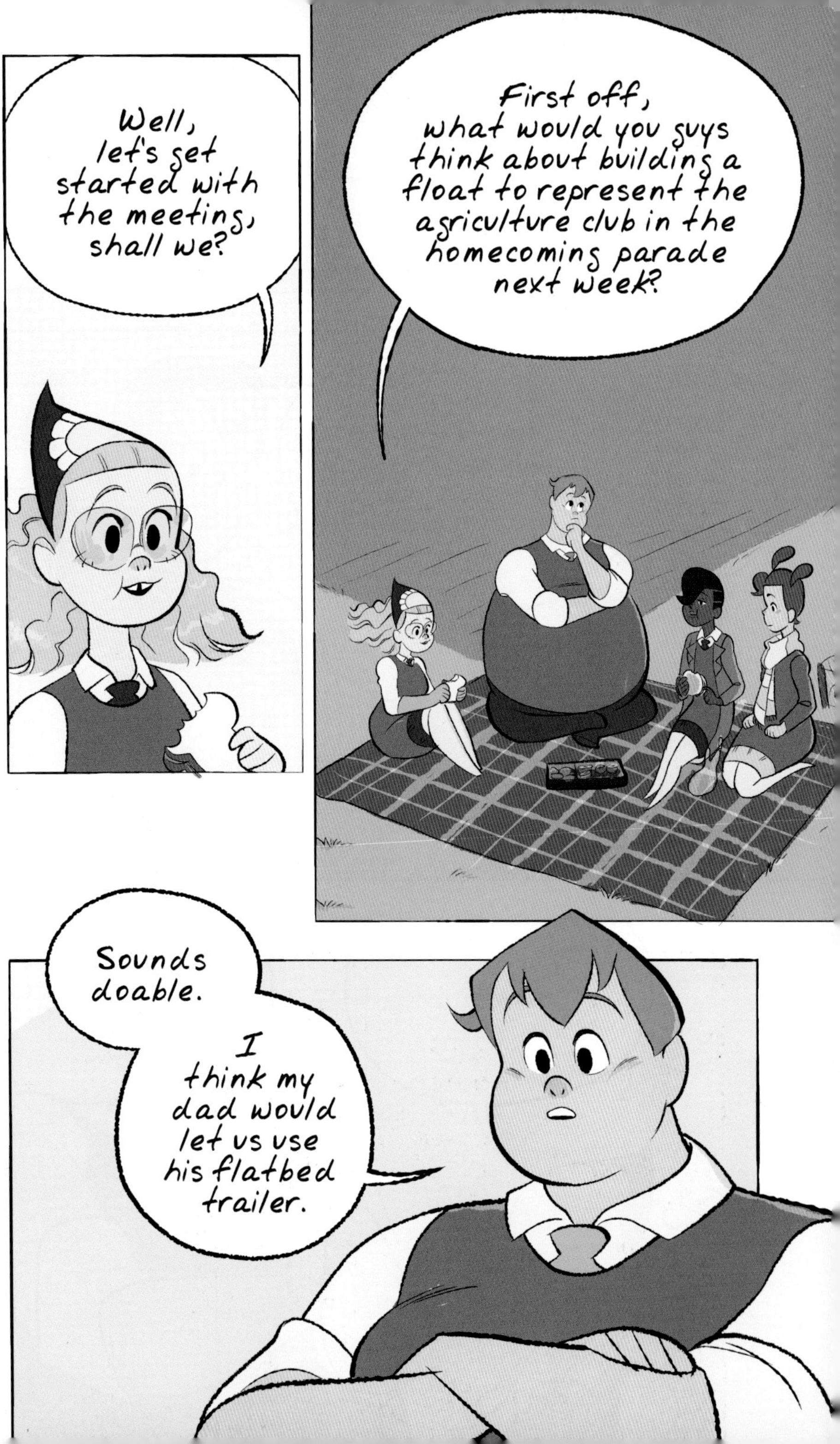
Well, let's get started with the meeting, shall we?
First off, what would you guys think about building a float to represent the agriculture club in the homecoming parade next week?
Sounds doable.
I think my dad would let us use his flatbed trailer.

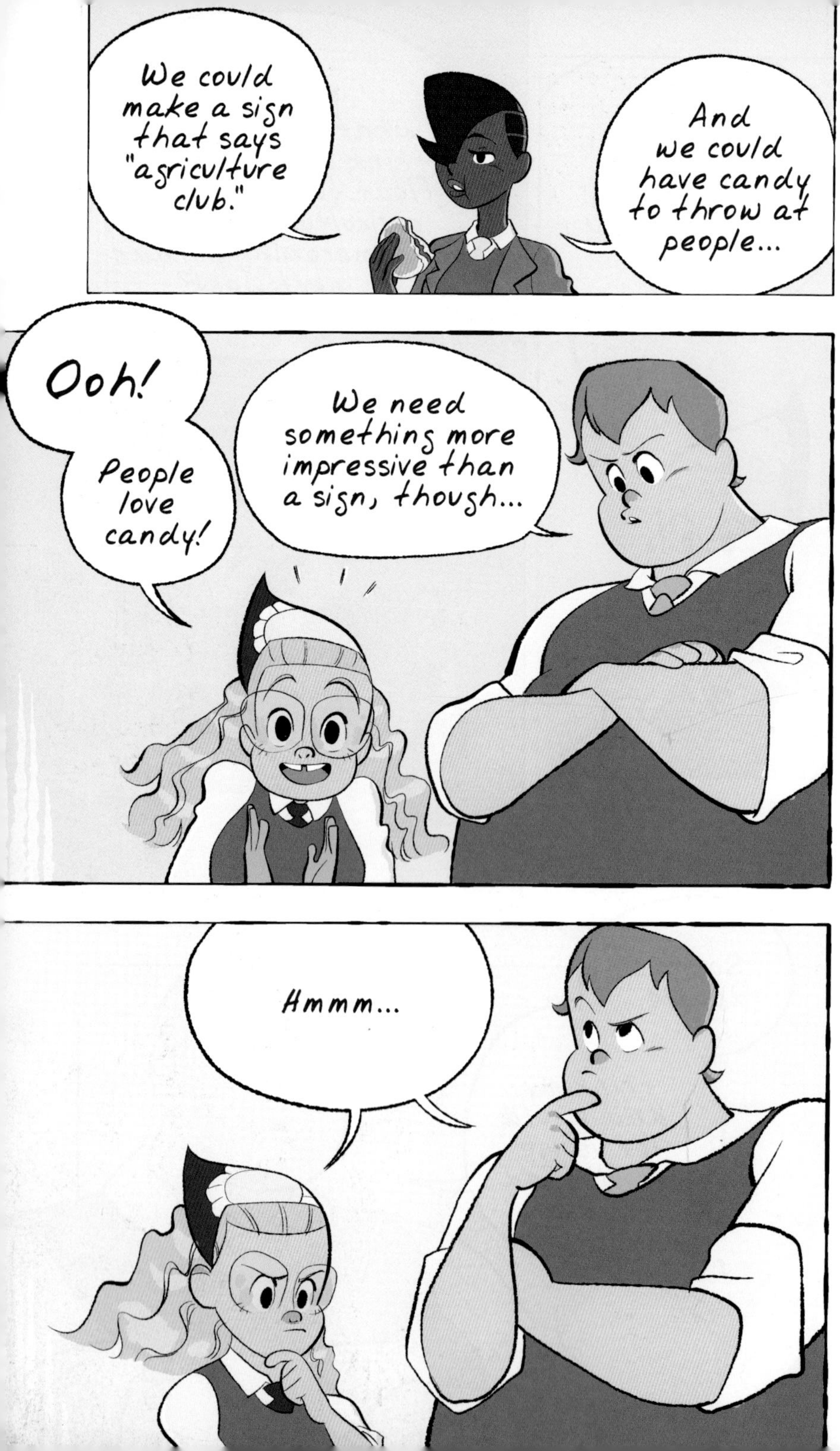
We could make a sign that says "agriculture club."
And we could have candy to throw at people...
Ooh!
People love candy!
We need something more impressive than a sign, though...
Hmmm...

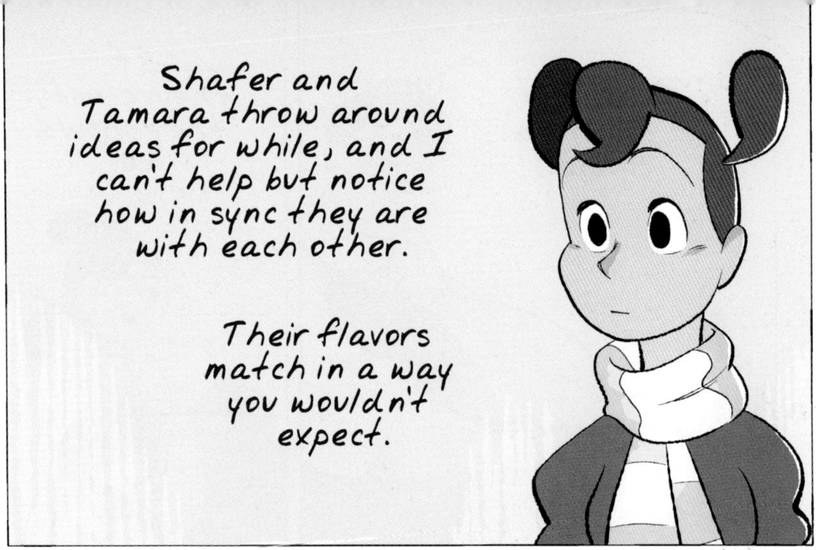
Shafer and Tamara throw around ideas for while, and I can't help but notice how in sync they are with each other.
Their flavors match in a way you wouldn't expect.

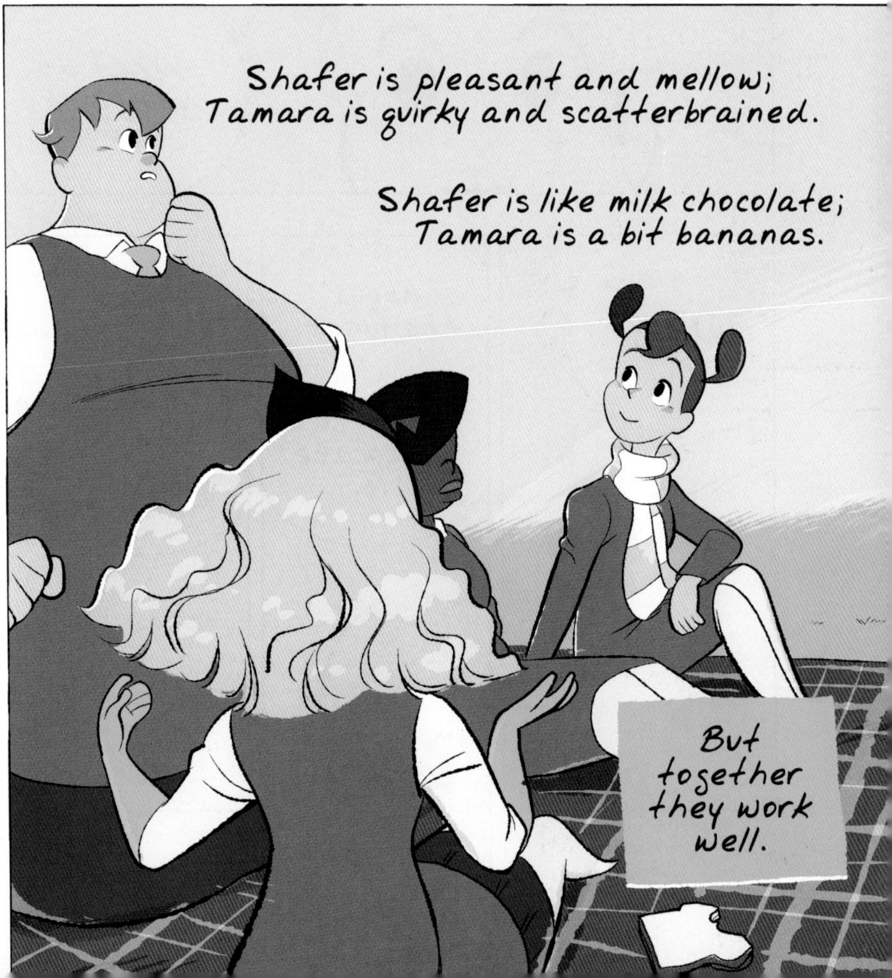
Shafer is pleasant and mellow; Tamara is quirky and scatterbrained.
Shafer is like milk chocolate; Tamara is a bit bananas.
But together they work well.

I wonder if they're a couple?

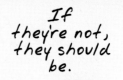

If they're not, they should be.

What do you think, Amy?

What?

About the float.

How to decorate it.

Oh, uh...

What if we went with, like, a fall theme?

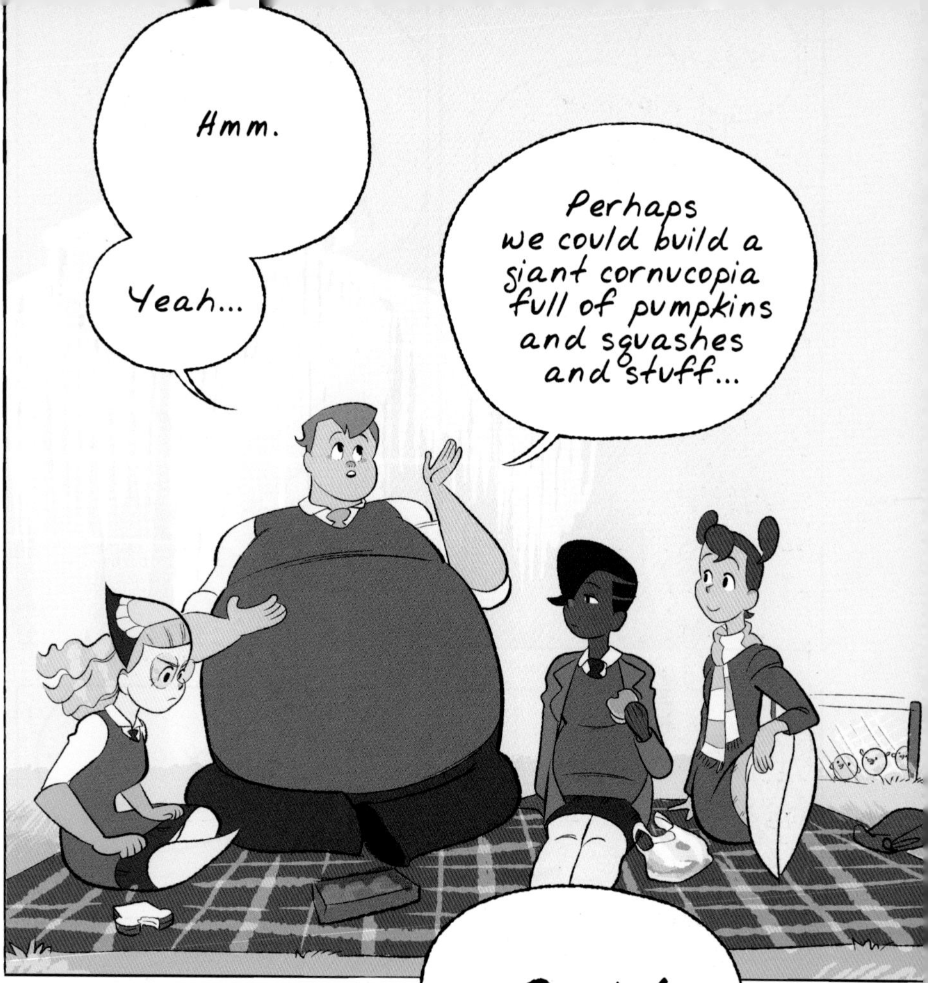
Hmm.
Yeah...
Perhaps we could build a giant cornucopia full of pumpkins and squashes and stuff...

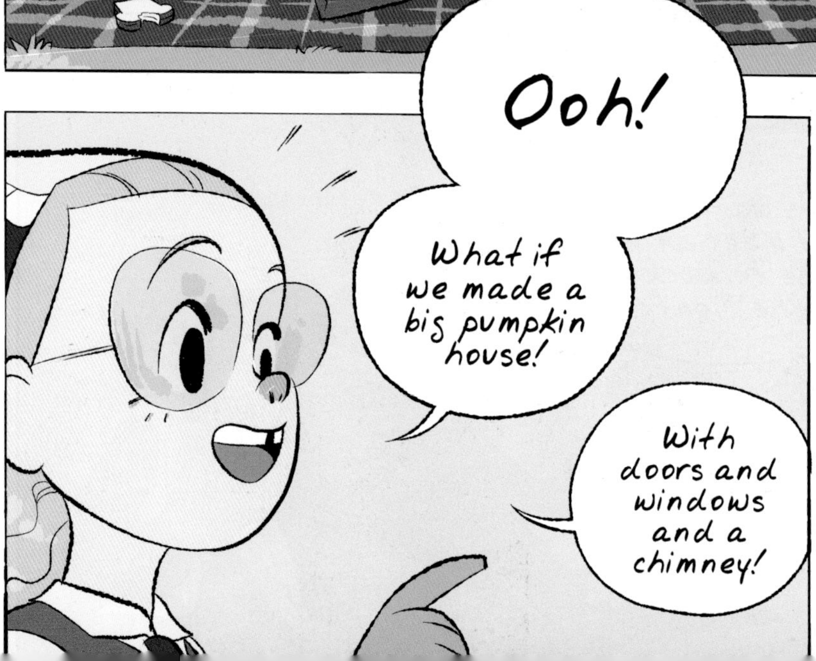
Ooh!
What if we made a big pumpkin house!
With doors and windows and a chimney!

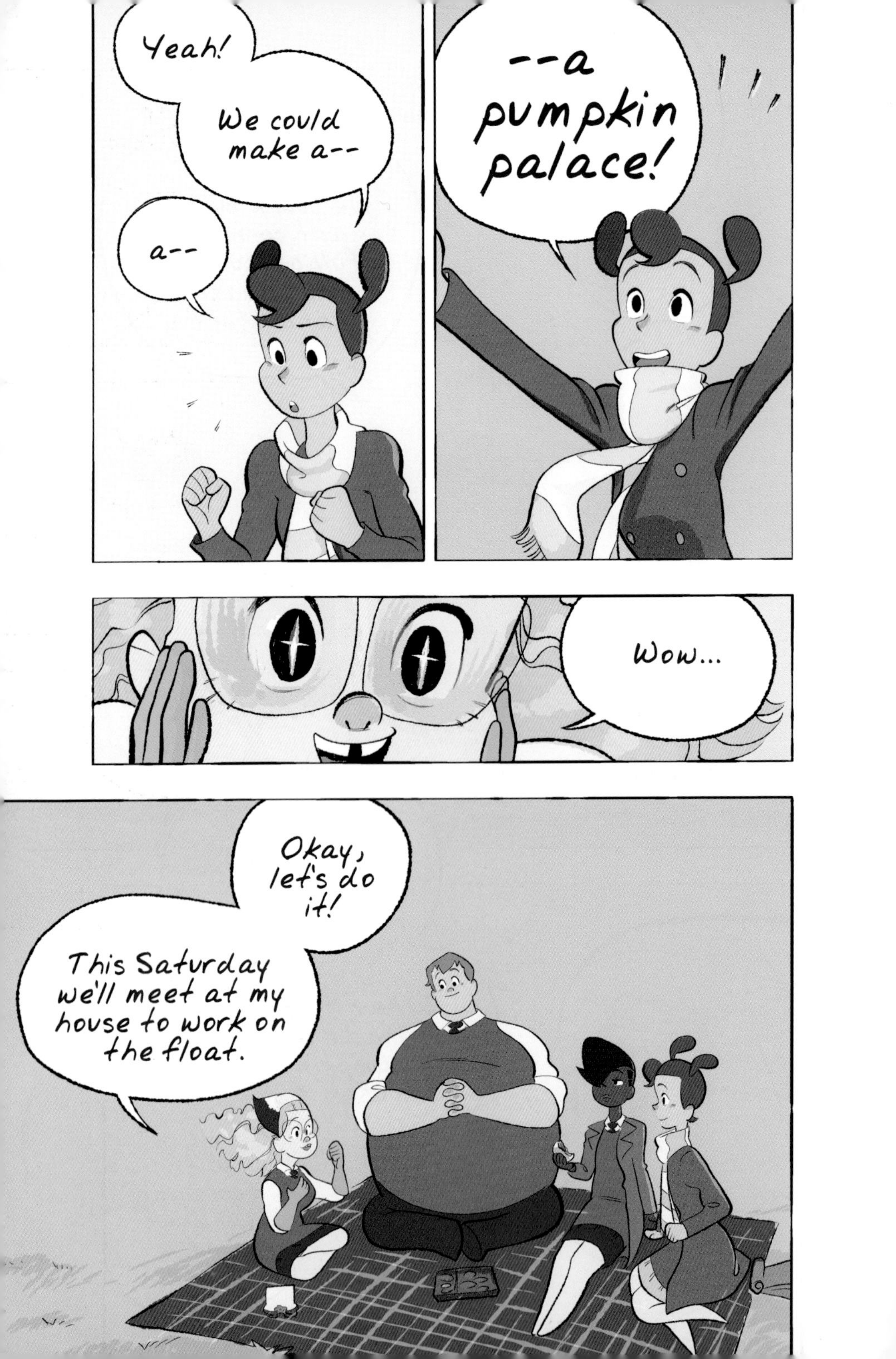
Yeah!
We could make a--
a--
--a pumpkin palace!
Wow...
Okay, let's do it!
This Saturday we'll meet at my house to work on the float.

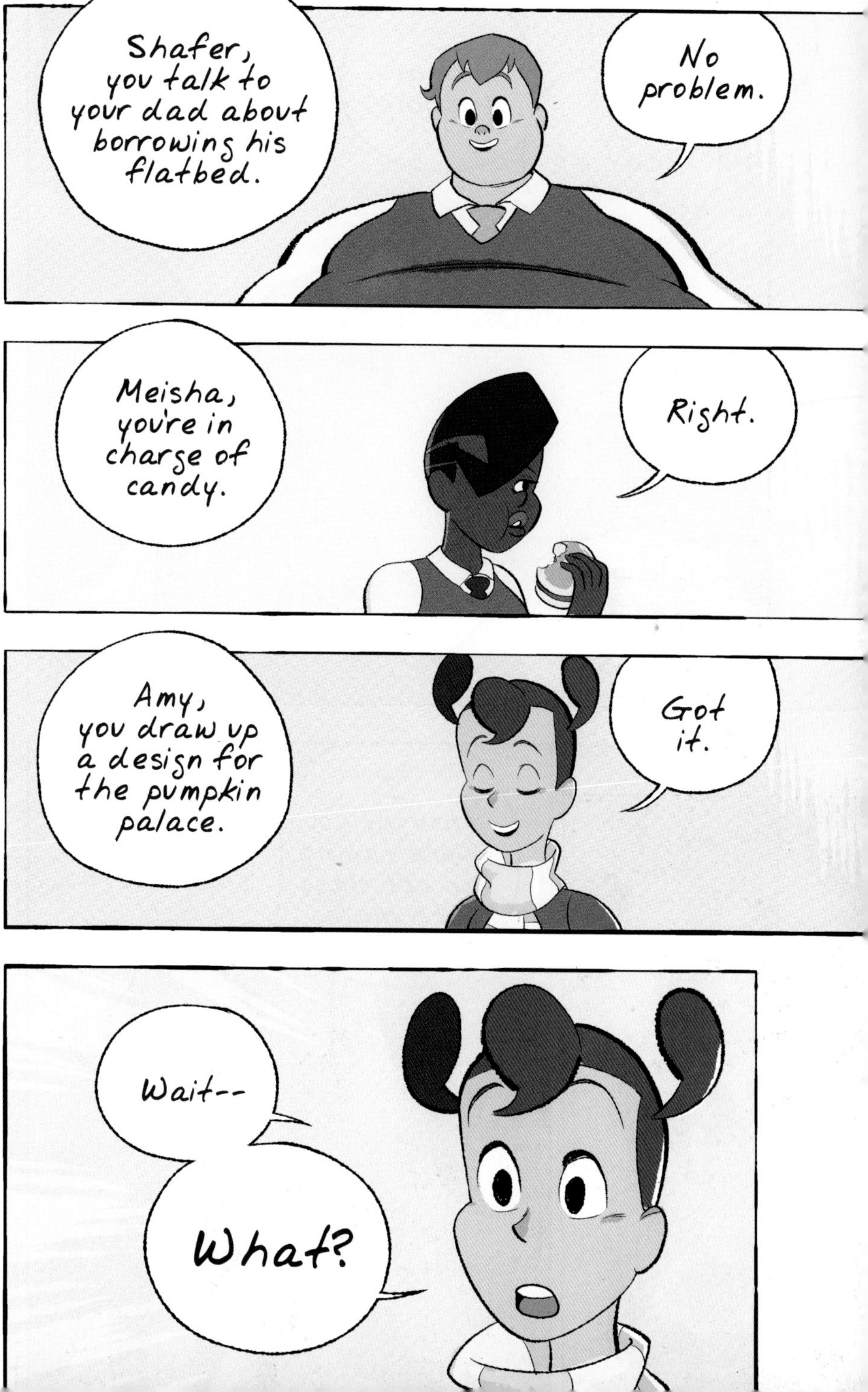
Shafer, you talk to your dad about borrowing his flatbed.
No problem.
Meisha, you're in charge of candy.
Right.
Amy, you draw up a design for the pumpkin palace.
Got it.
Wait--
What?

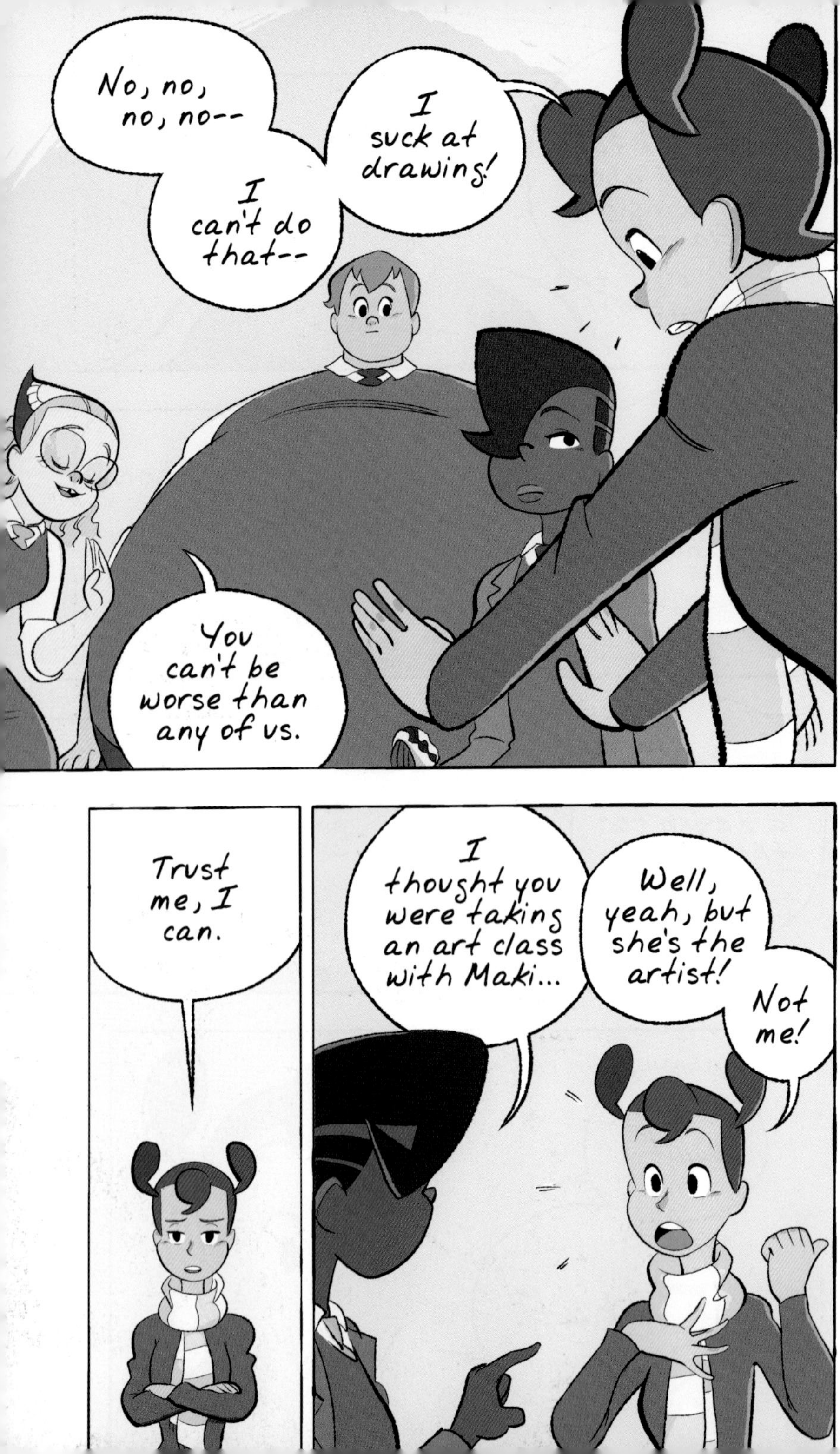
No, no, no, no--
I suck at drawing!
I can't do that--
You can't be worse than any of us.
Trust me, I can.
I thought you were taking an art class with Maki...
Well, yeah, but she's the artist!
Not me!

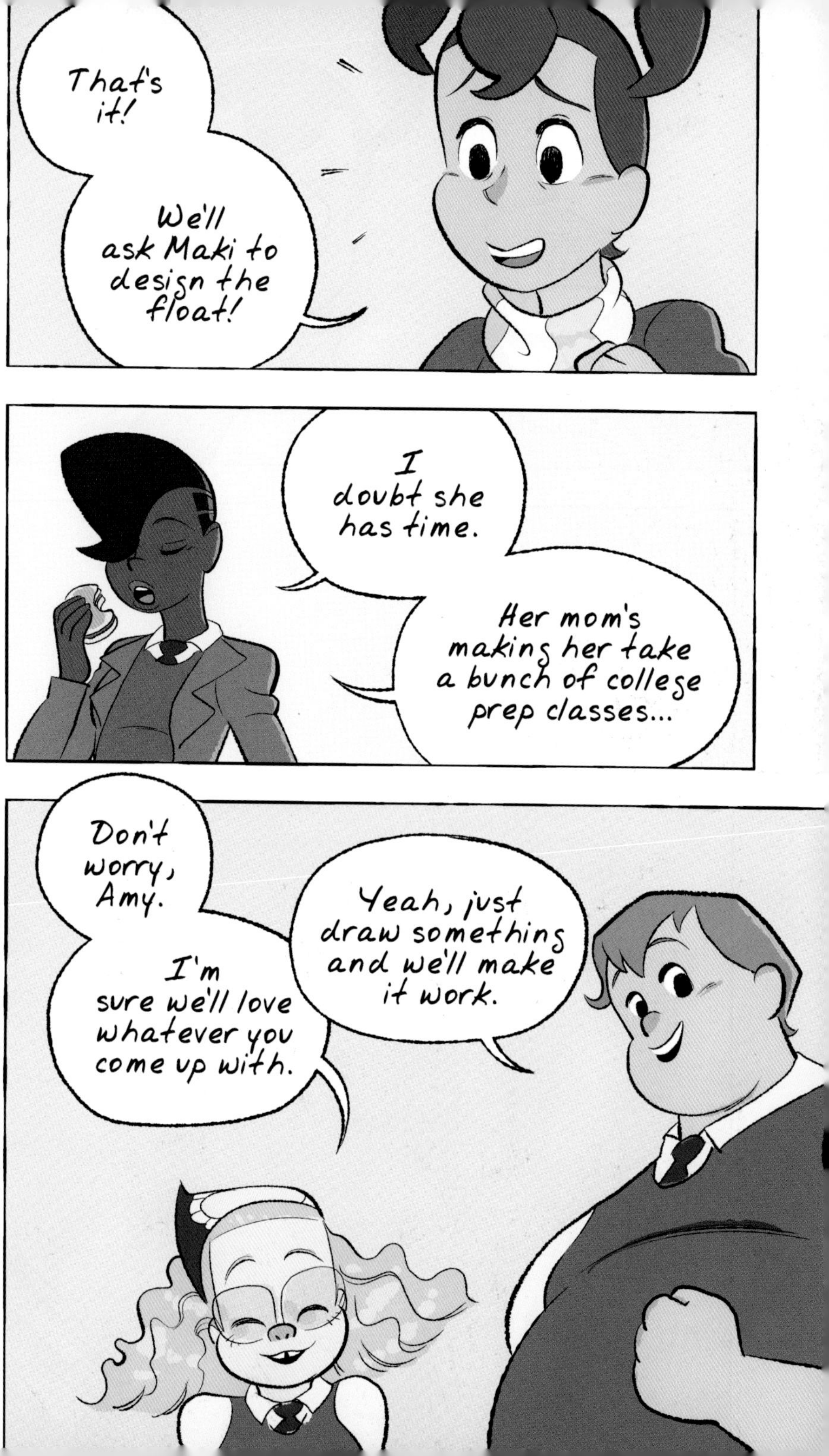
That's it!
We'll ask Maki to design the float!
I doubt she has time.
Her mom's making her take a bunch of college prep classes...
Don't worry, Amy.
I'm sure we'll love whatever you come up with.
Yeah, just draw something and we'll make it work.

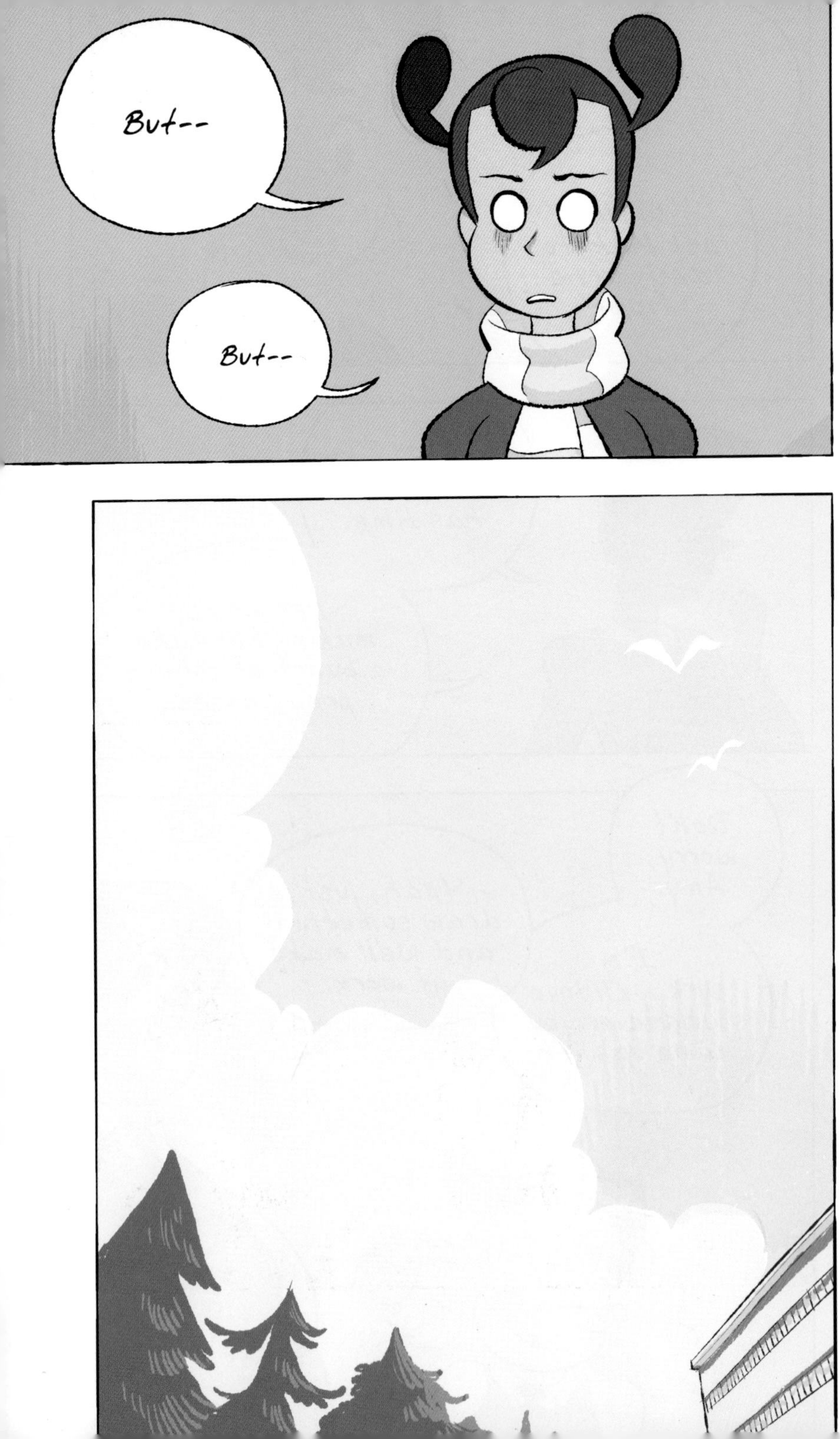
But--
But--

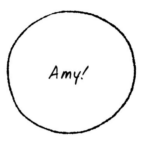

Amy!

Hey!

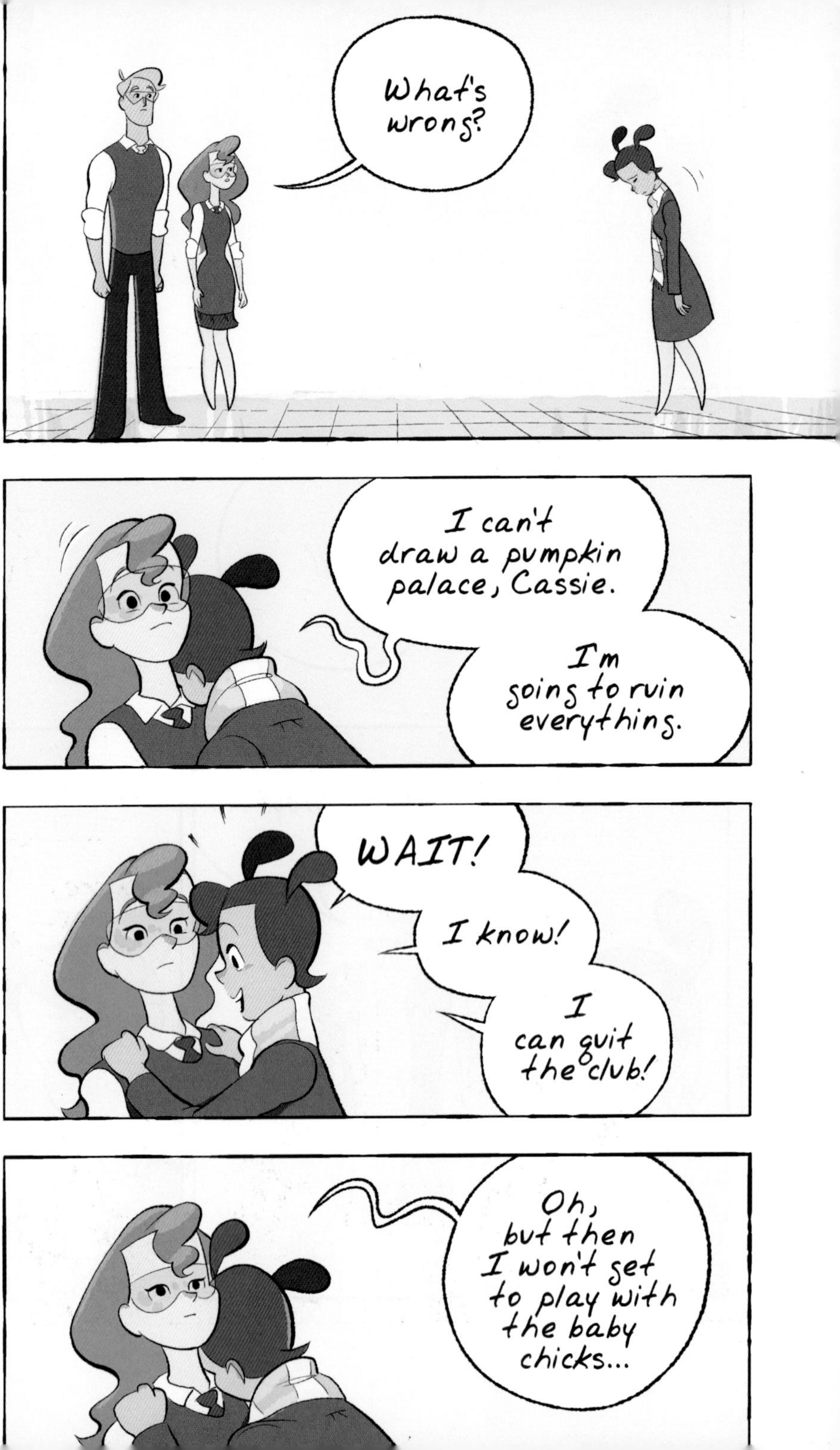
What's wrong?
I can't draw a pumpkin palace, Cassie.
I'm going to ruin everything.
WAIT!
I know!
I can quit the club!
Oh, but then I won't get to play with the baby chicks...

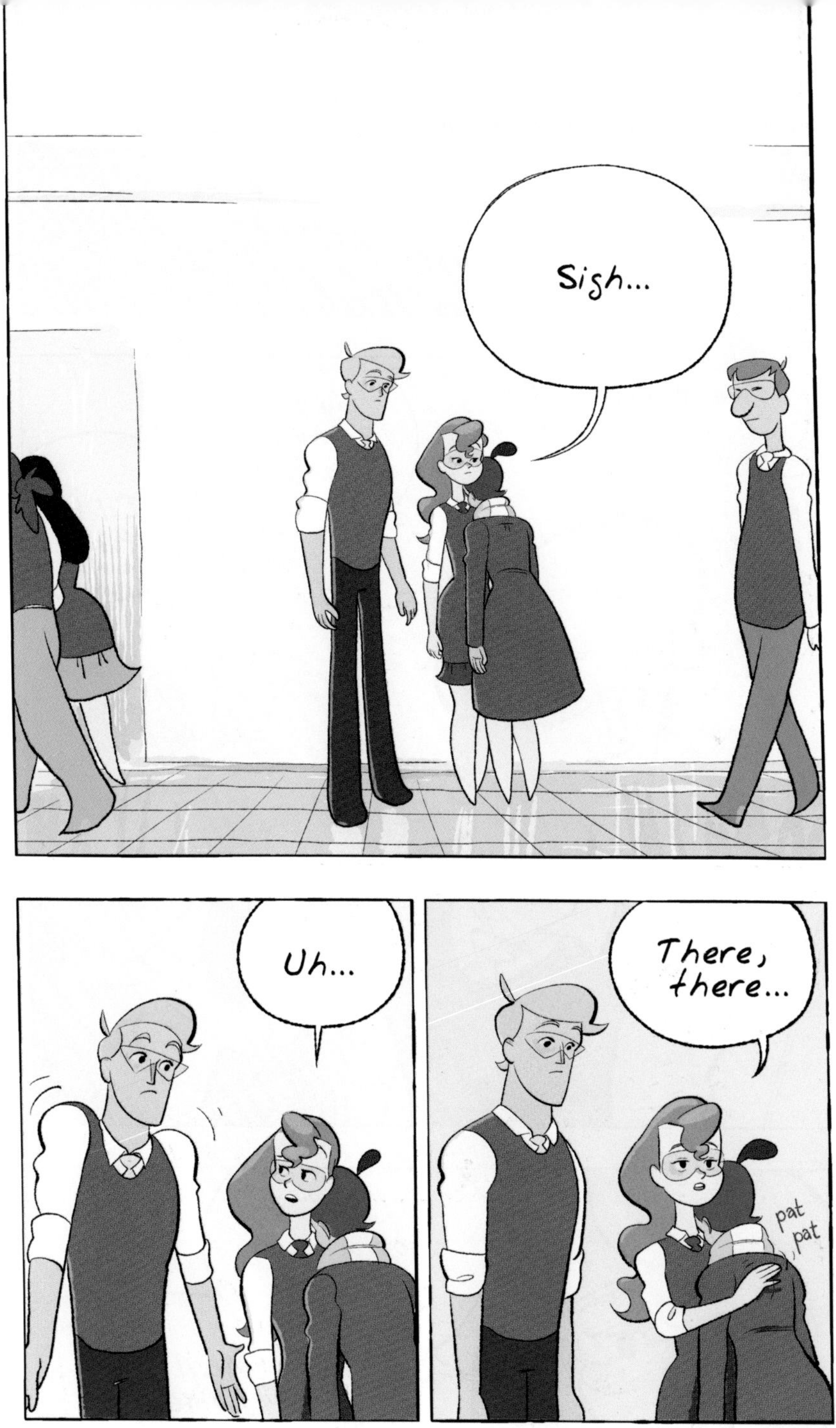
Sigh...
Uh...
There, there...
pat pat

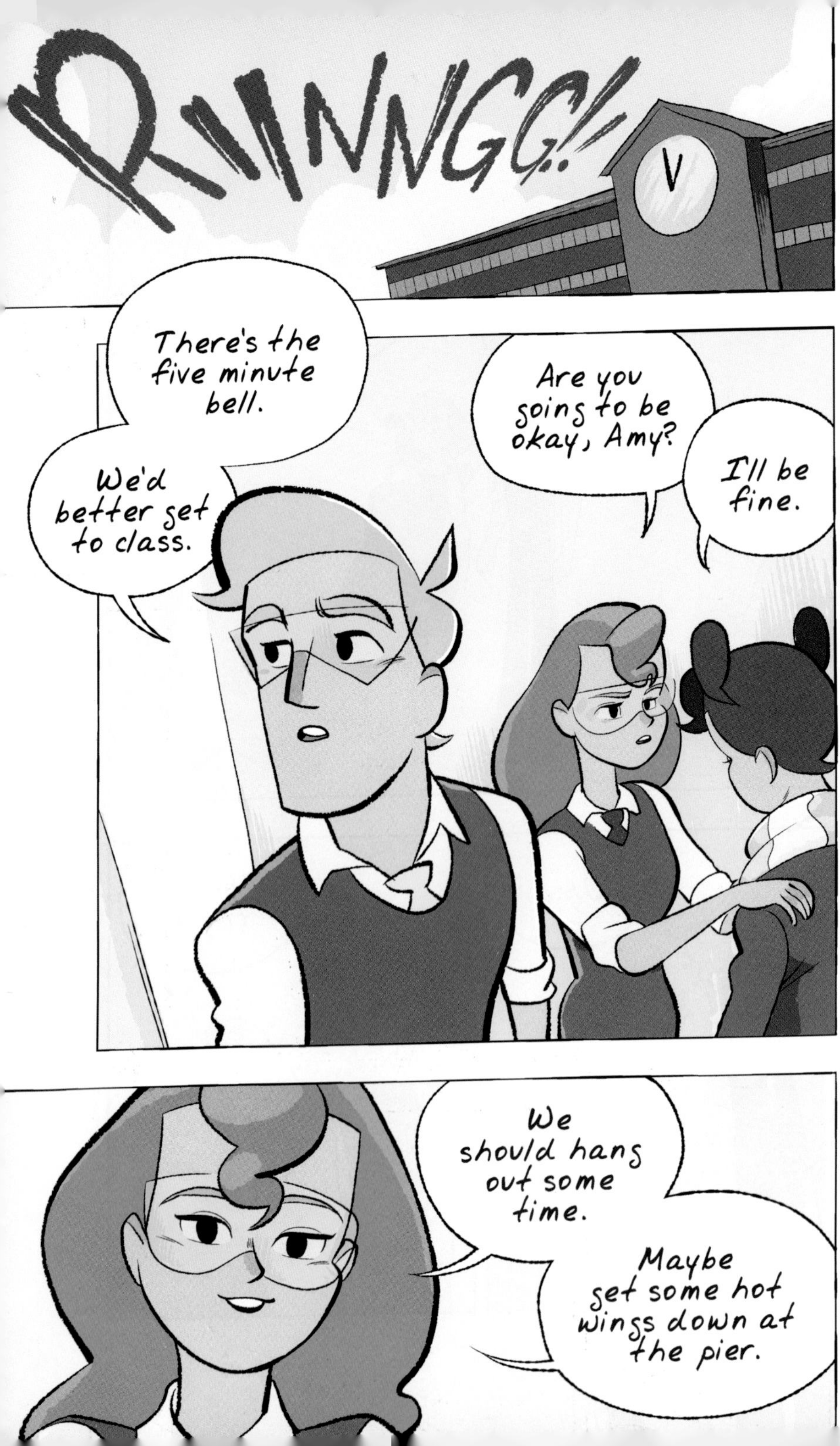
RIIINGG!!
There's the five minute bell.
We'd better get to class.
Are you going to be okay, Amy?
I'll be fine.
We should hang out some time.
Maybe get some hot wings down at the pier.

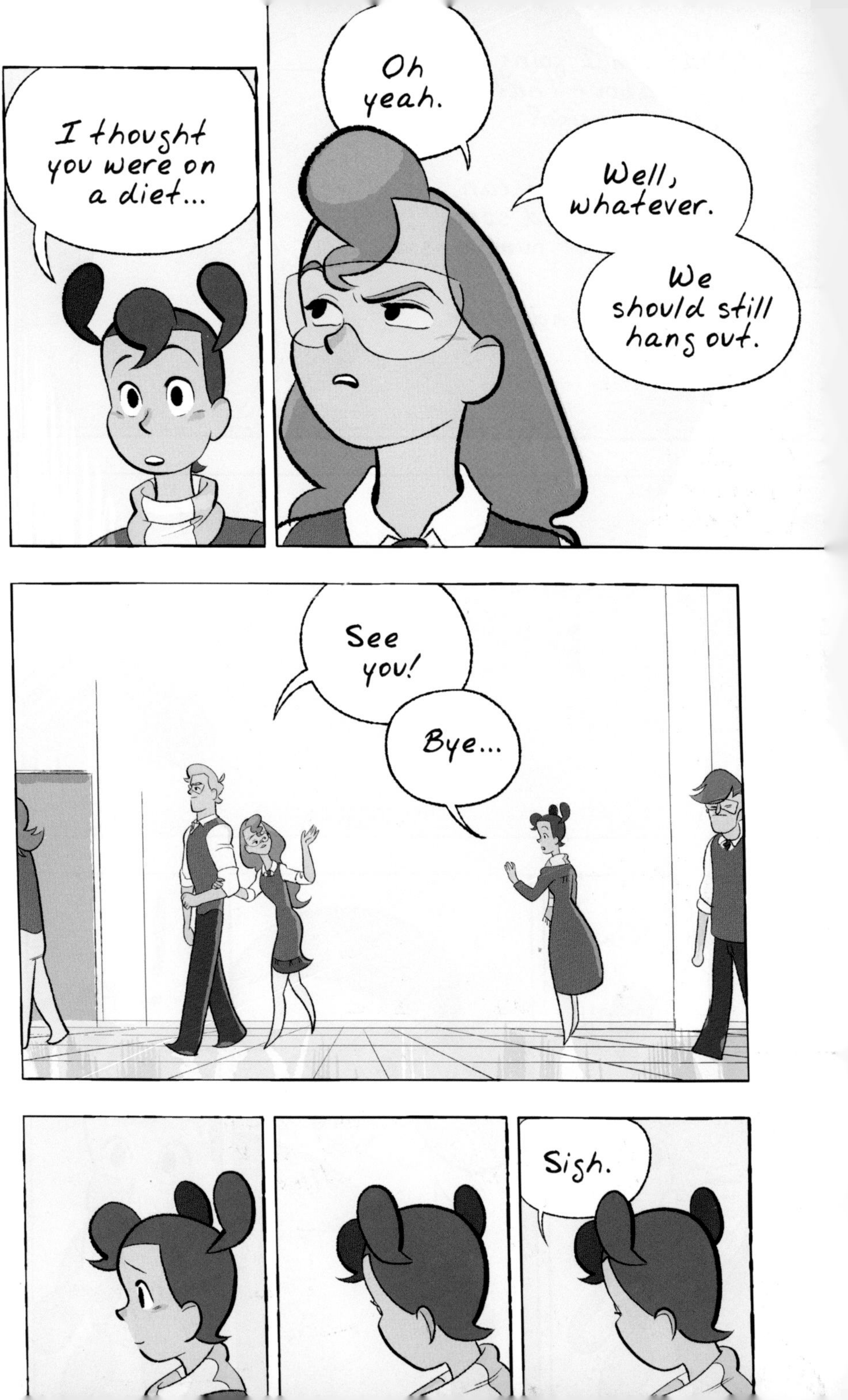
I thought you were on a diet...
Oh yeah.
Well, whatever.
We should still hang out.
See you!
Bye...
Sigh.

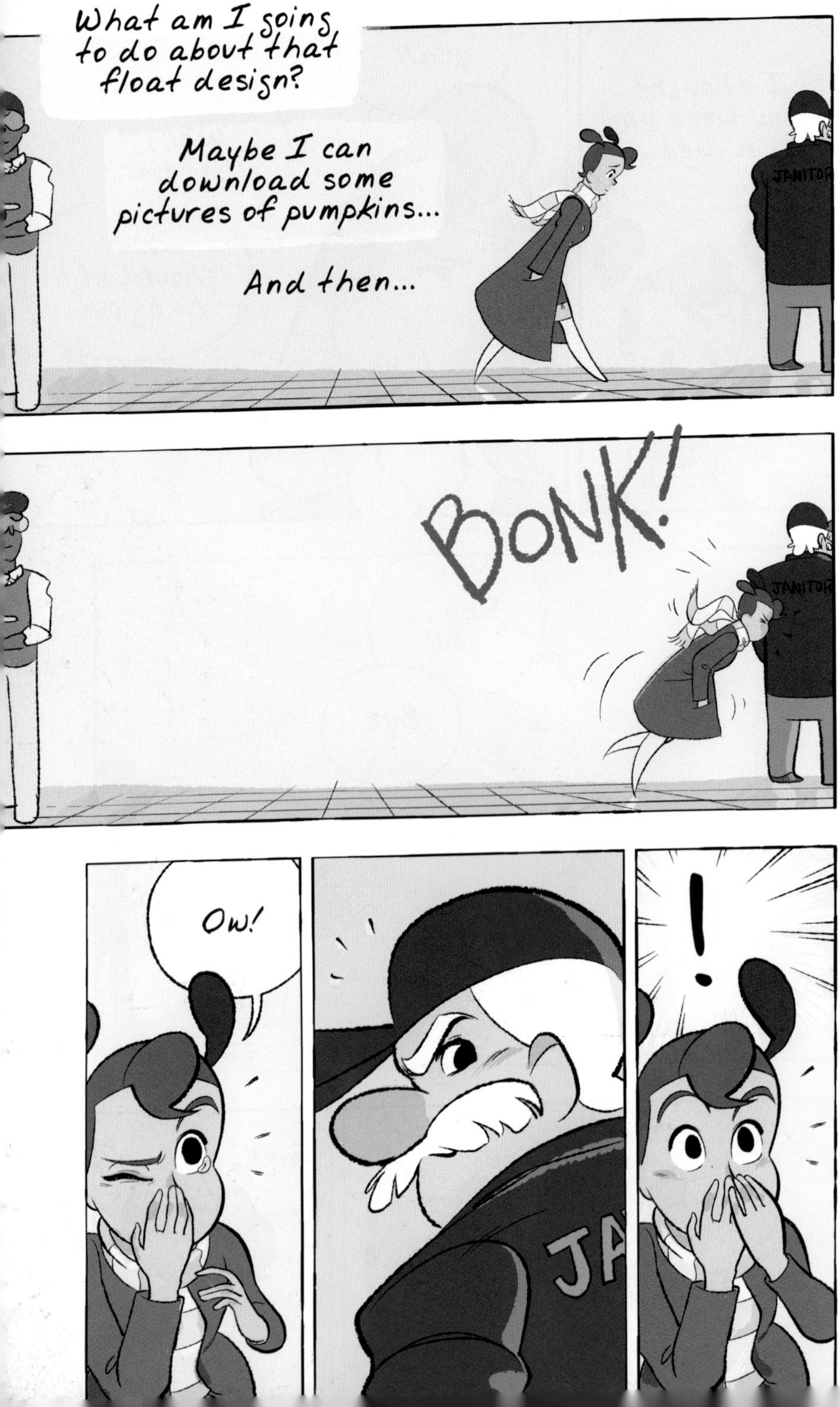
What am I going to do about that float design?
Maybe I can download some pictures of pumpkins...
And then...
JANITOR
BONK!
JANITOR
Ow!
JA
!

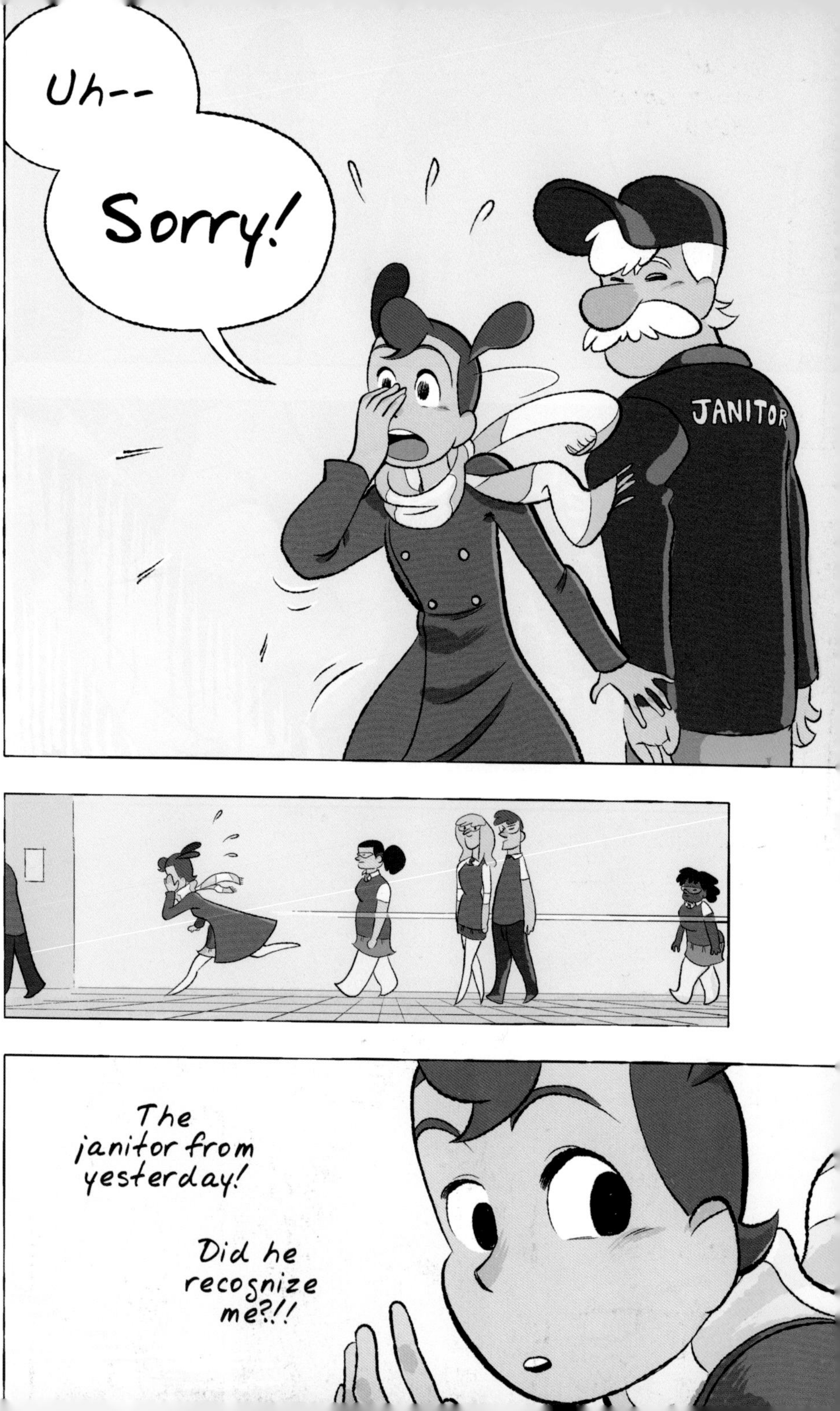
Uh--
Sorry!
JANITOR
The janitor from yesterday!
Did he recognize me?!!

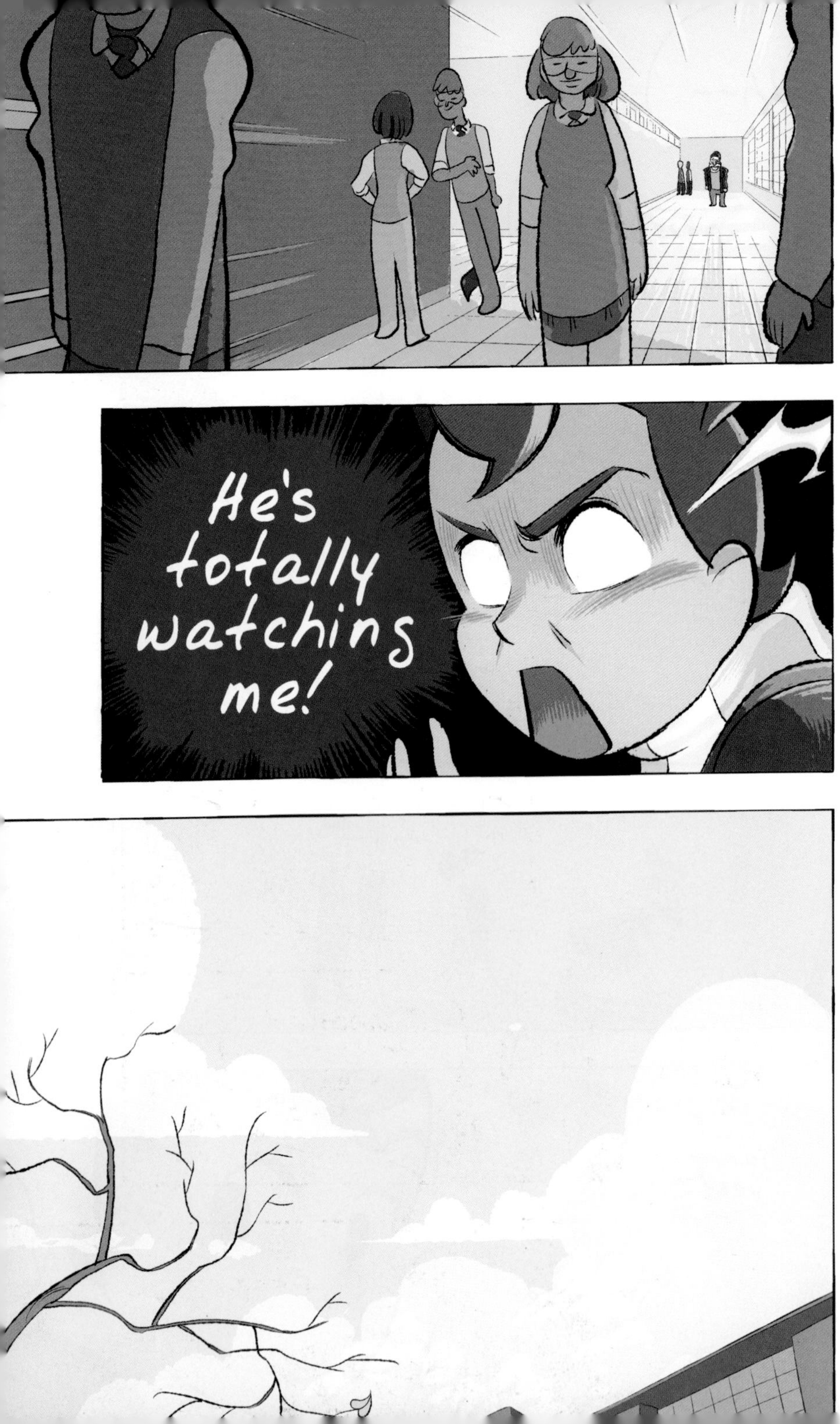
He's totally watching me!

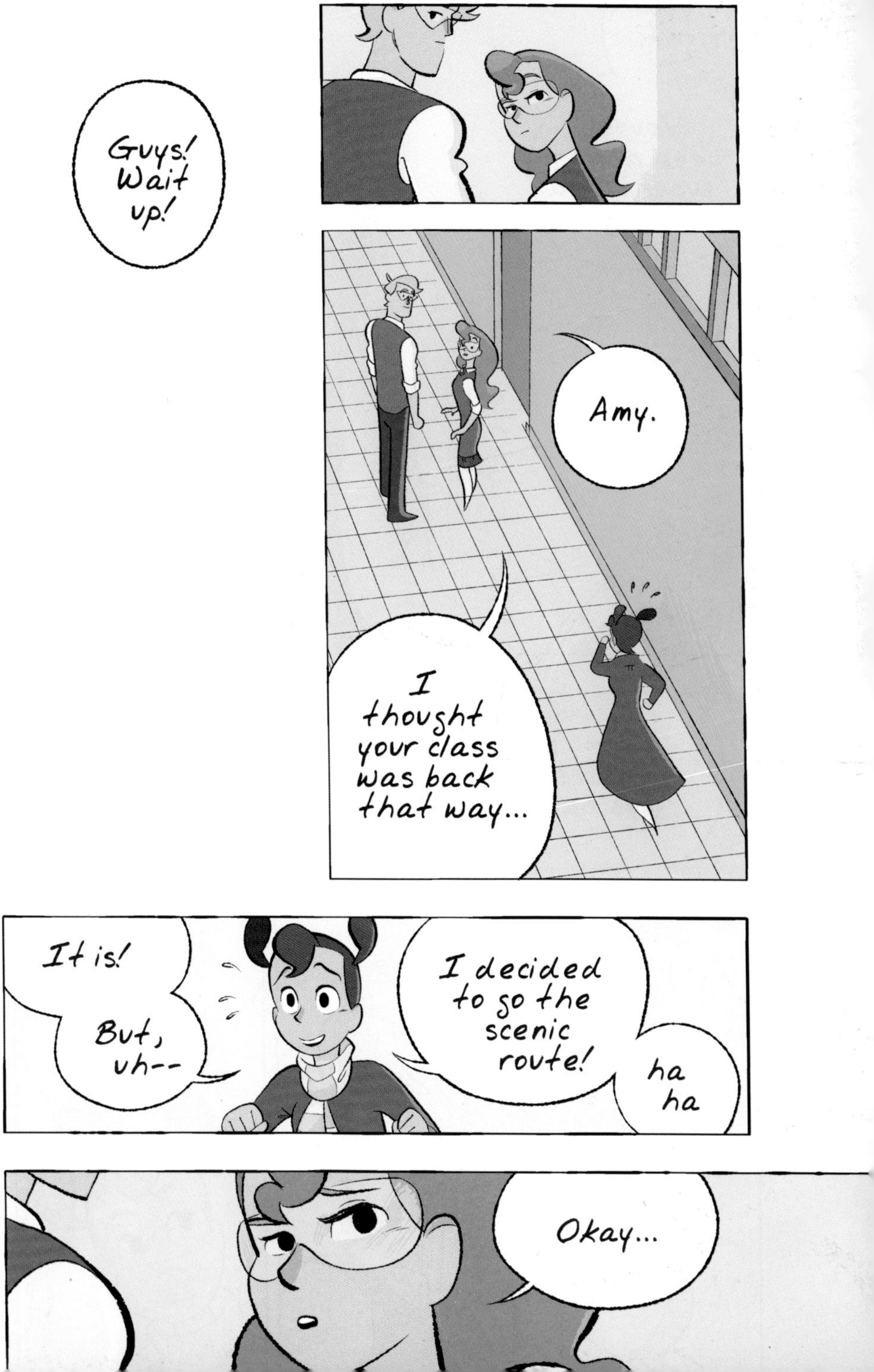
Guys! Wait up!
Amy.
I thought your class was back that way...
It is!
But, uh--
I decided to go the scenic route!
ha ha
Okay...

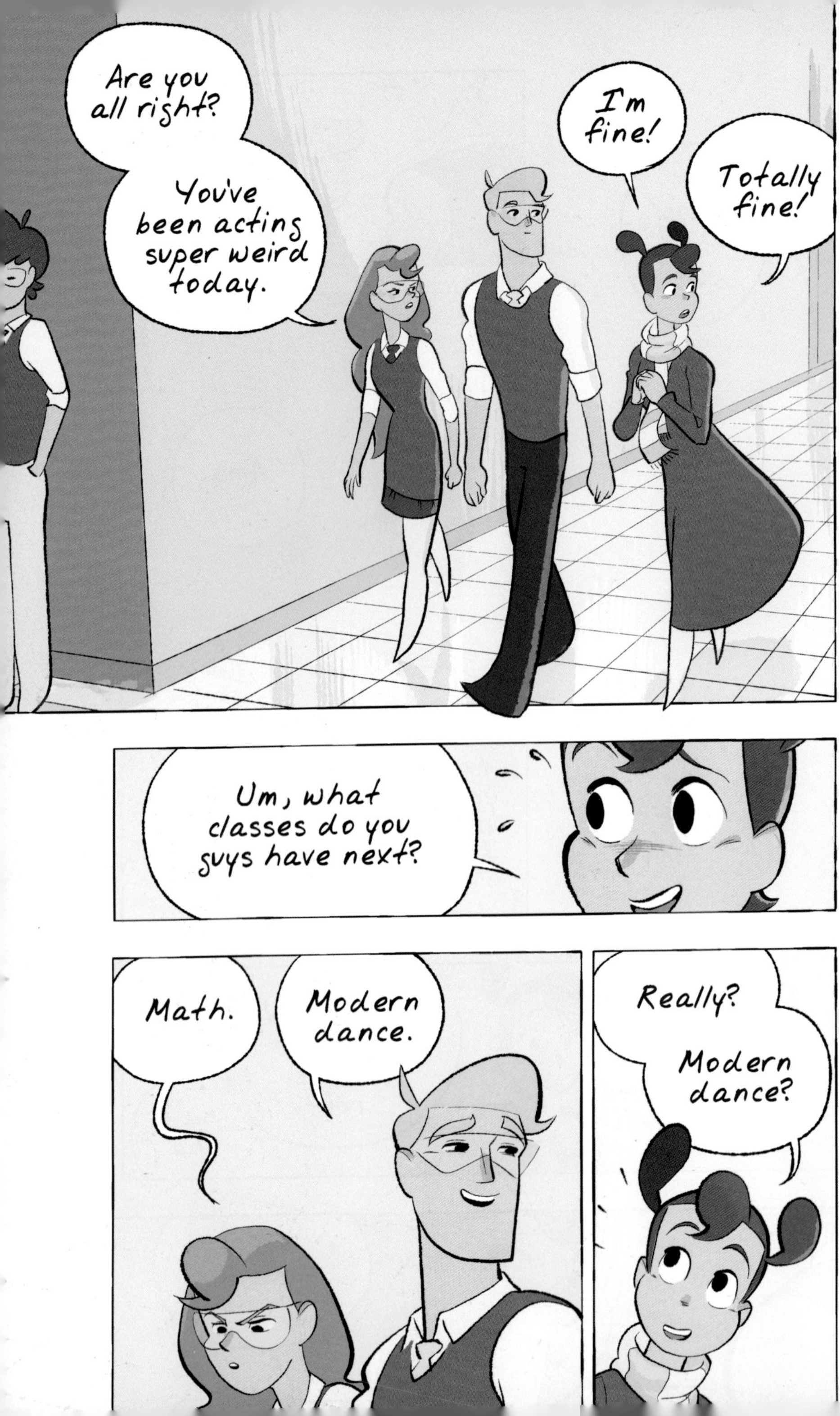
Are you all right?
You've been acting super weird today.
I'm fine!
Totally fine!
Um, what classes do you guys have next?
Math.
Modern dance.
Really?
Modern dance?

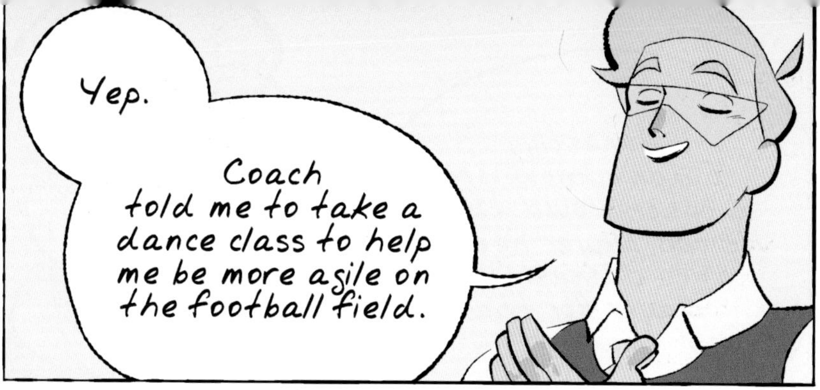
Yep.
Coach told me to take a dance class to help me be more agile on the football field.

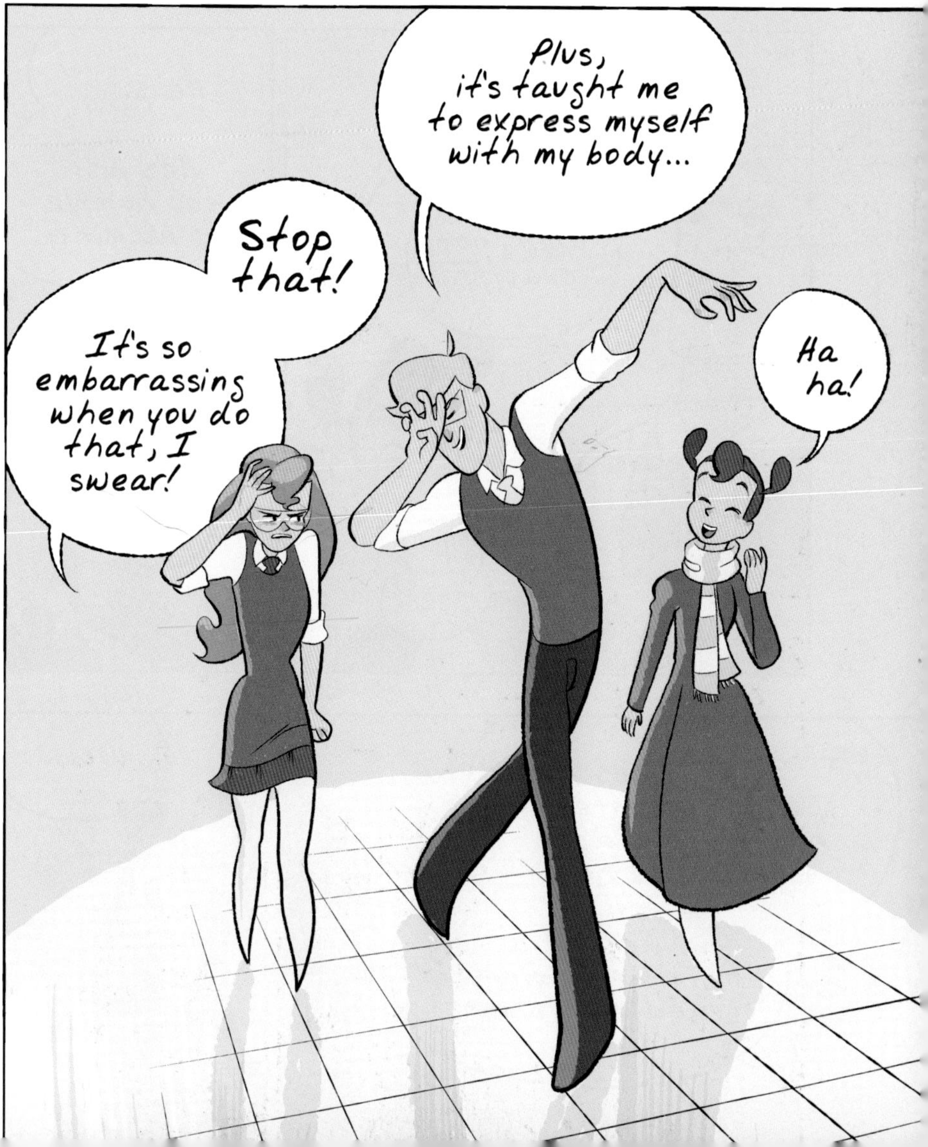
Plus, it's taught me to express myself with my body...
Stop that!
It's so embarrassing when you do that, I swear!
Ha ha!

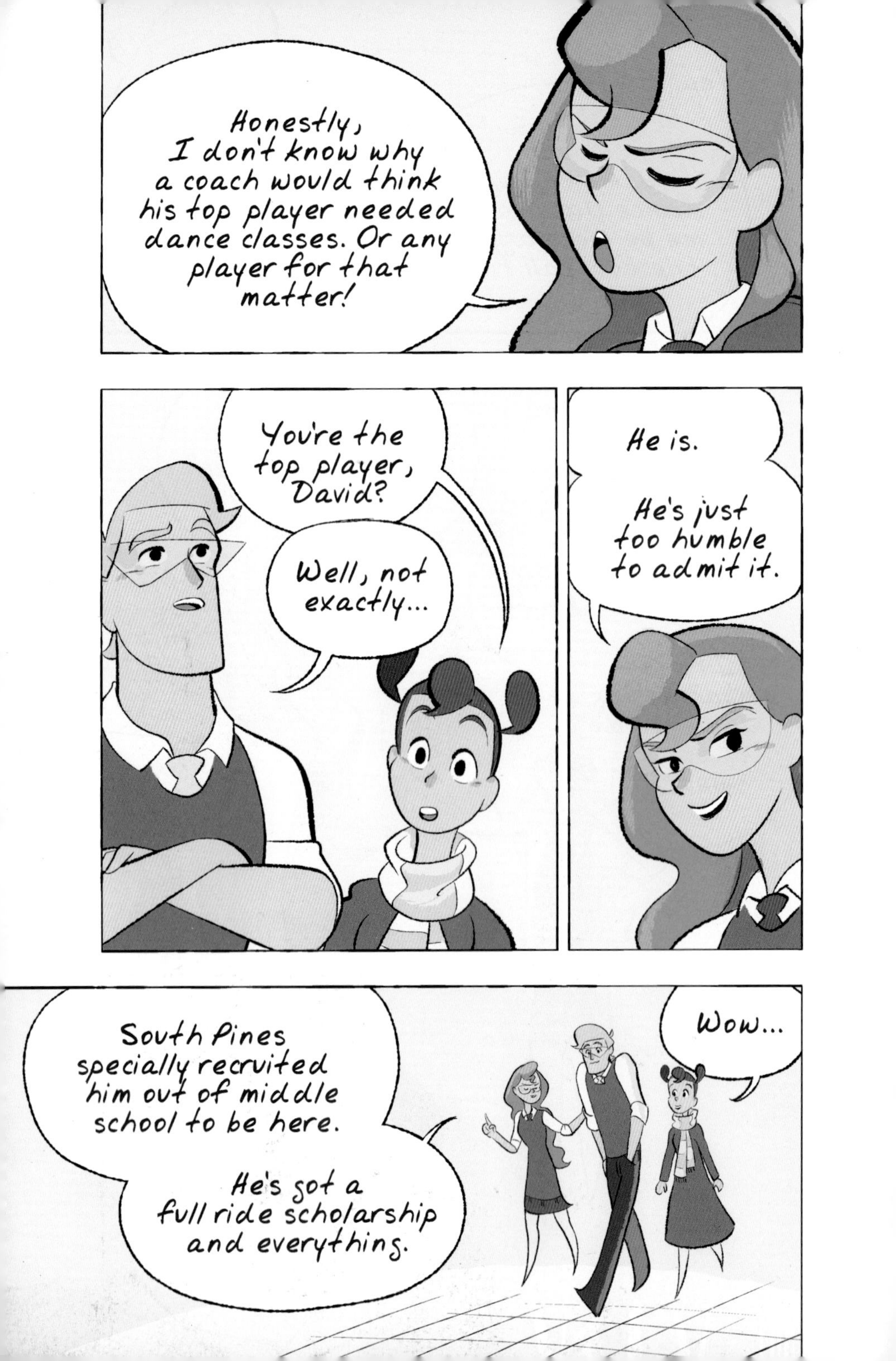
Honestly, I don't know why a coach would think his top player needed dance classes. Or any player for that matter!
You're the top player, David?
Well, not exactly...
He is.
He's just too humble to admit it.
South Pines specially recruited him out of middle school to be here.
He's got a full ride scholarship and everything.
Wow...

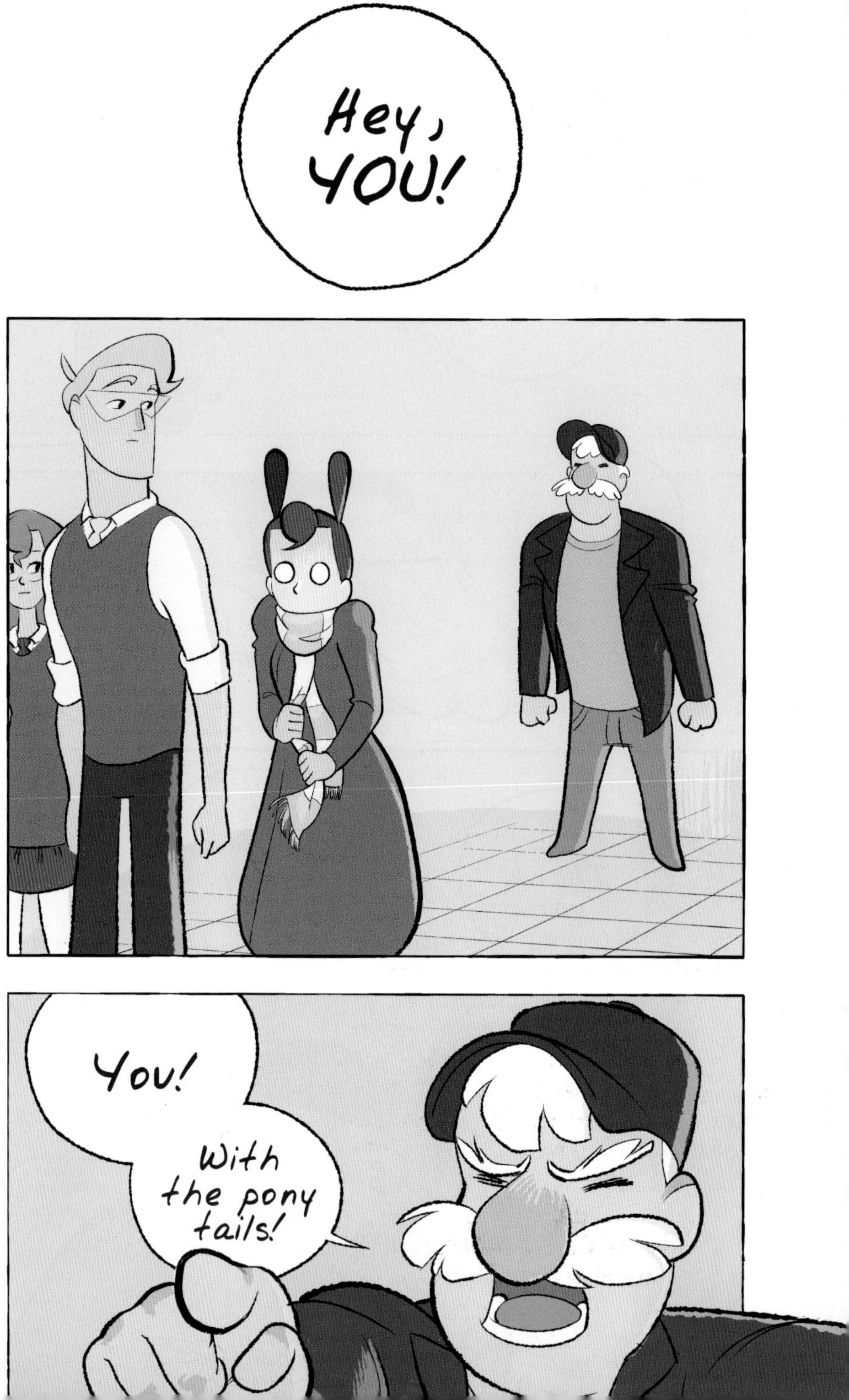
Hey, YOU!
You!
With the pony tails!

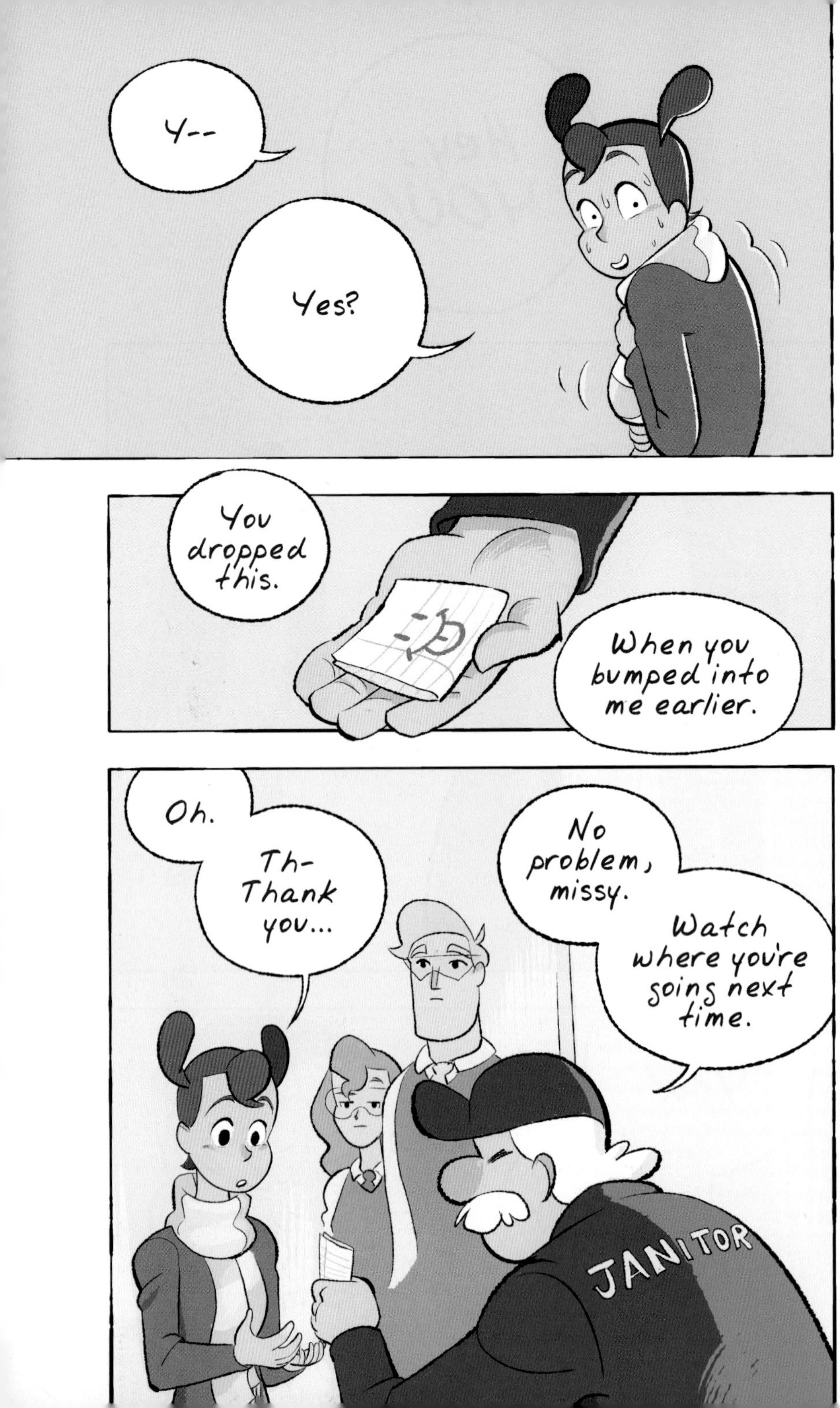
Y--
Yes?
You dropped this.
When you bumped into me earlier.
Oh.
Th- Thank you...
No problem, missy.
Watch where you're going next time.
JANITOR

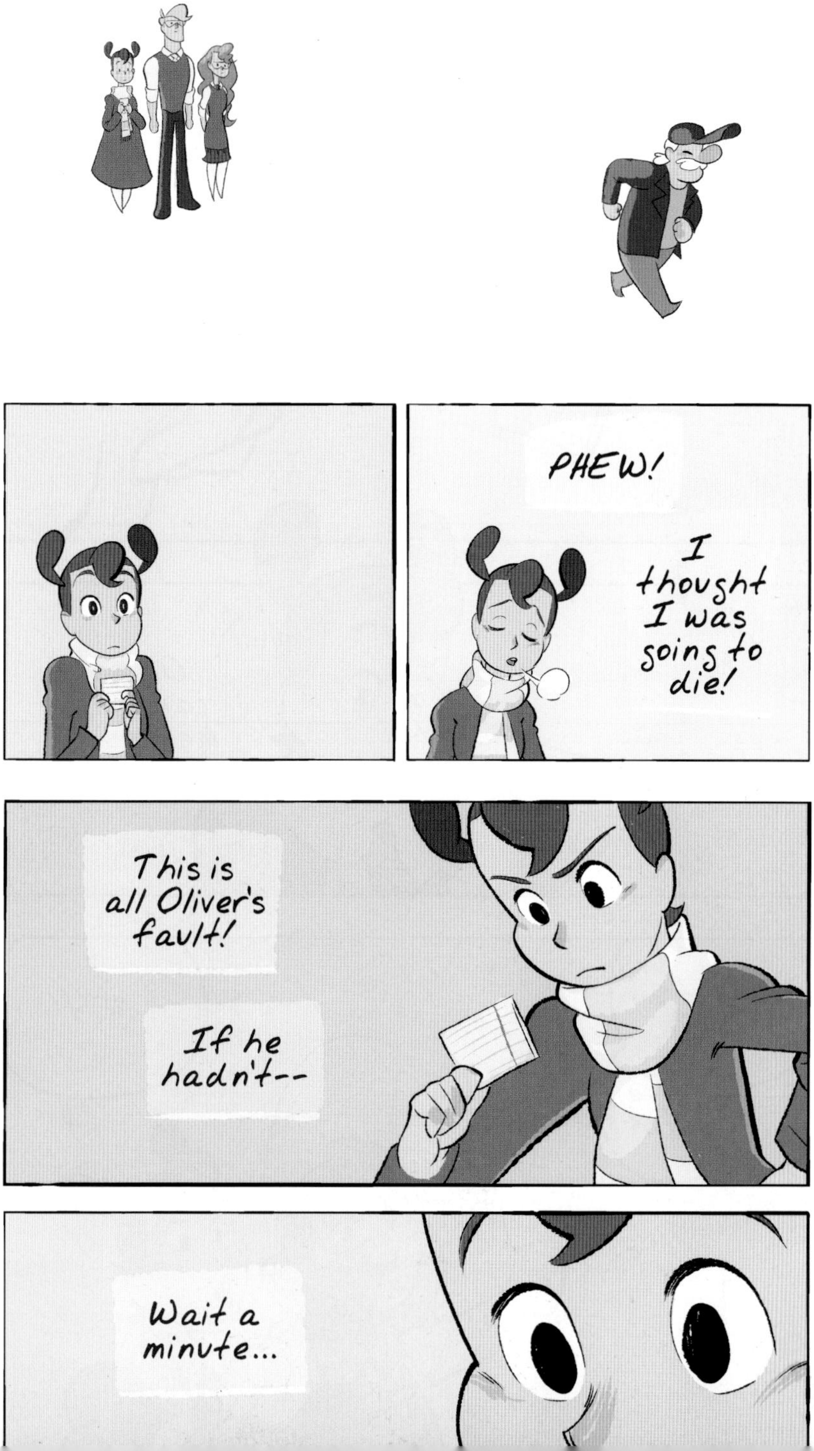
PHEW!
I thought I was going to die!
This is all Oliver's fault!
If he hadn't--
Wait a minute...

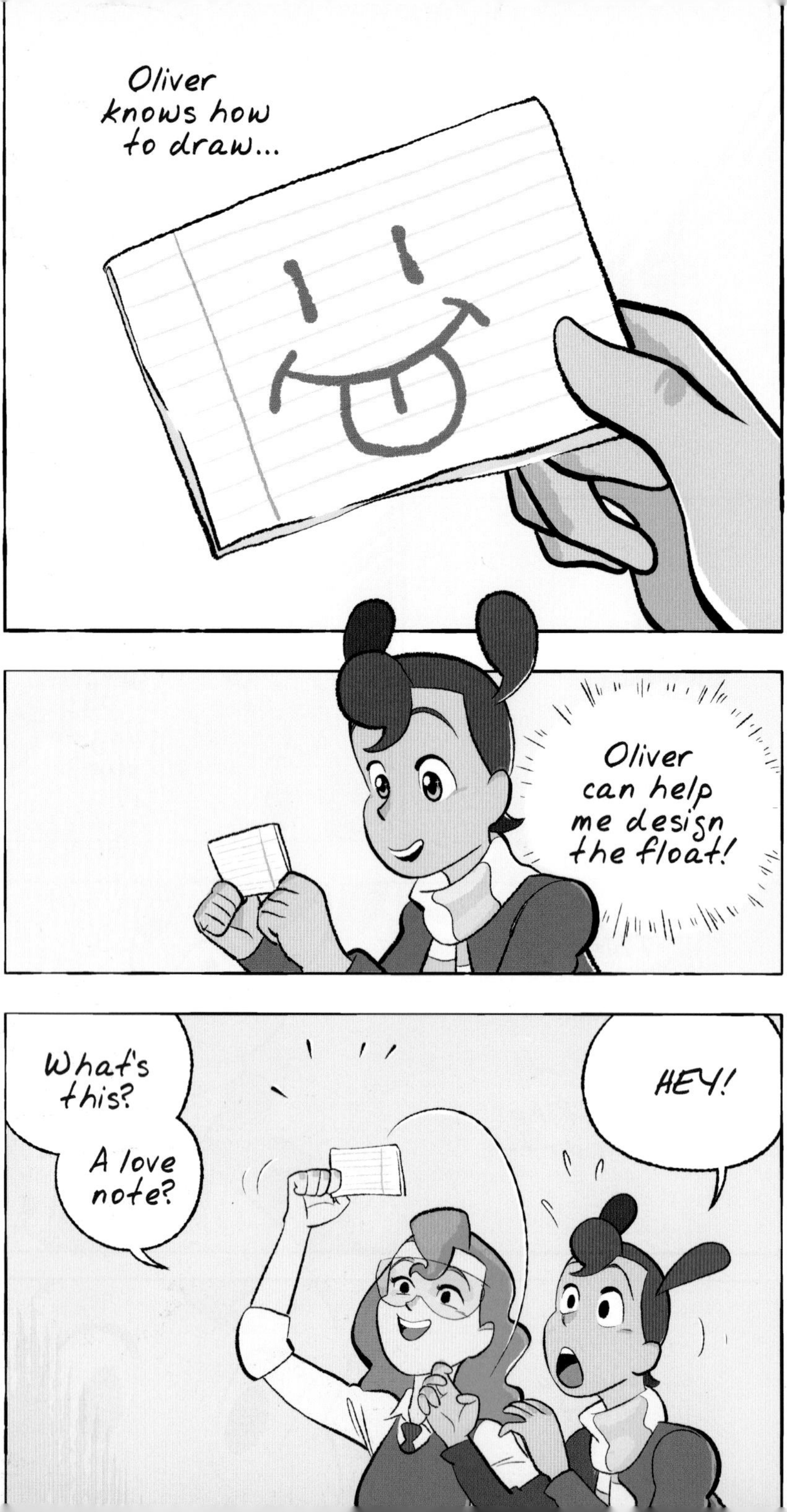
Oliver knows how to draw...
Oliver can help me design the float!
What's this?
A love note?
HEY!

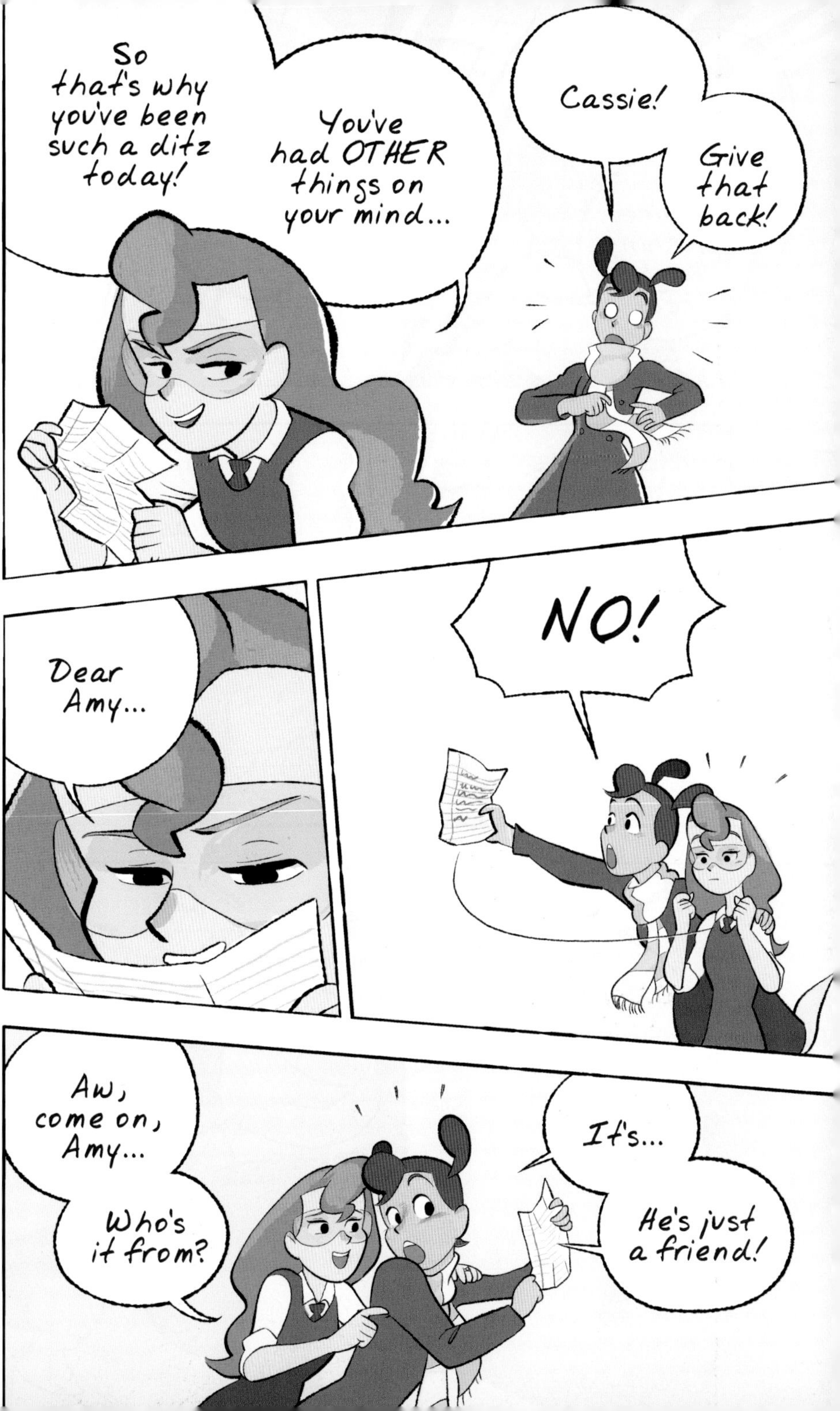
So that's why you've been such a ditz today!
You've had OTHER things on your mind...
Cassie!
Give that back!
Dear Amy...
NO!
Aw, come on, Amy...
Who's it from?
It's...
He's just a friend!

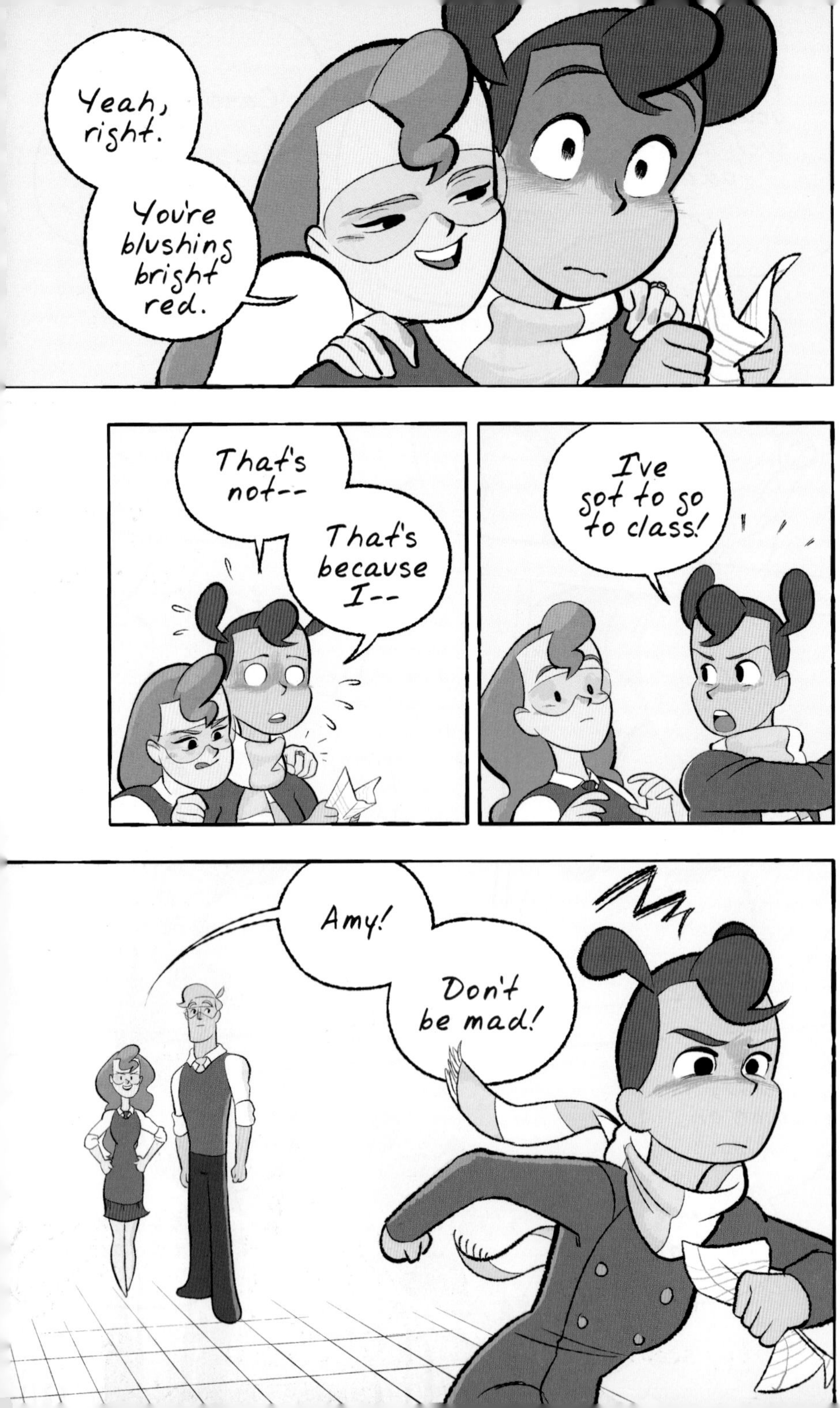
Yeah, right.
You're blushing bright red.
That's not--
That's because I--
I've got to go to class!
Amy!
Don't be mad!

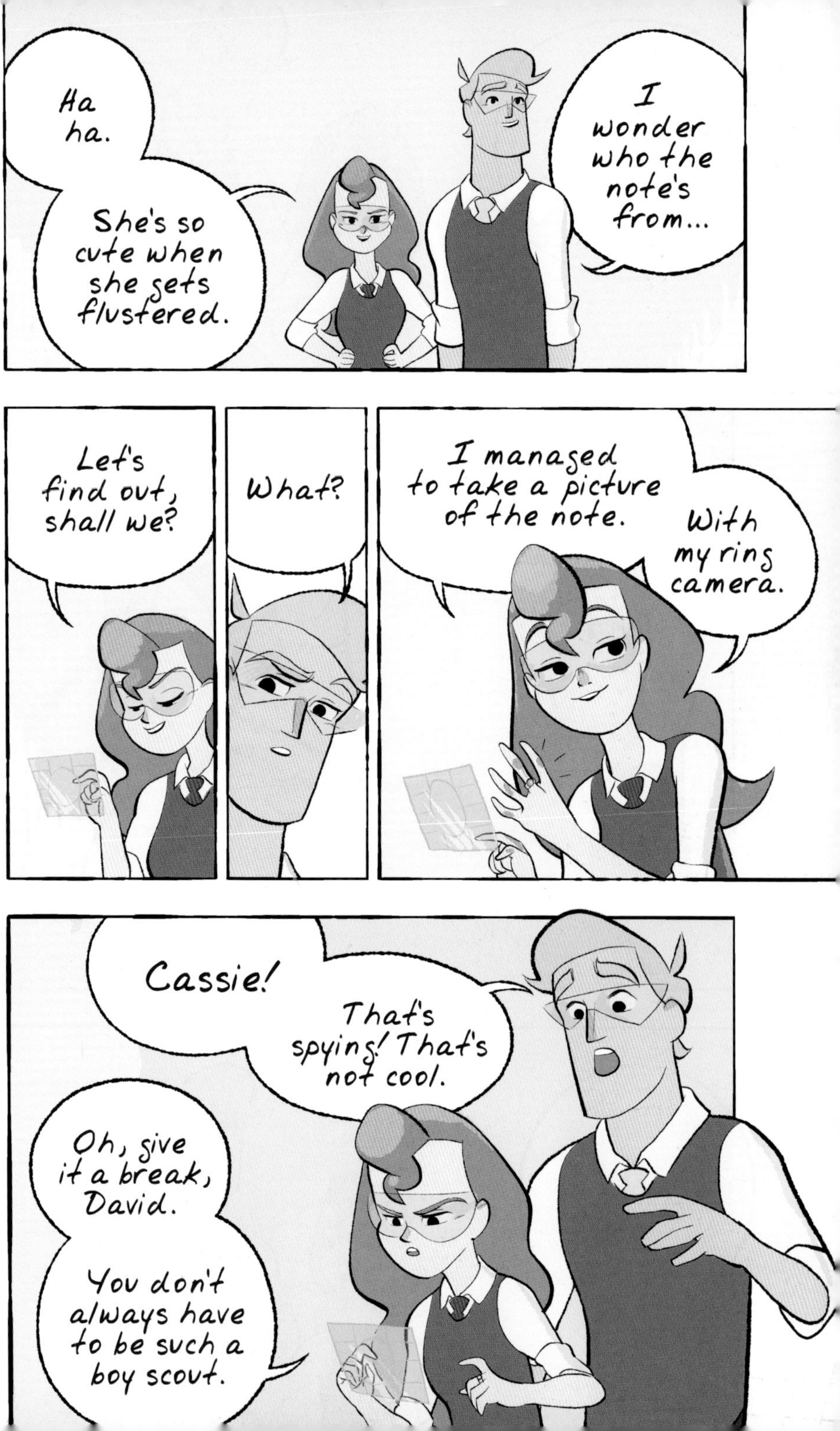
Ha ha.
She's so cute when she gets flustered.
I wonder who the note's from...
Let's find out, shall we?
What?
I managed to take a picture of the note.
With my ring camera.
Cassie!
That's spying! That's not cool.
Oh, give it a break, David.
You don't always have to be such a boy scout.

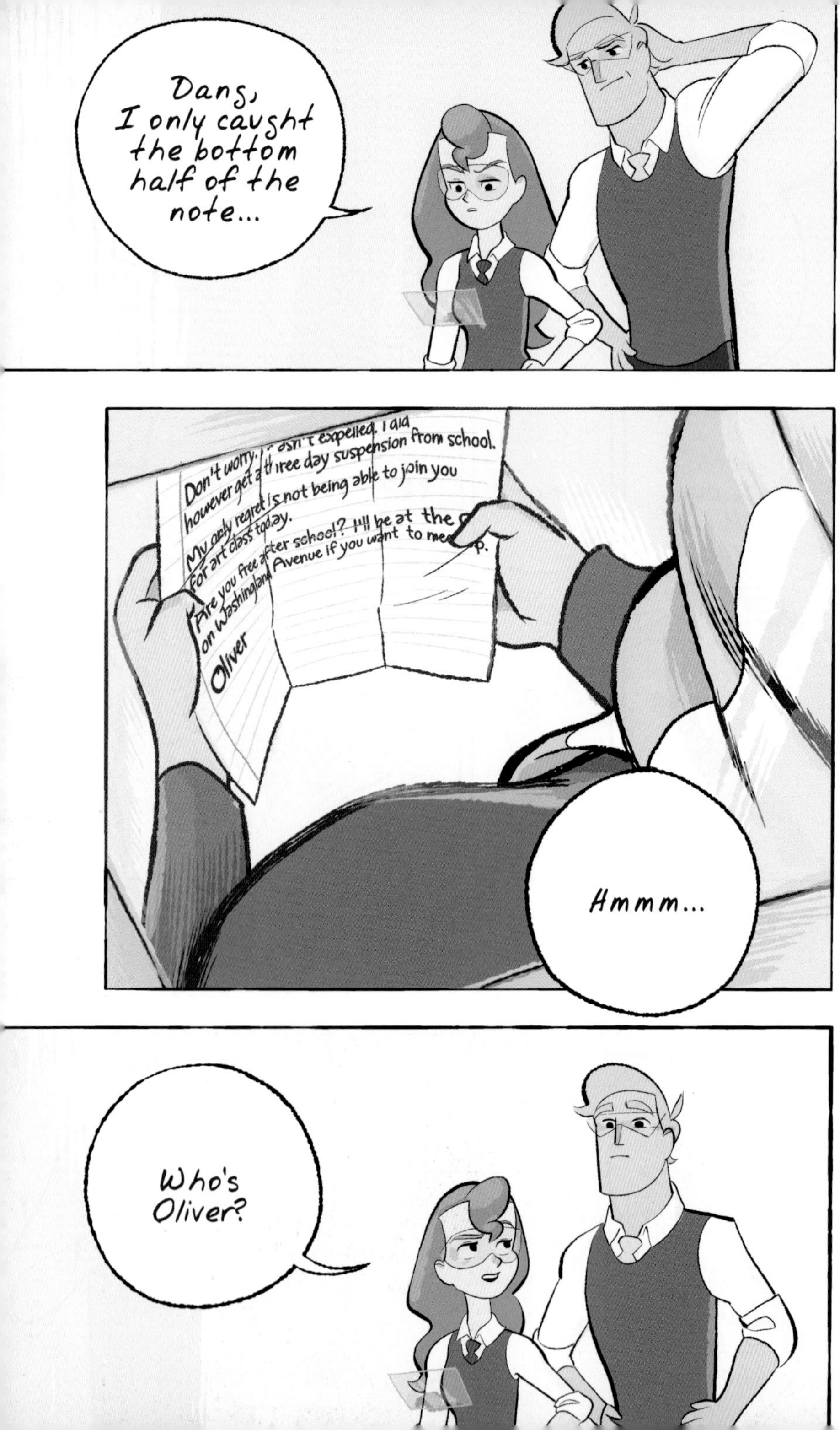
Dang, I only caught the bottom half of the note...
Don't worry,
expelled. I did
however get a three day suspension from school.
My only regret is not being able to join you
for art class today.
Are you free after school? I'll be at the
on Washington Avenue if you want to
Oliver
Hmmm...
Who's Oliver?

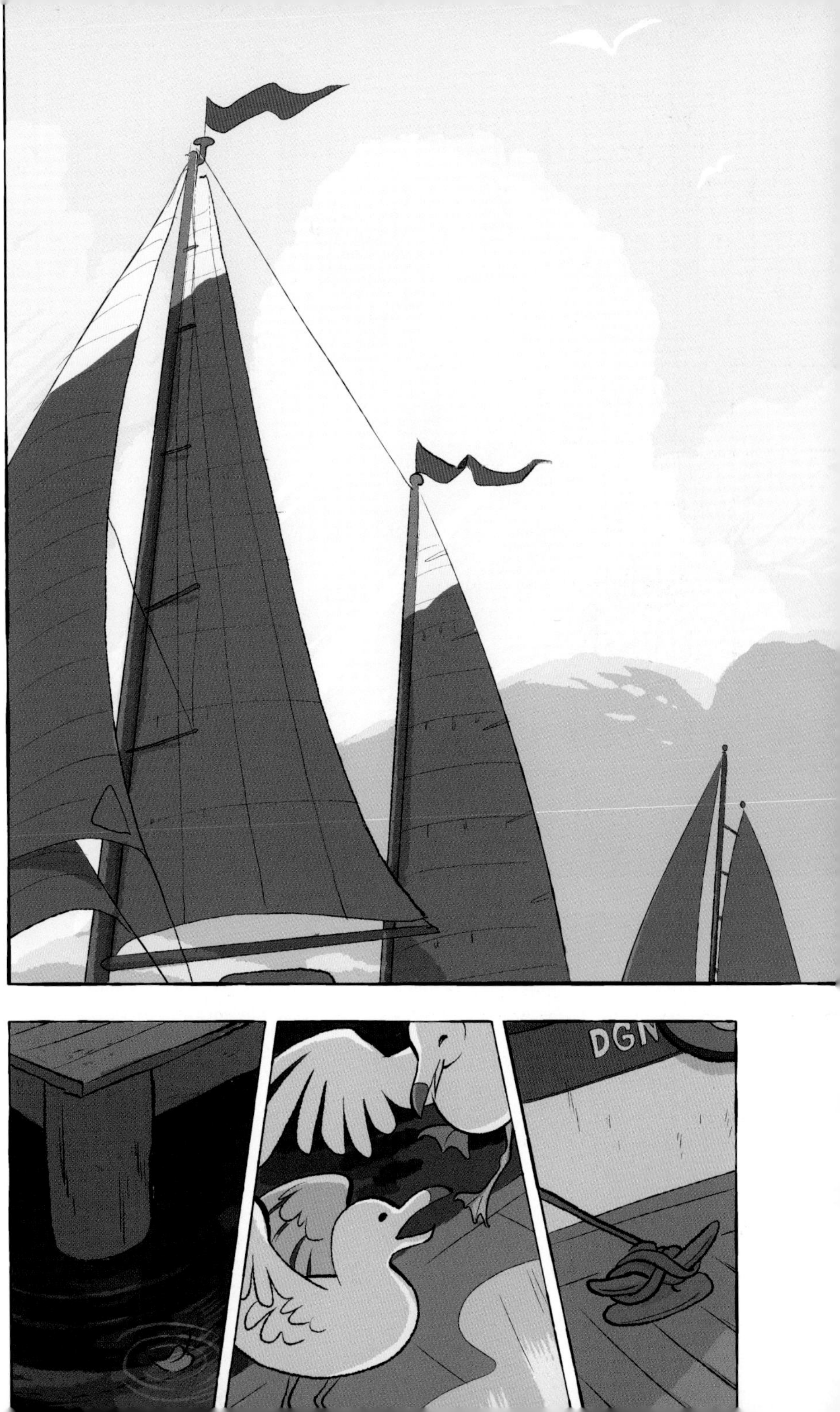
DGN

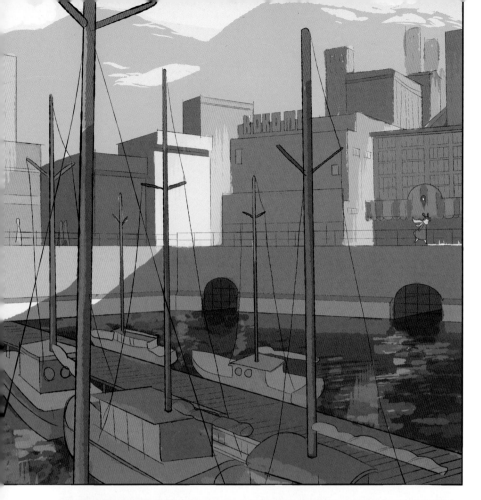

Brrr.

It's cold.

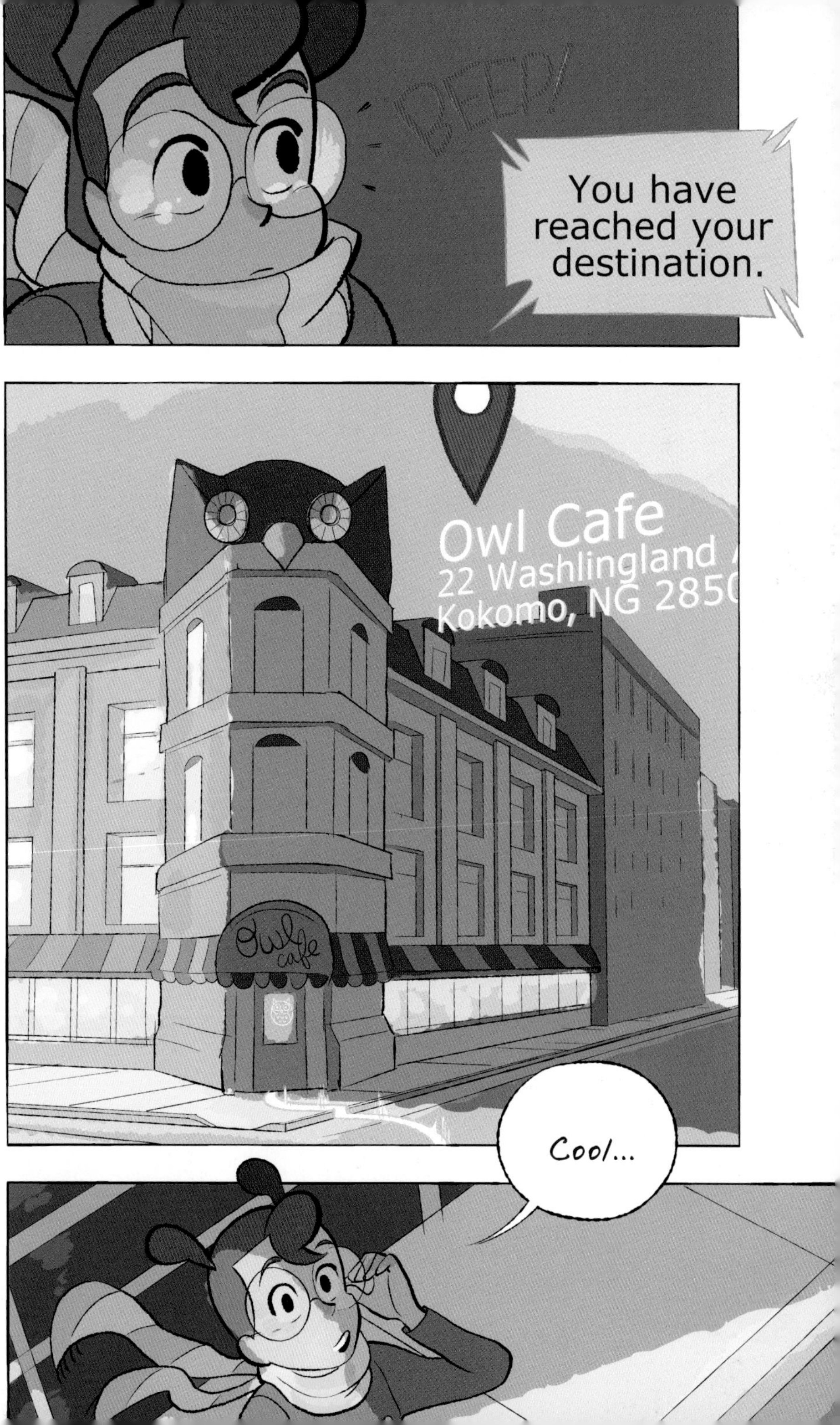
BEEP!
You have reached your destination.
Owl Cafe
22 Washlingland
Kokomo, NG 285
Owl cafe
Cool...

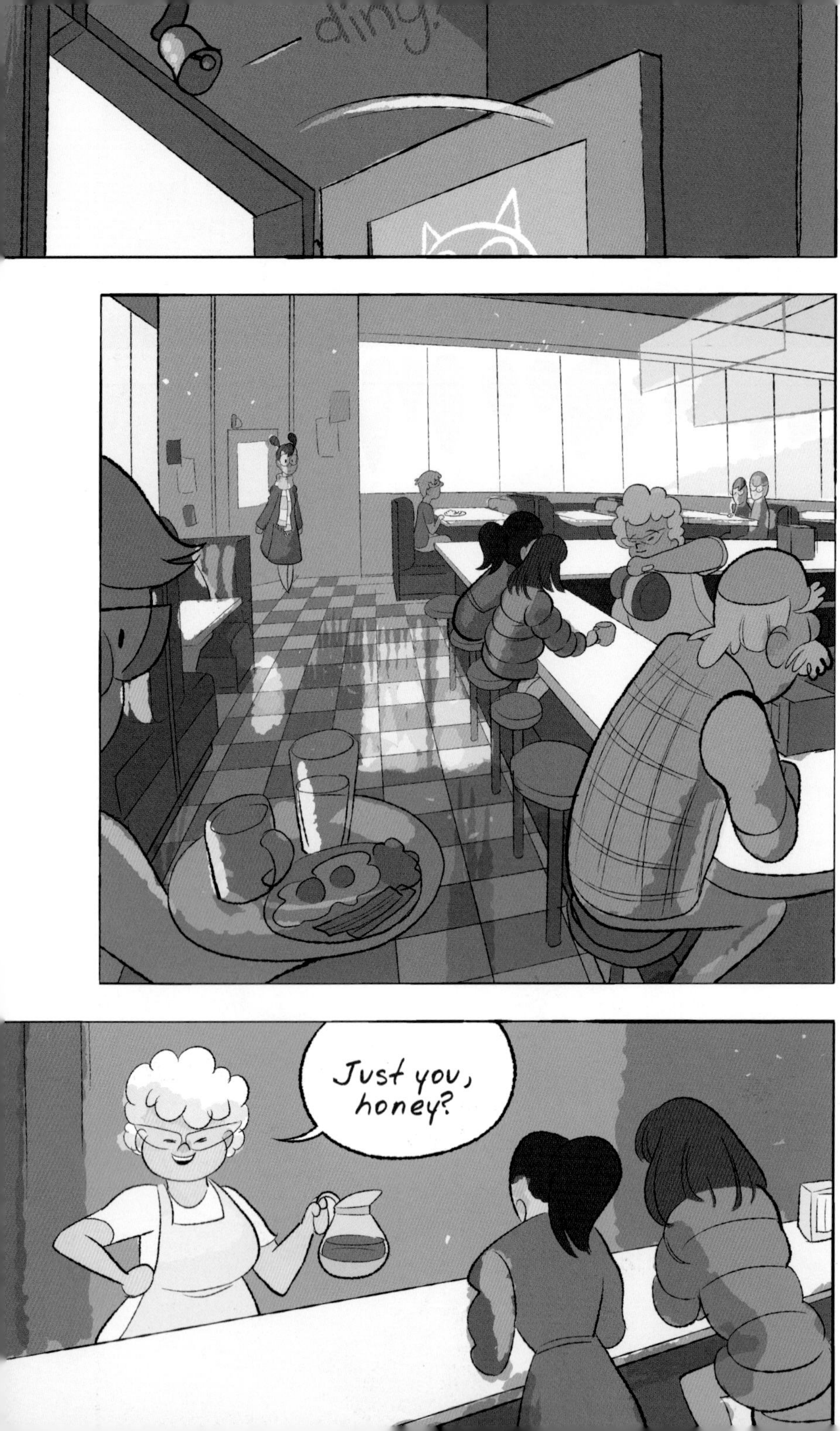
ding!
Just you, honey?

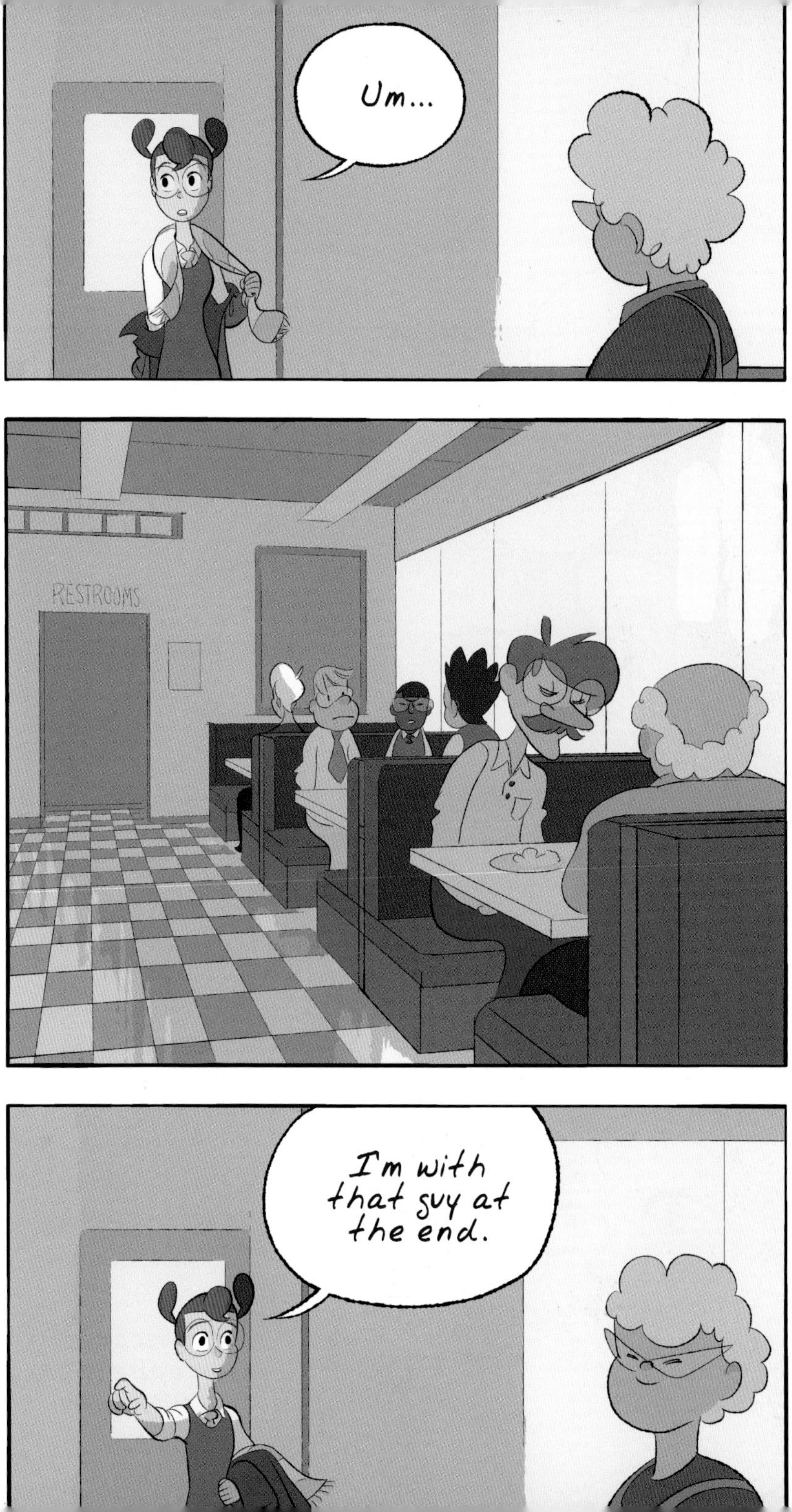
Um...
RESTROOMS
I'm with that guy at the end.

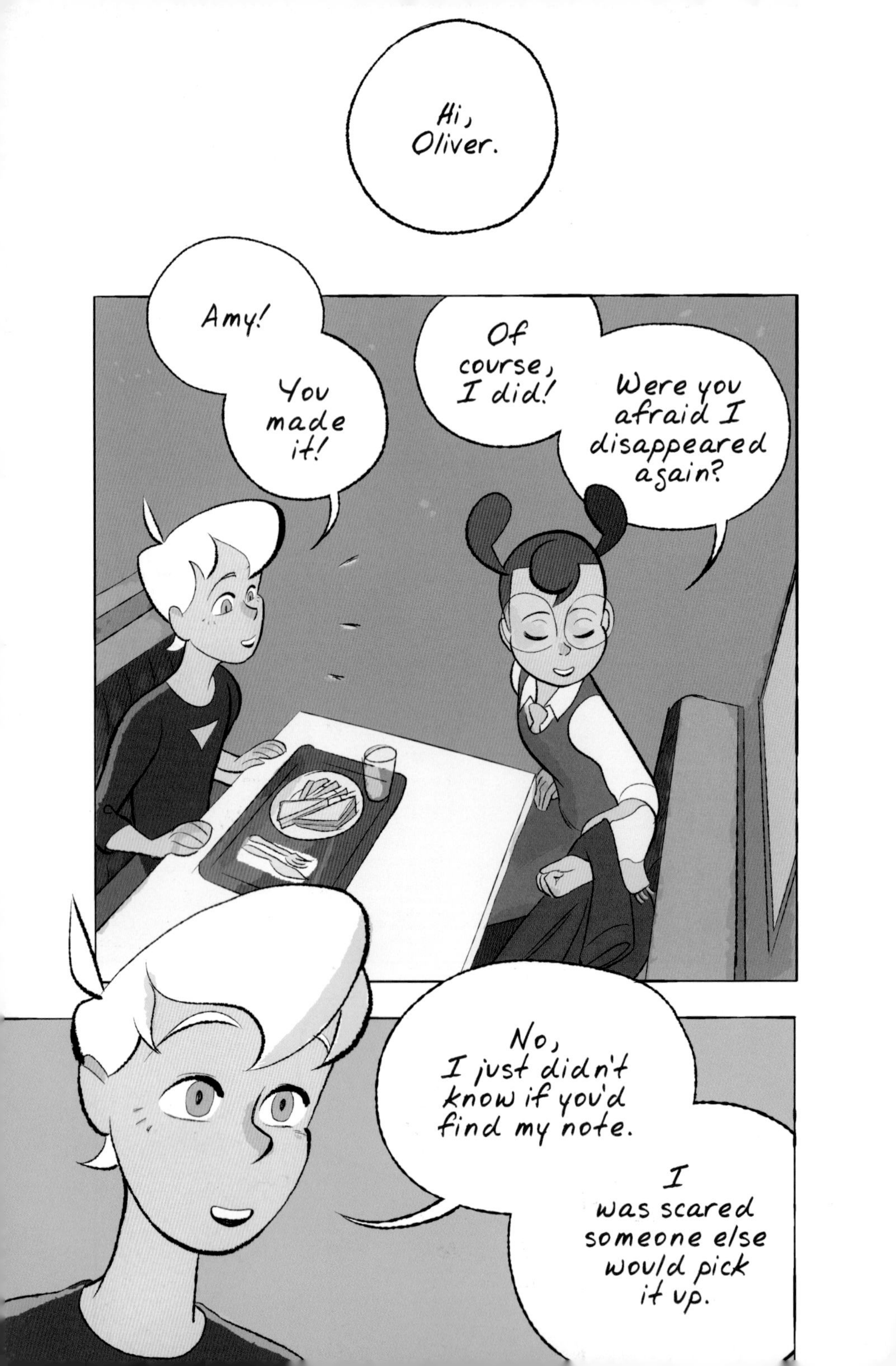

Hi, Oliver.
Amy!
You made it!
Of course, I did!
Were you afraid I disappeared again?
No, I just didn't know if you'd find my note.
I was scared someone else would pick it up.

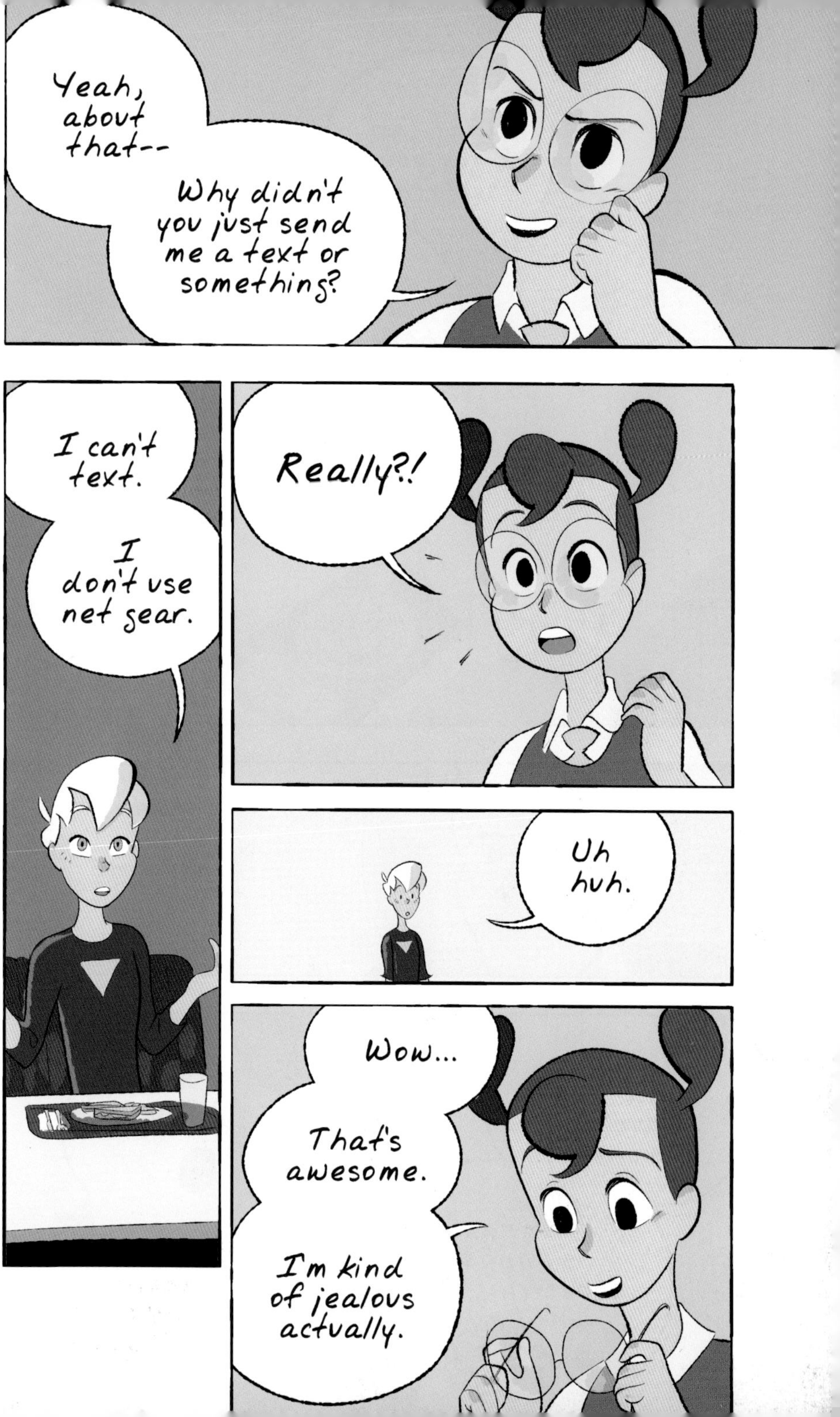
Yeah, about that--
Why didn't you just send me a text or something?
I can't text.
I don't use net gear.
Really?!
Uh huh.
Wow...
That's awesome.
I'm kind of jealous actually.

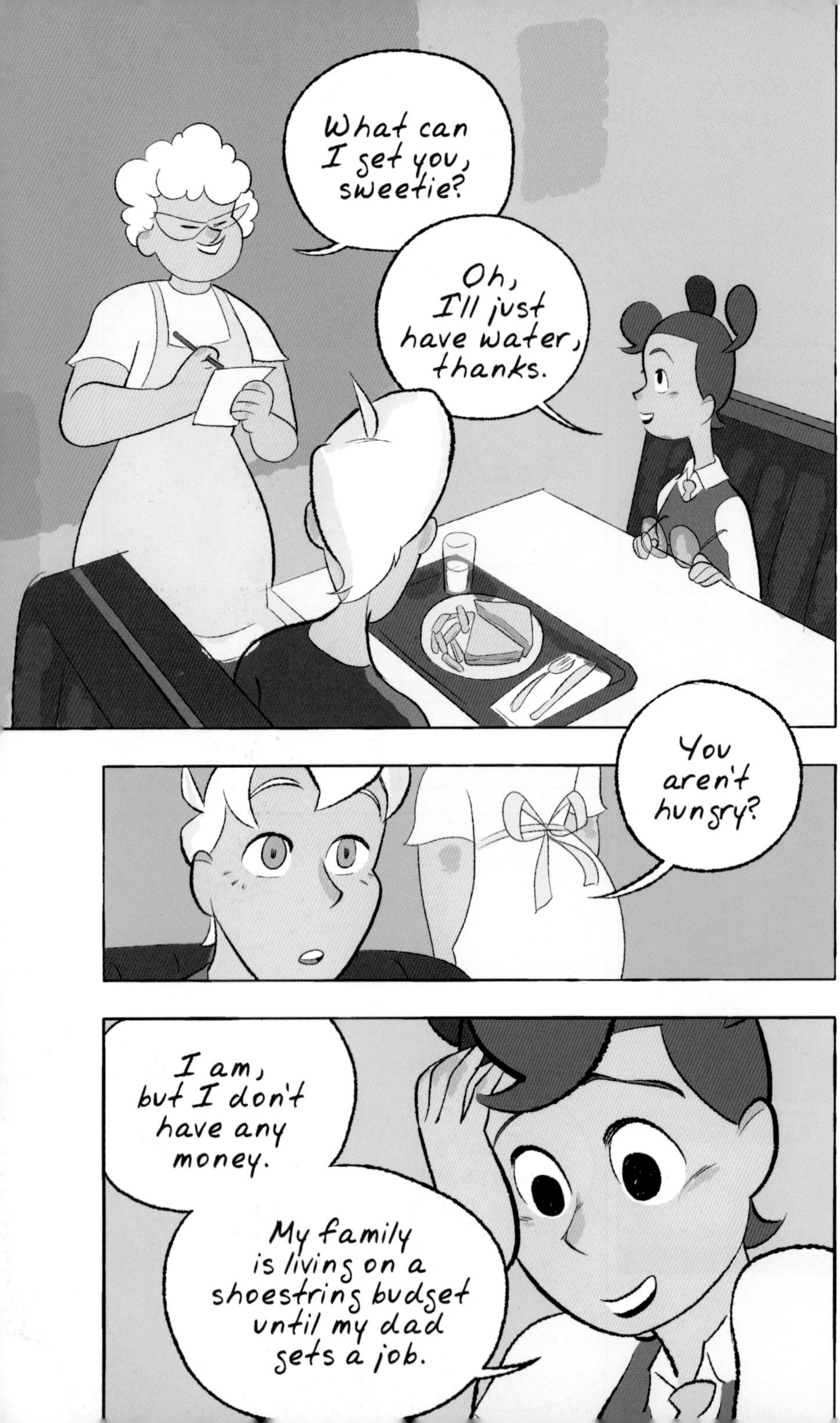
What can I get you, sweetie?
Oh, I'll just have water, thanks.
You aren't hungry?
I am, but I don't have any money.
My family is living on a shoestring budget until my dad gets a job.

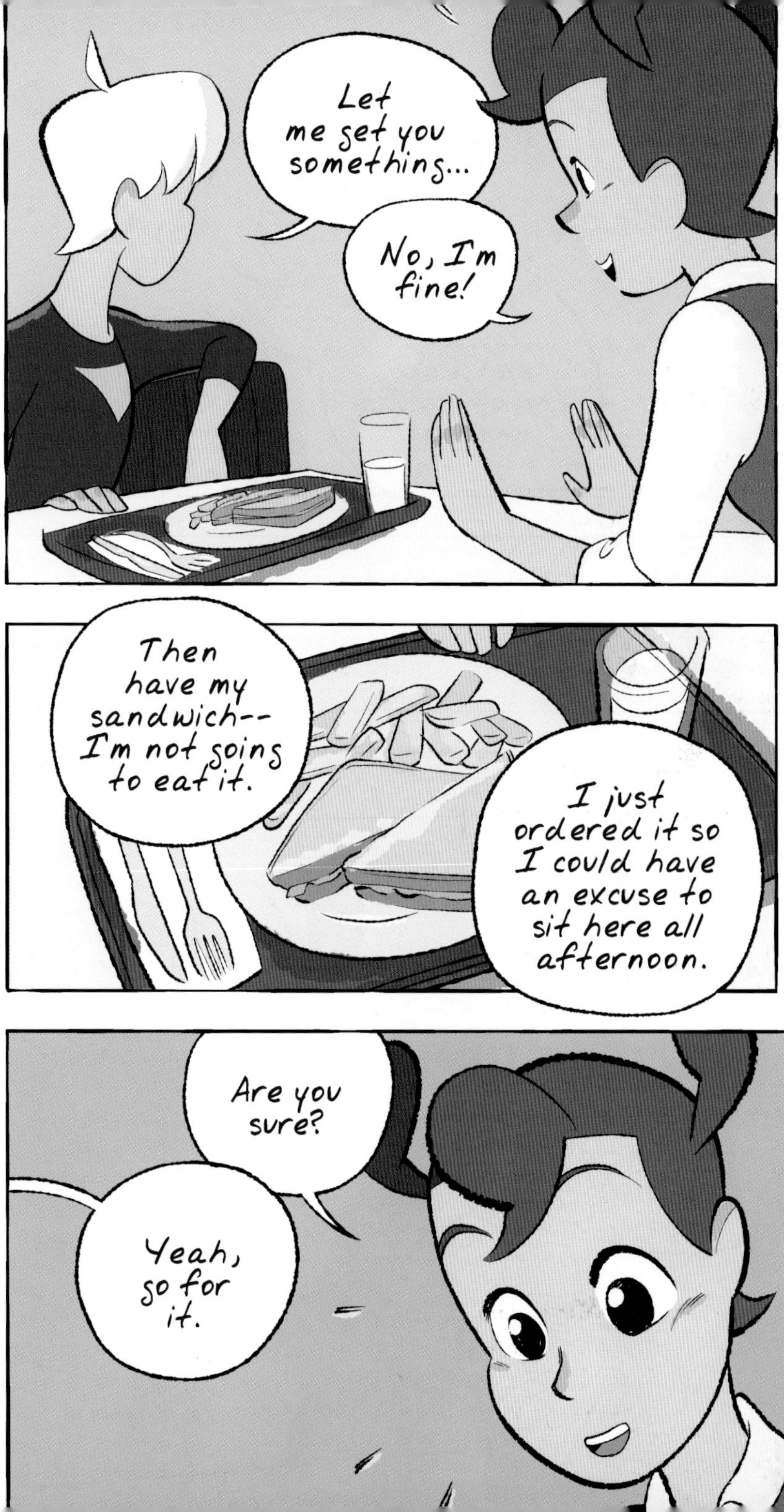
Let me get you something...
No, I'm fine!
Then have my sandwich-- I'm not going to eat it.
I just ordered it so I could have an excuse to sit here all afternoon.
Are you sure?
Yeah, go for it.

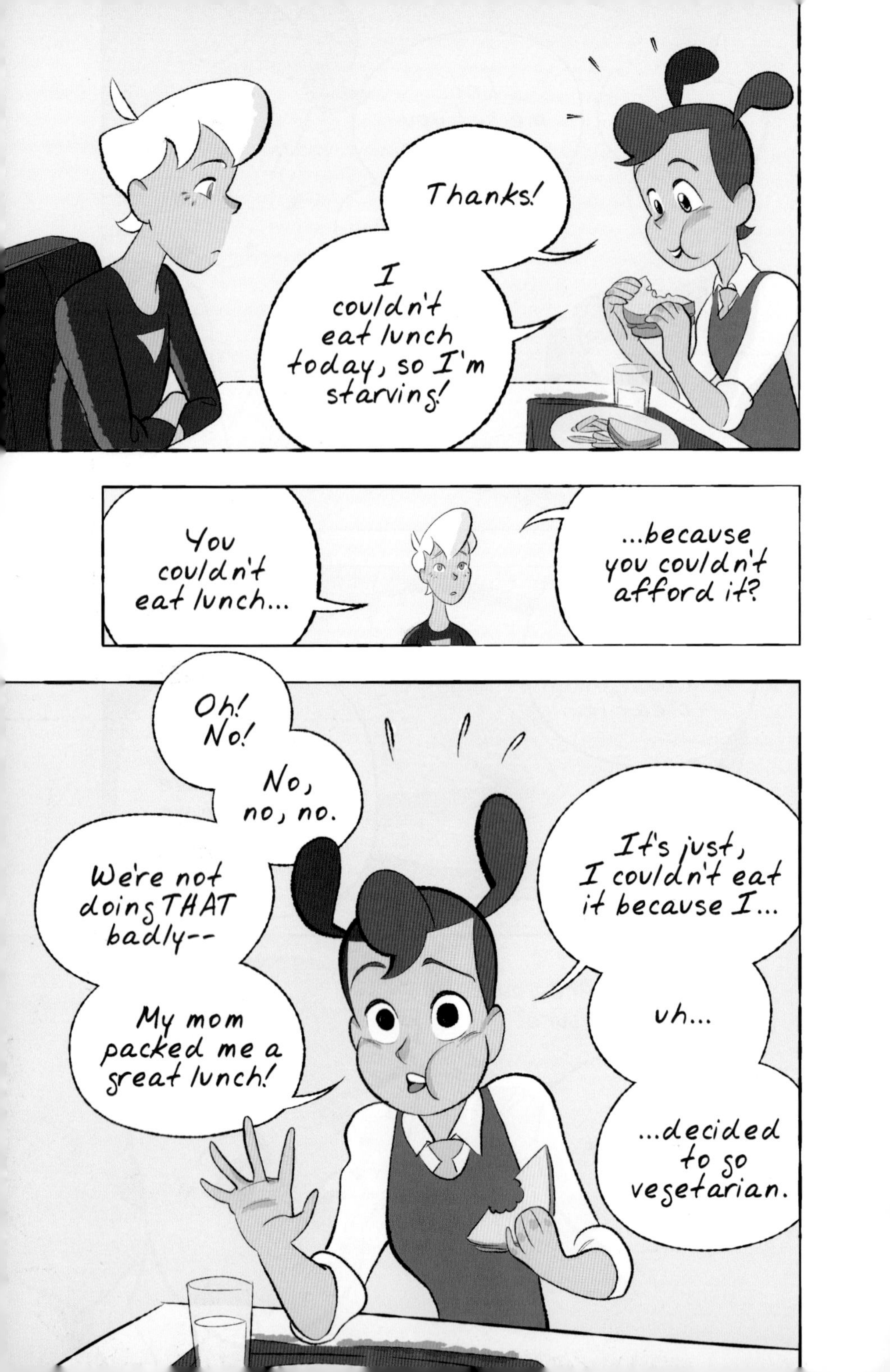
Thanks!
I couldn't eat lunch today, so I'm starving!
You couldn't eat lunch...
...because you couldn't afford it?
Oh! No!
No, no, no.
We're not doing THAT badly--
My mom packed me a great lunch!
It's just, I couldn't eat it because I...
uh...
...decided to go vegetarian.

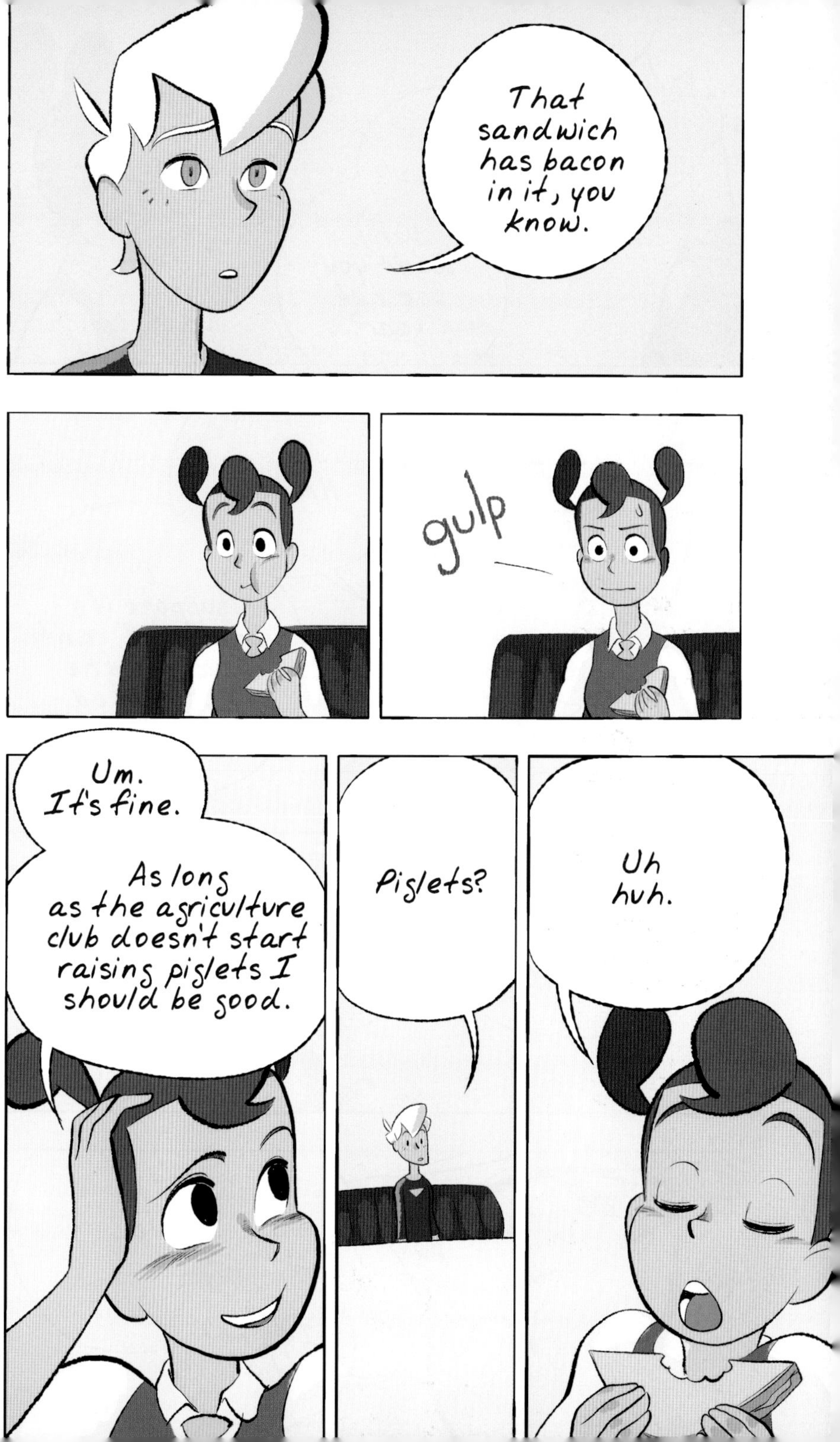
That sandwich has bacon in it, you know.
gulp
Um. It's fine.
As long as the agriculture club doesn't start raising piglets I should be good.
Piglets?
Uh huh.

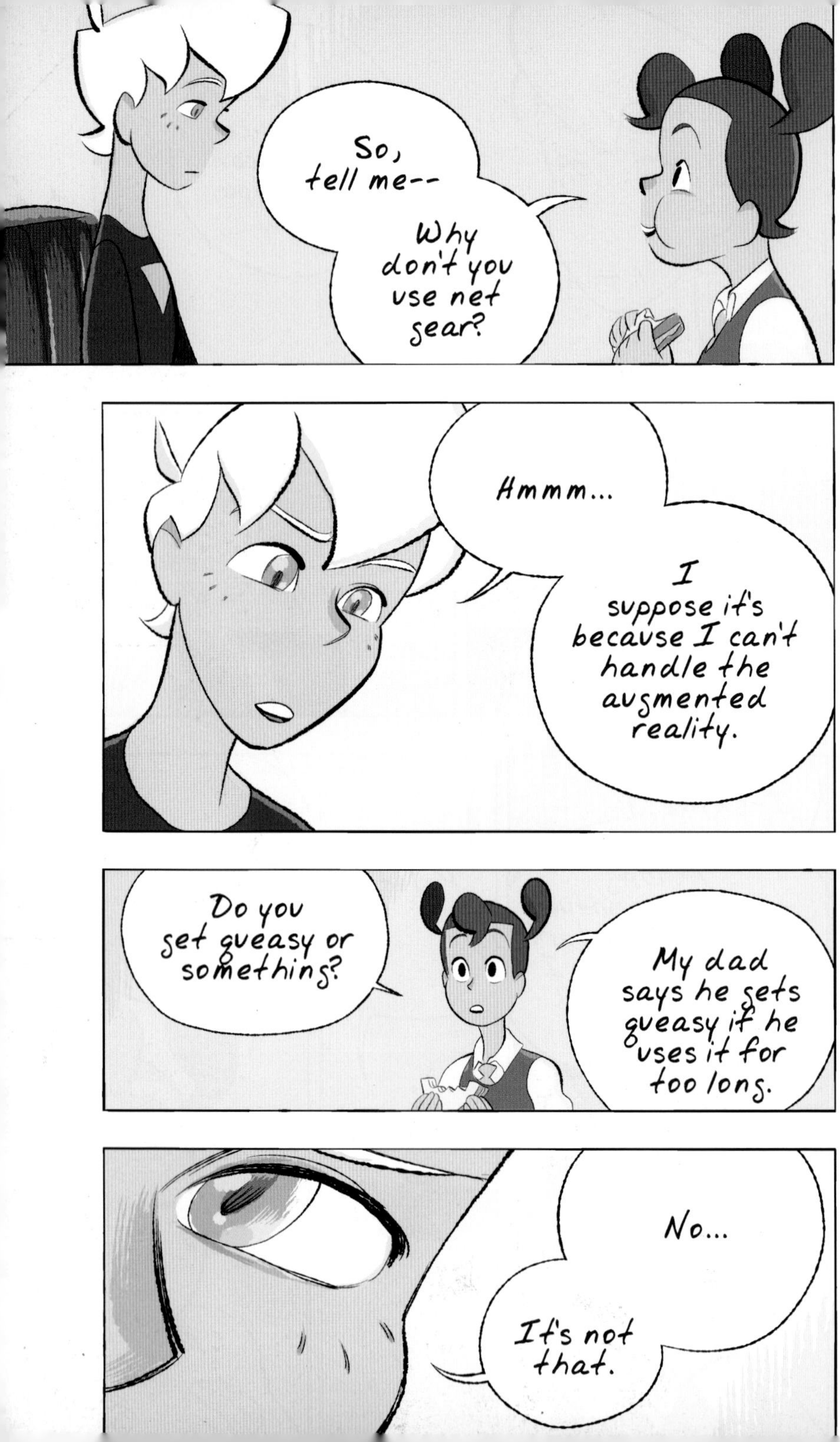
So, tell me--
Why don't you use net gear?
Hmmm...
I suppose it's because I can't handle the augmented reality.
Do you get queasy or something?
My dad says he gets queasy if he uses it for too long.
No...
It's not that.

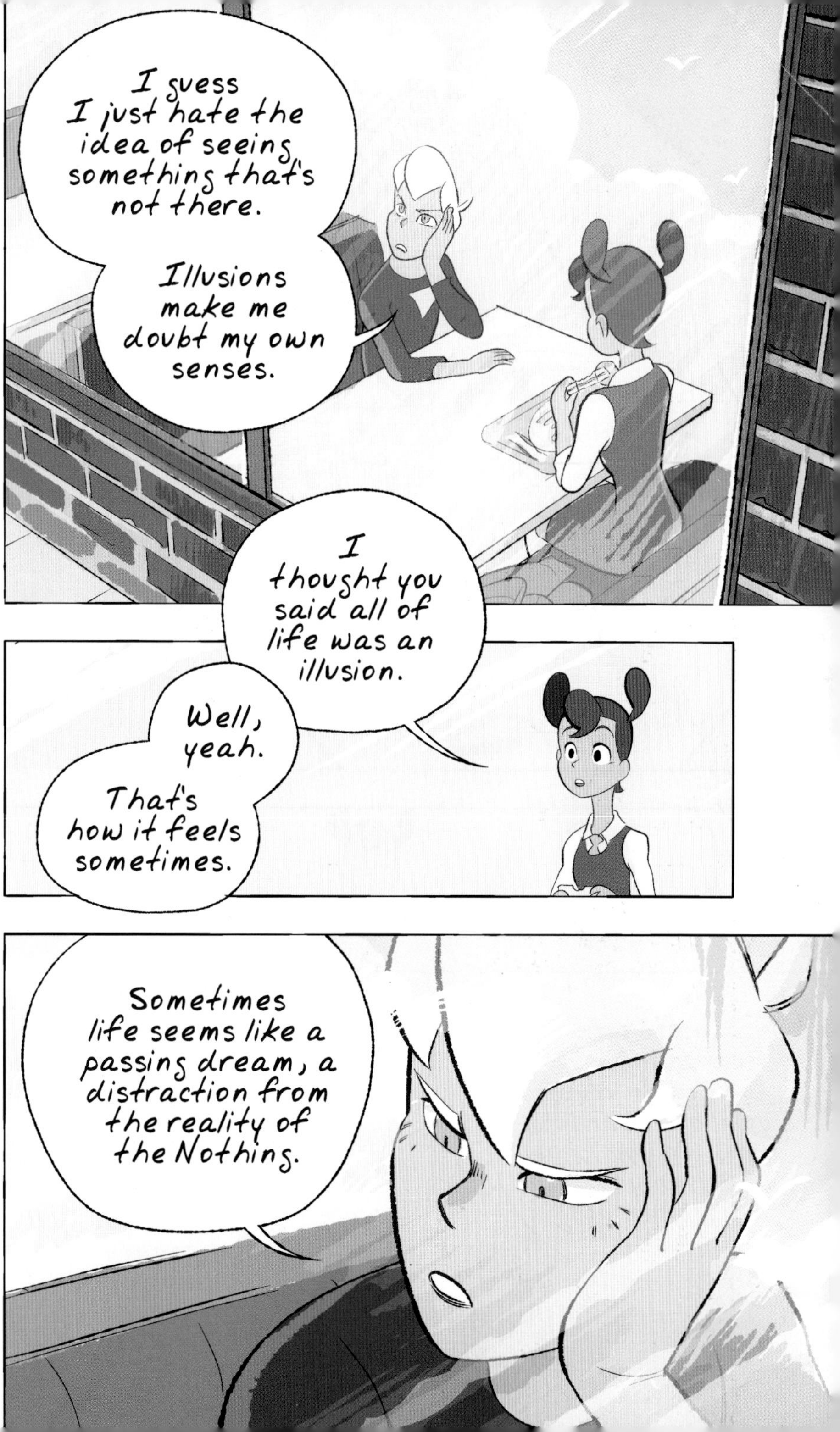
I guess I just hate the idea of seeing something that's not there.
Illusions make me doubt my own senses.
I thought you said all of life was an illusion.
Well, yeah.
That's how it feels sometimes.
Sometimes life seems like a passing dream, a distraction from the reality of the Nothing.

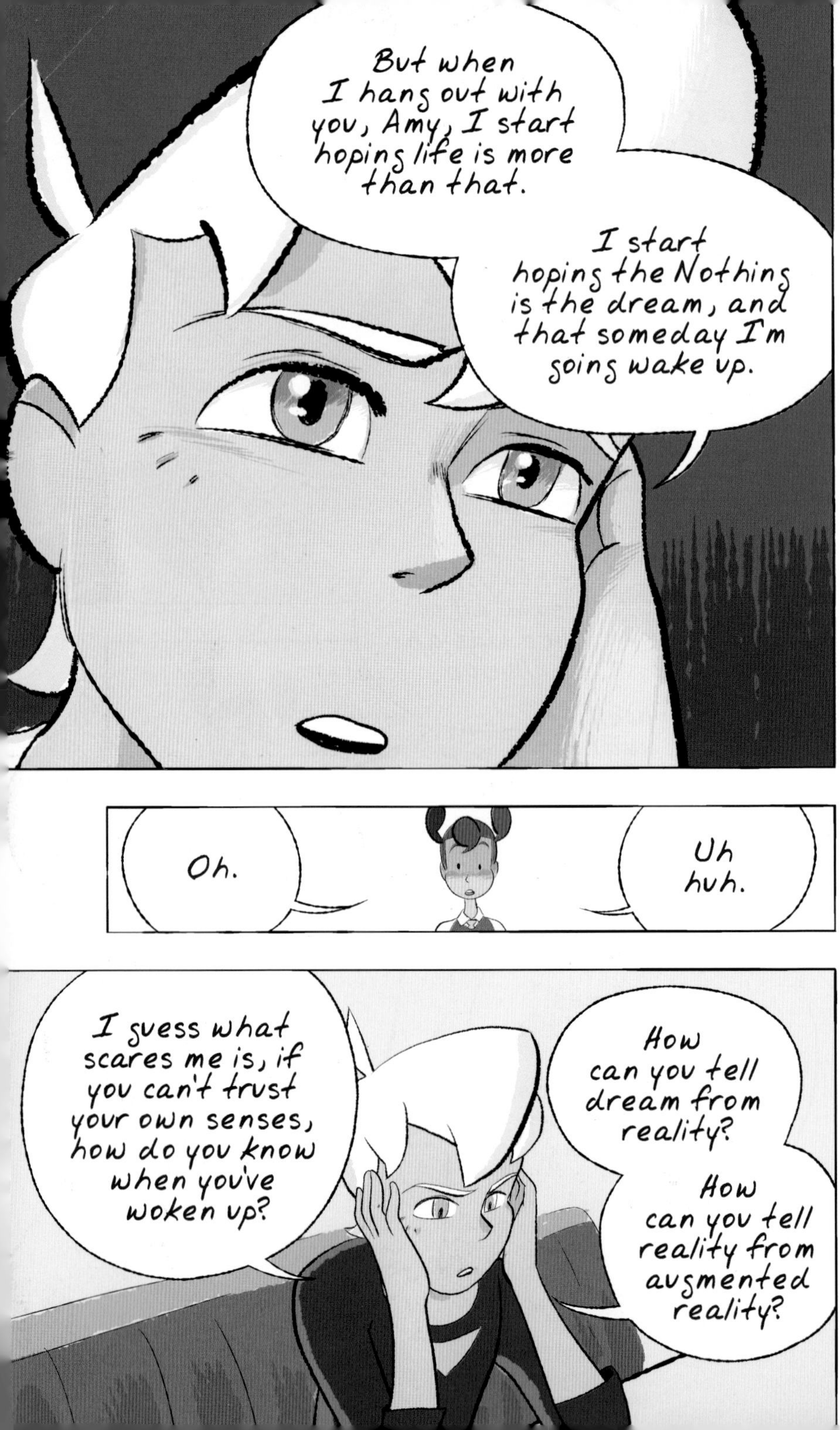

But when I hang out with you, Amy, I start hoping life is more than that.
I start hoping the Nothing is the dream, and that someday I'm going wake up.
Oh.
Uh huh.
I guess what scares me is, if you can't trust your own senses, how do you know when you've woken up?
How can you tell dream from reality?
How can you tell reality from augmented reality?

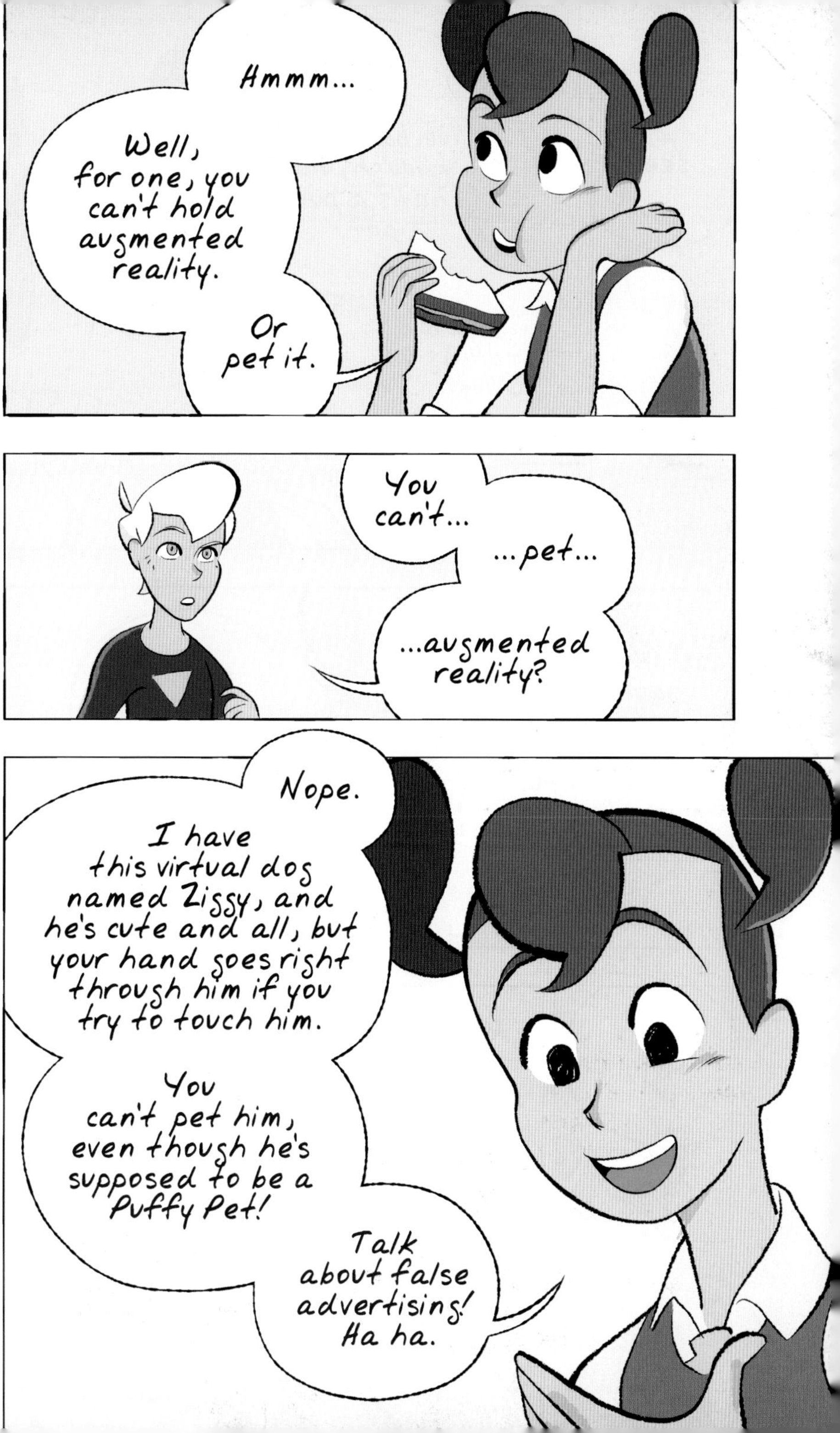
Hmmm...
Well, for one, you can't hold augmented reality.
Or pet it.
You can't...
...pet...
...augmented reality?
Nope.
I have this virtual dog named Ziggy, and he's cute and all, but your hand goes right through him if you try to touch him.
You can't pet him, even though he's supposed to be a Puffy Pet!
Talk about false advertising! Ha ha.

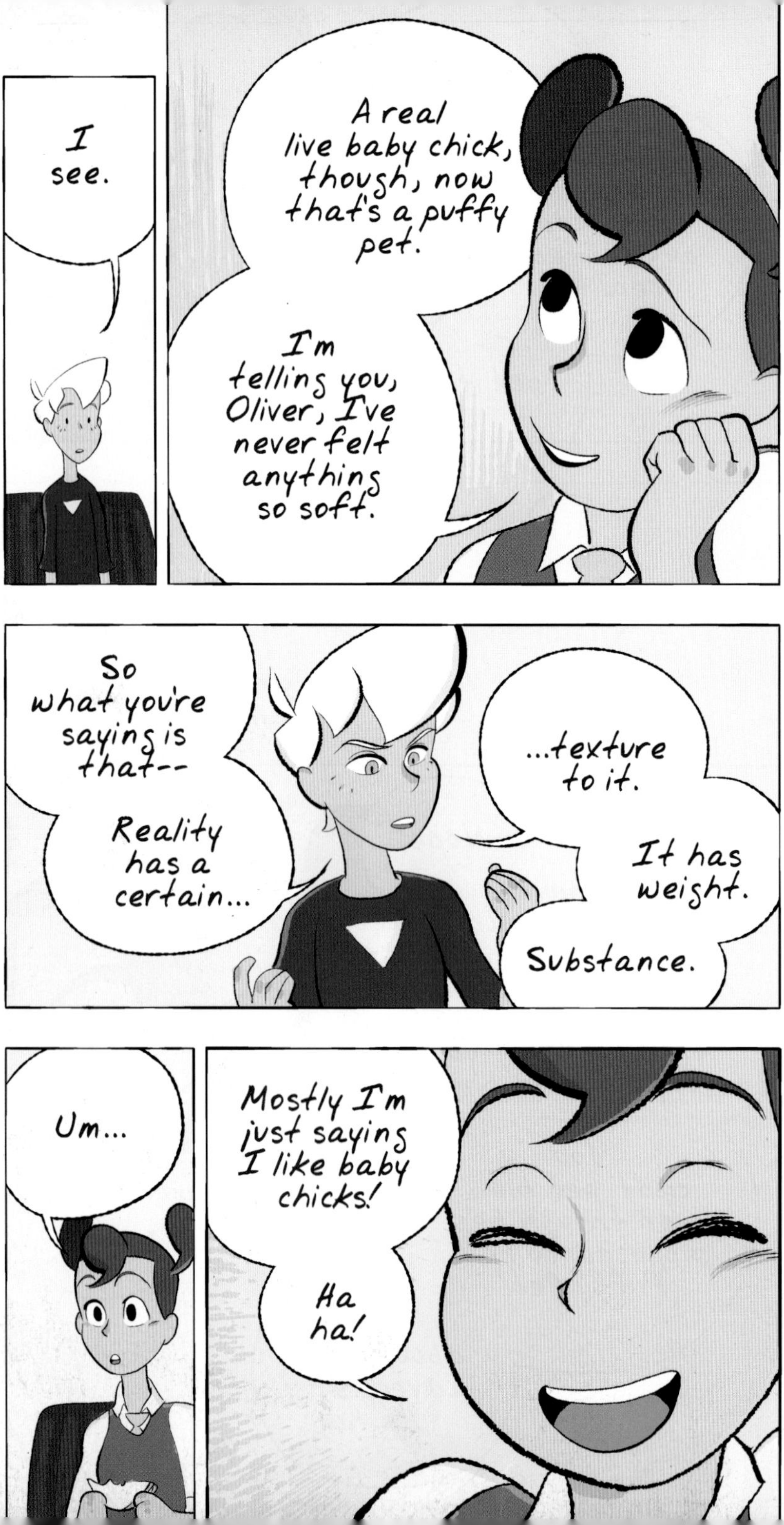
I see.
A real live baby chick, though, now that's a puffy pet.
I'm telling you, Oliver, I've never felt anything so soft.
So what you're saying is that--
Reality has a certain...
...texture to it.
It has weight.
Substance.
Um...
Mostly I'm just saying I like baby chicks!
Ha ha!

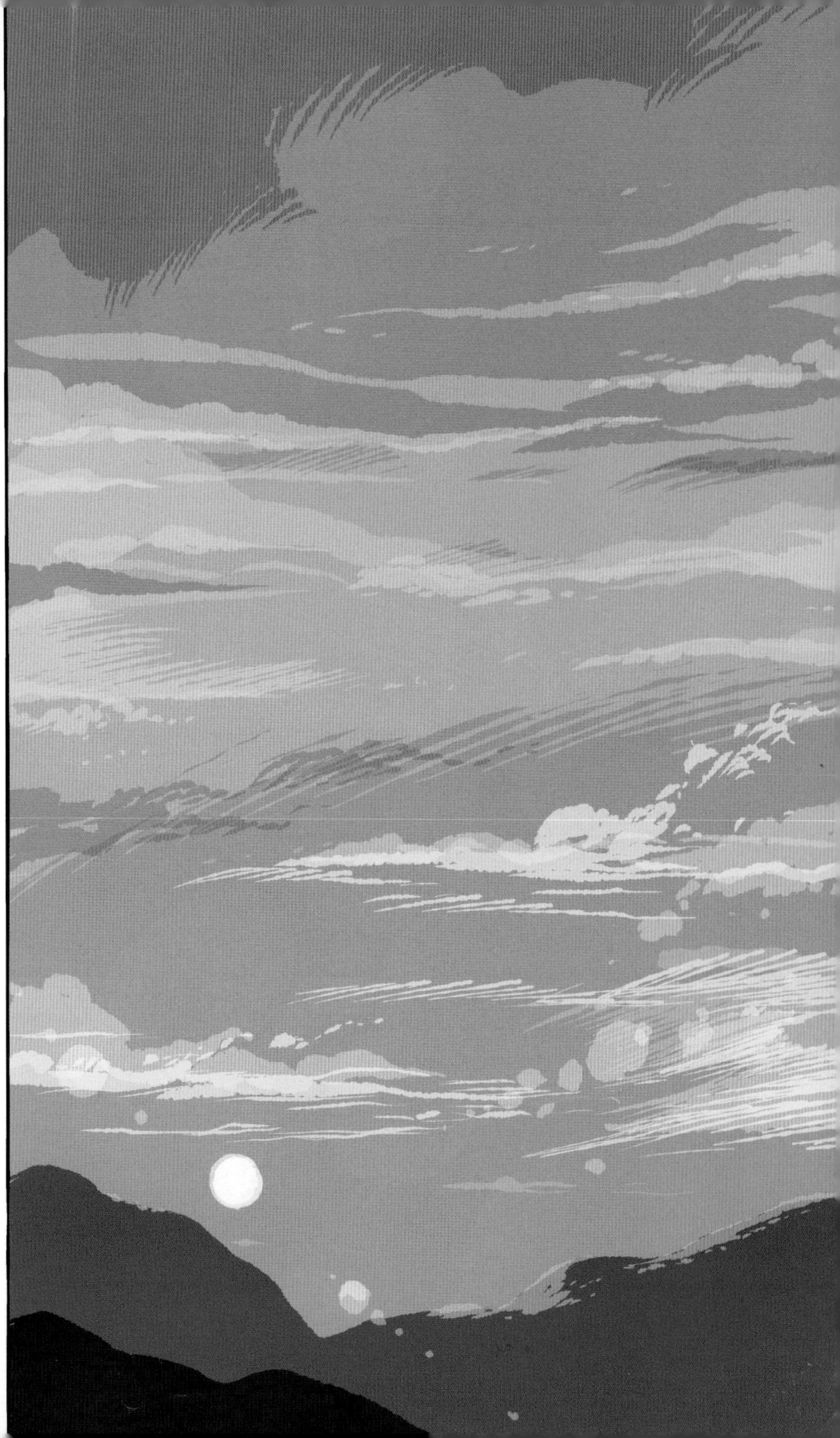

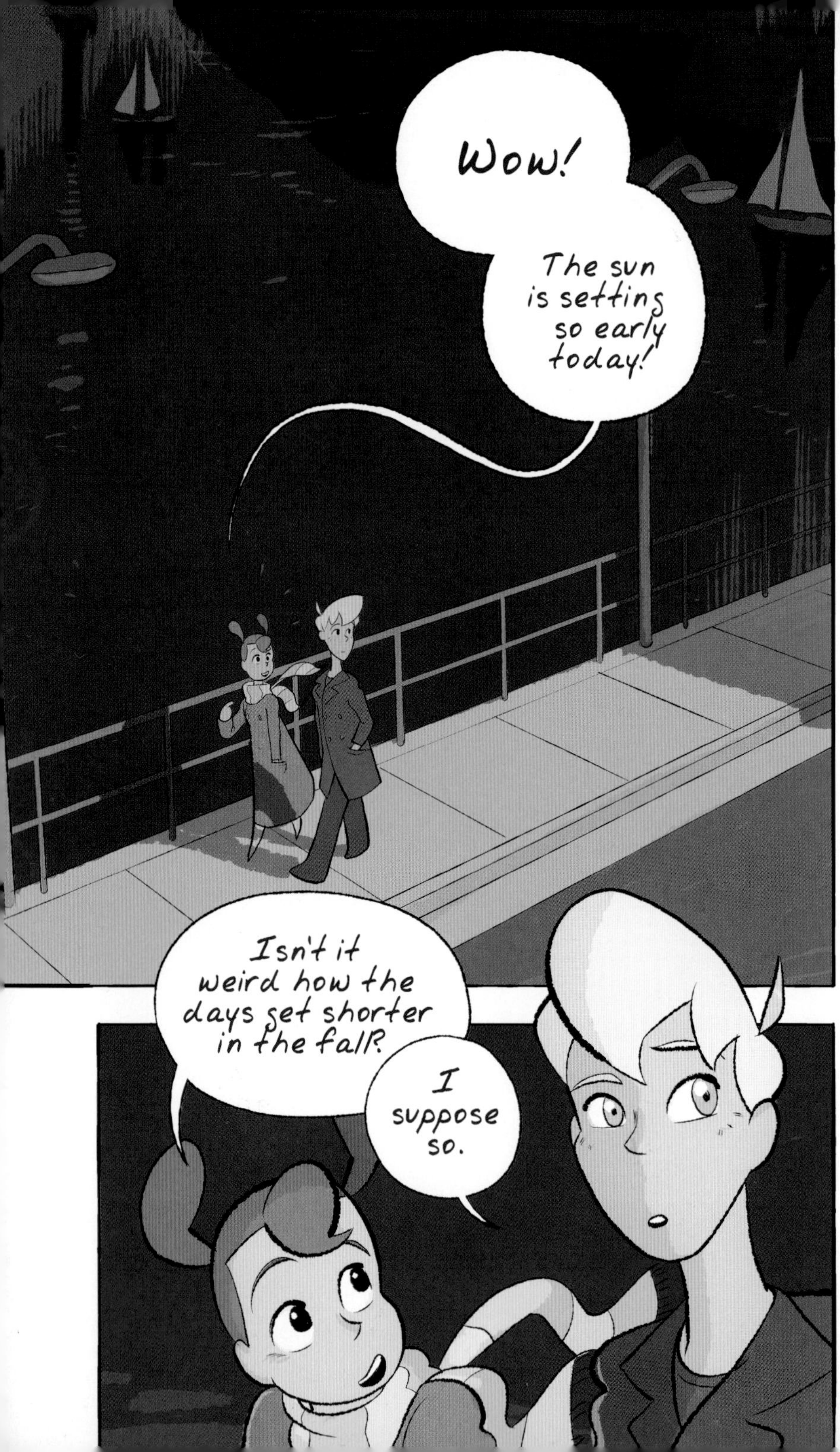
Wow!
The sun is setting so early today!
Isn't it weird how the days get shorter in the fall?
I suppose so.

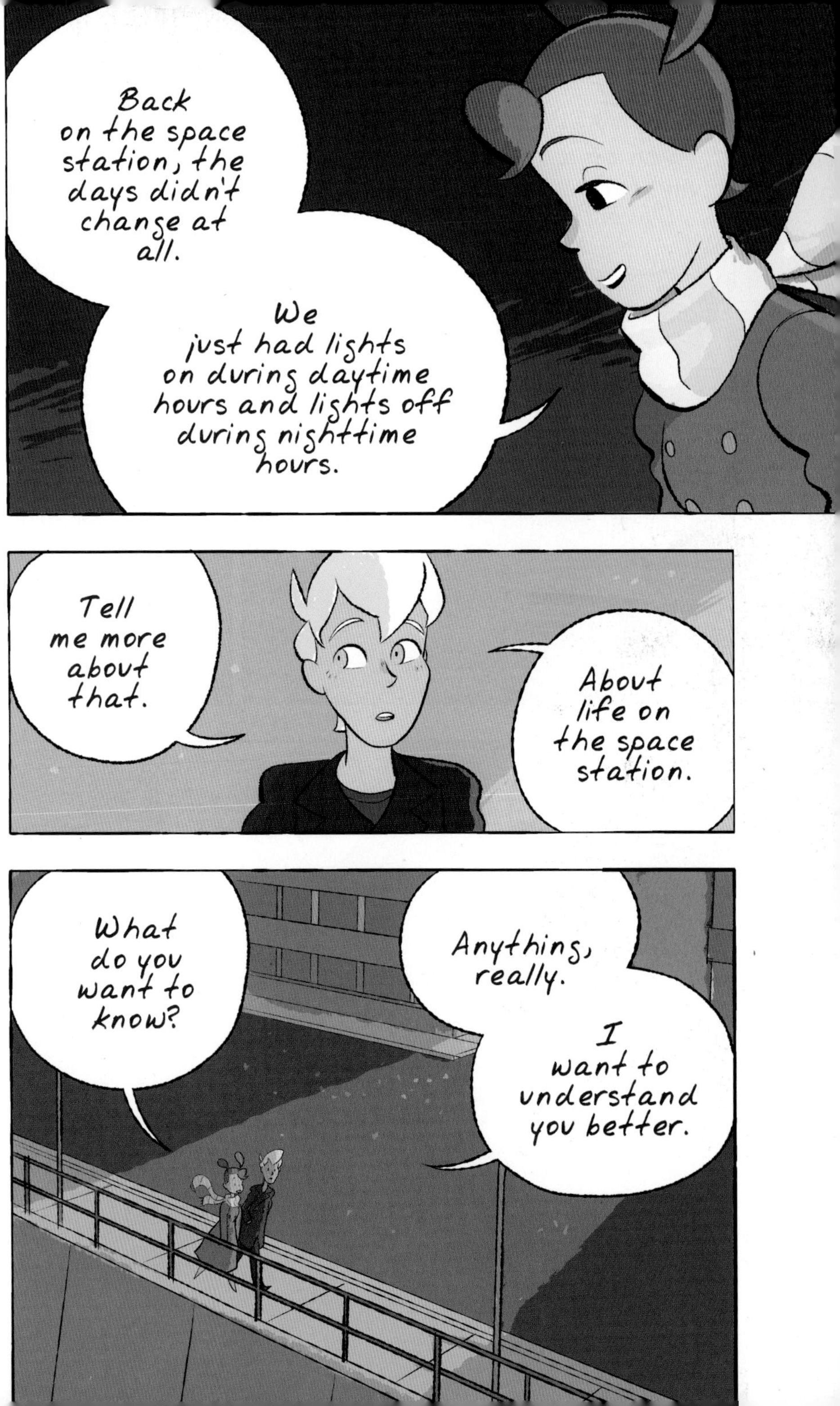
Back on the space station, the days didn't change at all.
We just had lights on during daytime hours and lights off during nighttime hours.
Tell me more about that.
About life on the space station.
What do you want to know?
Anything, really.
I want to understand you better.

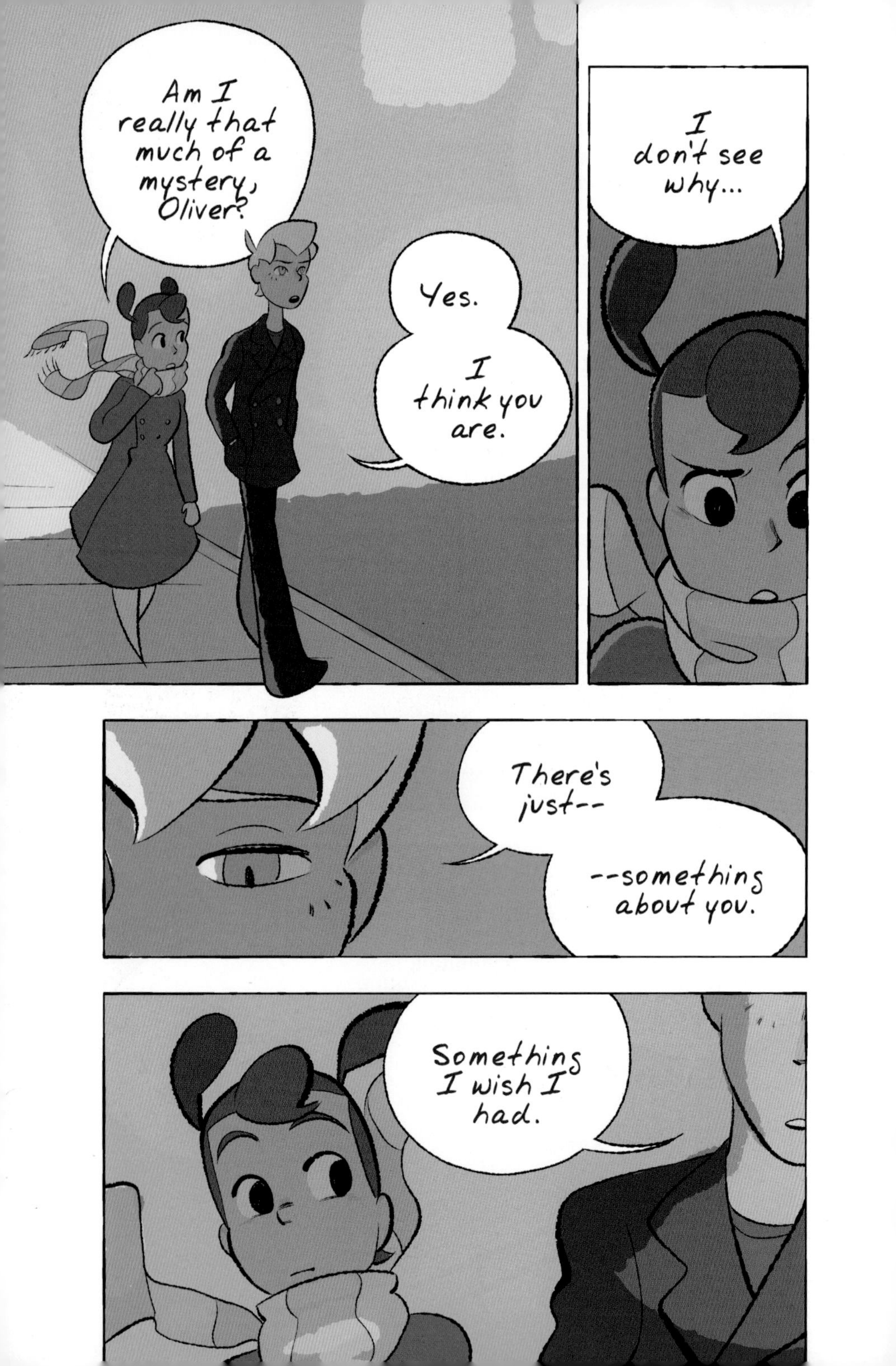
Am I really that much of a mystery, Oliver?
Yes.
I think you are.
I don't see why...
There's just--
--somethins about you.
Somethins I wish I had.

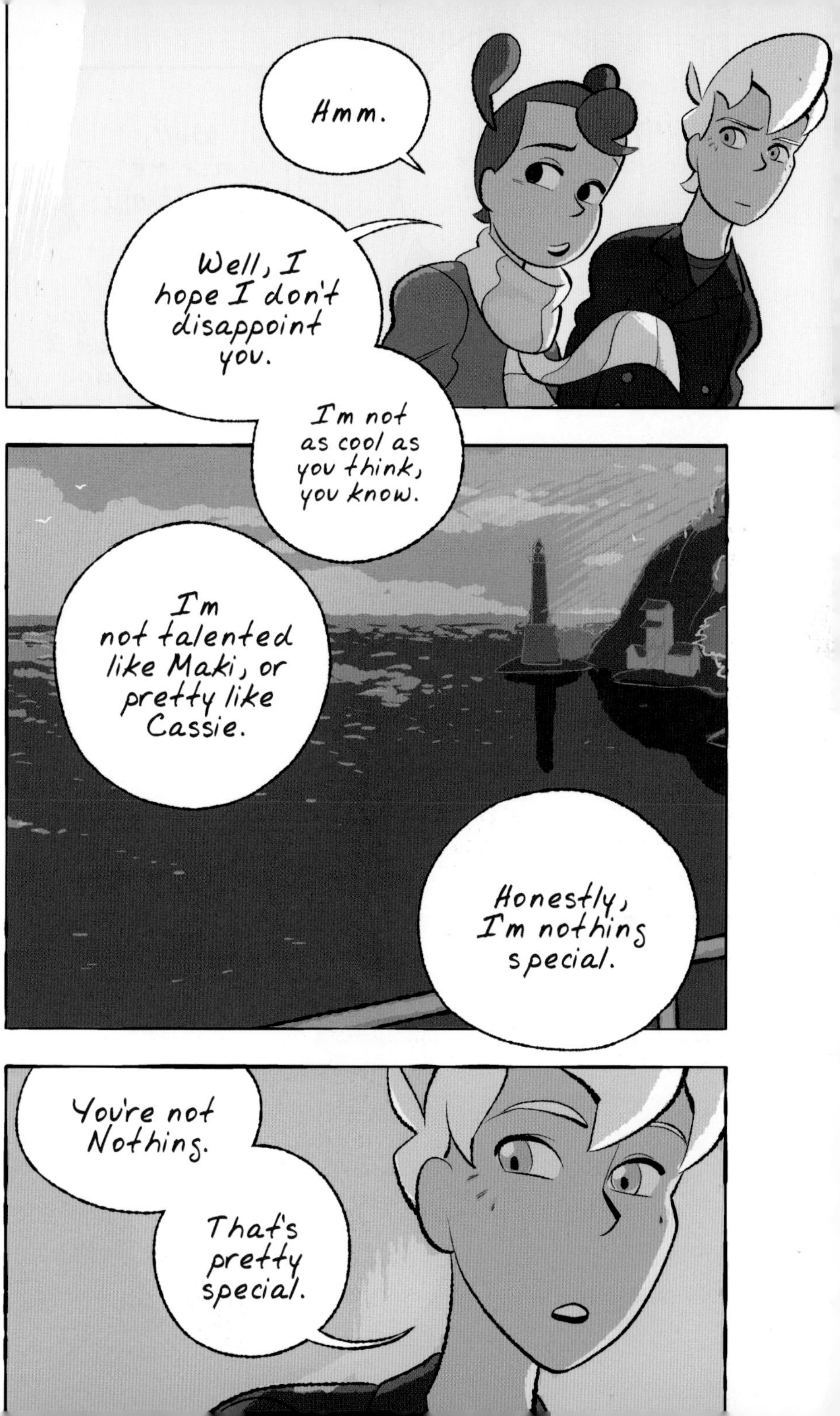
Hmm.
Well, I hope I don't disappoint you.
I'm not as cool as you think, you know.
I'm not talented like Maki, or pretty like Cassie.
Honestly, I'm nothing special.
You're not Nothing.
That's pretty special.

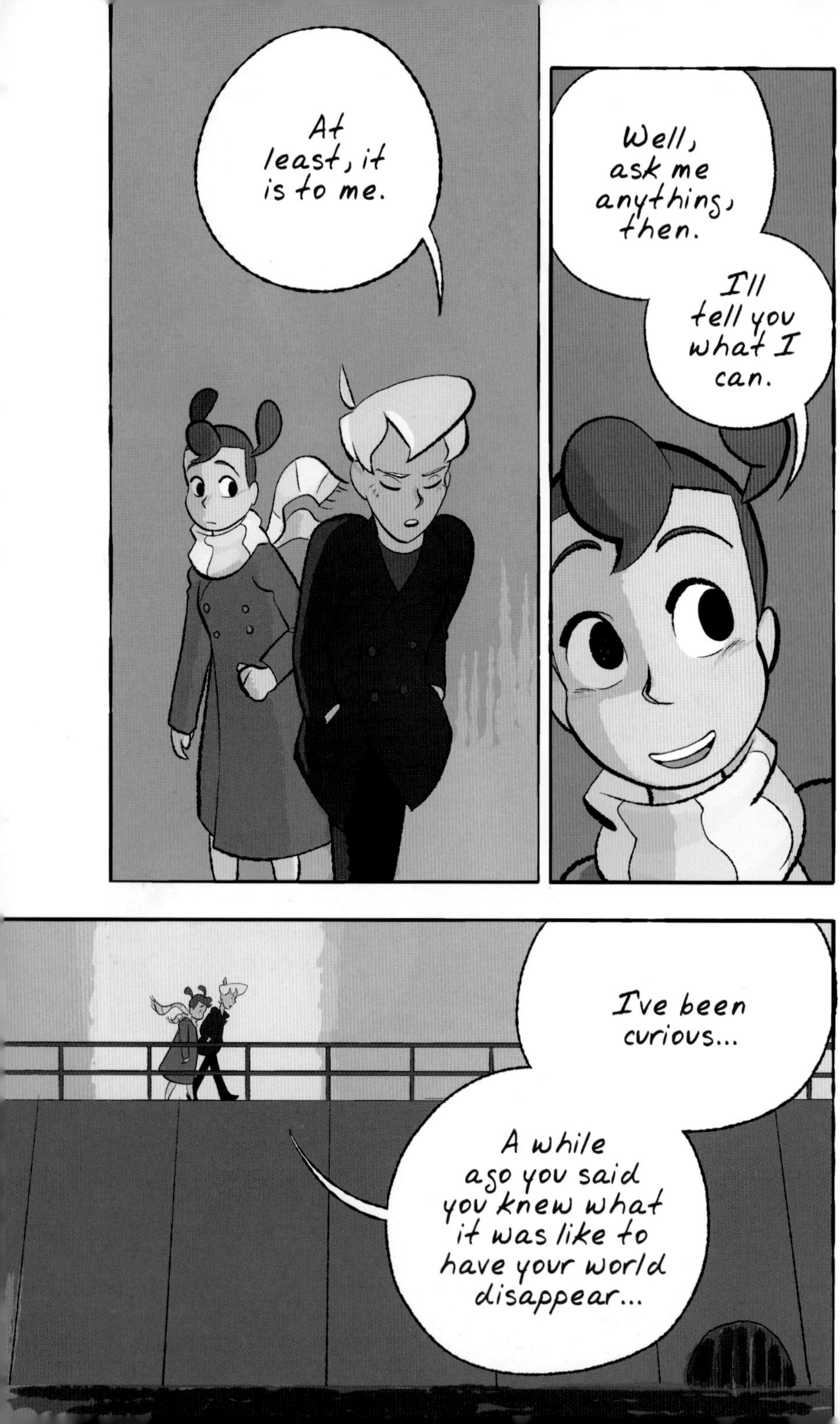
At least, it is to me.
Well, ask me anything, then.
I'll tell you what I can.
I've been curious...
A while ago you said you knew what it was like to have your world disappear...

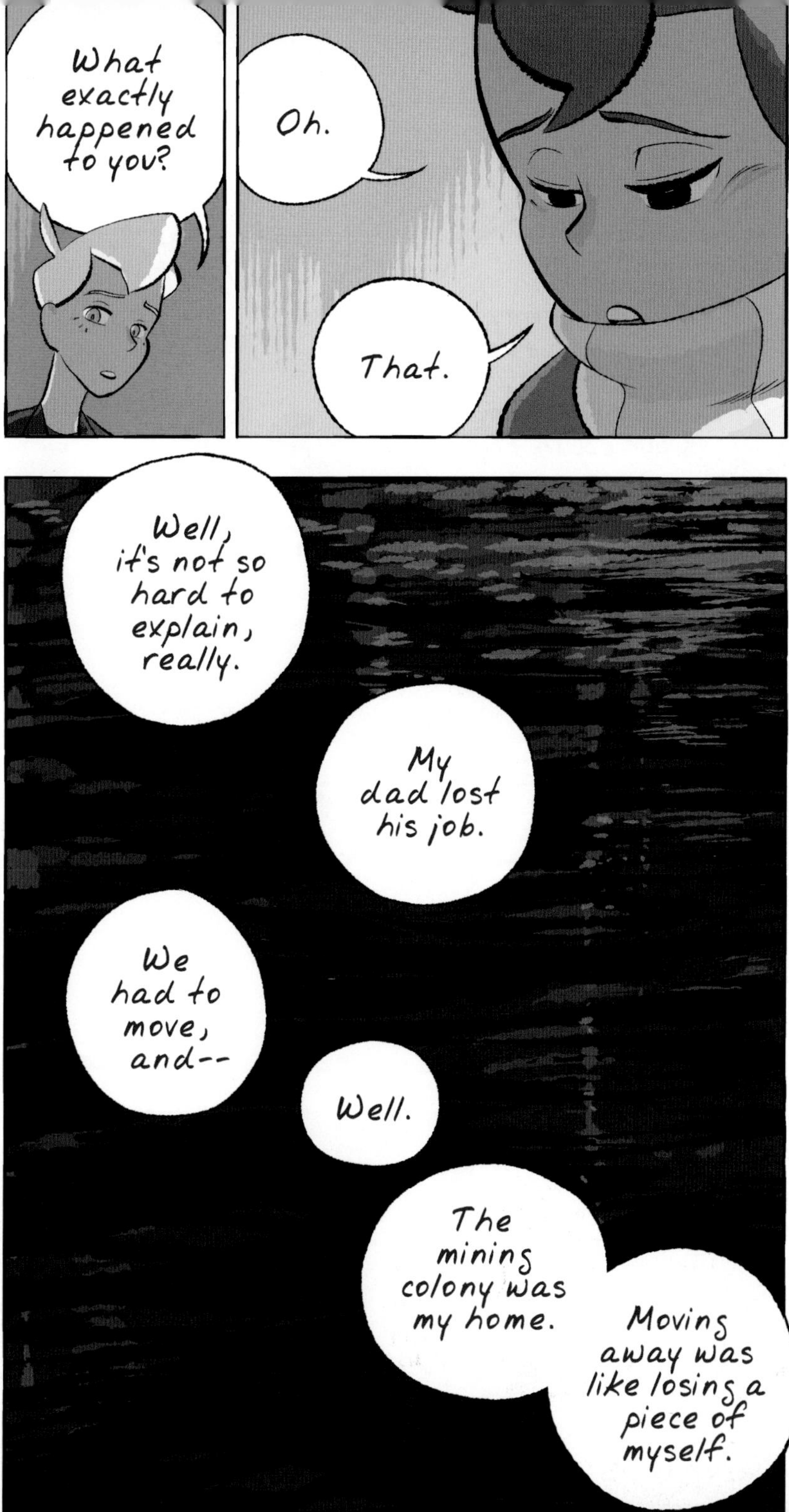
What exactly happened to you?
Oh.
That.
Well, it's not so hard to explain, really.
My dad lost his job.
We had to move, and--
Well.
The mining colony was my home.
Moving away was like losing a piece of myself.

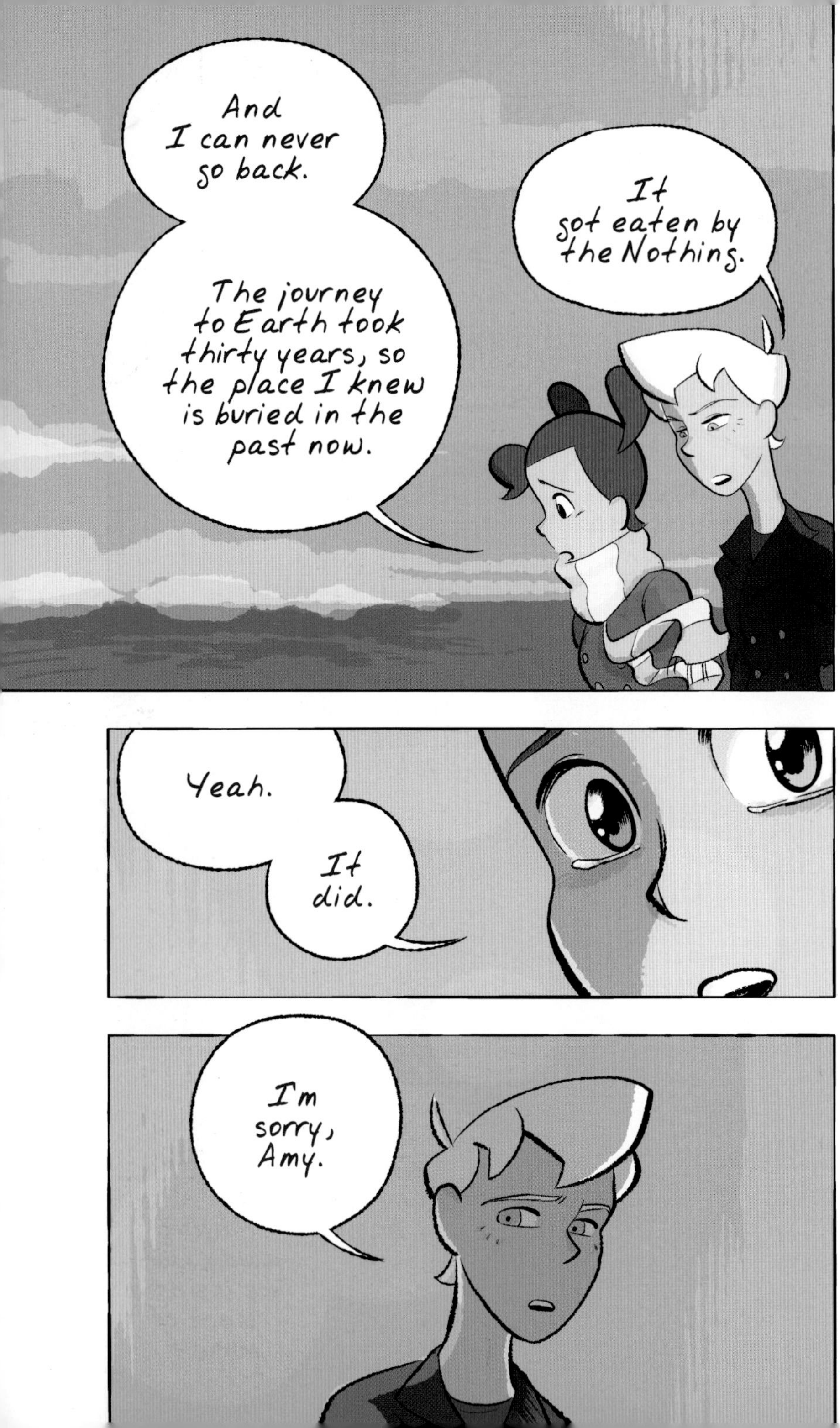
And I can never go back.
The journey to Earth took thirty years, so the place I knew is buried in the past now.
It got eaten by the Nothing.
Yeah.
It did.
I'm sorry, Amy.

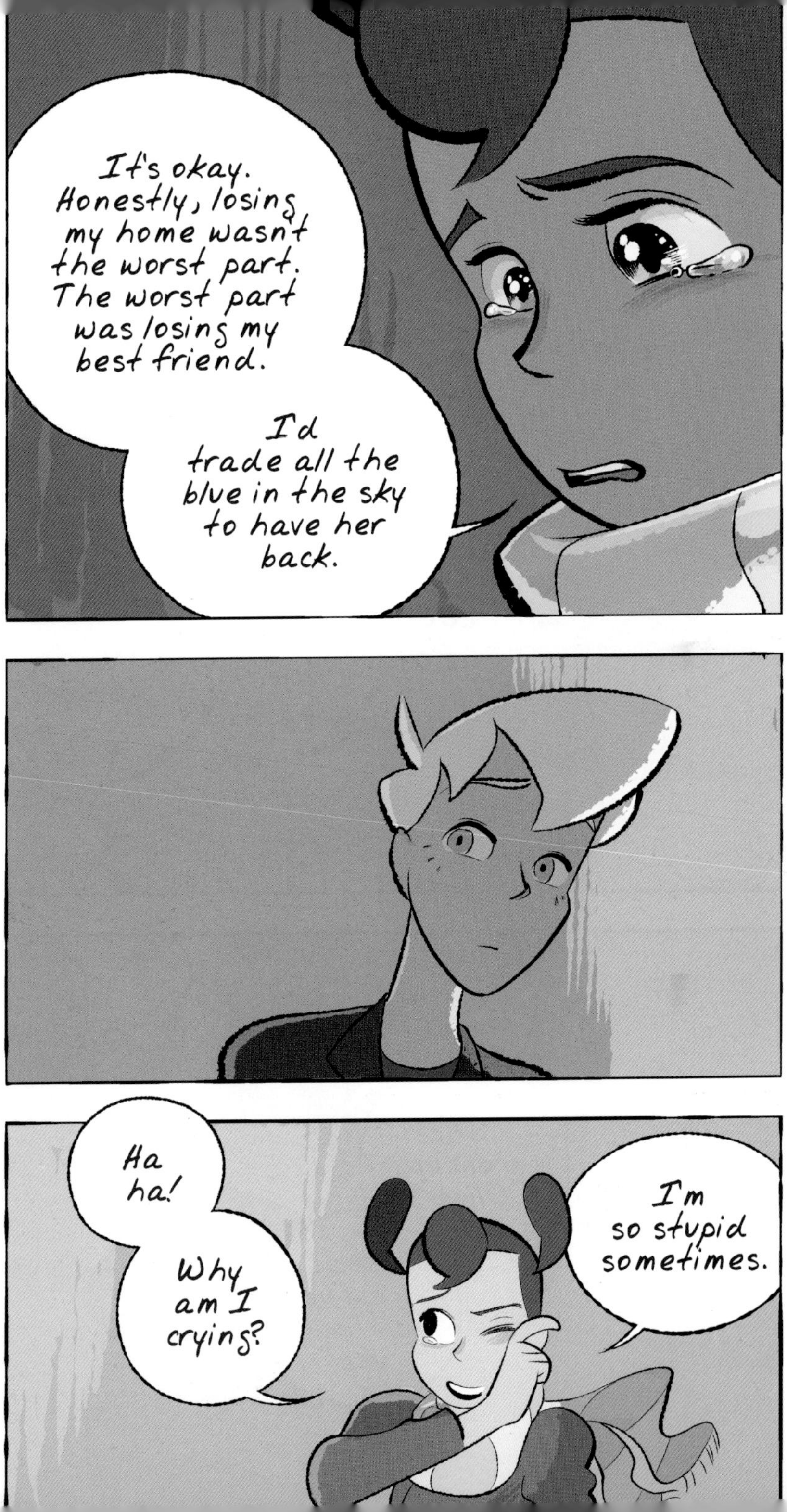
It's okay. Honestly, losing my home wasn't the worst part. The worst part was losing my best friend.
I'd trade all the blue in the sky to have her back.
Ha ha!
Why am I crying?
I'm so stupid sometimes.

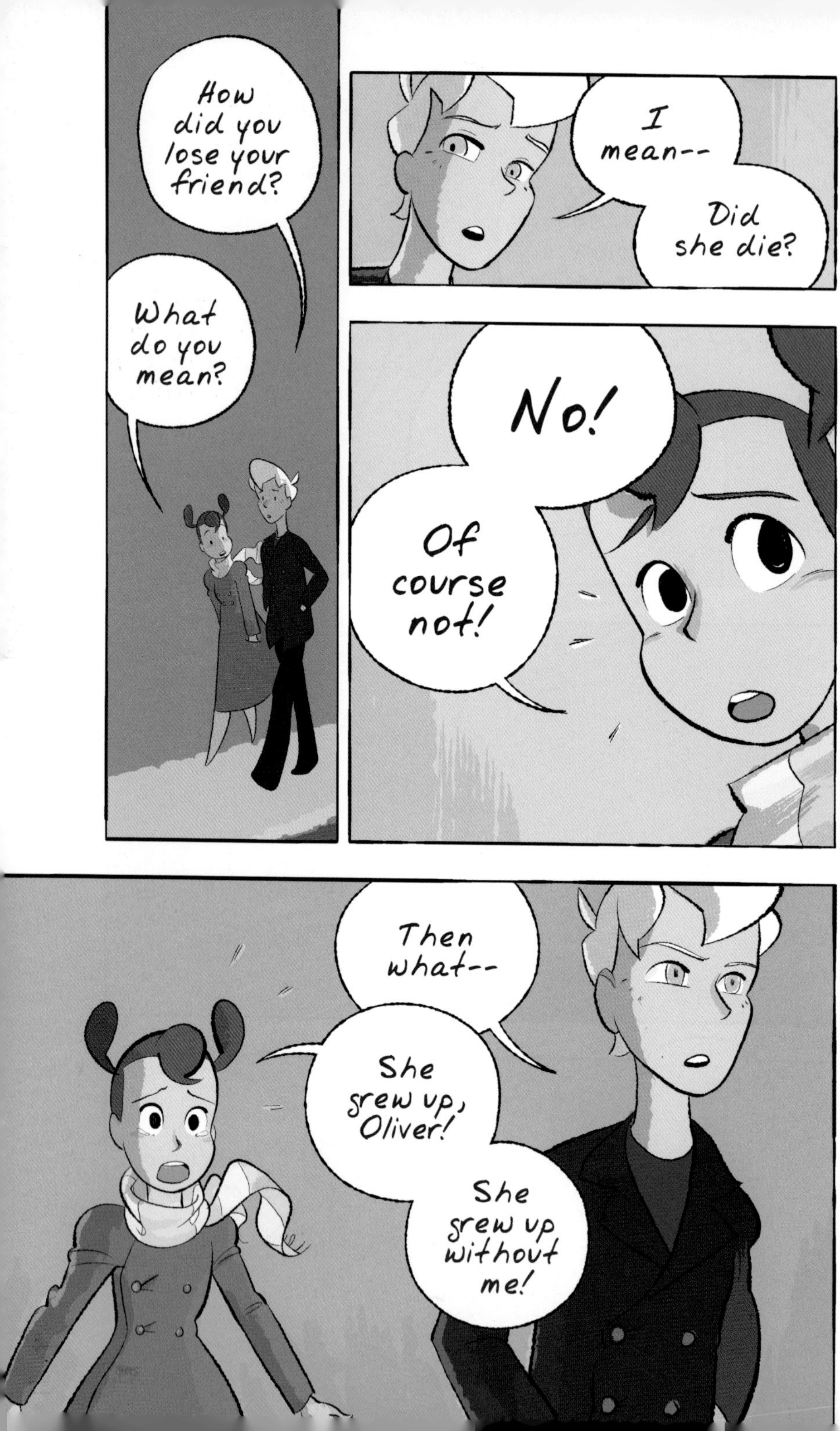
How did you lose your friend?
What do you mean?
I mean--
Did she die?
No!
Of course not!
Then what--
She grew up, Oliver!
She grew up without me!

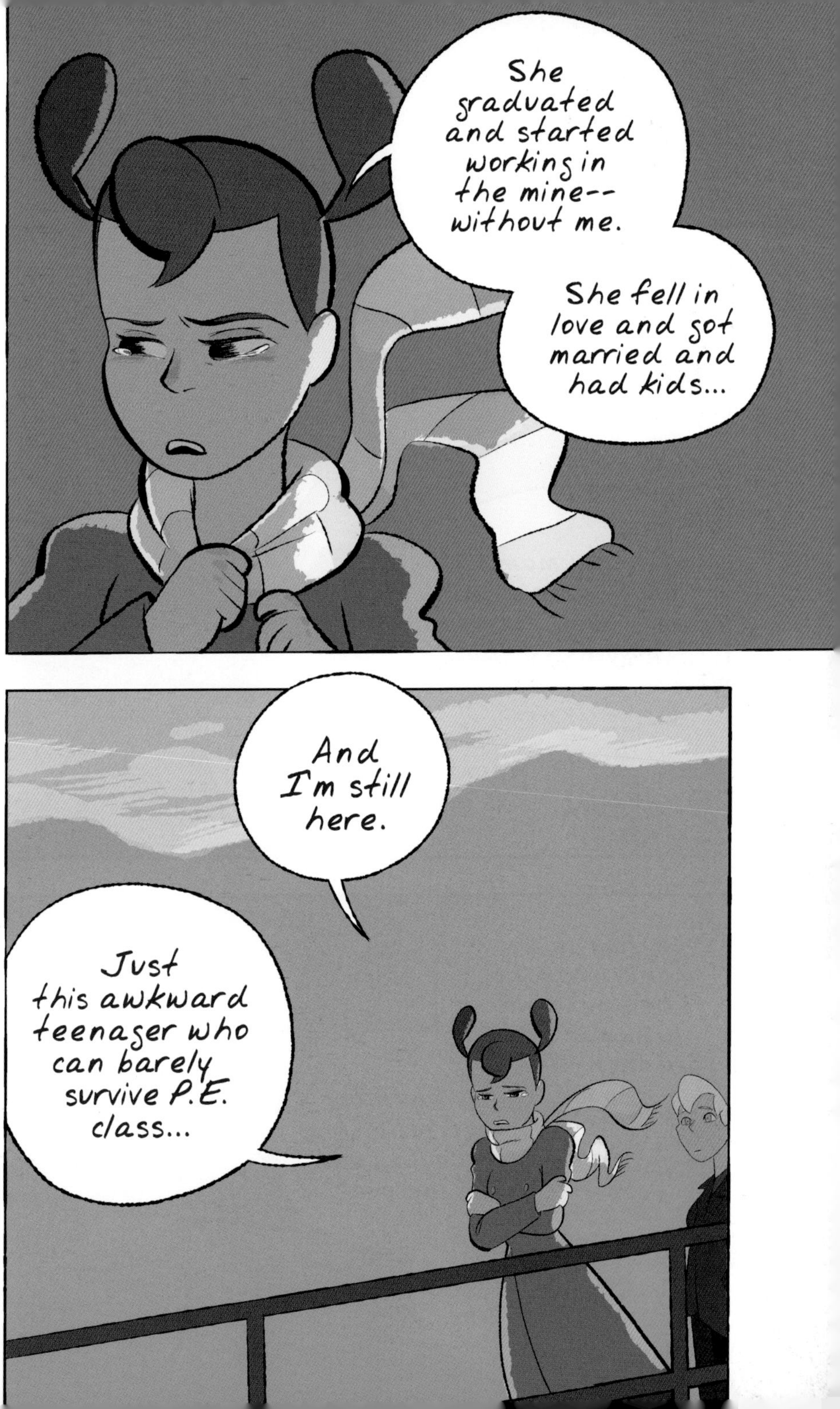
She gradvated and started workins in the mine-- without me.
She fell in love and sot married and had kids...
And I'm still here.
Just this awkward teenaser who can barely survive P.E. class...

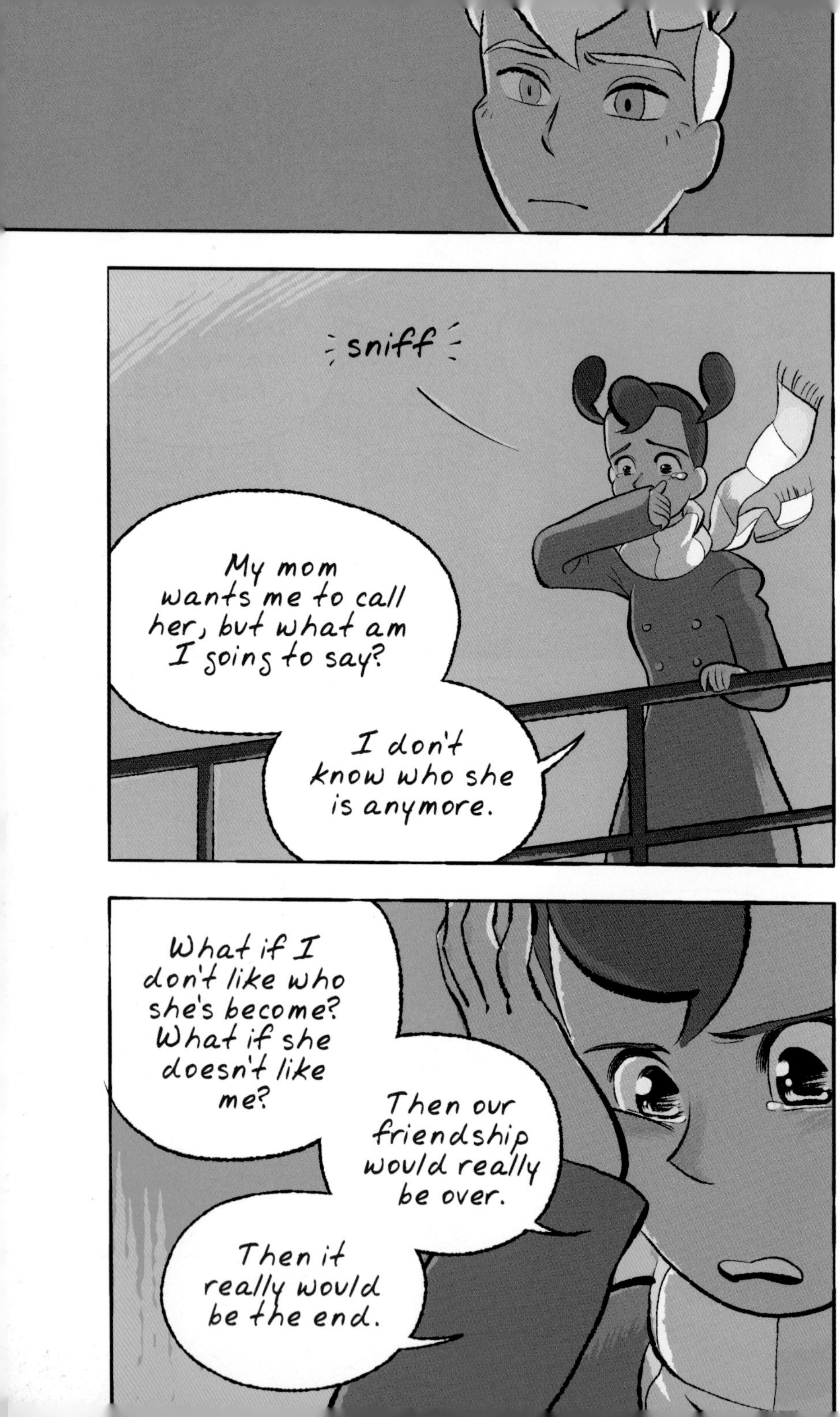
sniff
My mom wants me to call her, but what am I going to say?
I don't know who she is anymore.
What if I don't like who she's become? What if she doesn't like me?
Then our friendship would really be over.
Then it really would be the end.

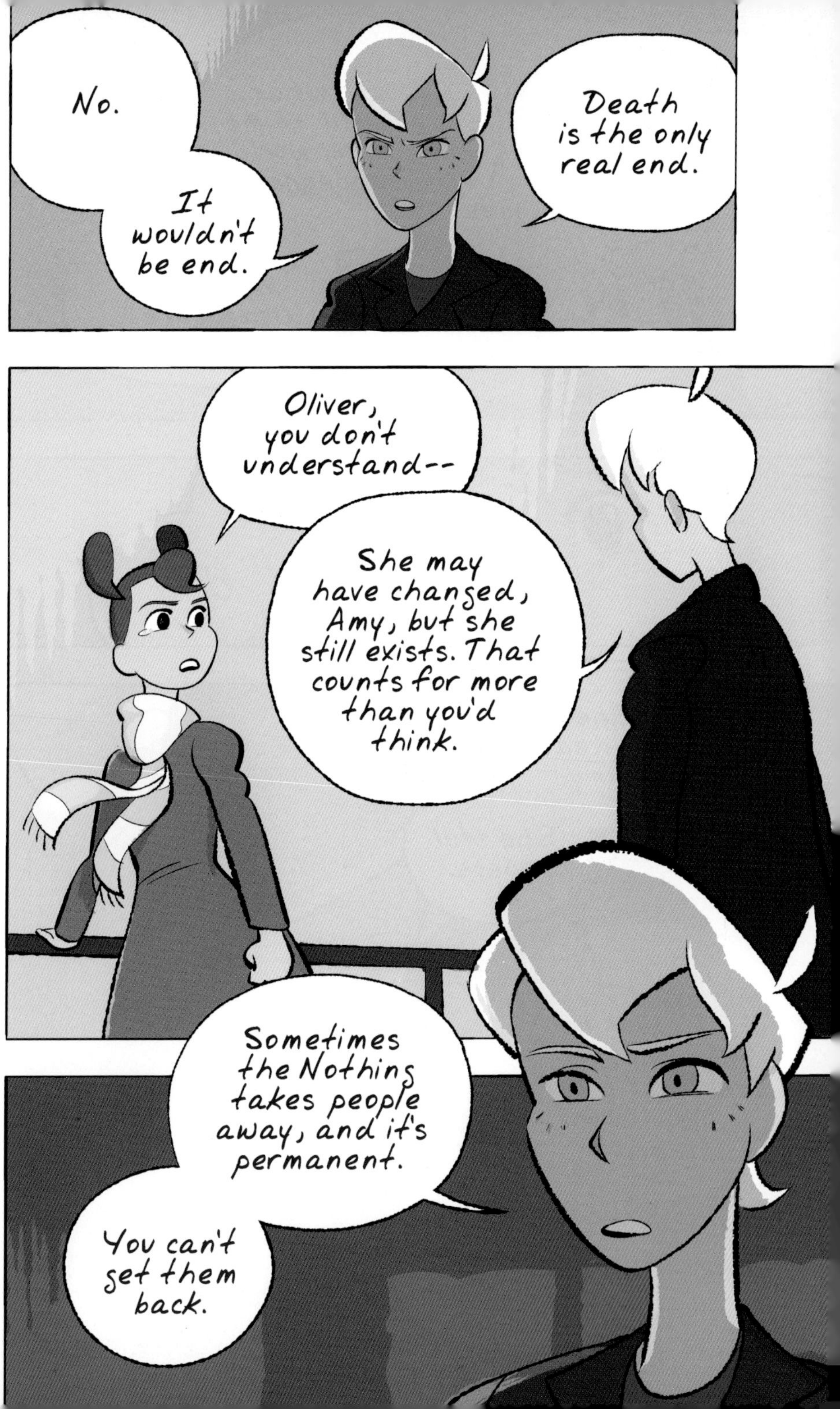
No.
It wouldn't be end.
Death is the only real end.
Oliver, you don't understand--
She may have changed, Amy, but she still exists. That counts for more than you'd think.
Sometimes the Nothing takes people away, and it's permanent.
You can't get them back.

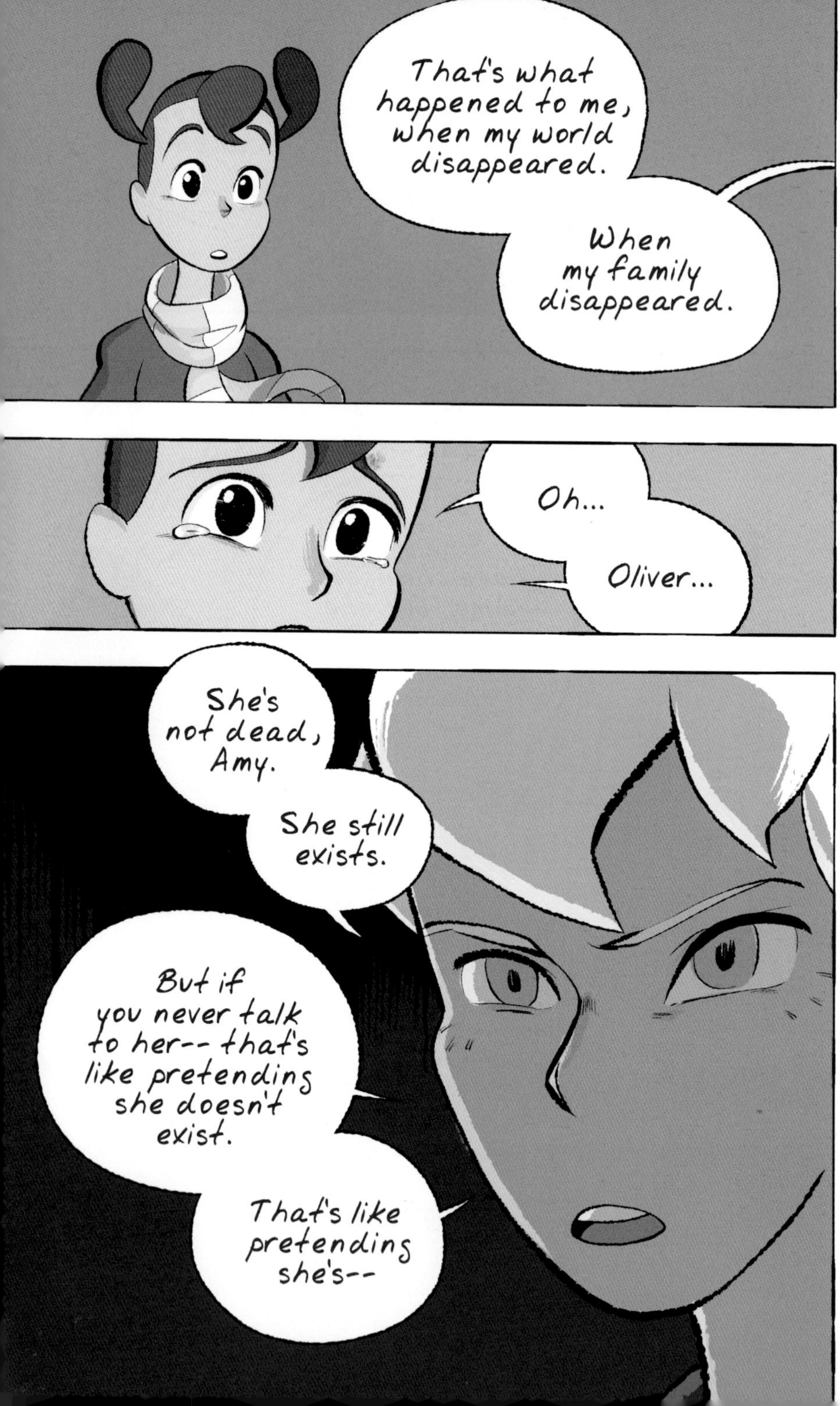
That's what happened to me, when my world disappeared.
When my family disappeared.
Oh...
Oliver...
She's not dead, Amy.
She still exists.
But if you never talk to her-- that's like pretending she doesn't exist.
That's like pretending she's--

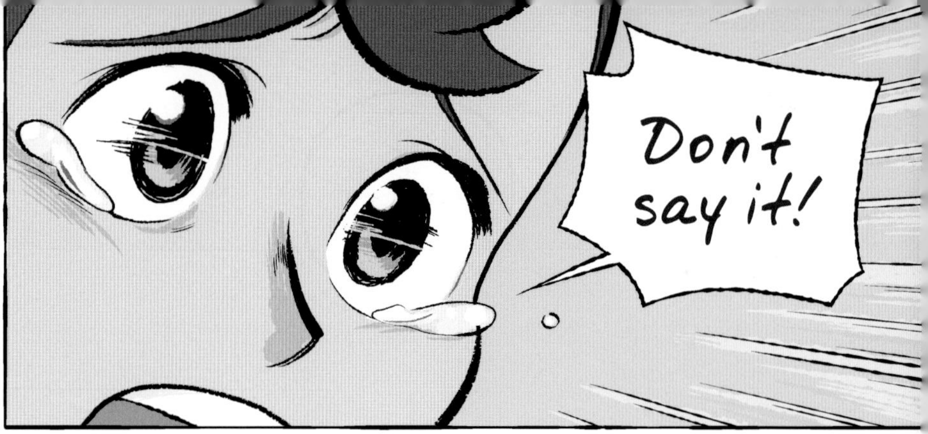
Don't say it!

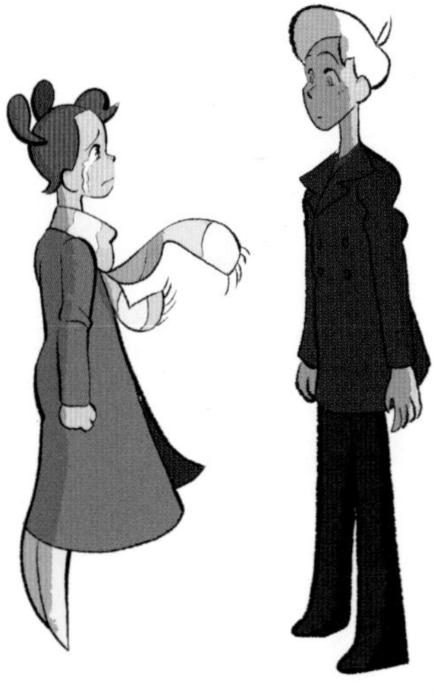

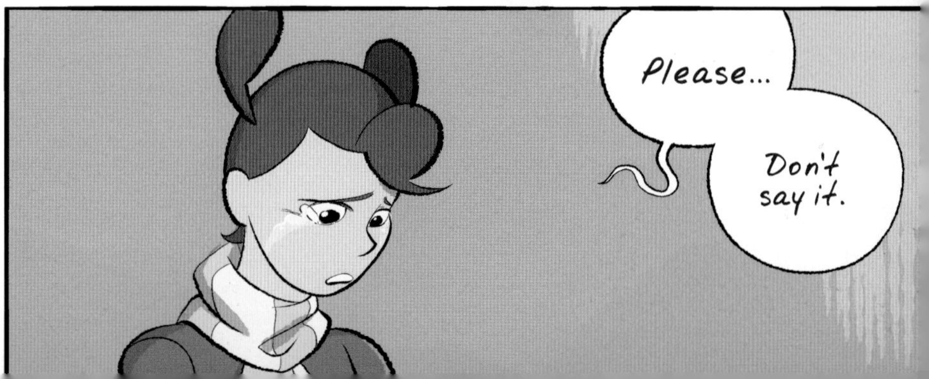
Please...
Don't say it.

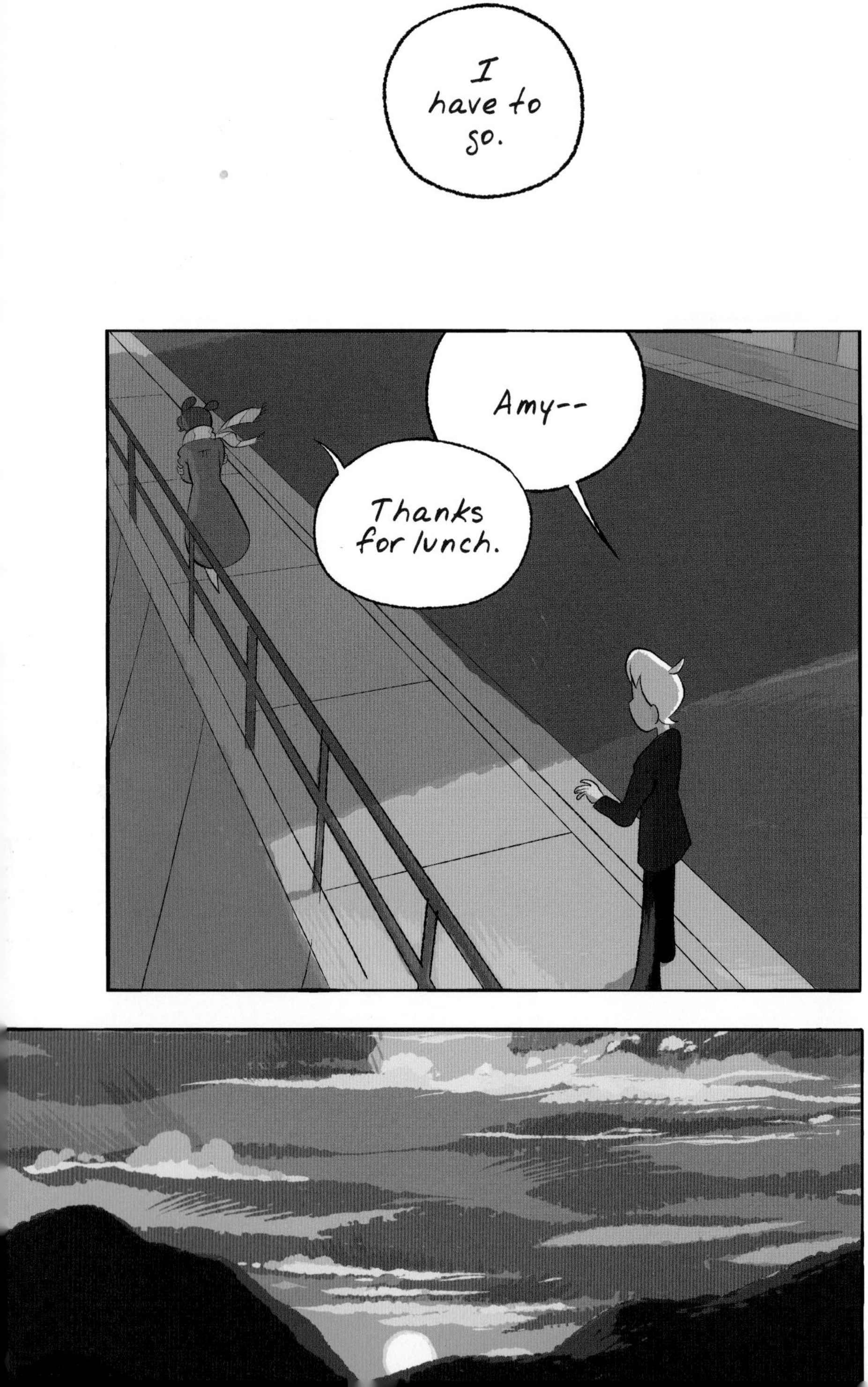

I have to go.
Amy--
Thanks for lunch.

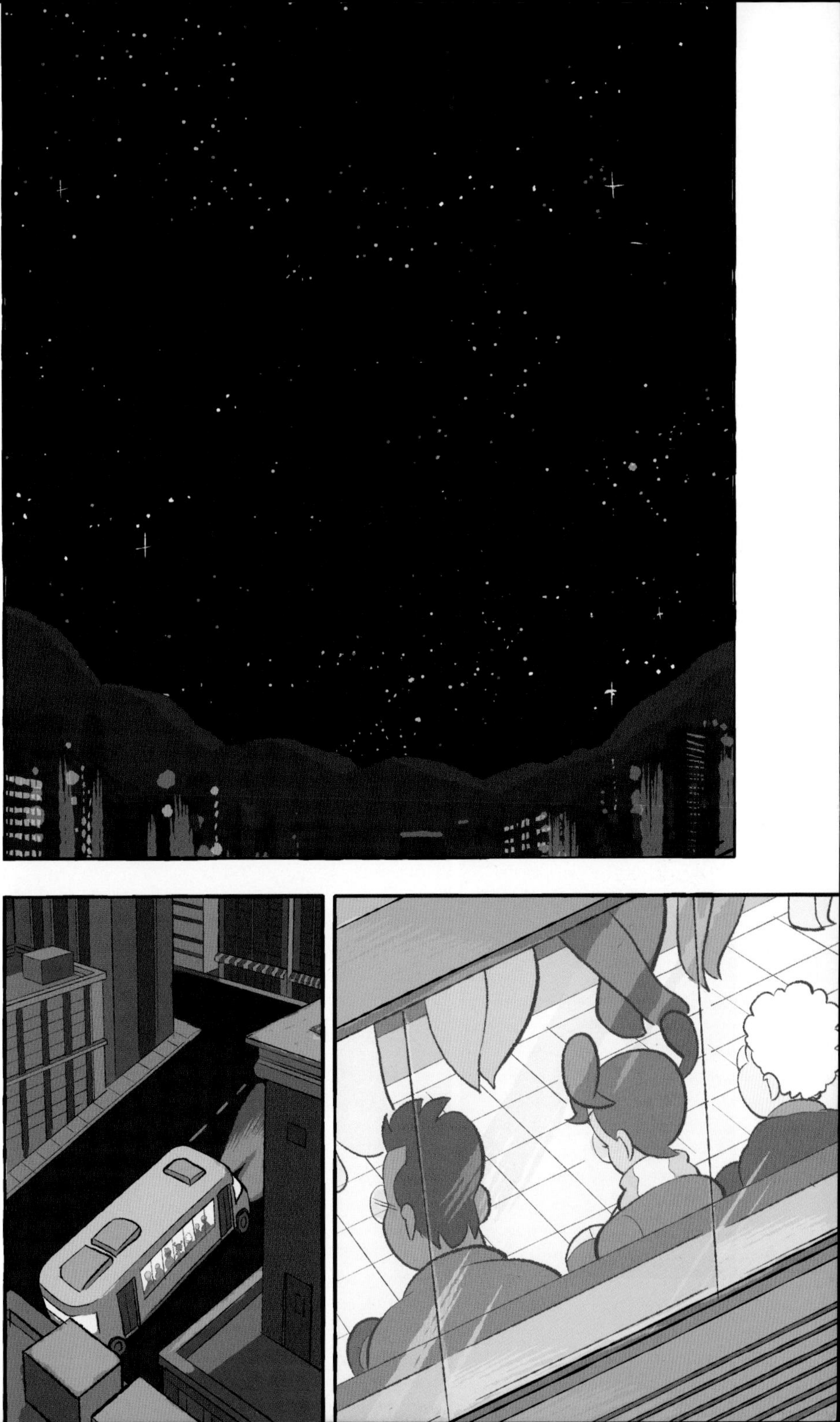

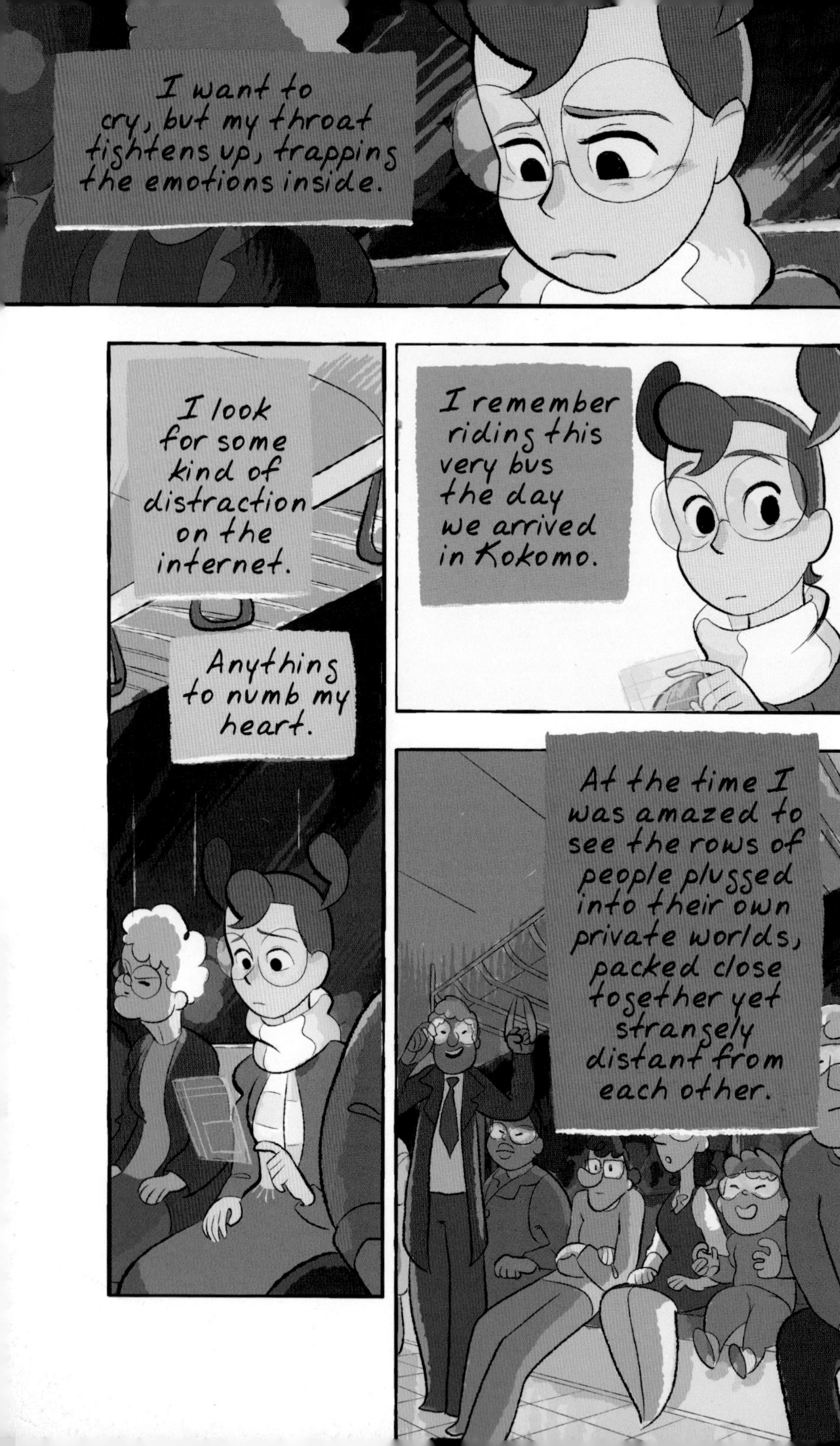
I want to cry, but my throat tightens up, trapping the emotions inside.
I look for some kind of distraction on the internet.
Anything to numb my heart.
I remember riding this very bus the day we arrived in Kokomo.
At the time I was amazed to see the rows of people plugged into their own private worlds, packed close together yet strangely distant from each other.

Now I am one of them, and
I am thankful for the distance,
thankful to be ignored.

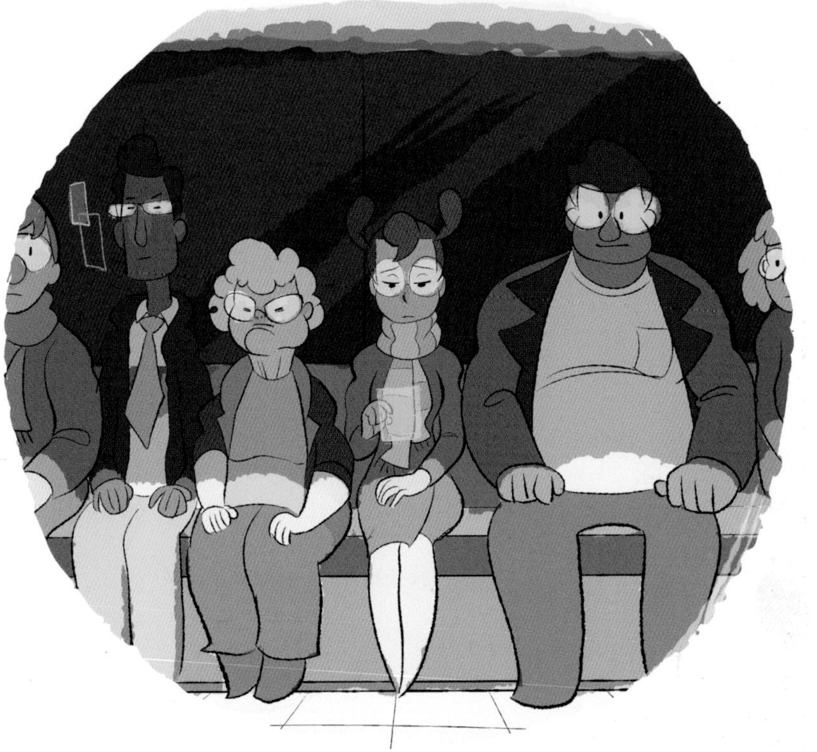

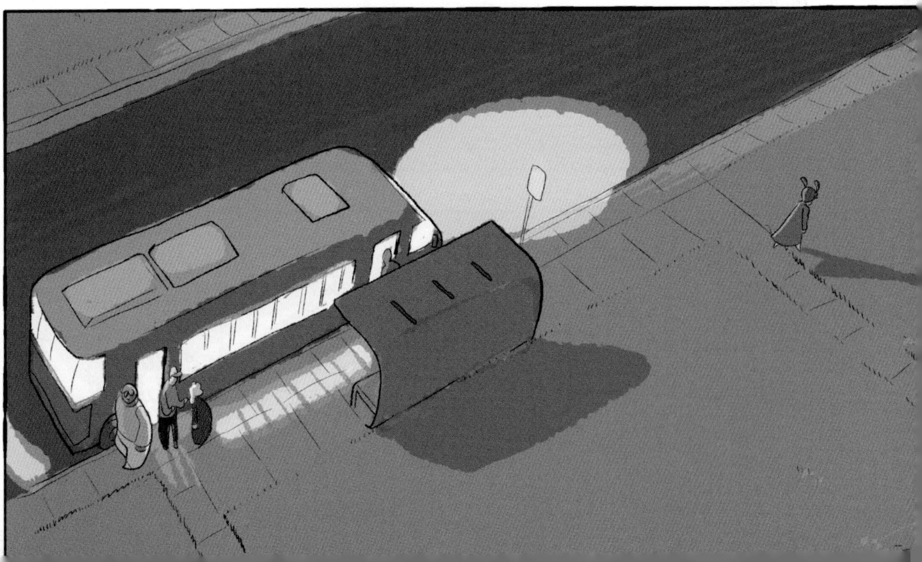

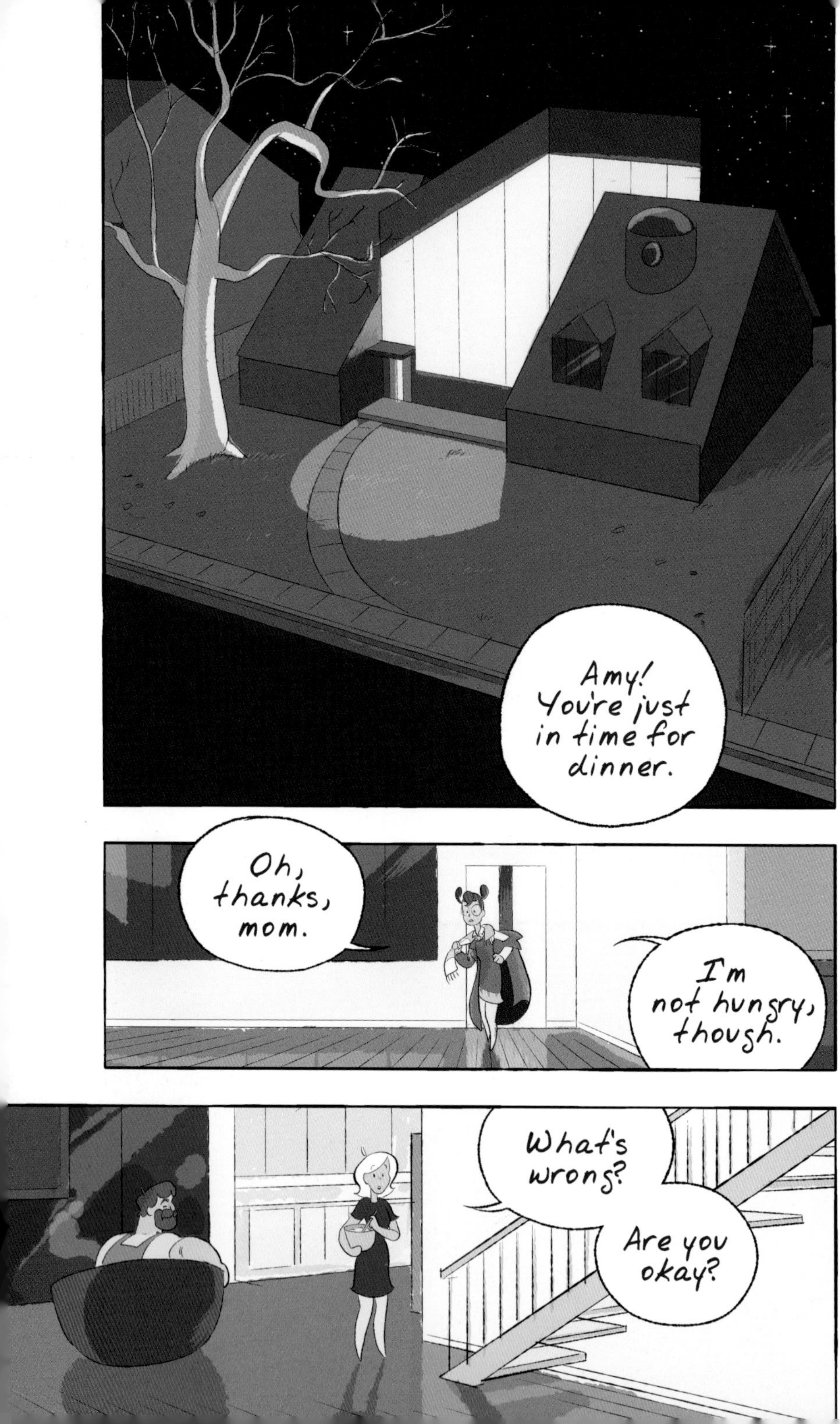
Amy! You're just in time for dinner.
Oh, thanks, mom.
I'm not hungry, though.
What's wrong?
Are you okay?

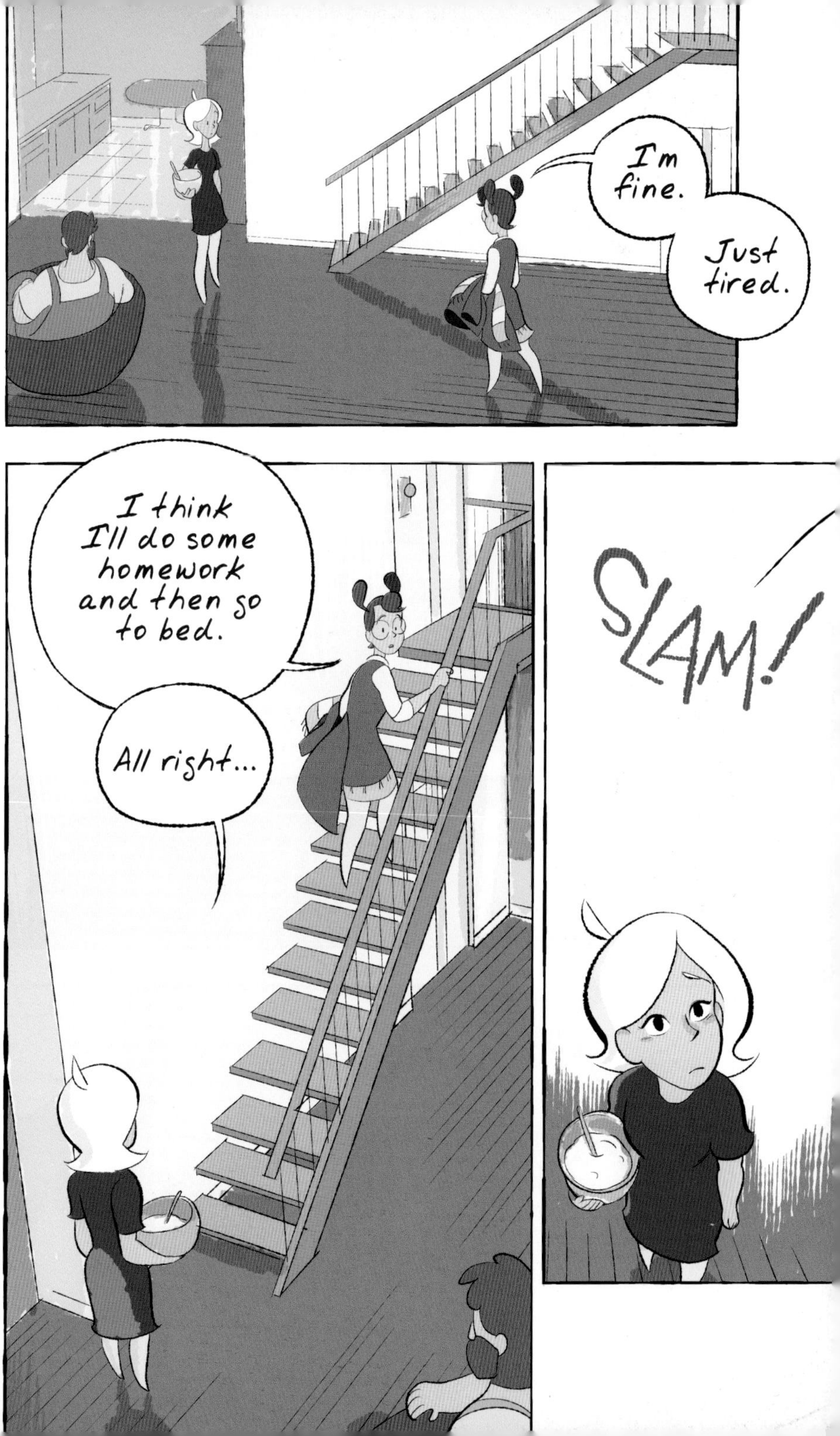
I'm fine.
Just tired.
I think I'll do some homework and then go to bed.
All right...
SLAM!

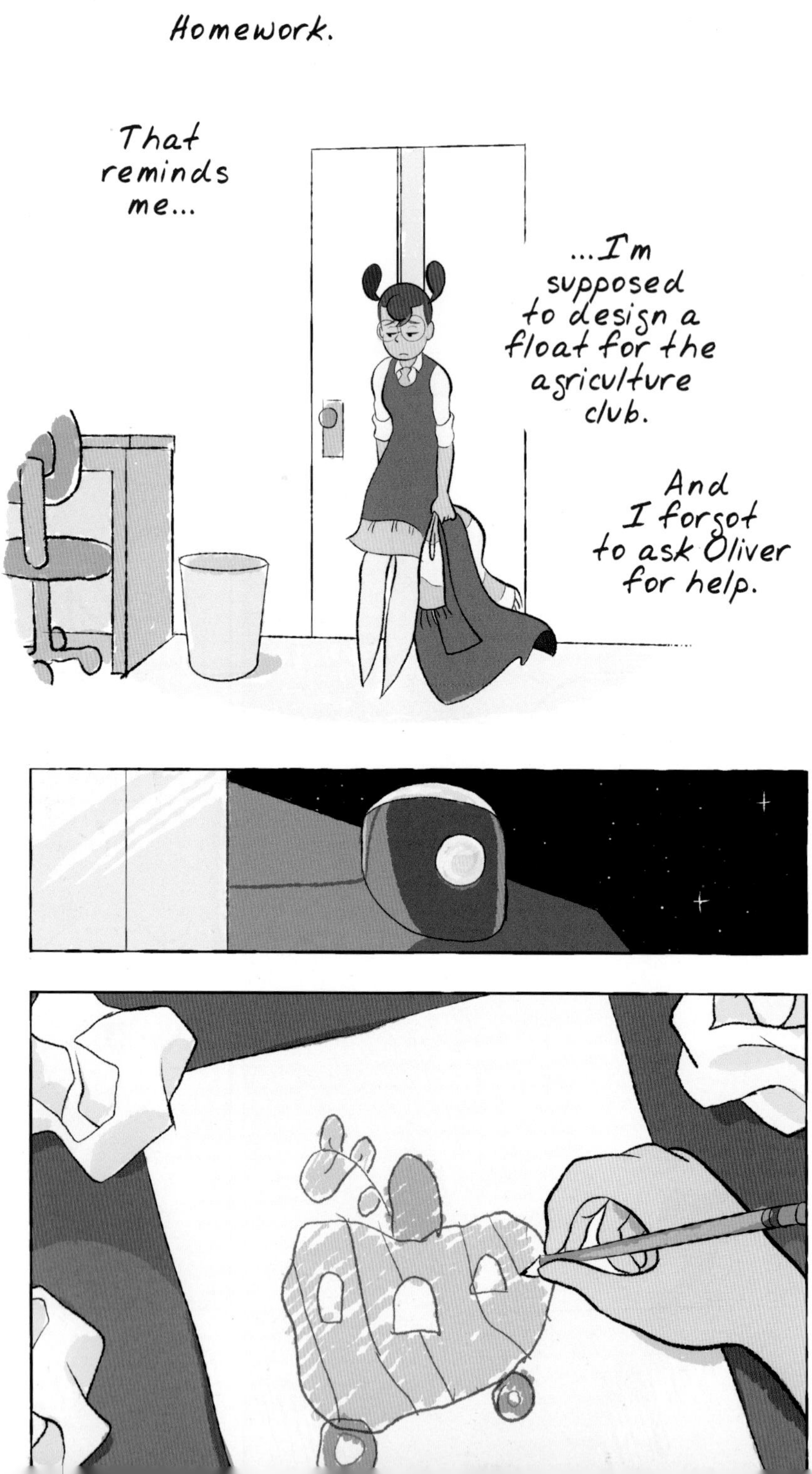
Homework.
That reminds me...
...I'm supposed to design a float for the agriculture club.
And I forgot to ask Oliver for help.

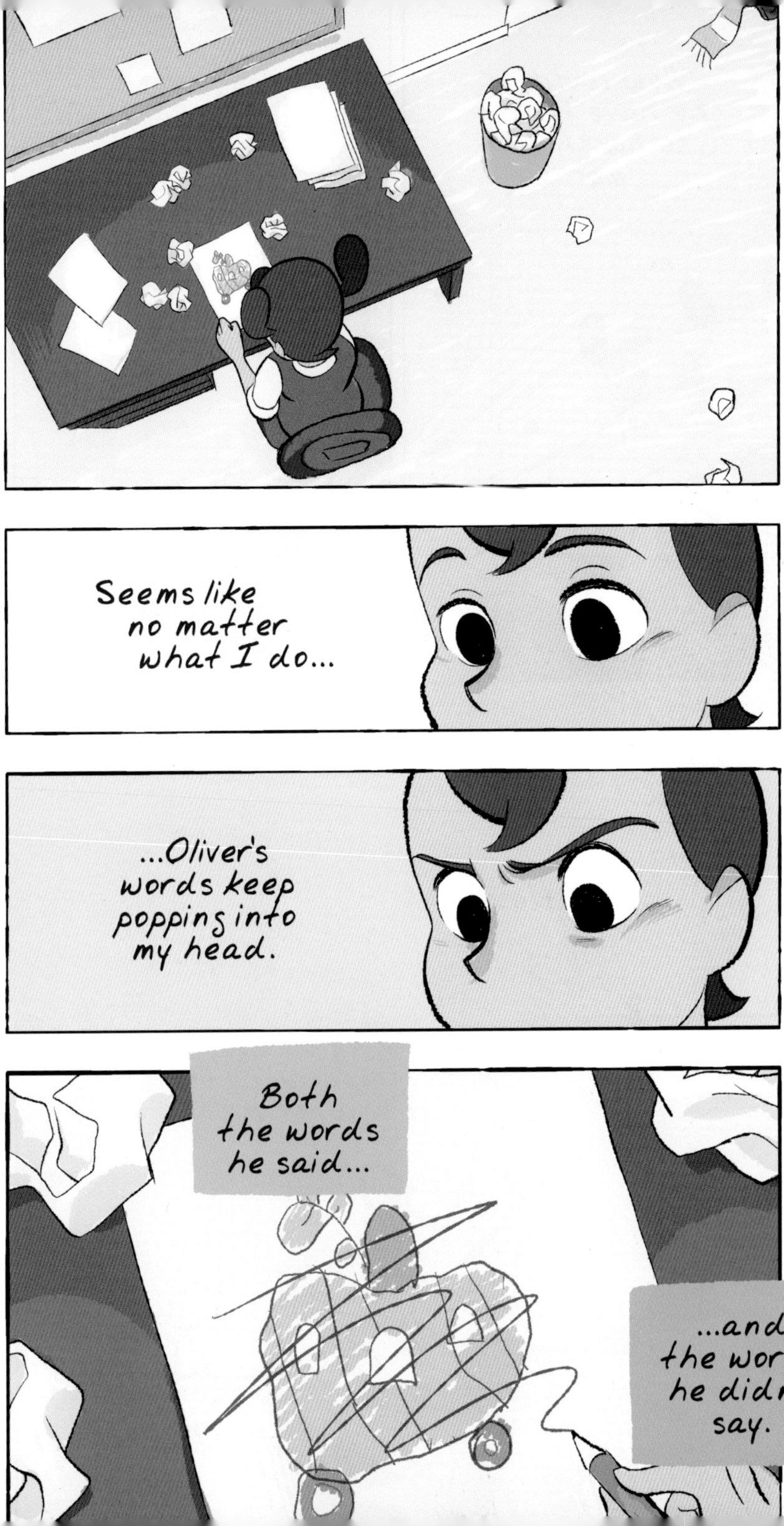
Seems like no matter what I do...
...Oliver's words keep popping into my head.
Both the words he said...
...and the words he didn't say.

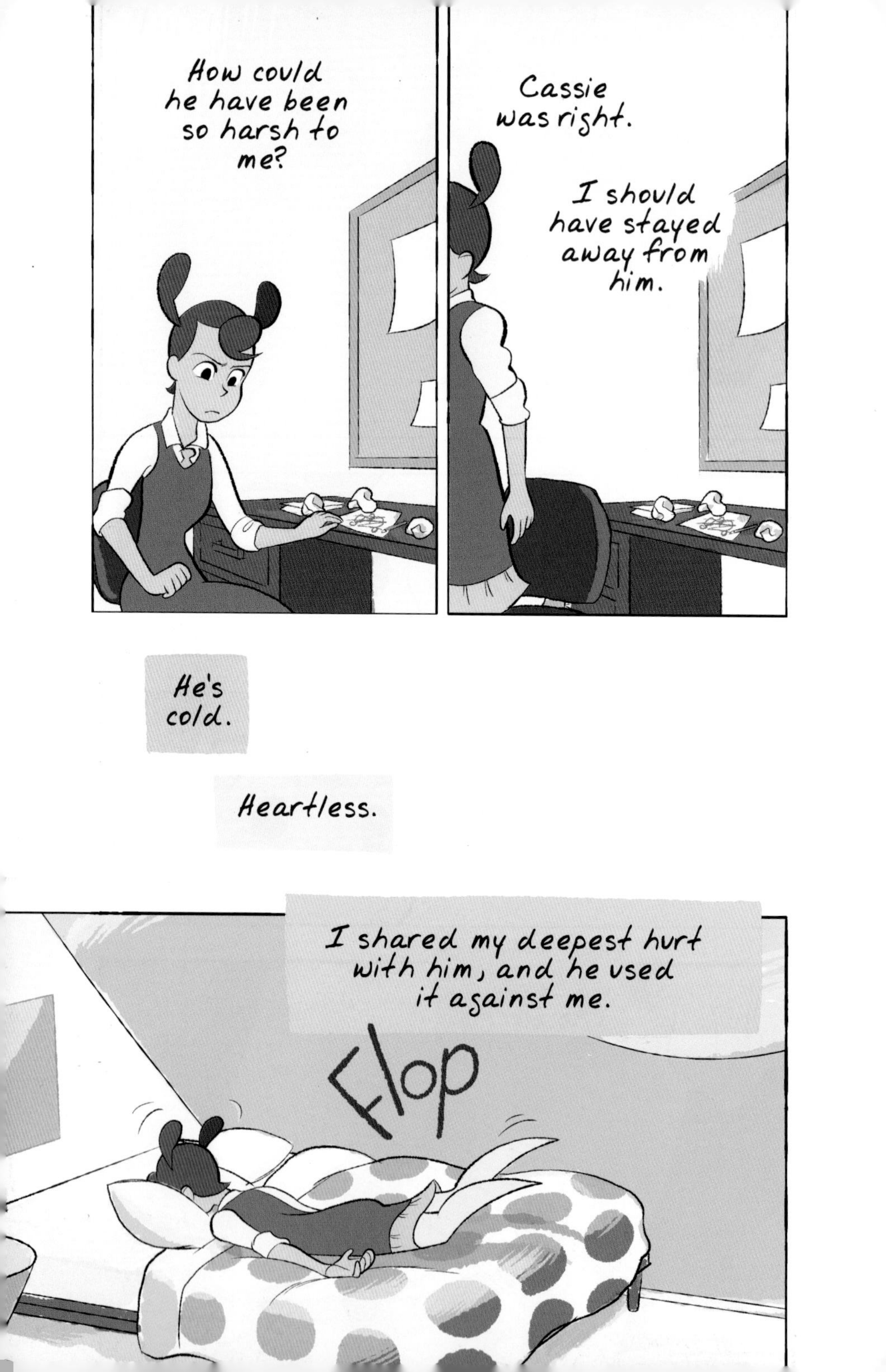
How could he have been so harsh to me?
Cassie was right.
I should have stayed away from him.
He's cold.
Heartless.
I shared my deepest hurt with him, and he used it against me.
Flop

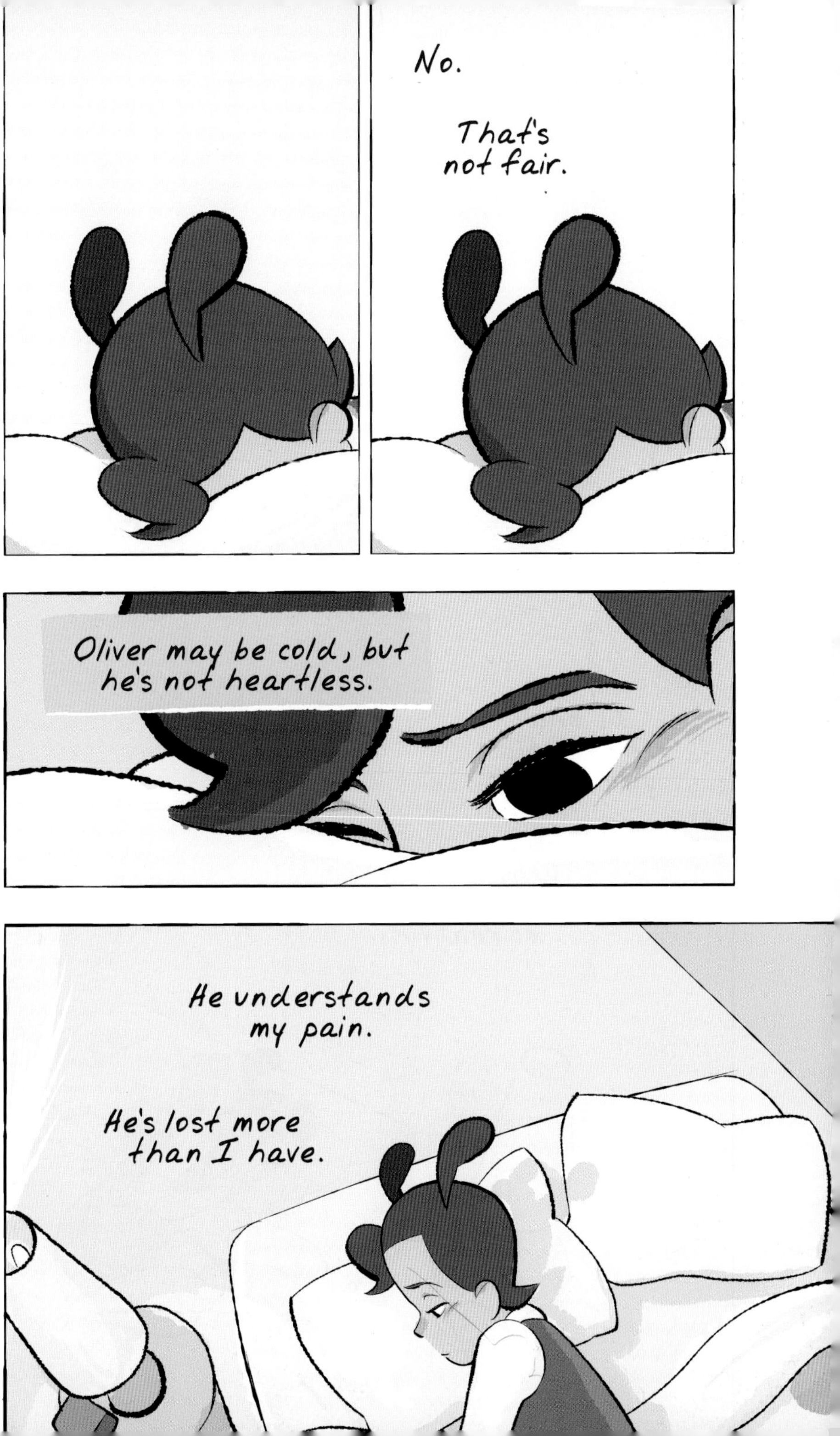
No.
That's not fair.
Oliver may be cold, but he's not heartless.
He understands my pain.
He's lost more than I have.

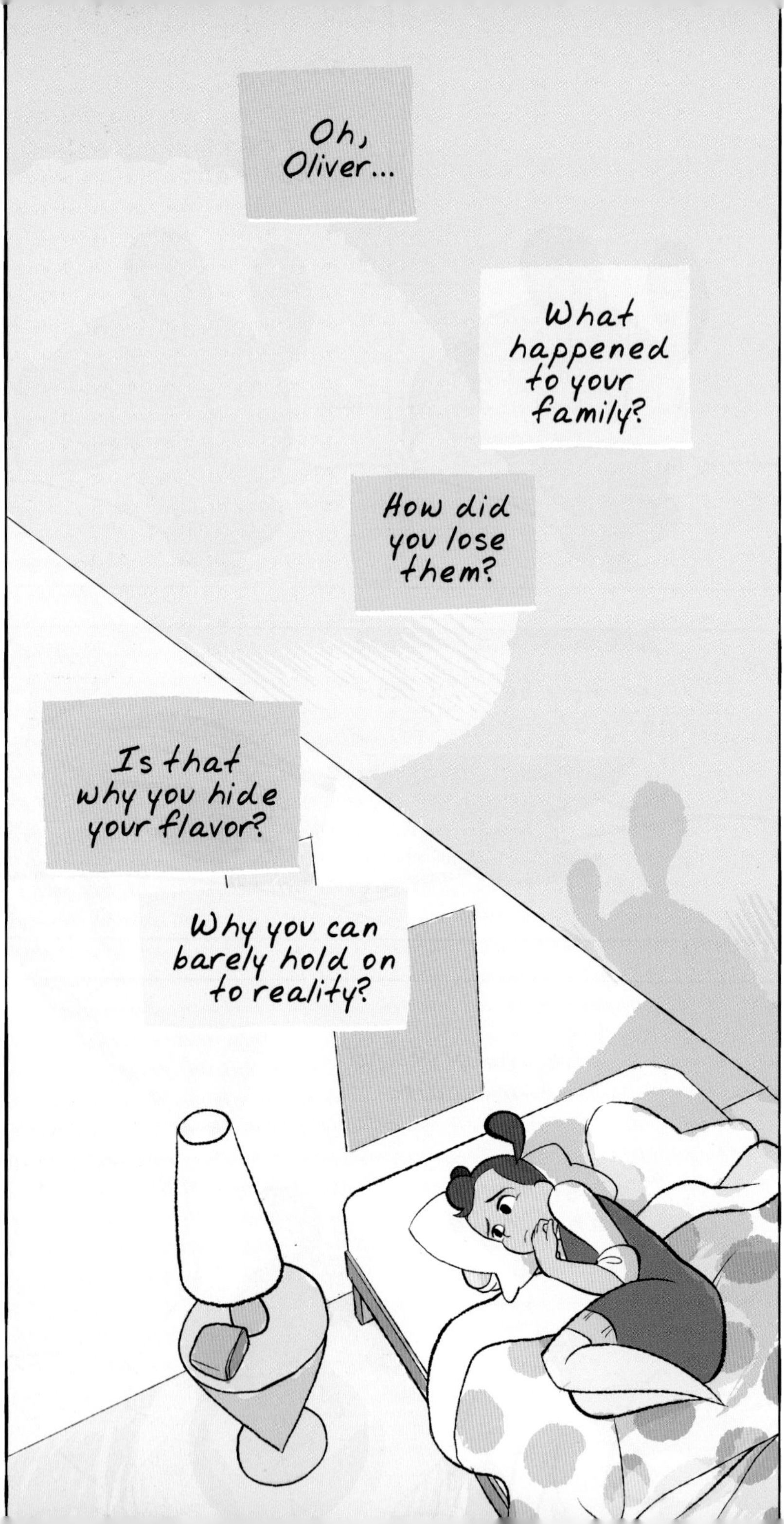
Oh, Oliver...
What happened to your family?
How did you lose them?
Is that why you hide your flavor?
Why you can barely hold on to reality?

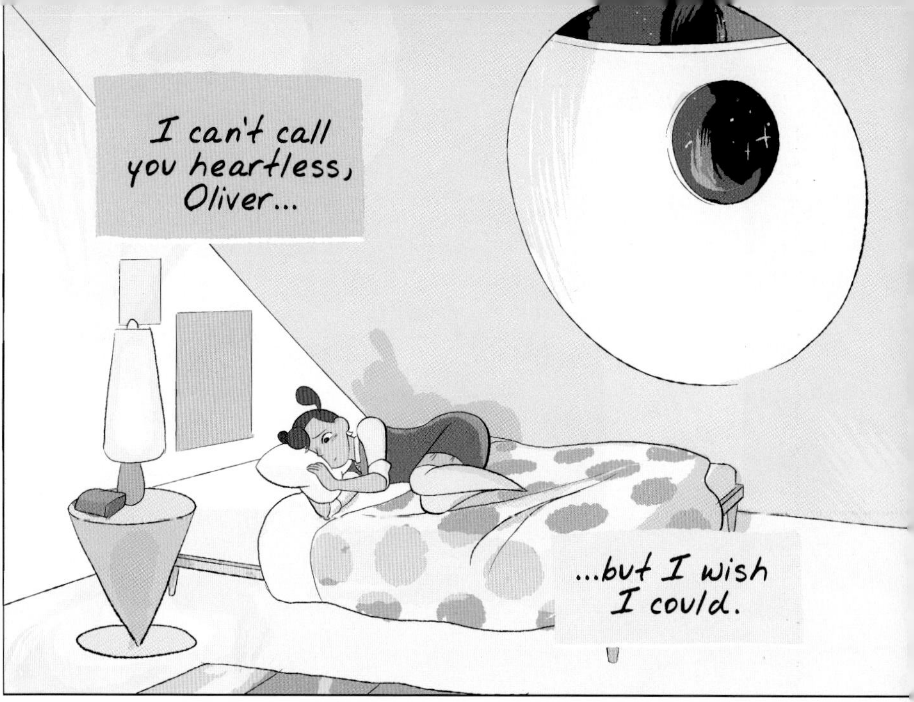
I can't call you heartless, Oliver...
...but I wish I could.

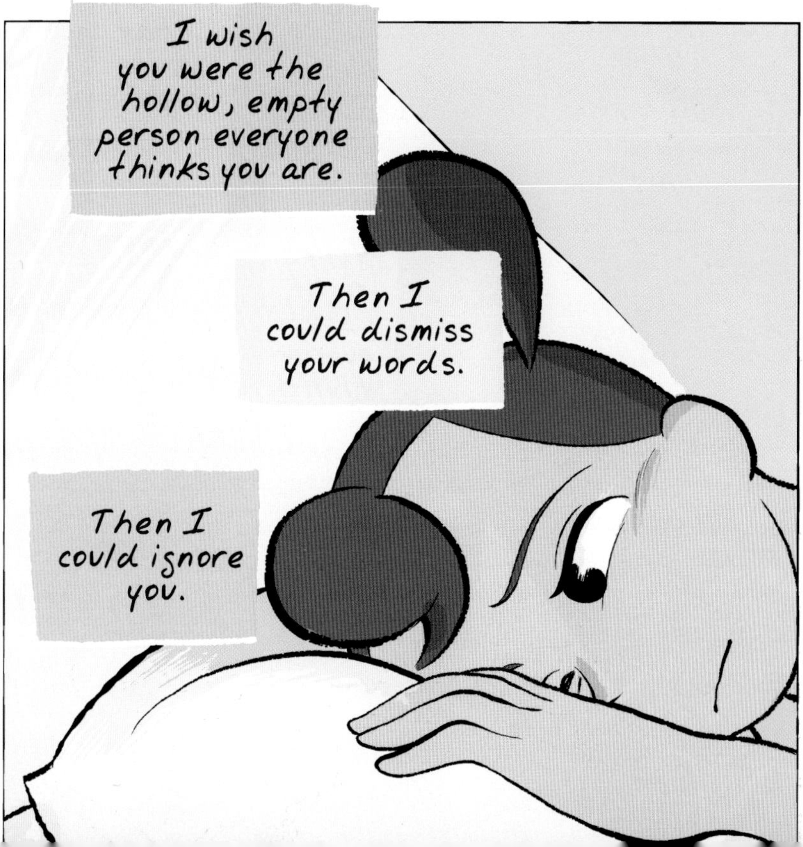
I wish you were the hollow, empty person everyone thinks you are.
Then I could dismiss your words.
Then I could ignore you.

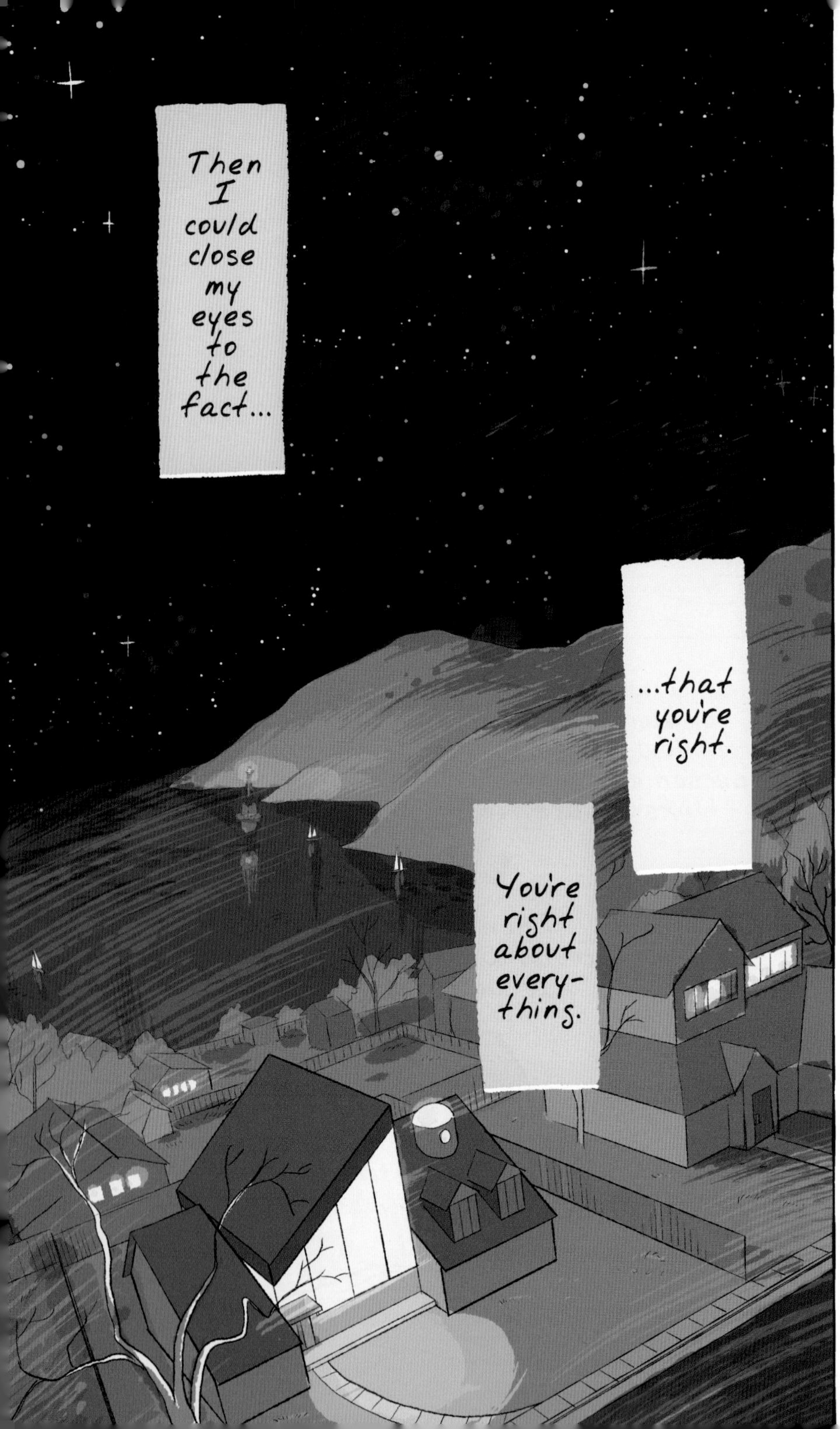
Then I could close my eyes to the fact...
...that you're right.
You're right about every-thing.

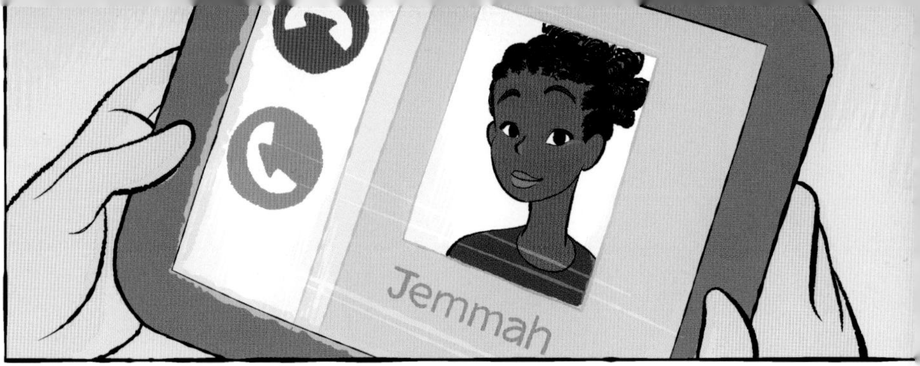
Jemmah
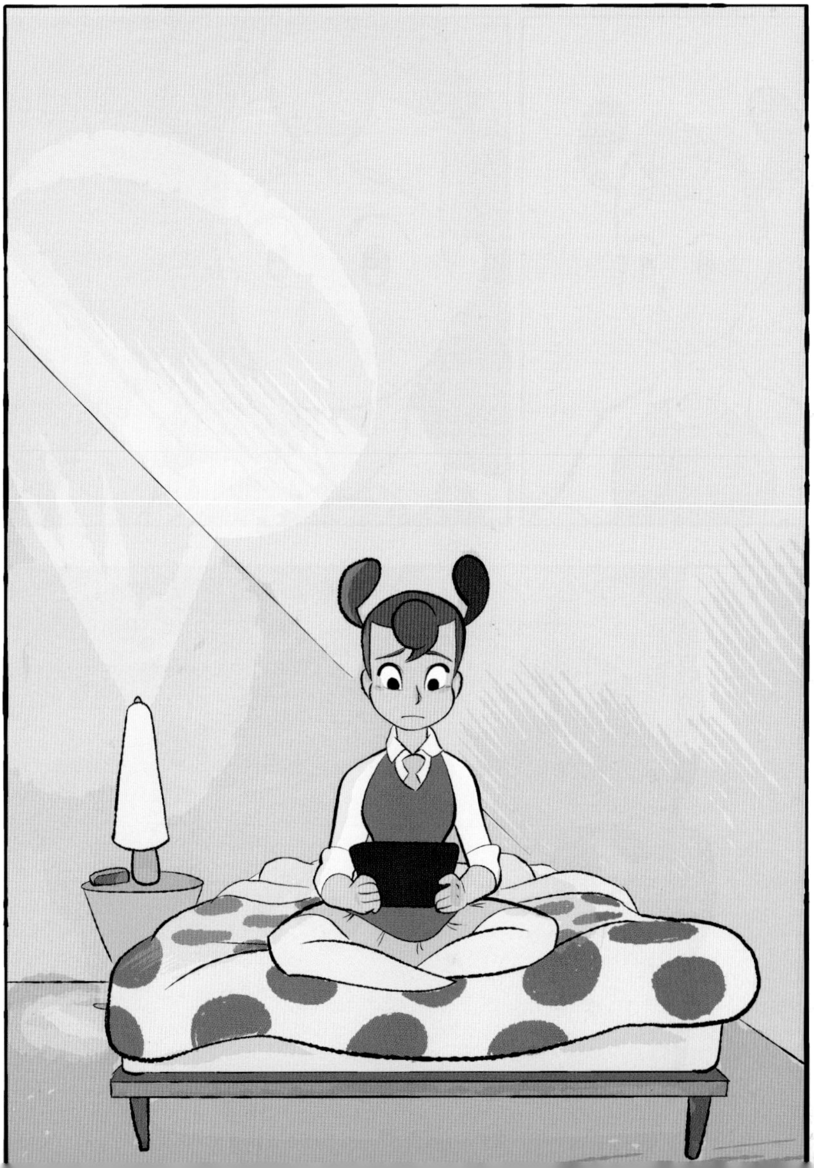

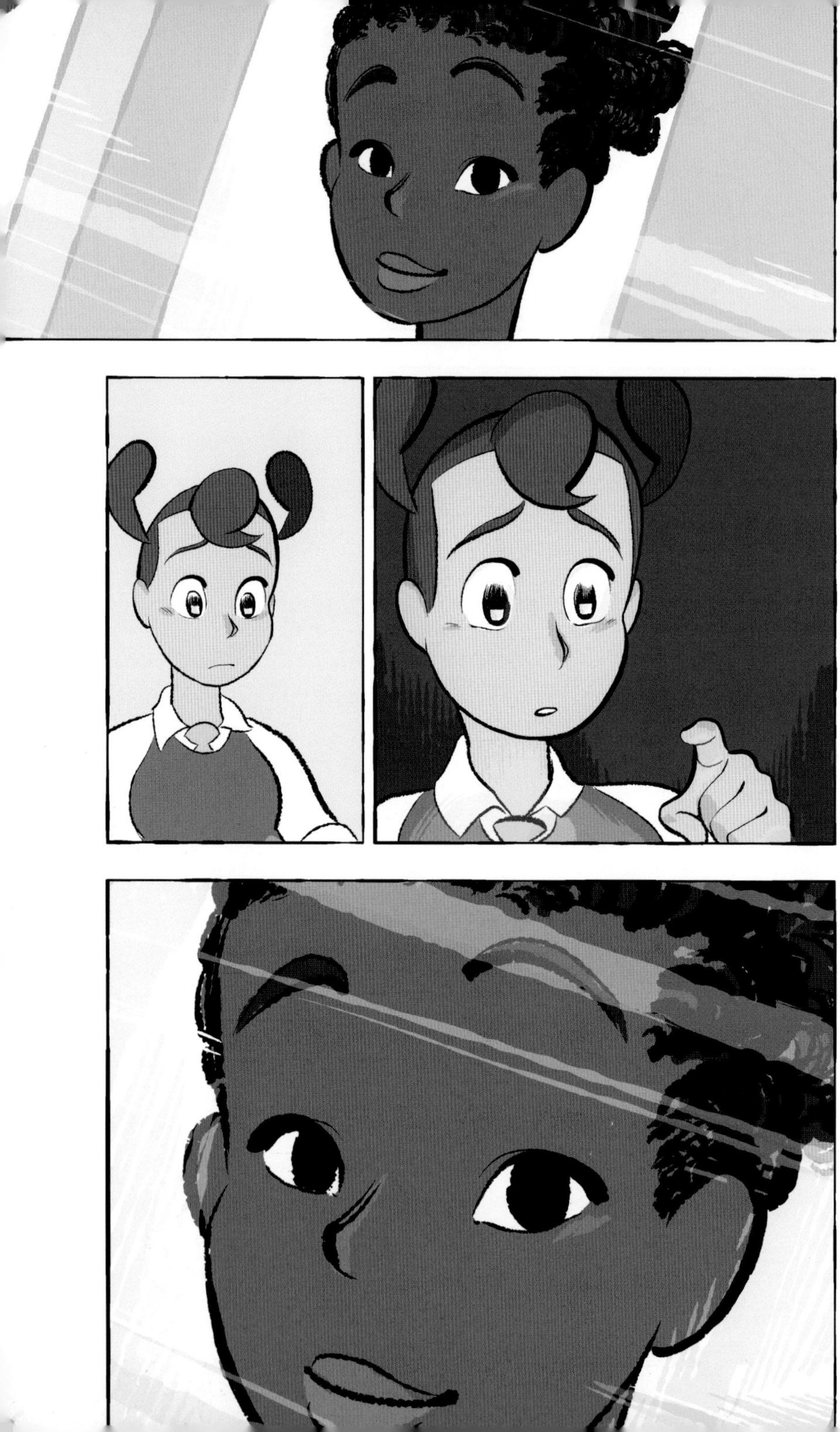

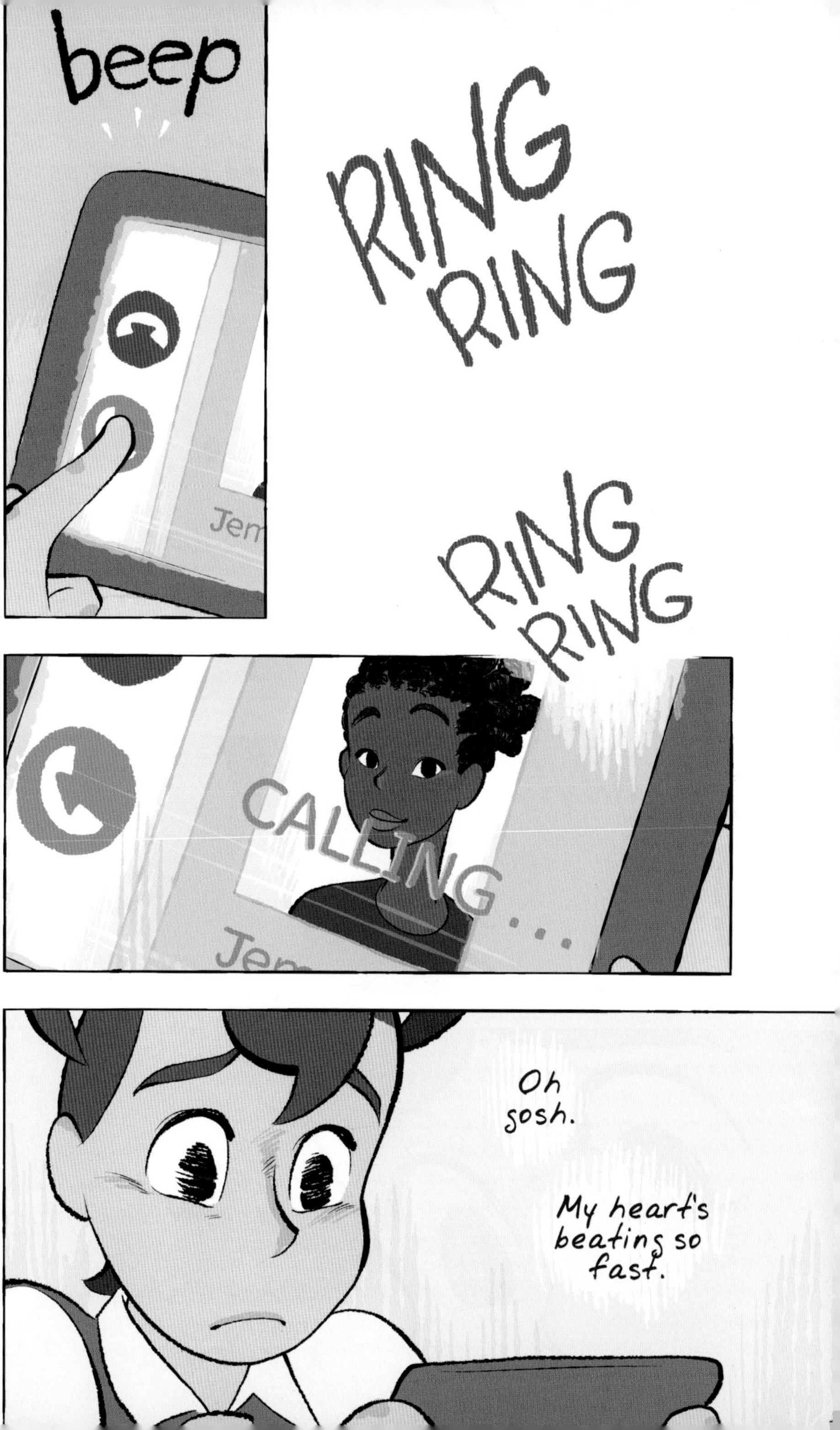
beep
RING
RING
Jem
RING
RING
CALLING...
Jem
Oh gosh.
My heart's beating so fast.

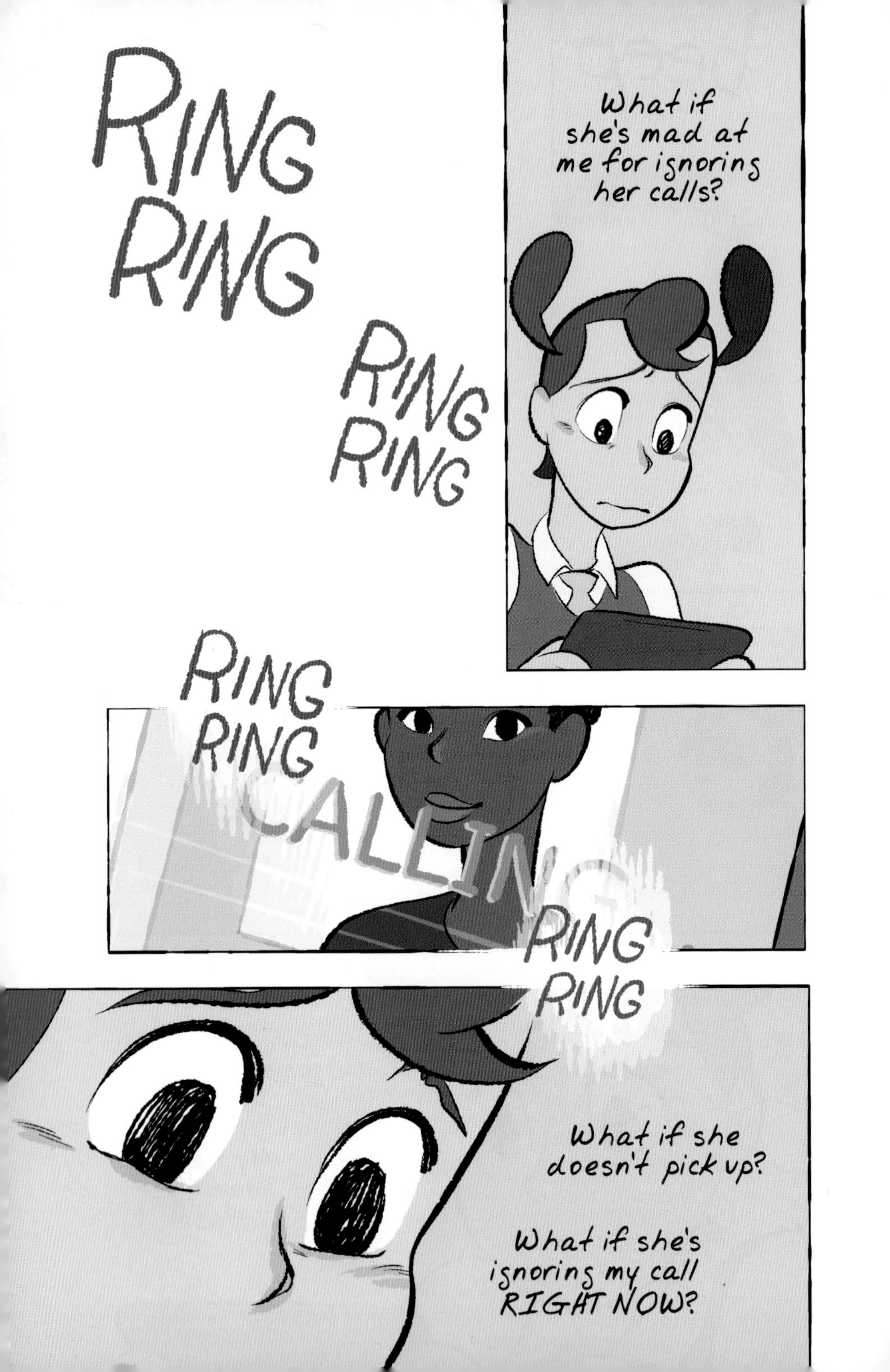
RING RING
RING RING
What if she's mad at me for ignorins her calls?
RING RING
CALLING
RING RING
What if she doesn't pick up?
What if she's ignorins my call RIGHT NOW?

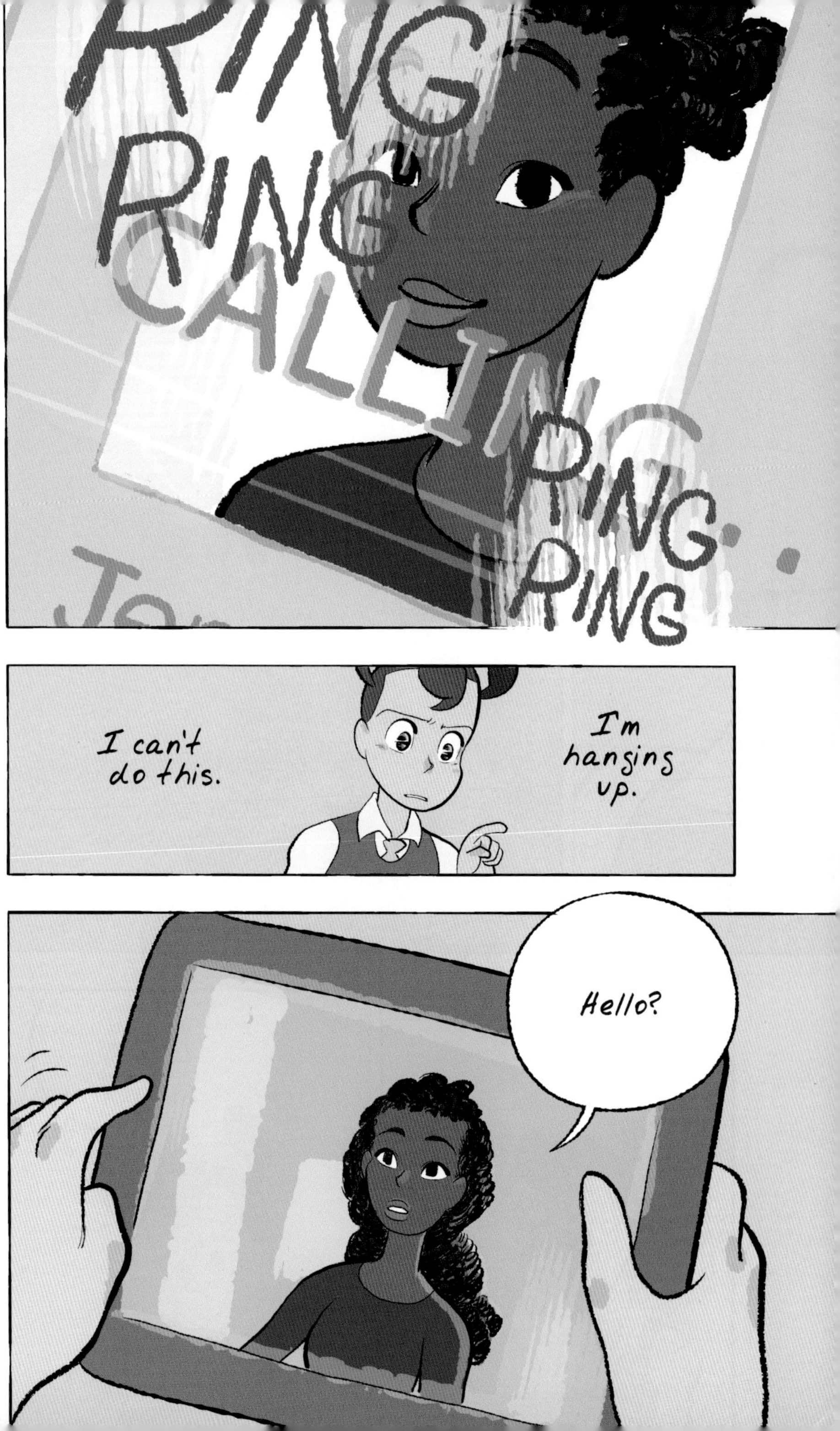
RING
RING
CALLING...
RING
RING
I can't do this.
I'm hanging up.
Hello?

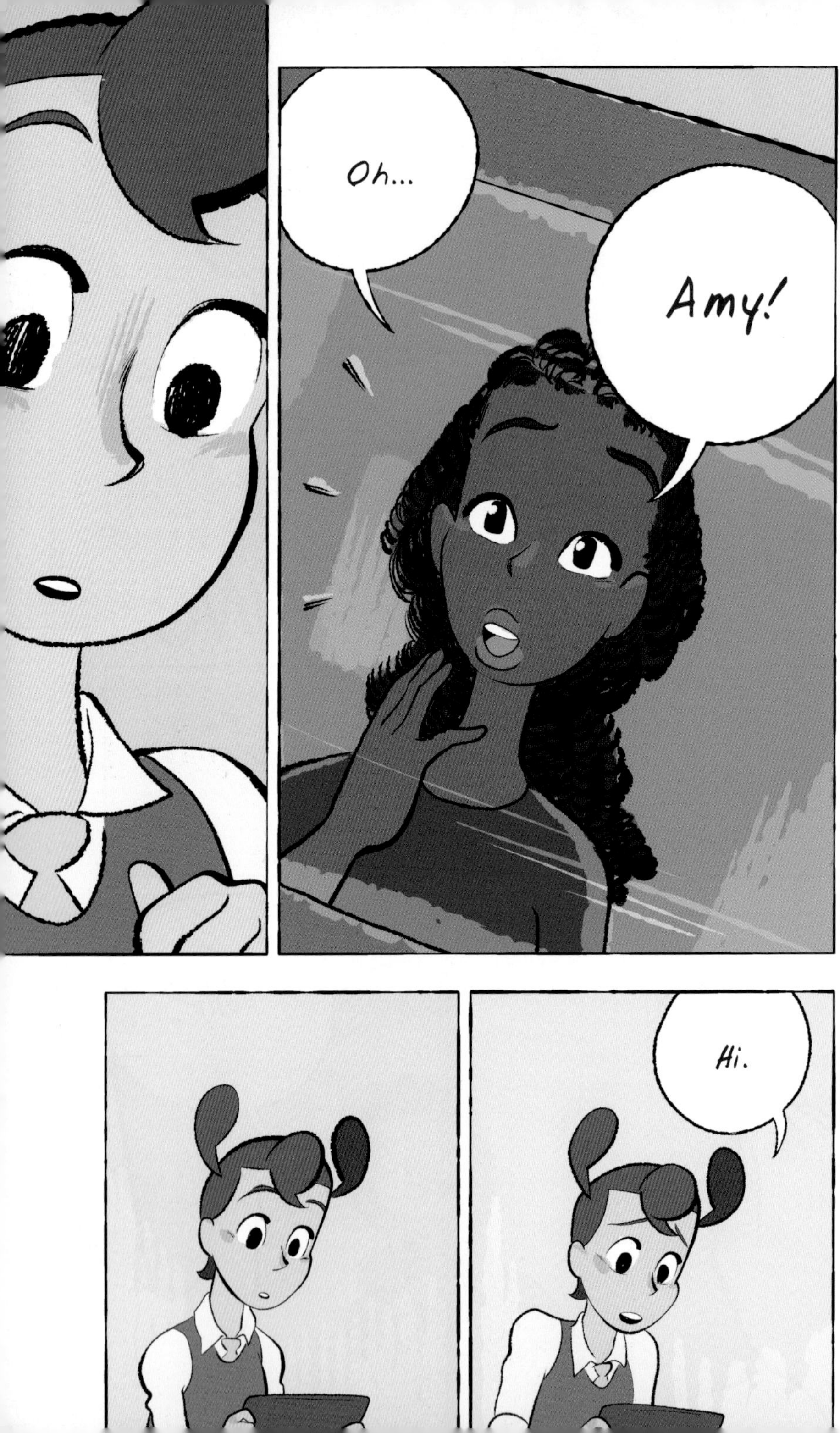
Oh...
Amy!
Hi.

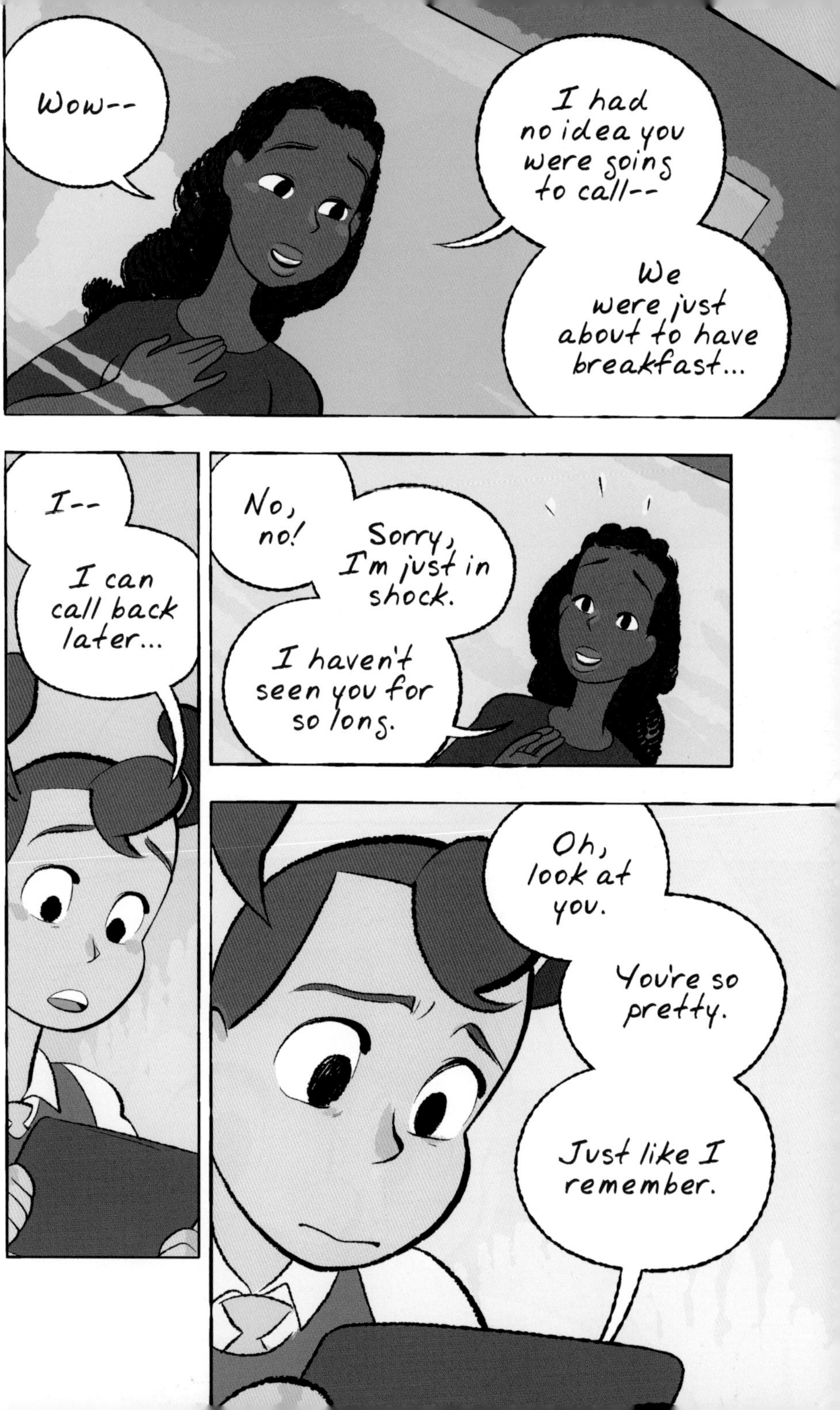
Wow--
I had no idea you were going to call--
We were just about to have breakfast...
I--
I can call back later...
No, no!
Sorry, I'm just in shock.
I haven't seen you for so long.
Oh, look at you.
You're so pretty.
Just like I remember.

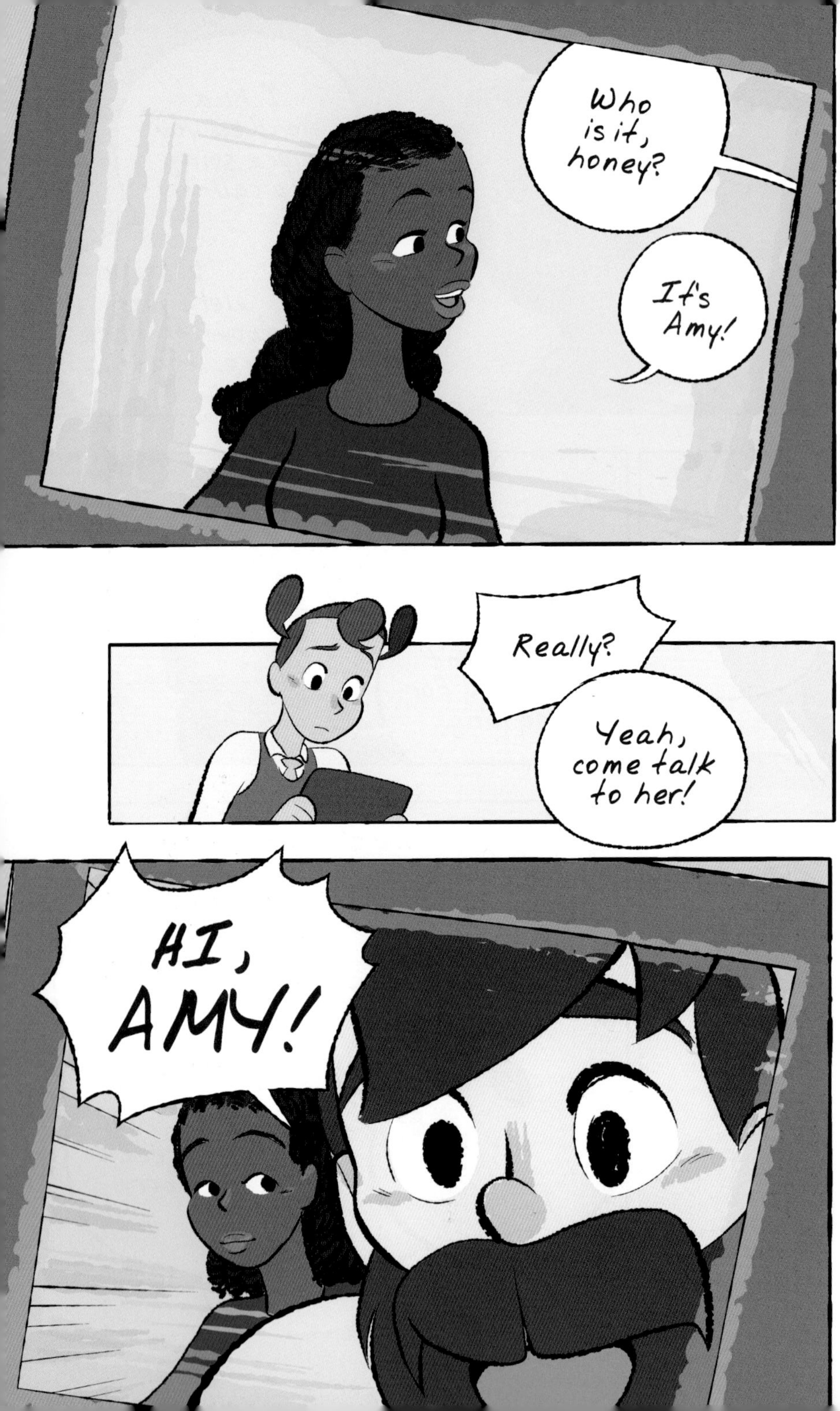

Who is it, honey?
It's Amy!
Really?
Yeah, come talk to her!
HI, AMY!

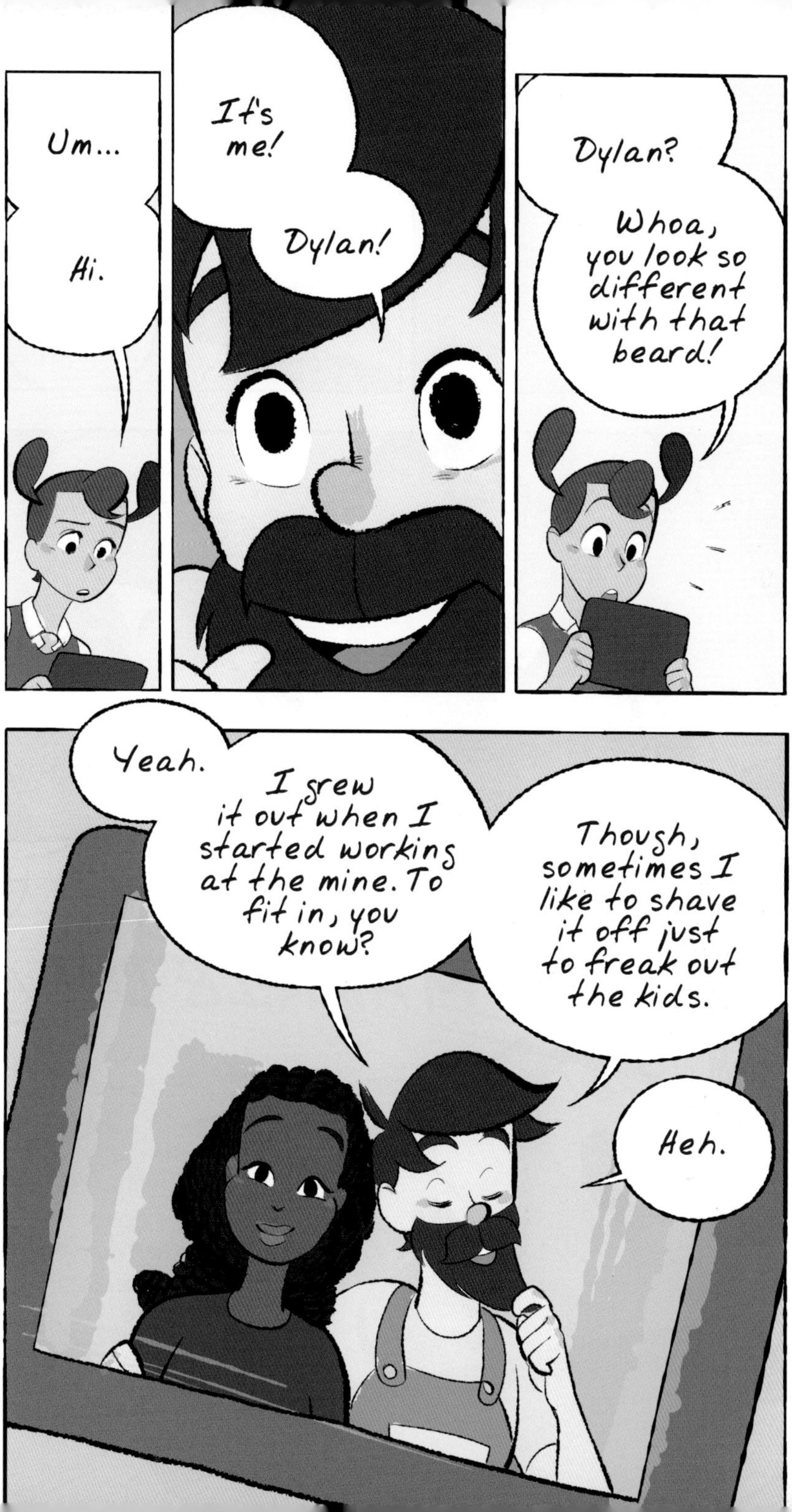
Um...
Hi.
It's me!
Dylan!
Dylan?
Whoa, you look so different with that beard!
Yeah.
I grew it out when I started working at the mine. To fit in, you know?
Though, sometimes I like to shave it off just to freak out the kids.
Heh.

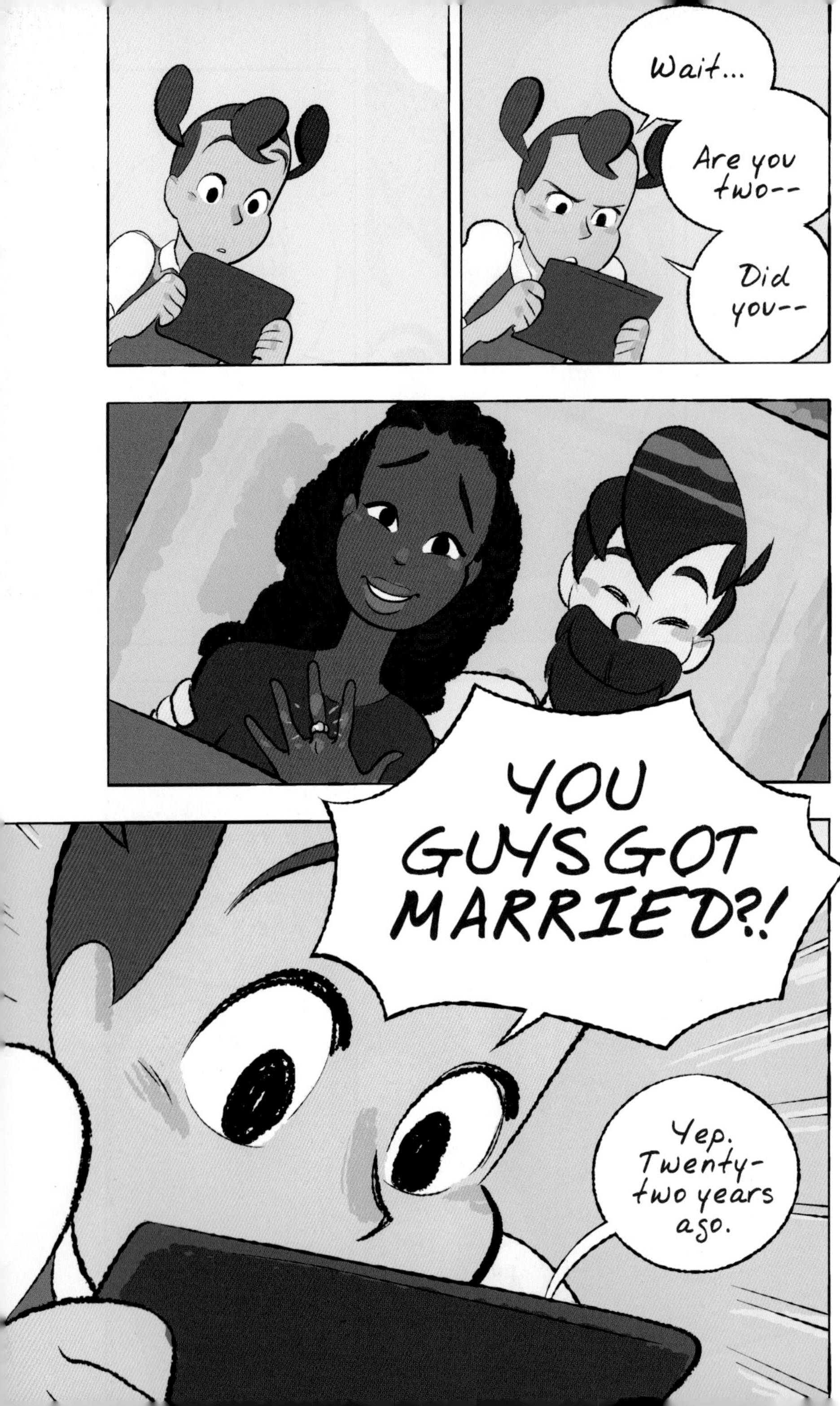
Wait...
Are you two--
Did you--
YOU GUYS GOT MARRIED?!
Yep. Twenty-two years ago.

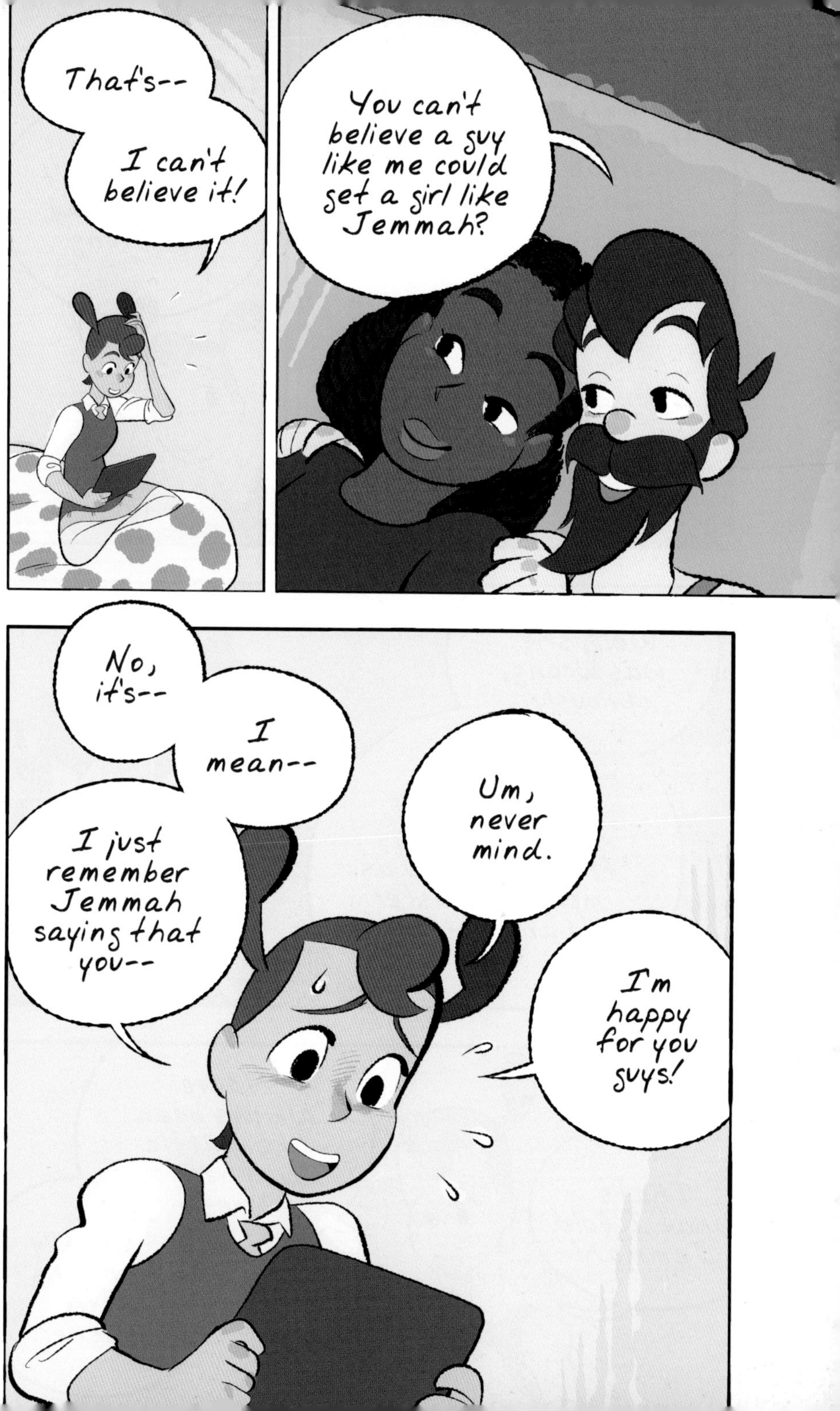
That's--
I can't believe it!
You can't believe a guy like me could get a girl like Jemmah?
No, it's--
I mean--
I just remember Jemmah saying that you--
Um, never mind.
I'm happy for you guys!

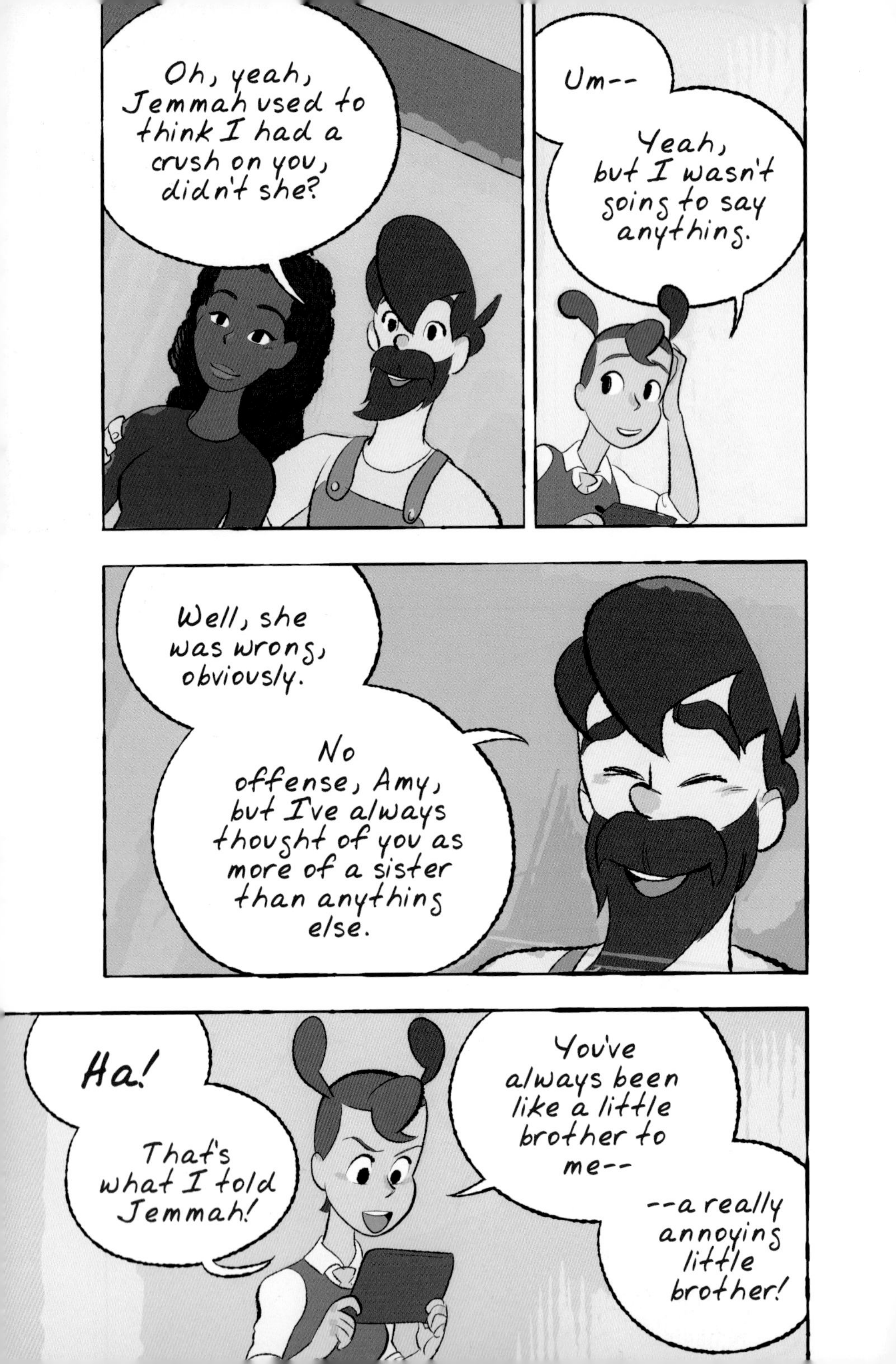

Oh, yeah, Jemmah used to think I had a crush on you, didn't she?
Um--
Yeah, but I wasn't going to say anything.
Well, she was wrong, obviously.
No offense, Amy, but I've always thought of you as more of a sister than anything else.
Ha!
That's what I told Jemmah!
You've always been like a little brother to me--
--a really annoying little brother!

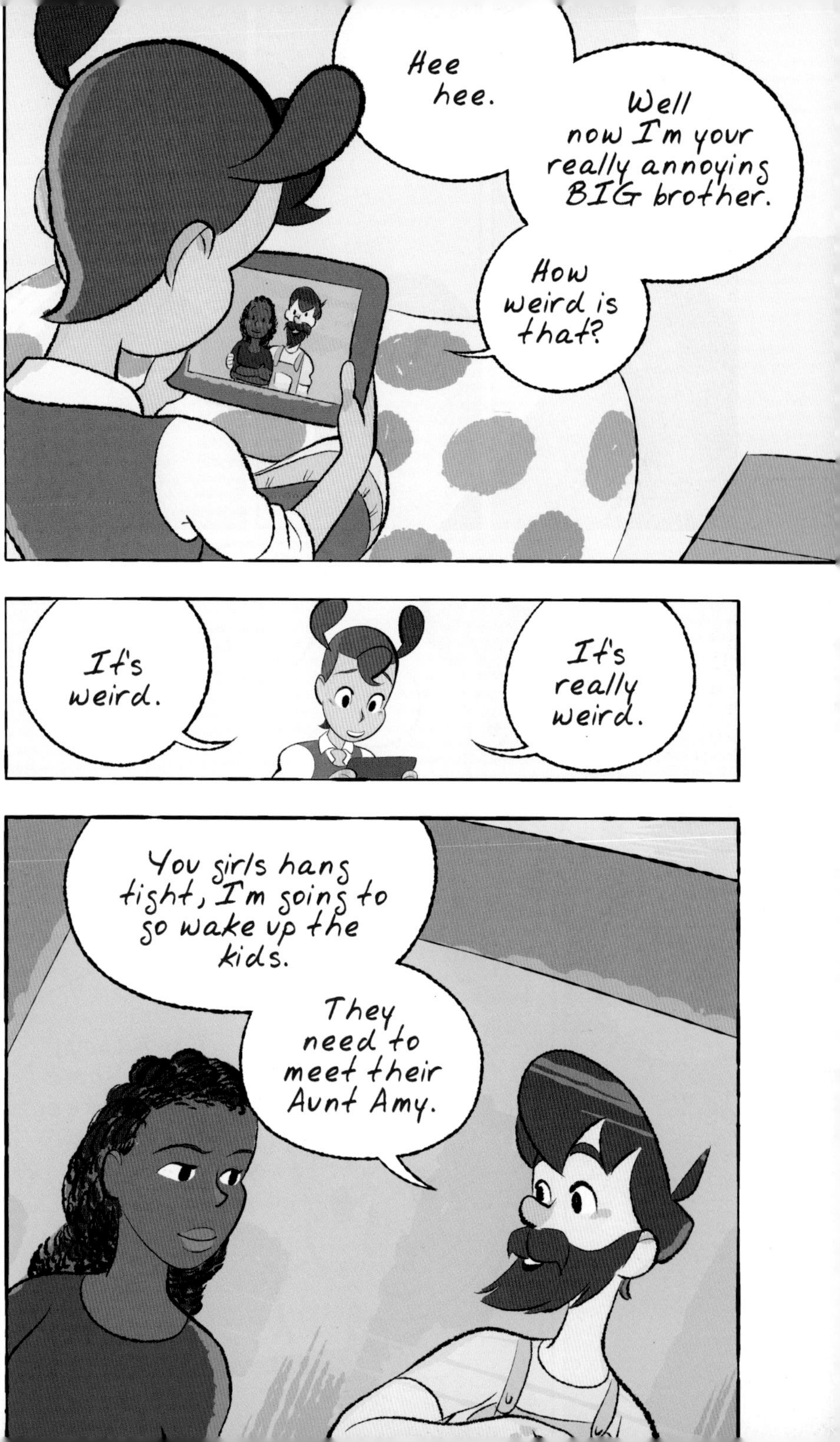
Hee hee.
Well now I'm your really annoying BIG brother.
How weird is that?
It's weird.
It's really weird.
You girls hang tight, I'm going to go wake up the kids.
They need to meet their Aunt Amy.

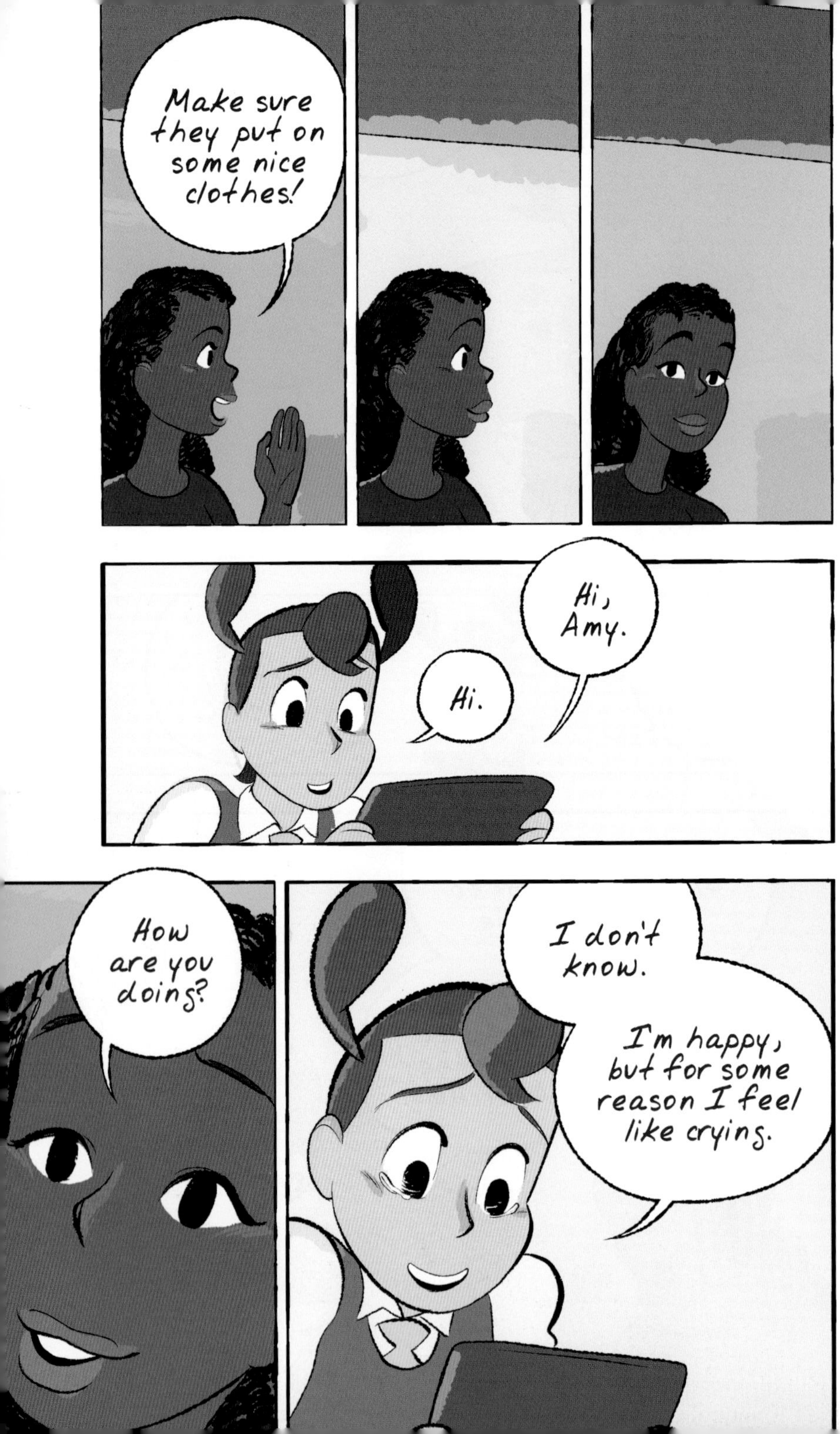
Make sure they put on some nice clothes!
Hi, Amy.
Hi.
How are you doing?
I don't know.
I'm happy, but for some reason I feel like crying.

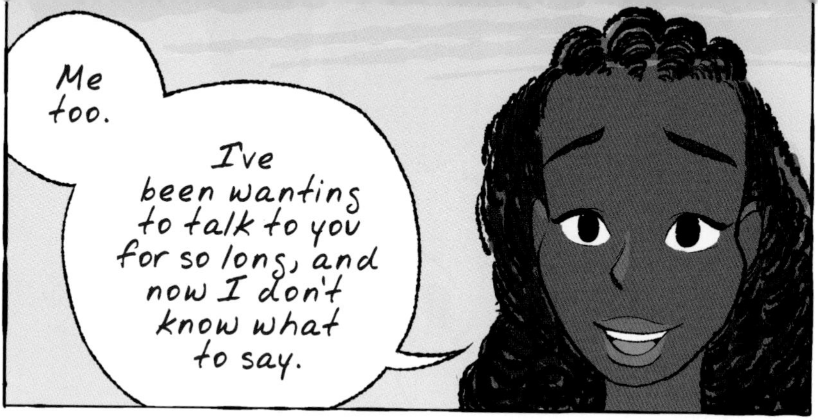
Me too.
I've been wanting to talk to you for so long, and now I don't know what to say.

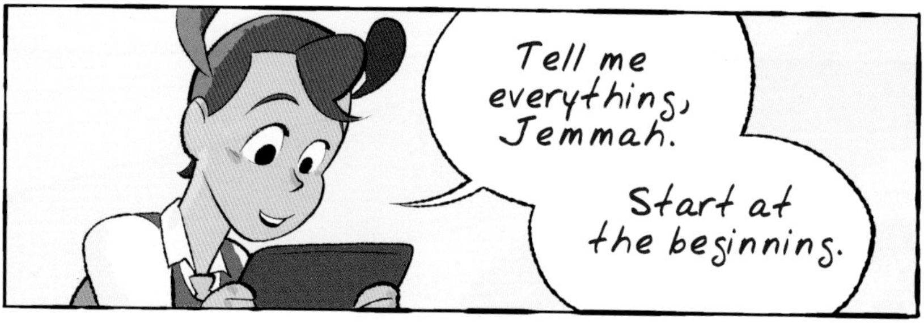
Tell me everything, Jemmah.
Start at the beginning.

And so she does.

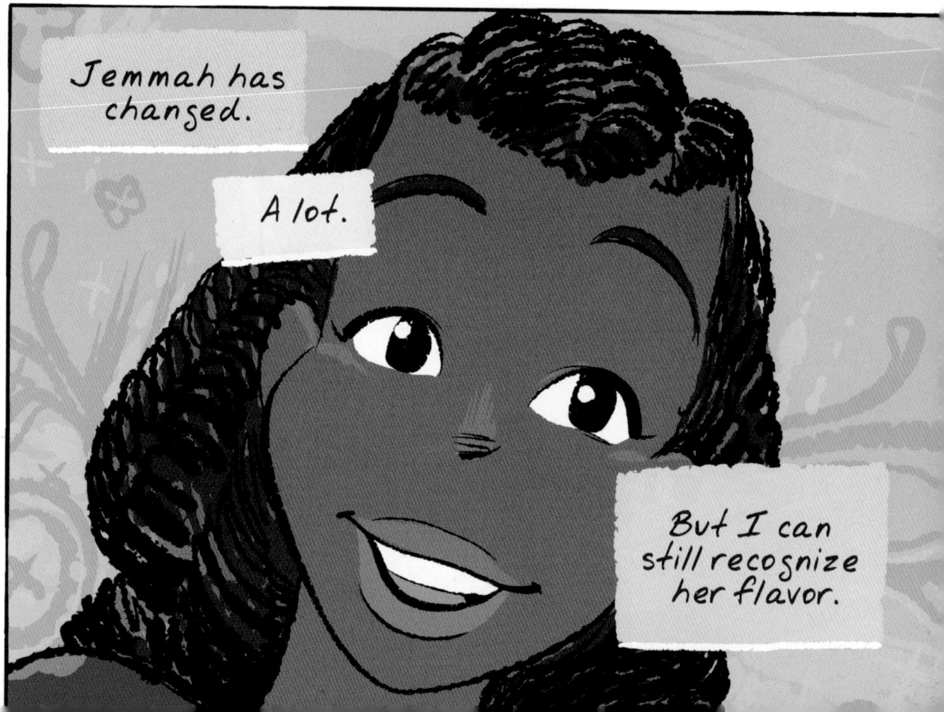
Jemmah has changed.
A lot.
But I can still recognize her flavor.

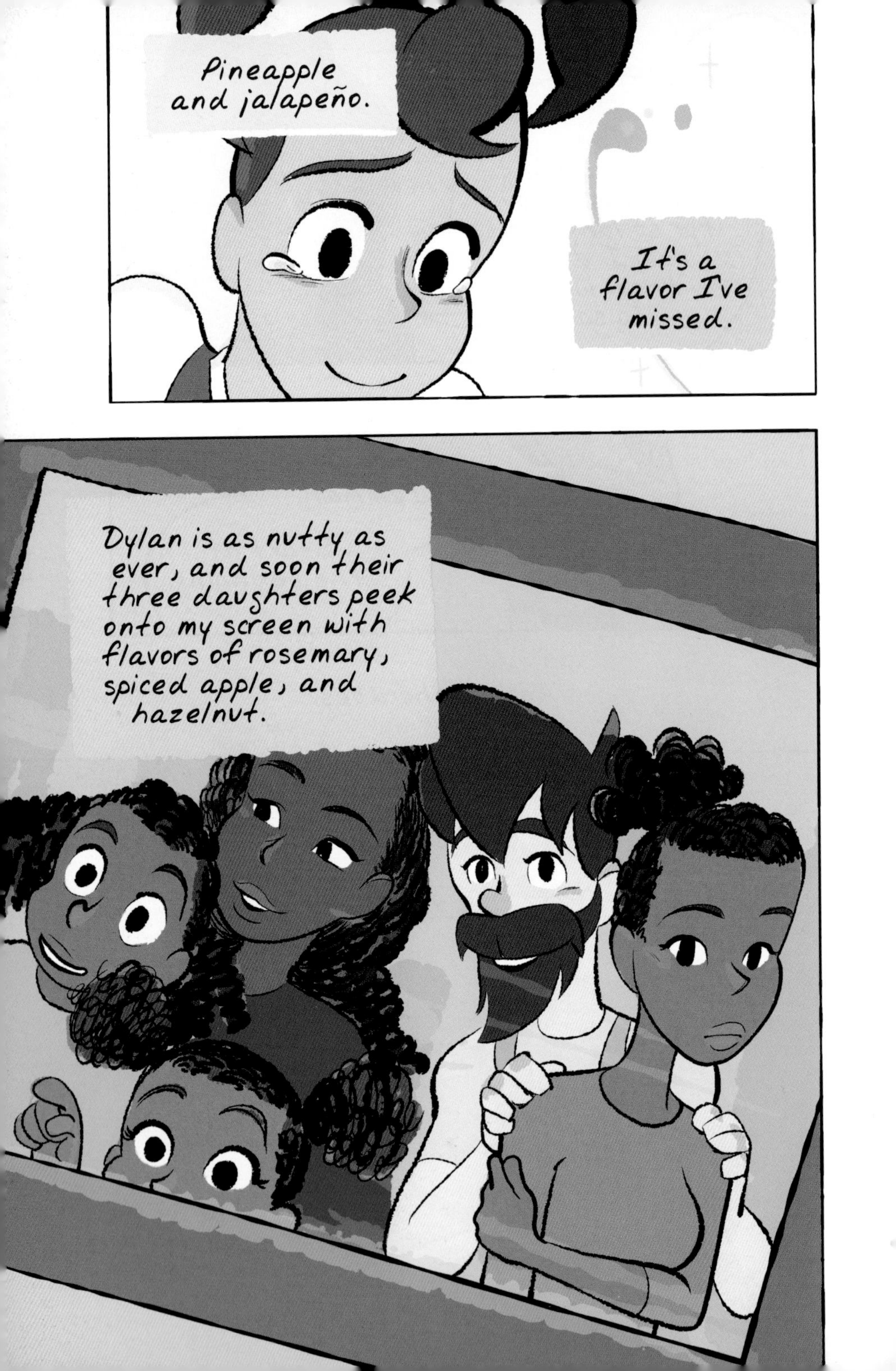
Pineapple and jalapeño.
It's a flavor I've missed.
Dylan is as nutty as ever, and soon their three daughters peek onto my screen with flavors of rosemary, spiced apple, and hazelnut.

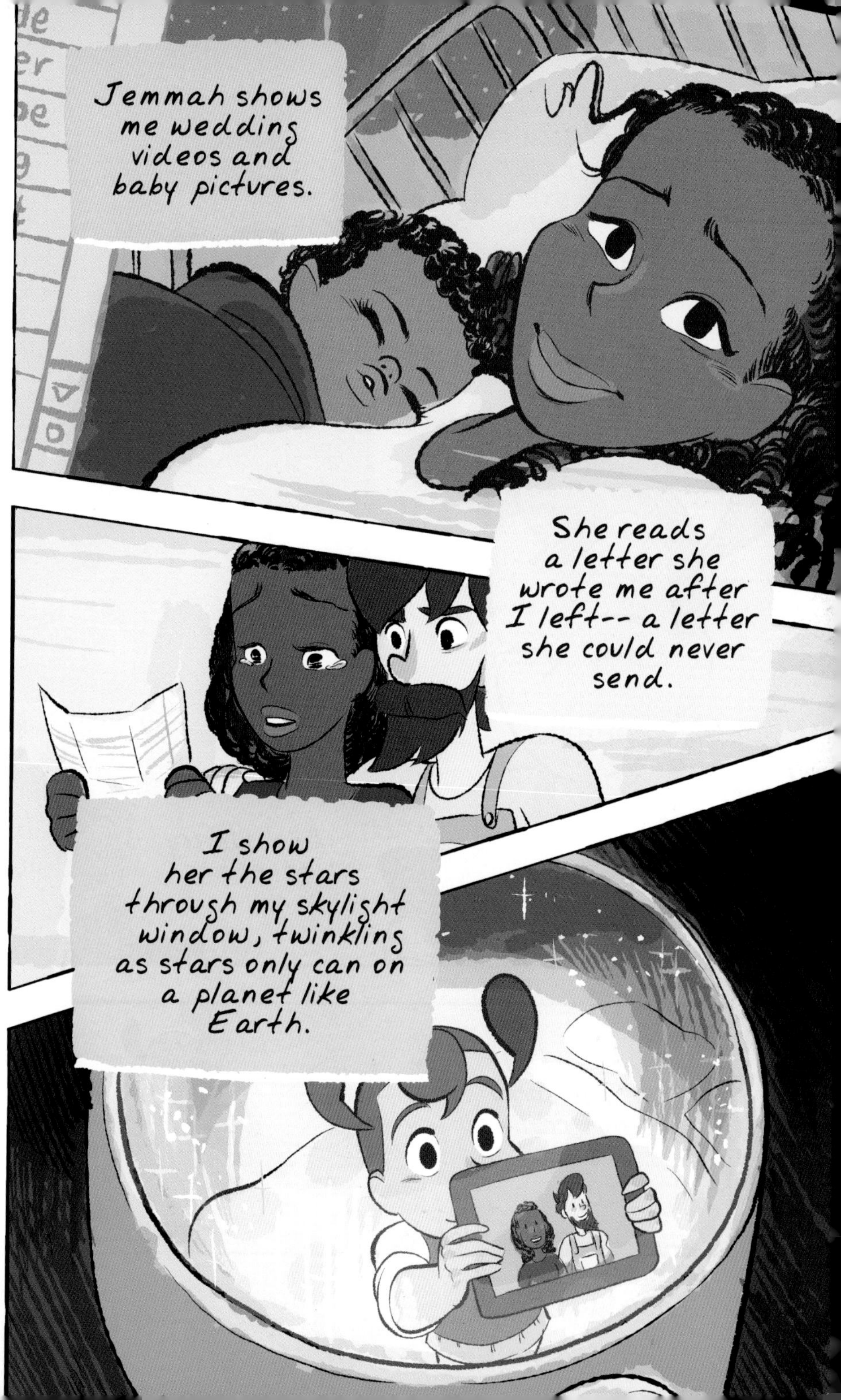
Jemmah shows me wedding videos and baby pictures.
She reads a letter she wrote me after I left-- a letter she could never send.
I show her the stars through my skylight window, twinkling as stars only can on a planet like Earth.

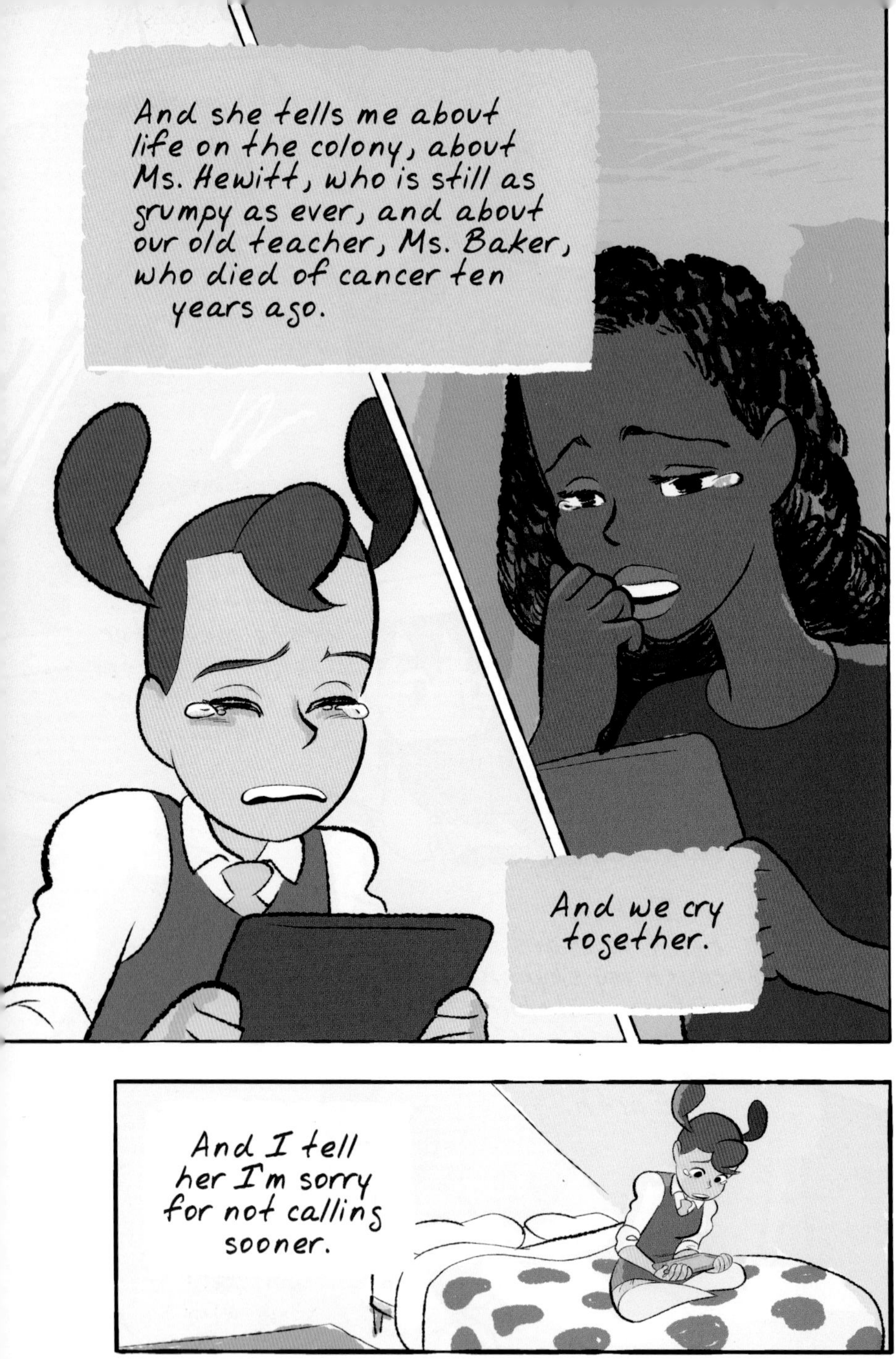
And she tells me about life on the colony, about Ms. Hewitt, who is still as grumpy as ever, and about our old teacher, Ms. Baker, who died of cancer ten years ago.
And we cry together.
And I tell her I'm sorry for not calling sooner.

And she just smiles and sticks out her tongue at me like always.

It's our secret sign...

...a sign we made up in the fourth grade...

...a sign that means...

...best friends forever.

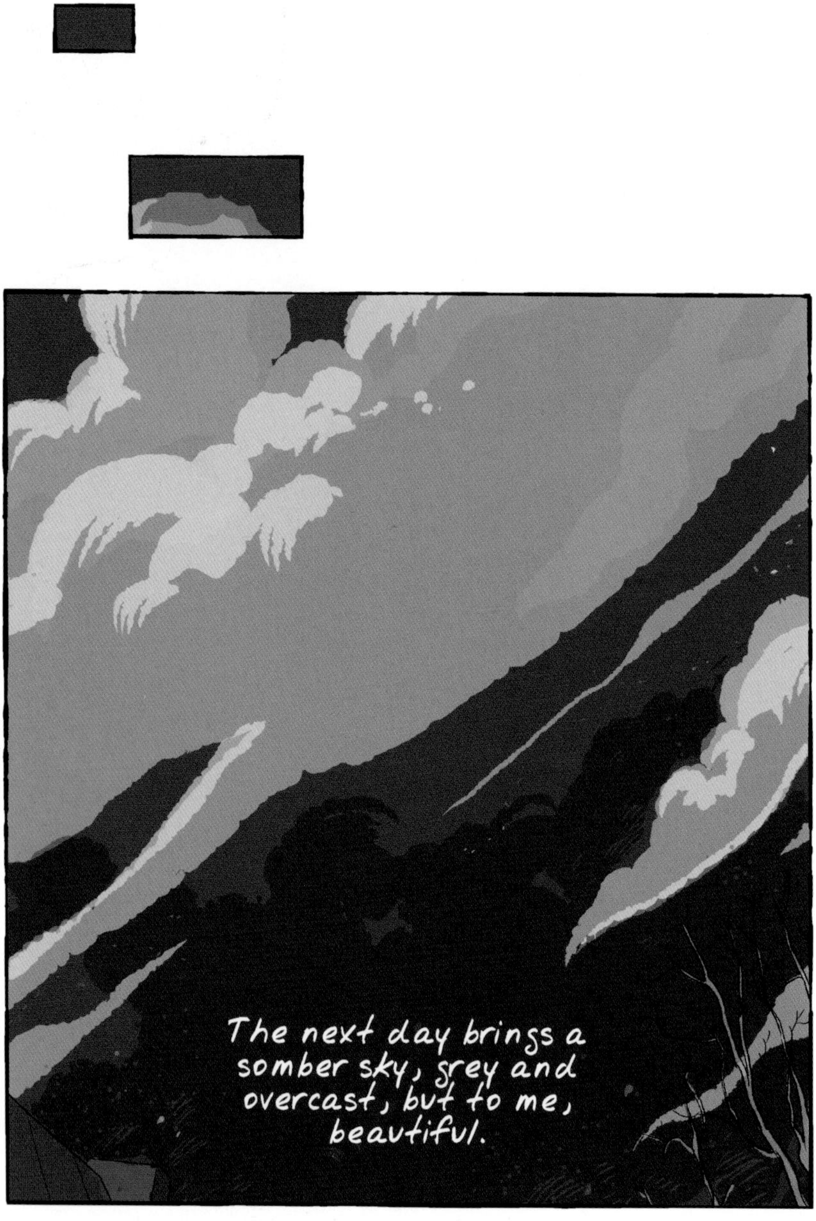
The next day brings a somber sky, grey and overcast, but to me, beautiful.

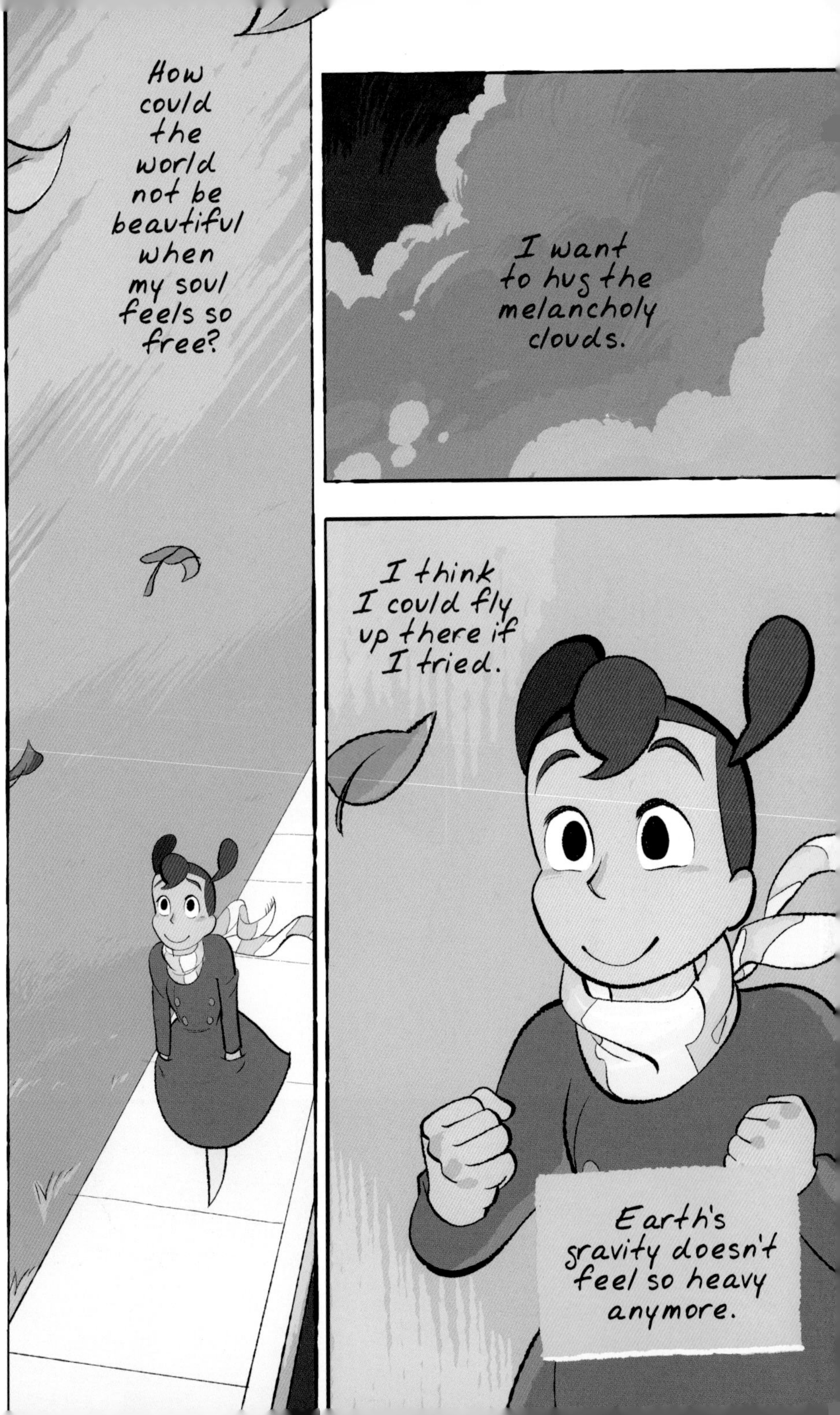
How could the world not be beautiful when my soul feels so free?
I want to hug the melancholy clouds.
I think I could fly up there if I tried.
Earth's gravity doesn't feel so heavy anymore.

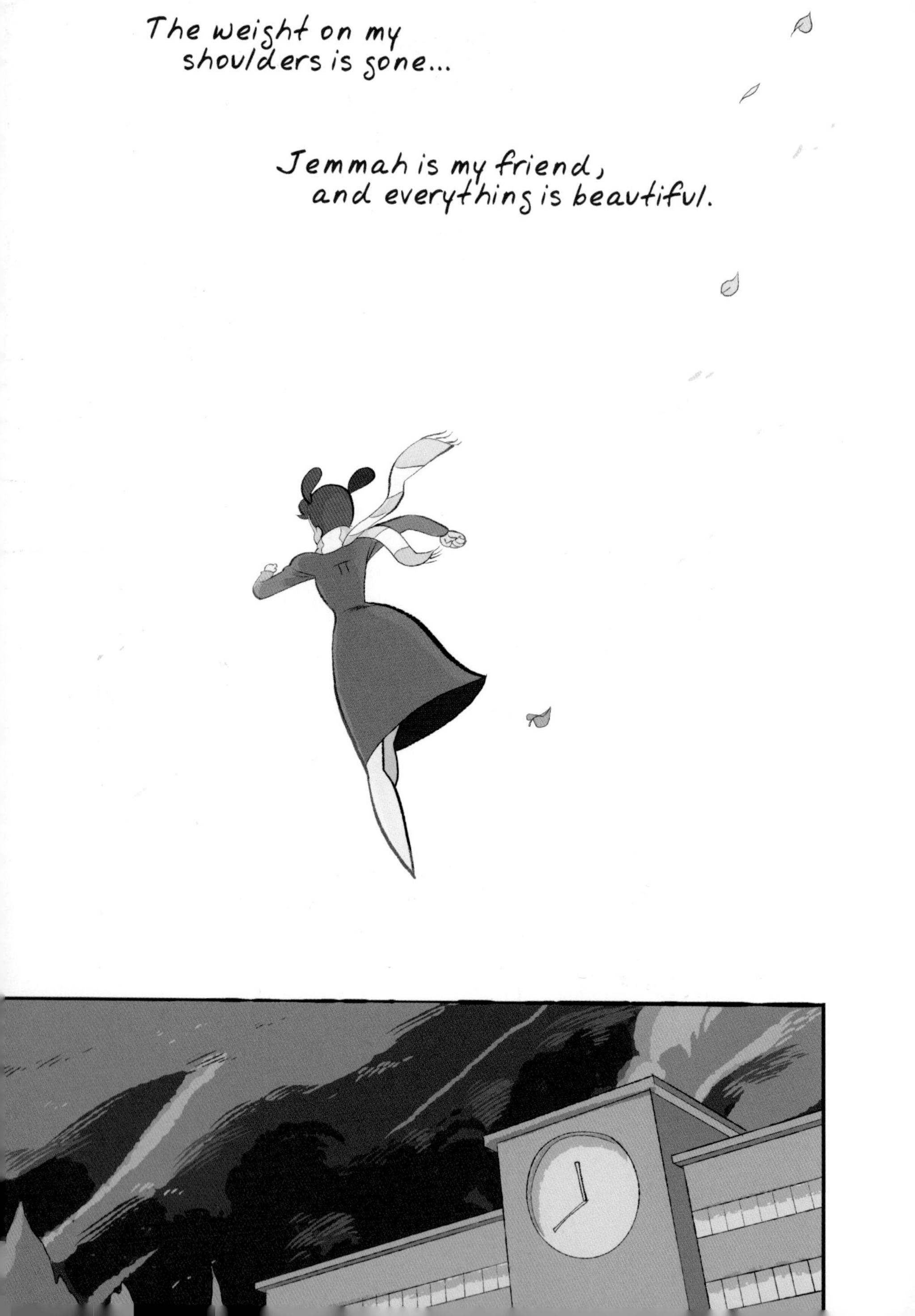
The weight on my shoulders is gone...
Jemmah is my friend, and everything is beautiful.

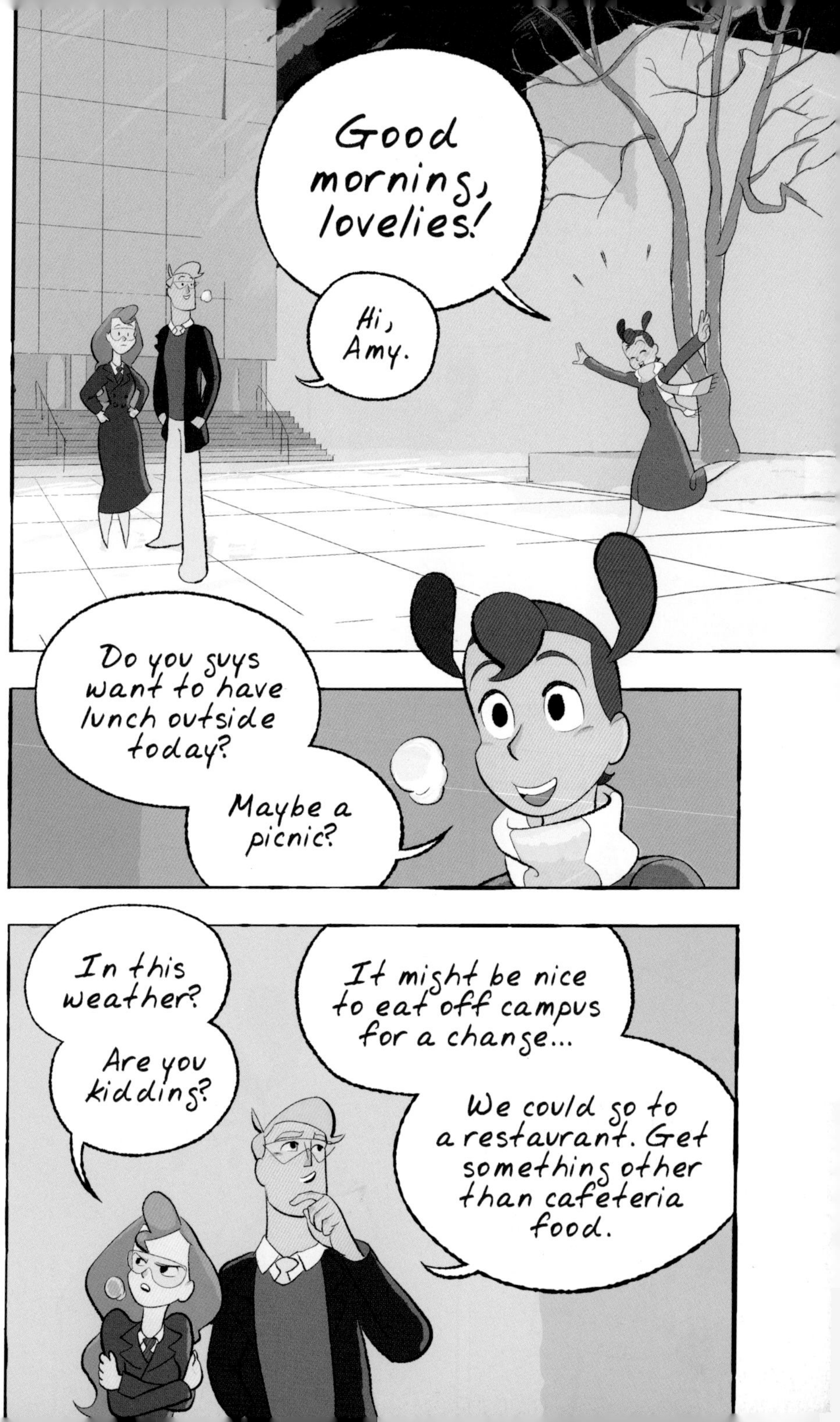
Good morning, lovelies!
Hi, Amy.
Do you guys want to have lunch outside today?
Maybe a picnic?
In this weather?
Are you kidding?
It might be nice to eat off campus for a change...
We could go to a restaurant. Get something other than cafeteria food.

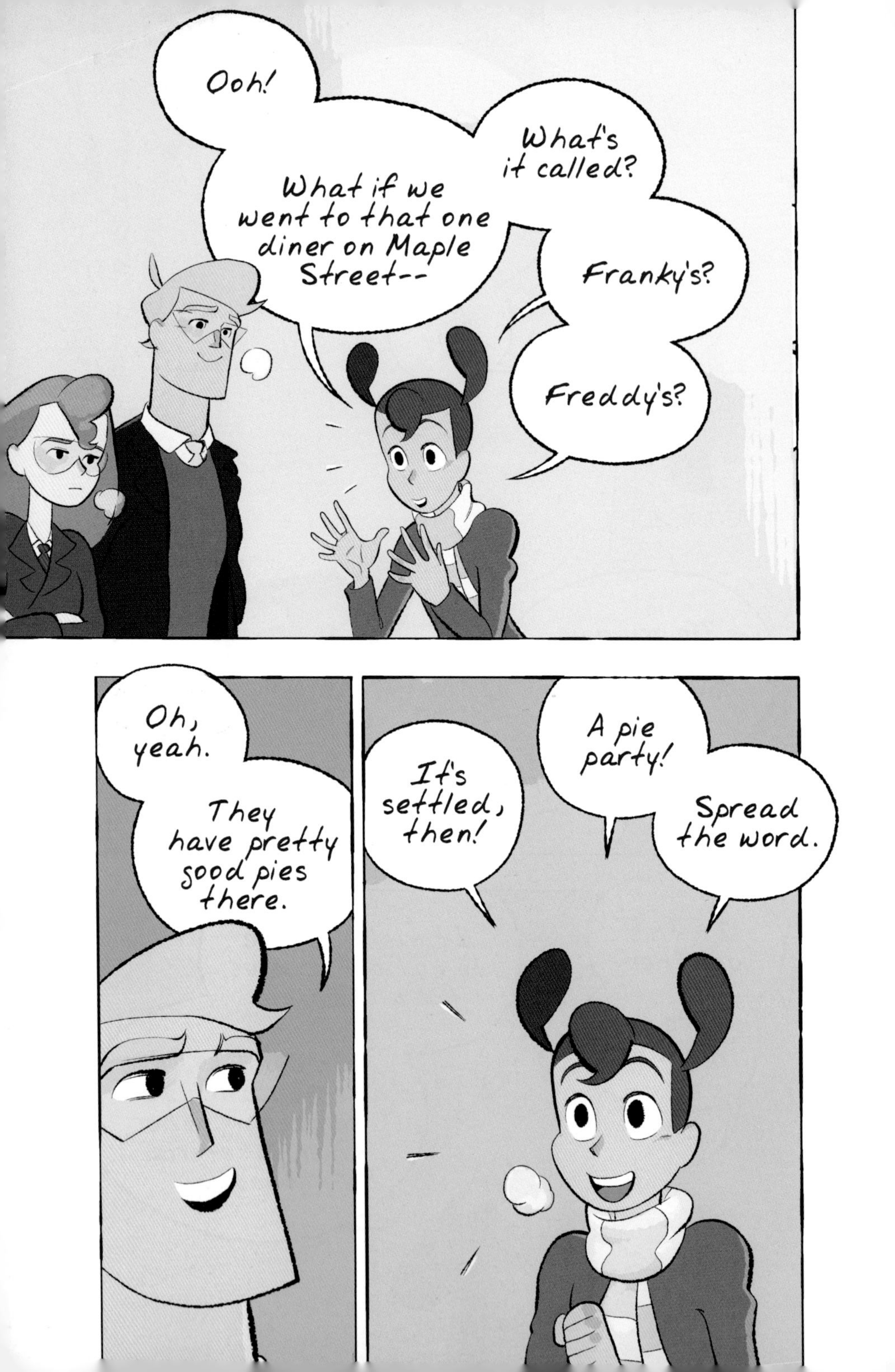
Ooh!
What if we went to that one diner on Maple Street--
What's it called?
Franky's?
Freddy's?
Oh, yeah.
They have pretty good pies there.
It's settled, then!
A pie party!
Spread the word.

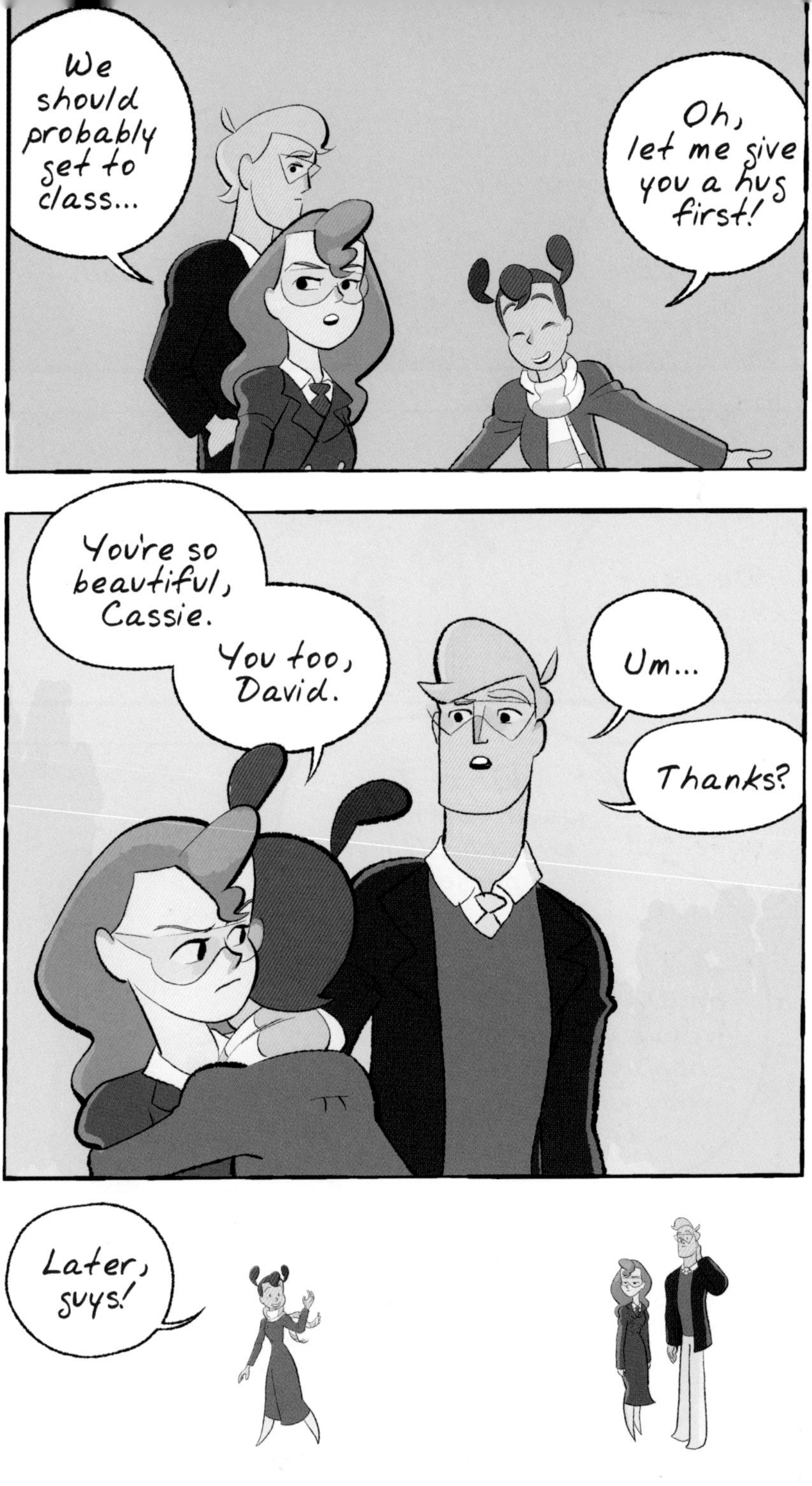

We should probably get to class...
Oh, let me give you a hug first!
You're so beautiful, Cassie.
You too, David.
Um...
Thanks?
Later, guys!

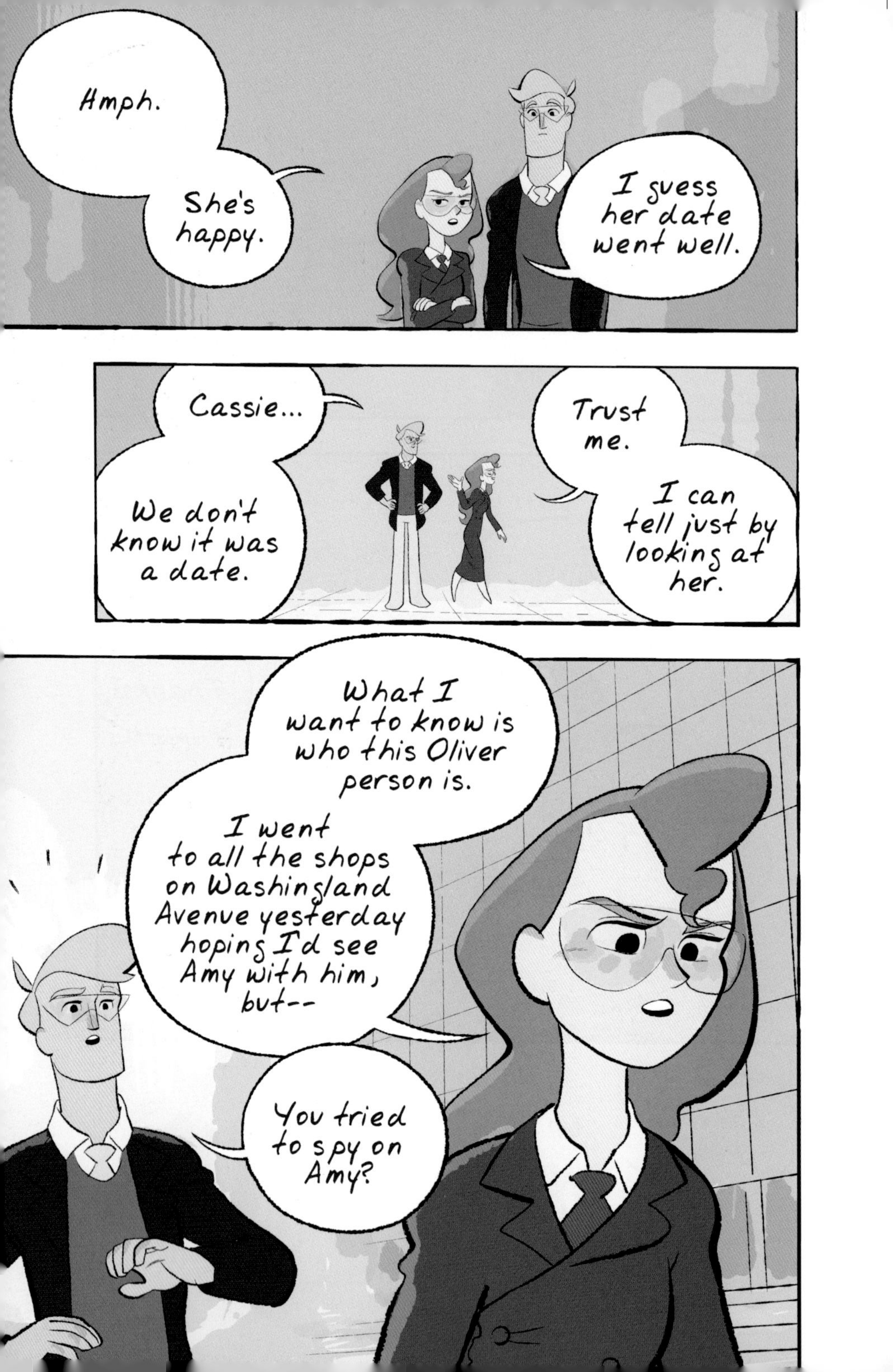
Hmph.
She's happy.
I guess her date went well.
Cassie...
We don't know it was a date.
Trust me.
I can tell just by looking at her.
What I want to know is who this Oliver person is.
I went to all the shops on Washingland Avenue yesterday hoping I'd see Amy with him, but--
You tried to spy on Amy?

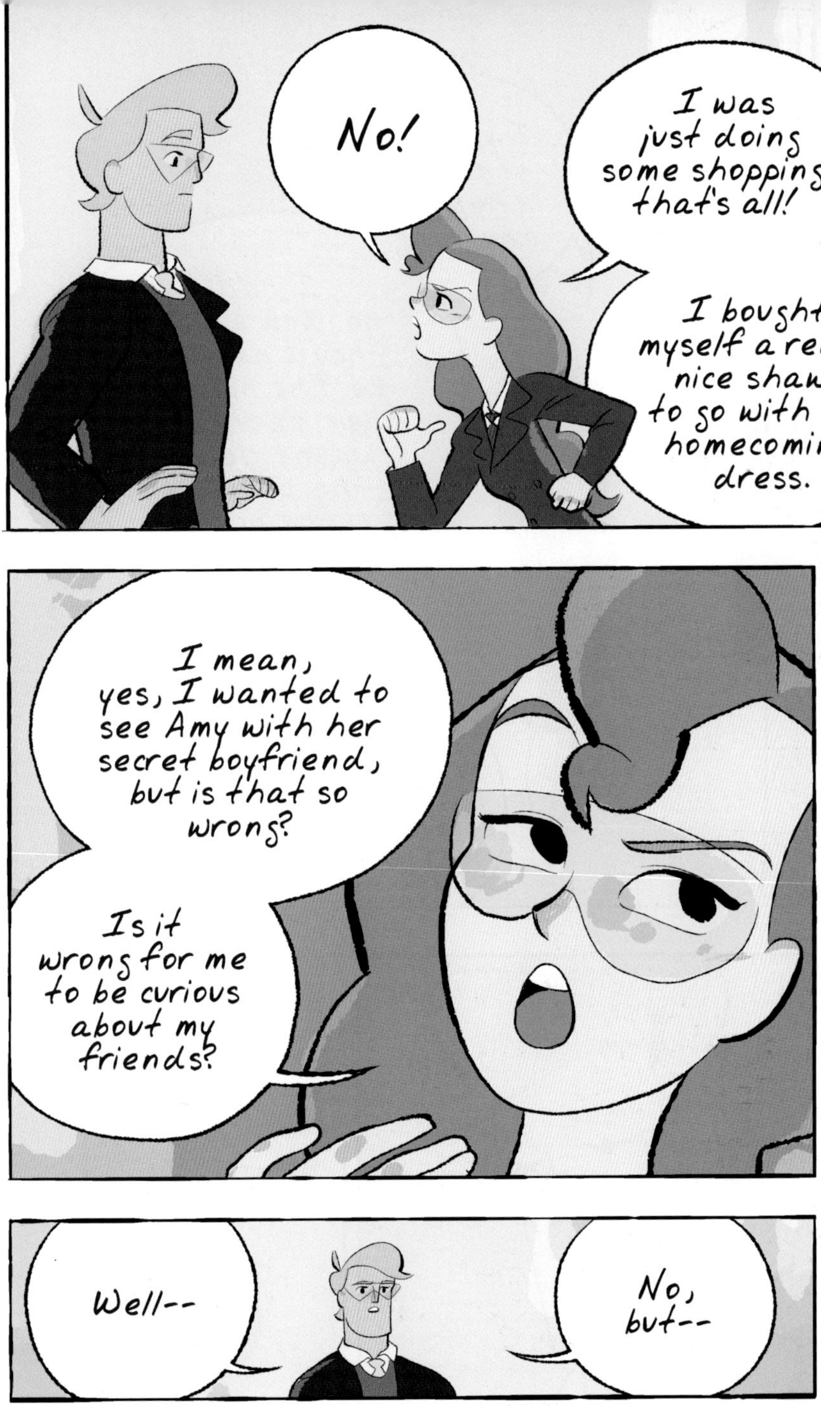
No!
I was just doing some shopping, that's all!
I bought myself a really nice shawl to go with my homecoming dress.
I mean, yes, I wanted to see Amy with her secret boyfriend, but is that so wrong?
Is it wrong for me to be curious about my friends?
Well--
No, but--

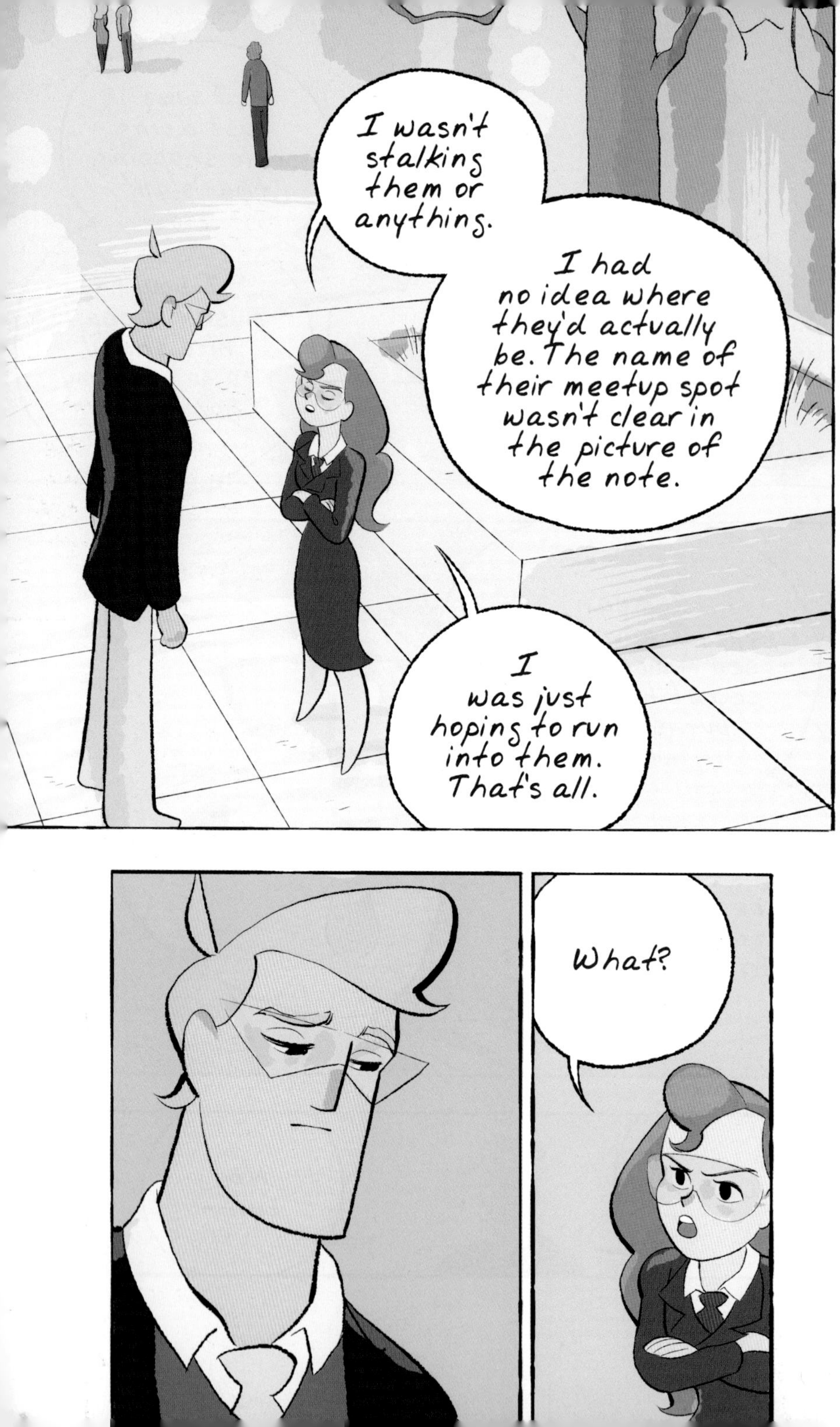
I wasn't stalking them or anything.
I had no idea where they'd actually be. The name of their meetup spot wasn't clear in the picture of the note.
I was just hoping to run into them. That's all.
What?

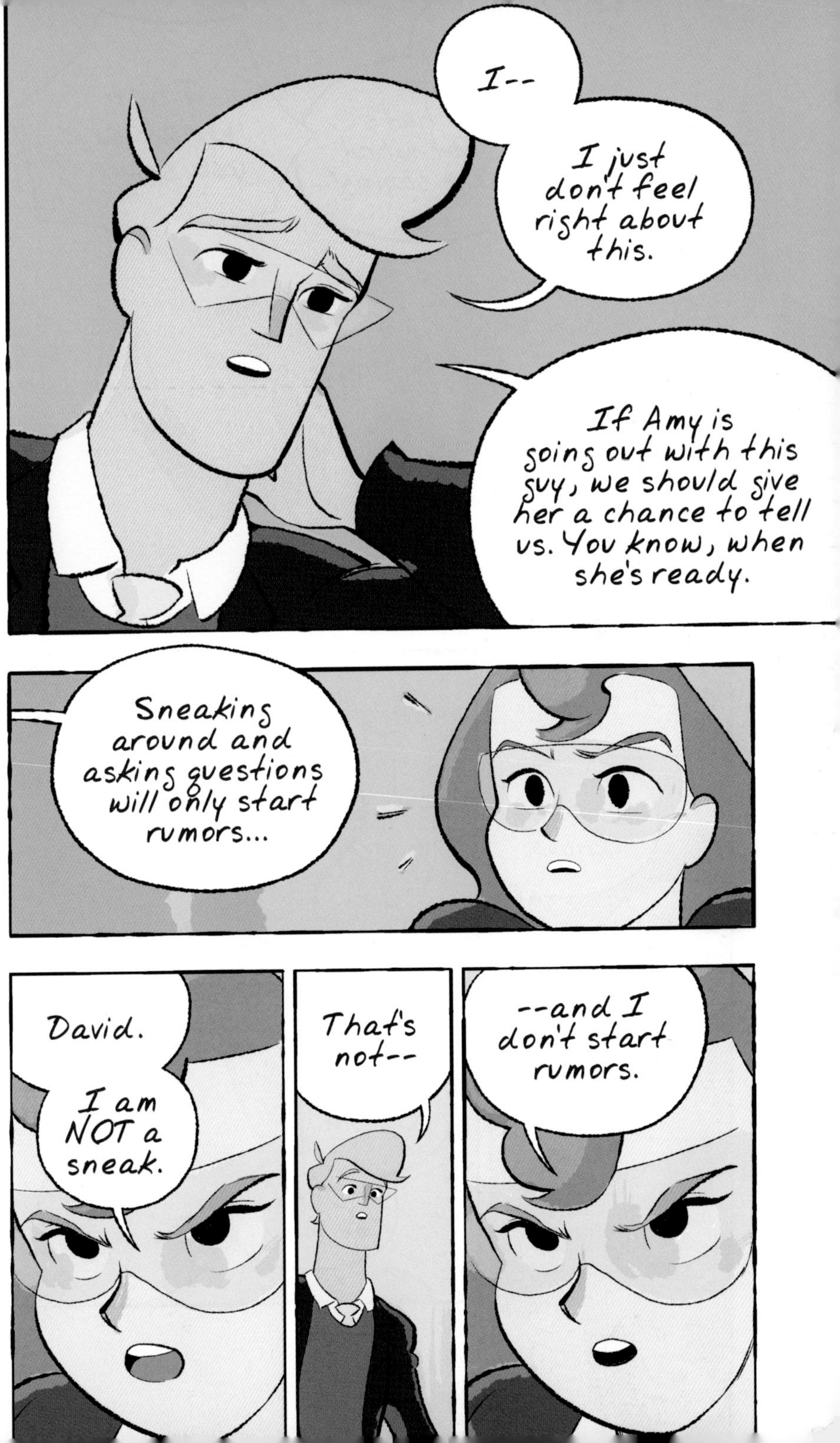
I--
I just don't feel right about this.
If Amy is going out with this guy, we should give her a chance to tell us. You know, when she's ready.
Sneaking around and asking questions will only start rumors...
David.
I am NOT a sneak.
That's not--
--and I don't start rumors.

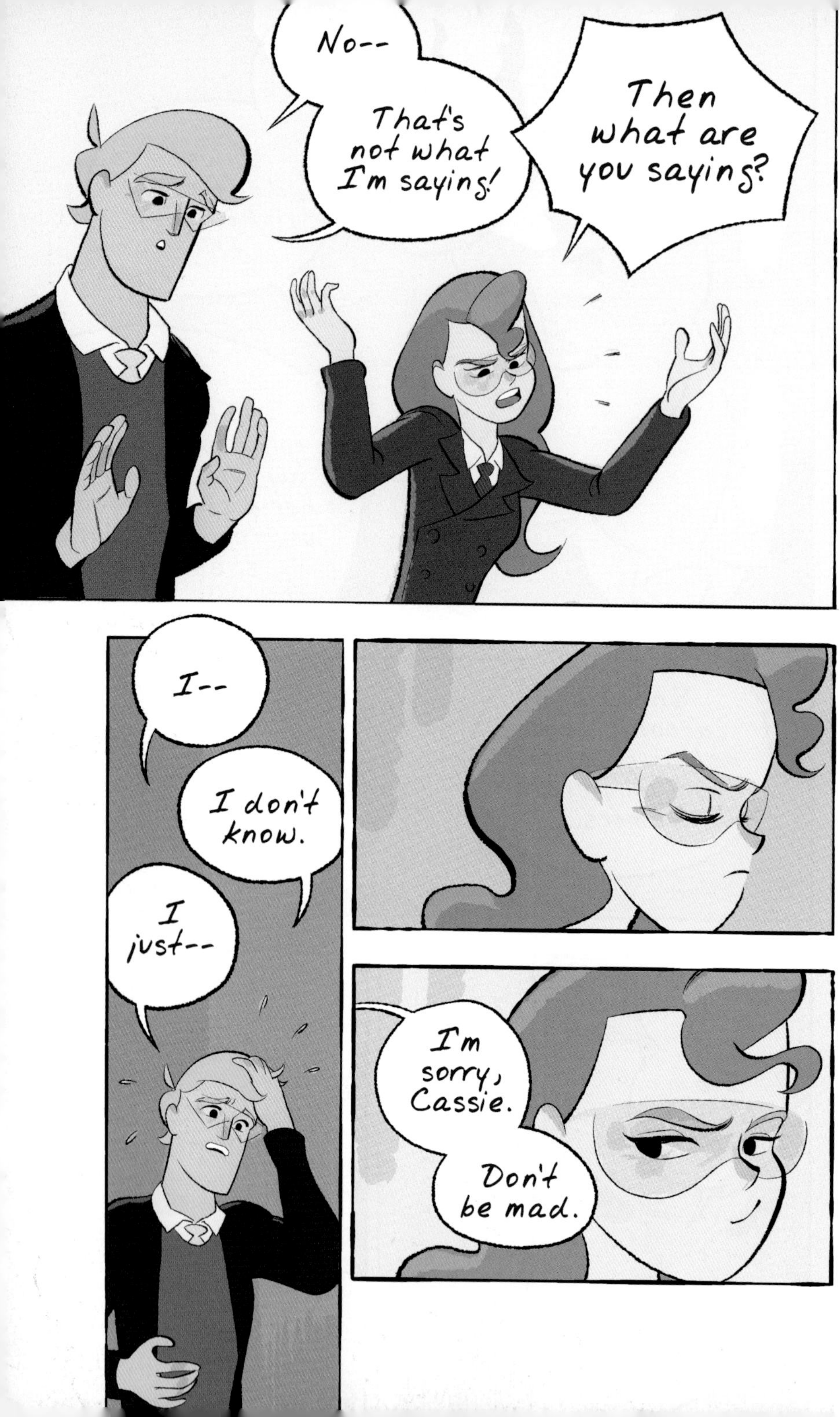
No--
That's not what I'm saying!
Then what are you saying?
I--
I don't know.
I just--
I'm sorry, Cassie.
Don't be mad.

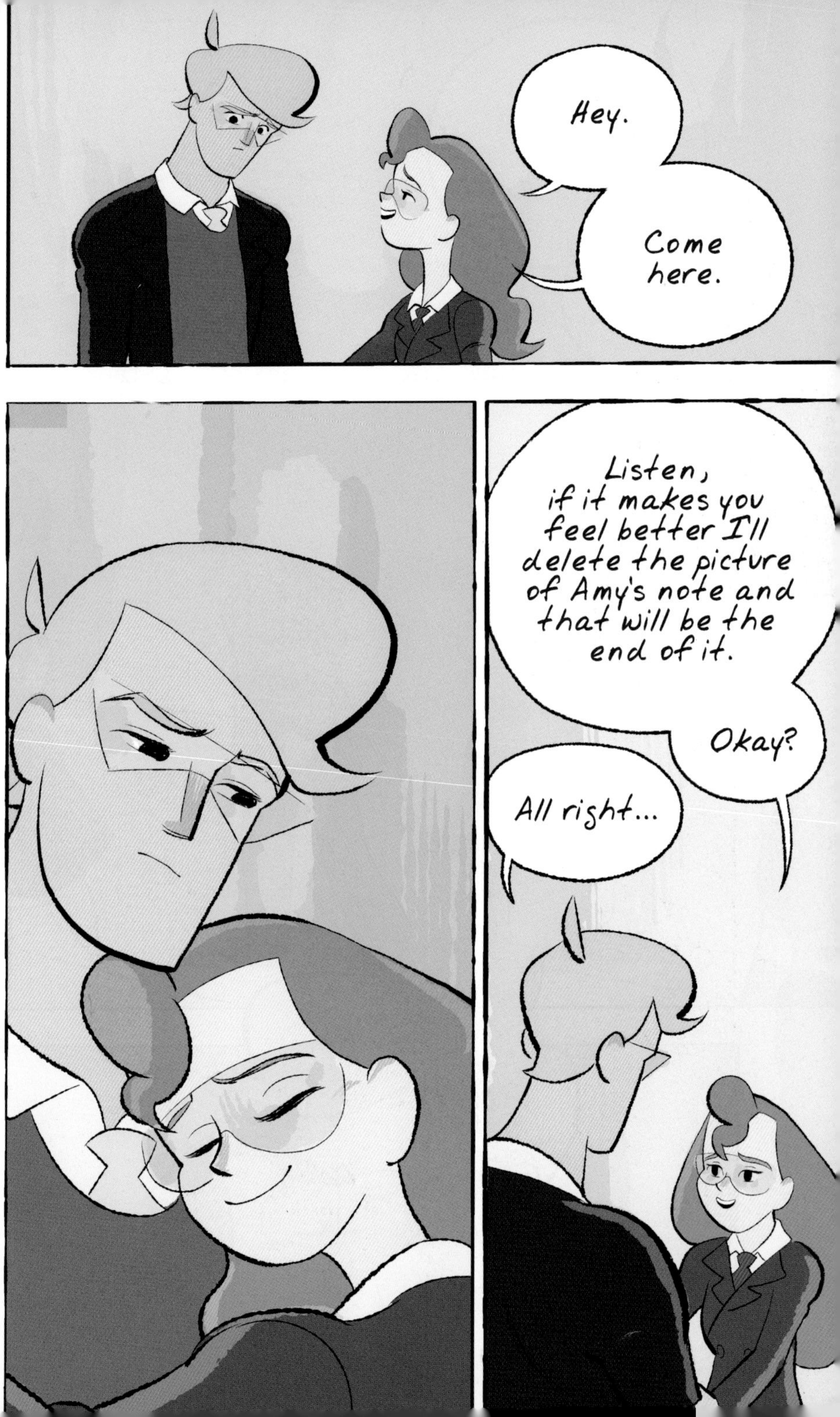
Hey.
Come here.
Listen, if it makes you feel better I'll delete the picture of Amy's note and that will be the end of it.
Okay?
All right...

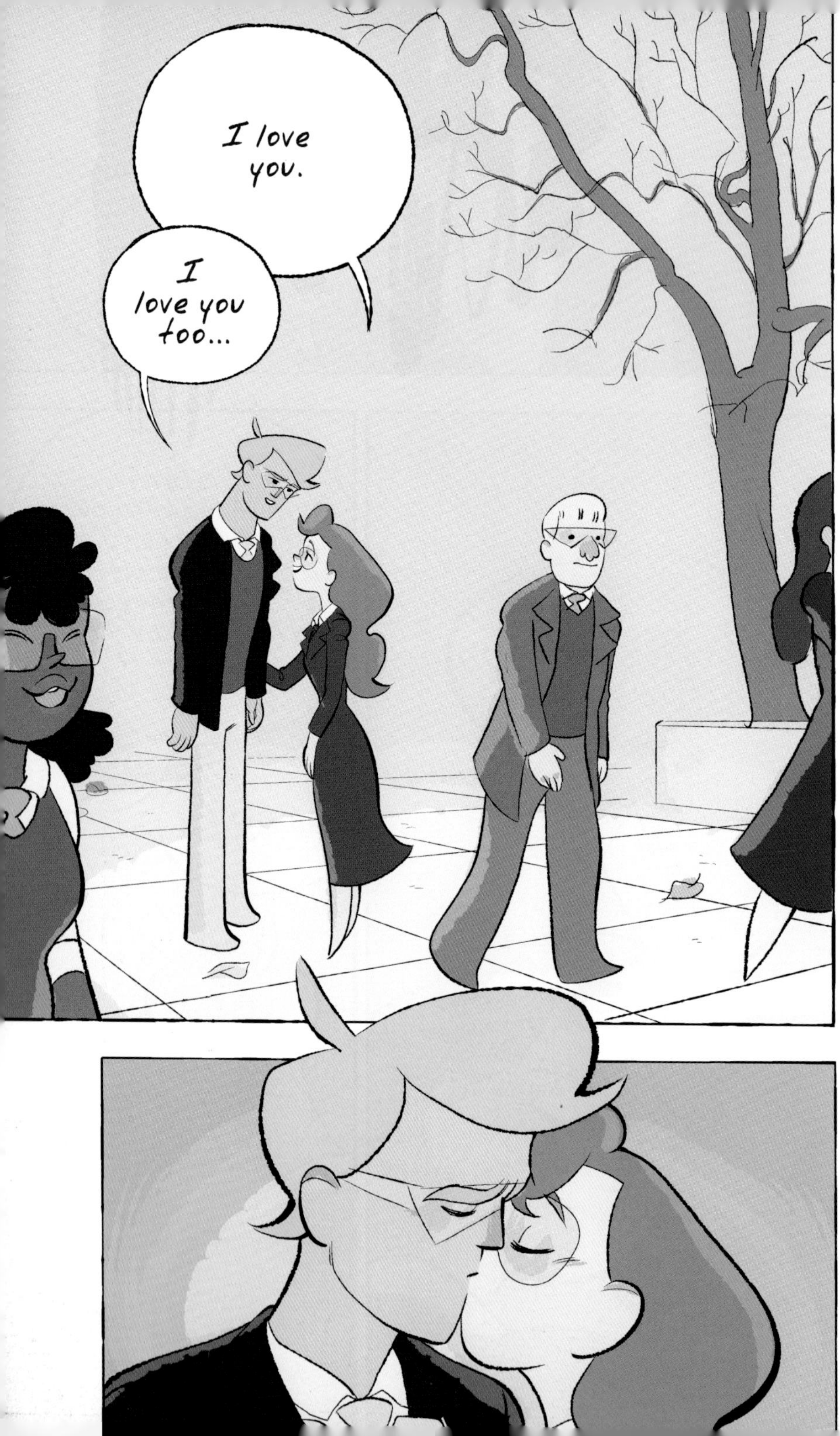

I love you.
I love you too...

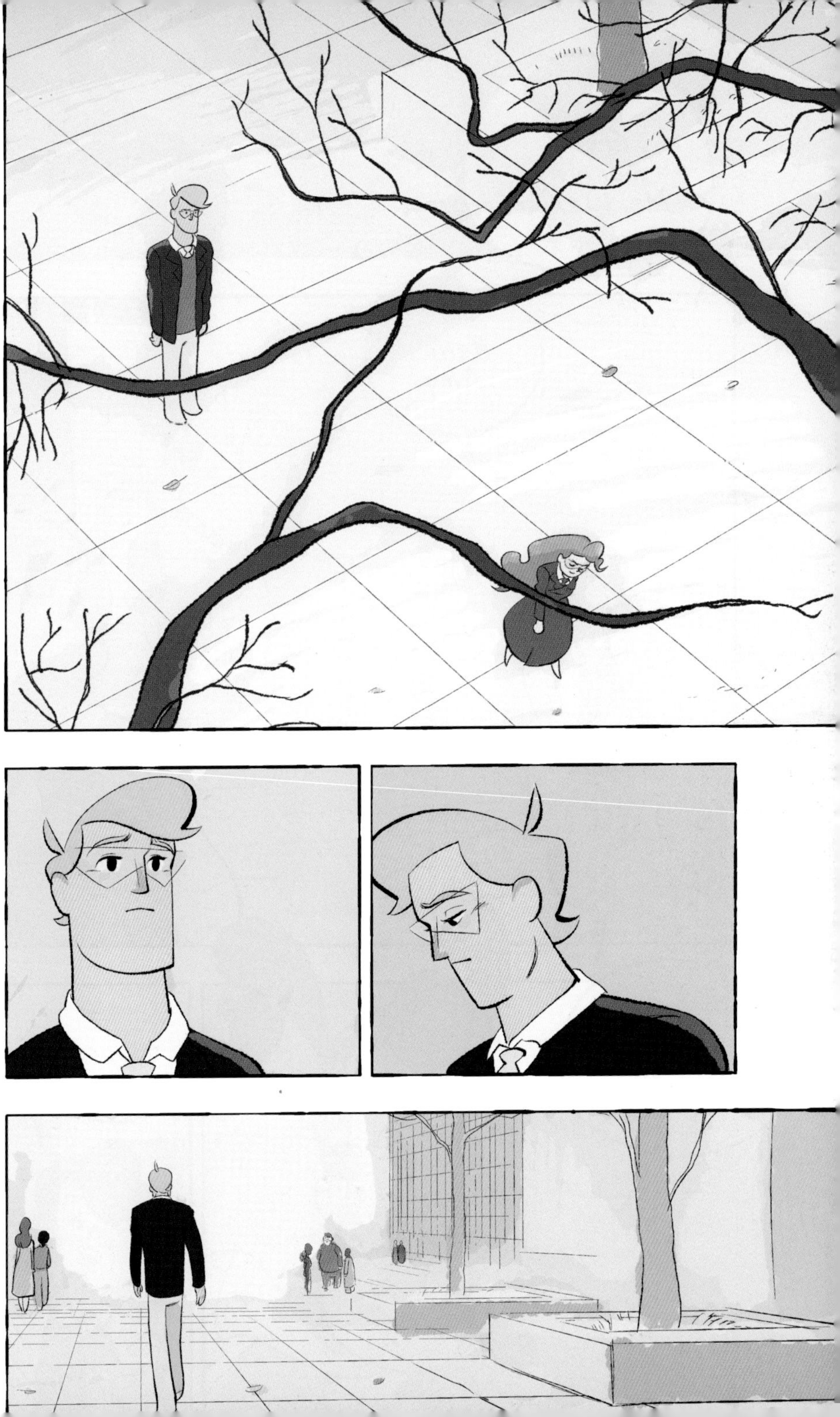

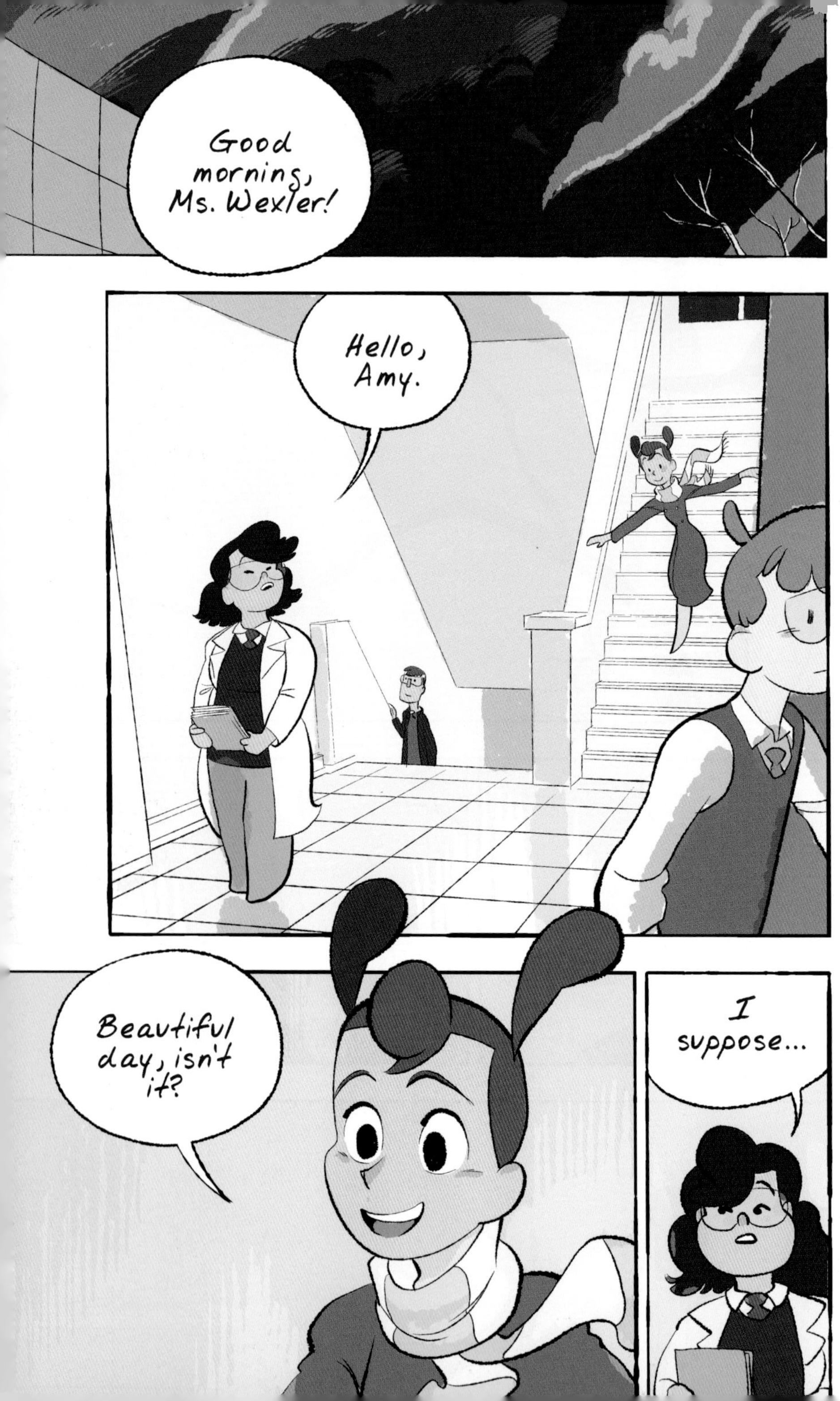
Good morning, Ms. Wexler!
Hello, Amy.
Beautiful day, isn't it?
I suppose...

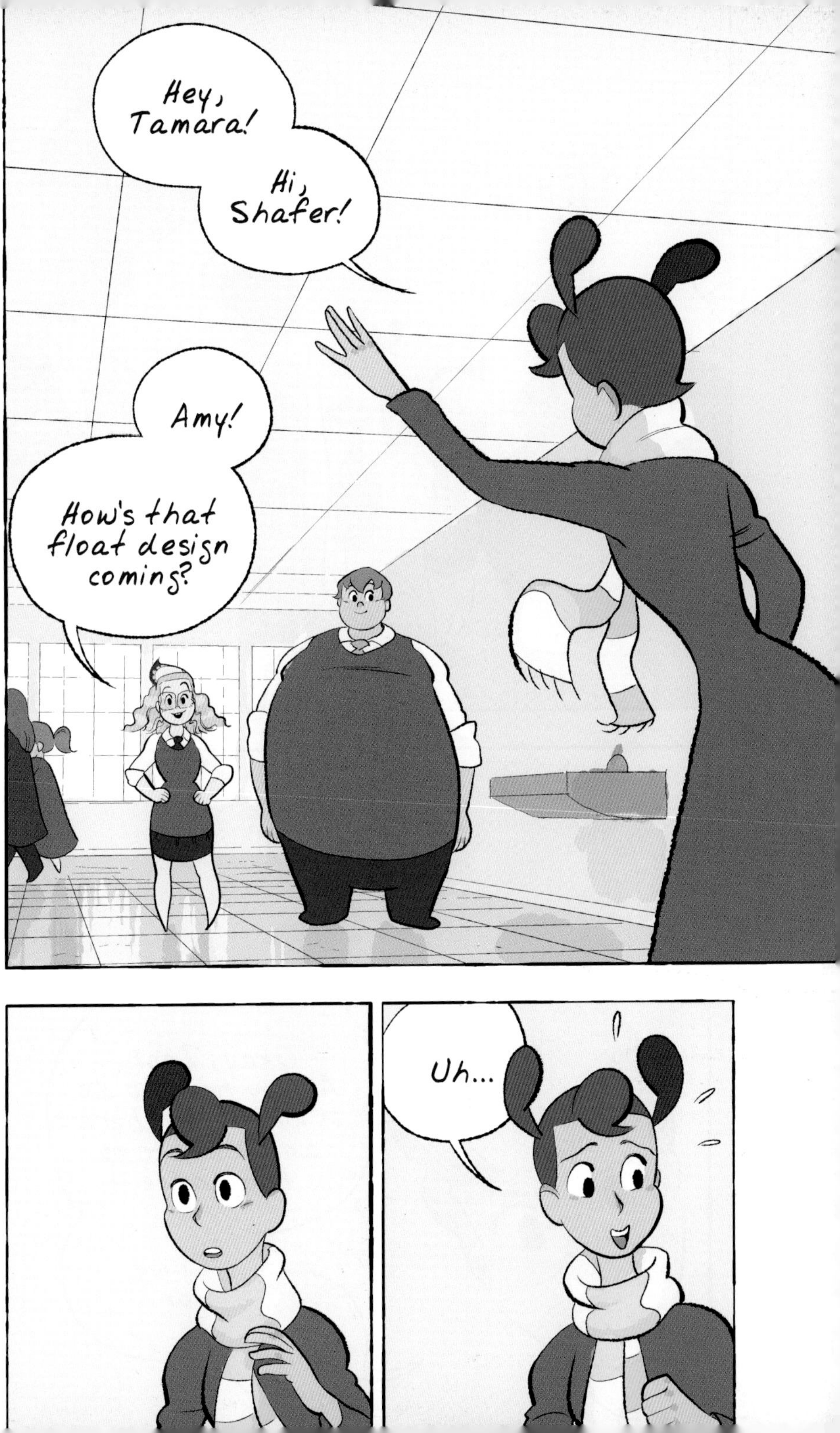
Hey, Tamara!
Hi, Shafer!
Amy!
How's that float design coming?
Uh...

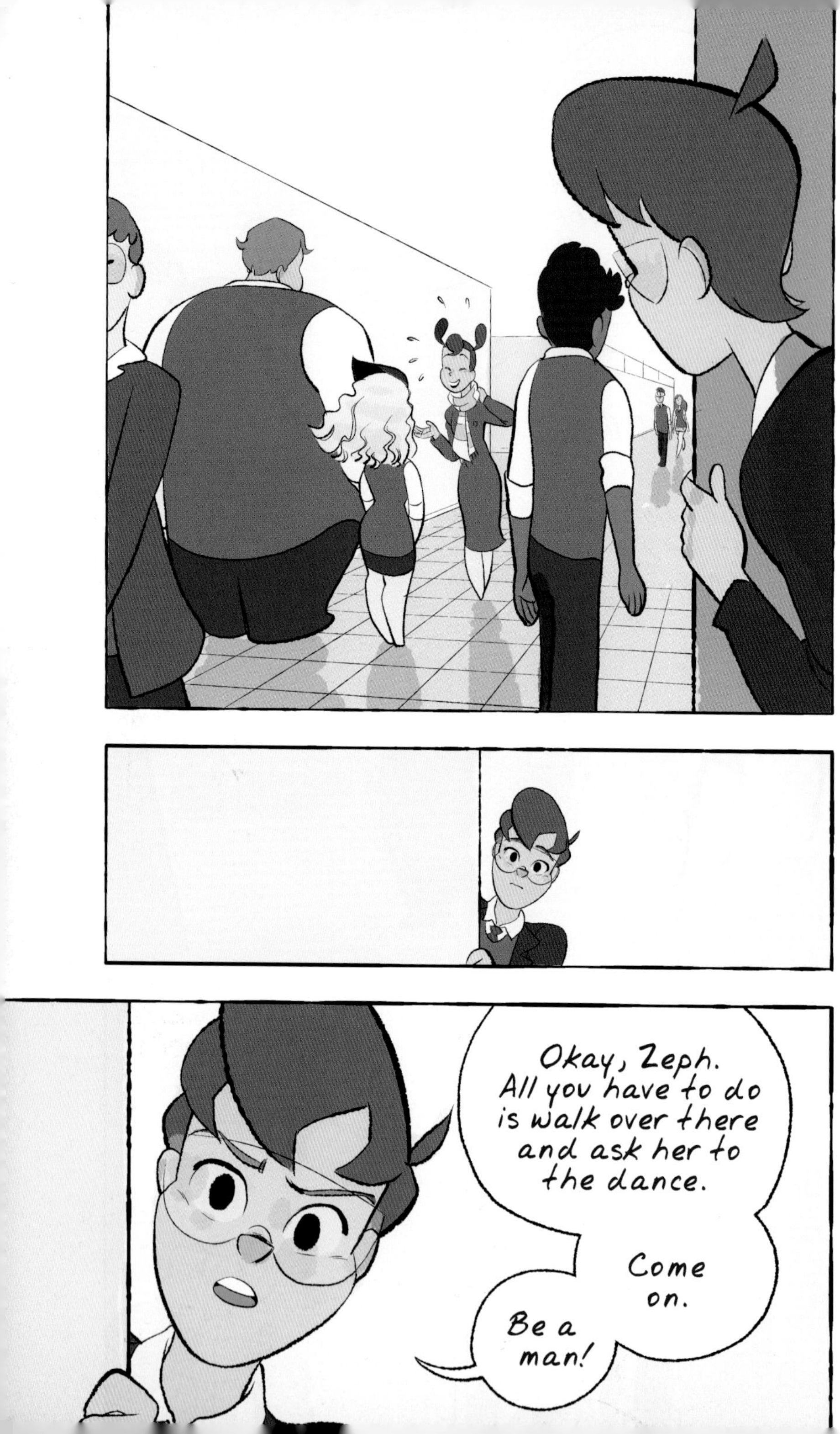
Okay, Zeph.
All you have to do
is walk over there
and ask her to
the dance.
Come
on.
Be a
man!

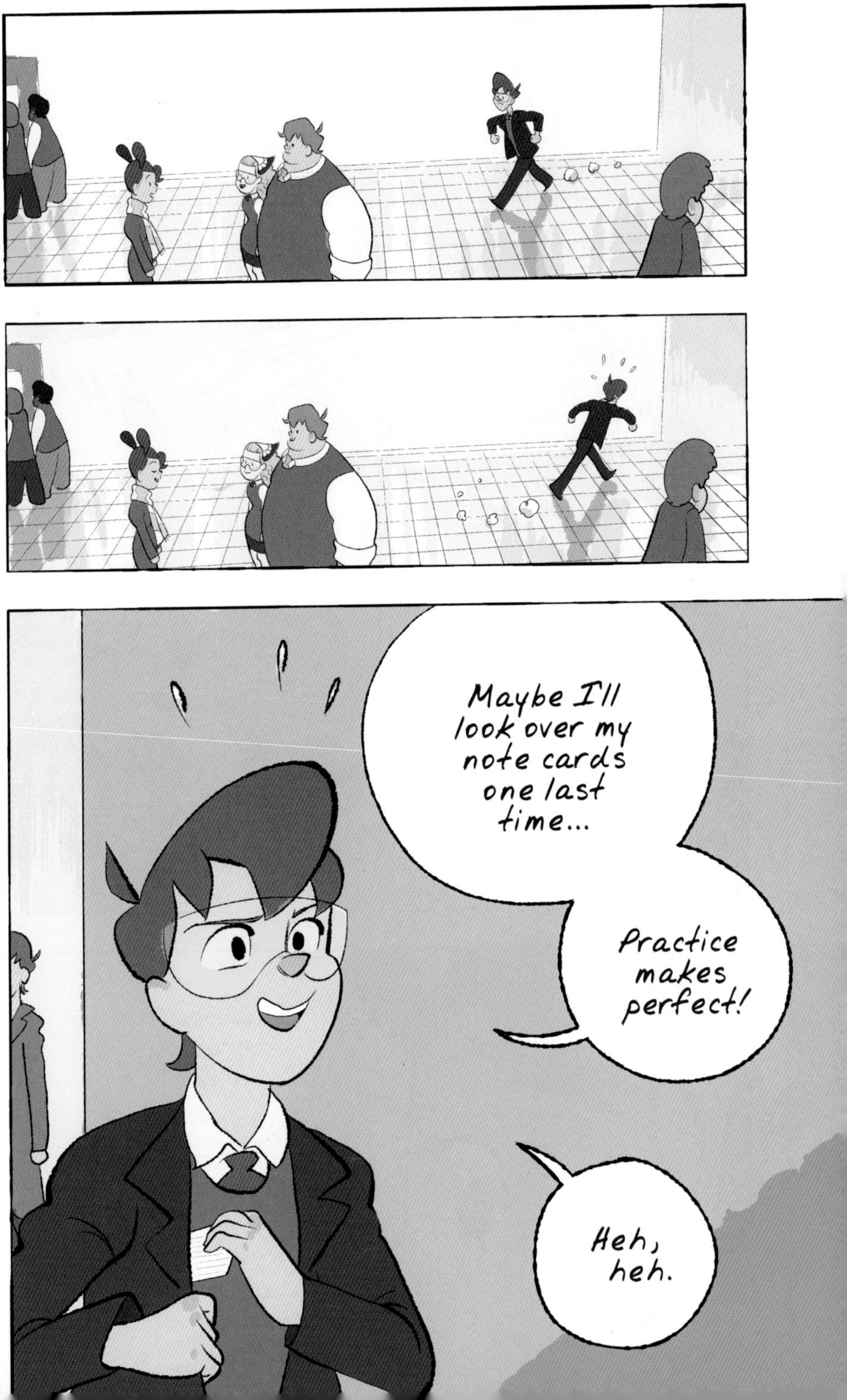
Maybe I'll look over my note cards one last time...
Practice makes perfect!
Heh, heh.

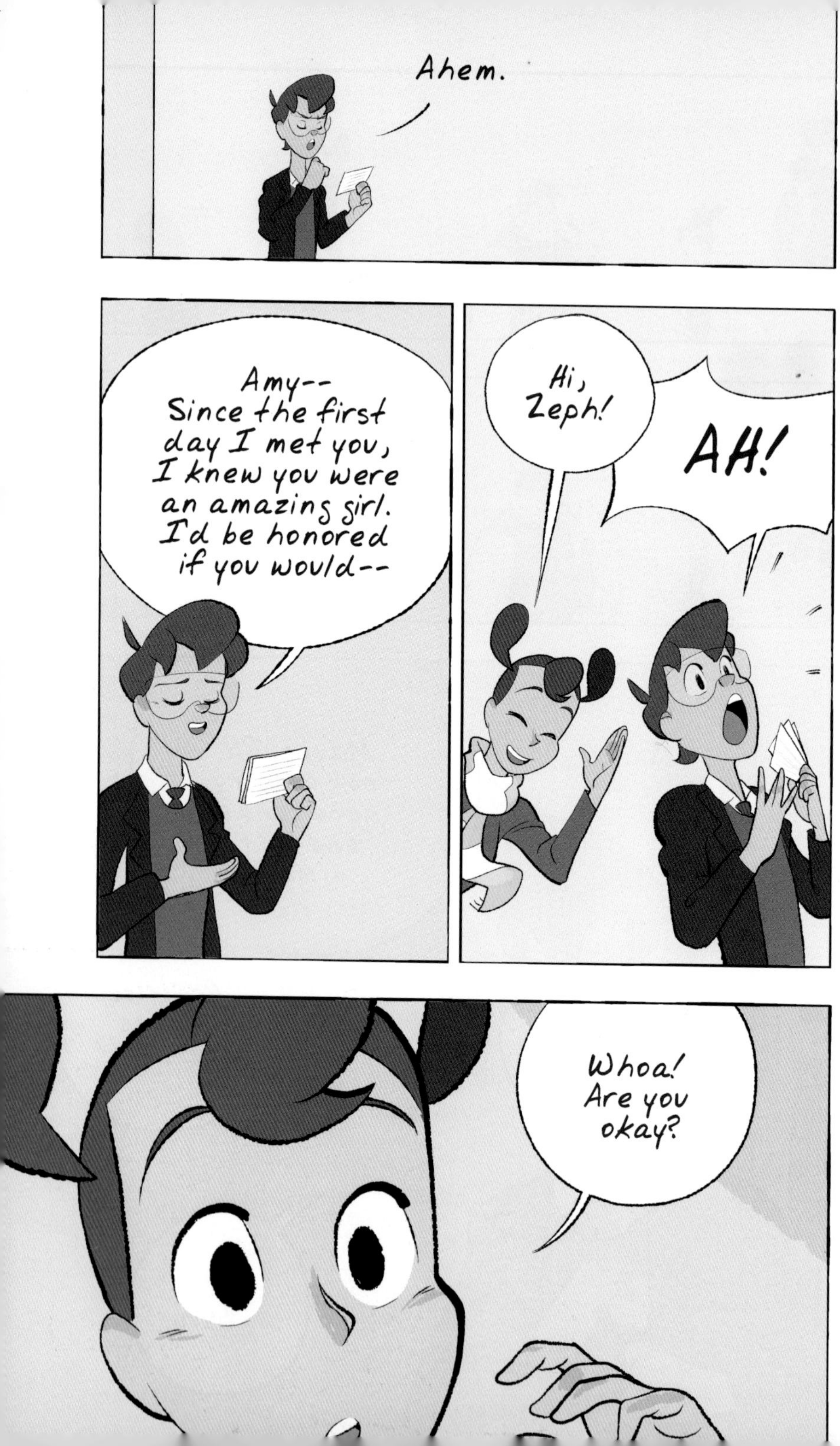
Ahem.
Amy-- Since the first day I met you, I knew you were an amazing girl. I'd be honored if you would--
Hi, Zeph!
AH!
Whoa! Are you okay?

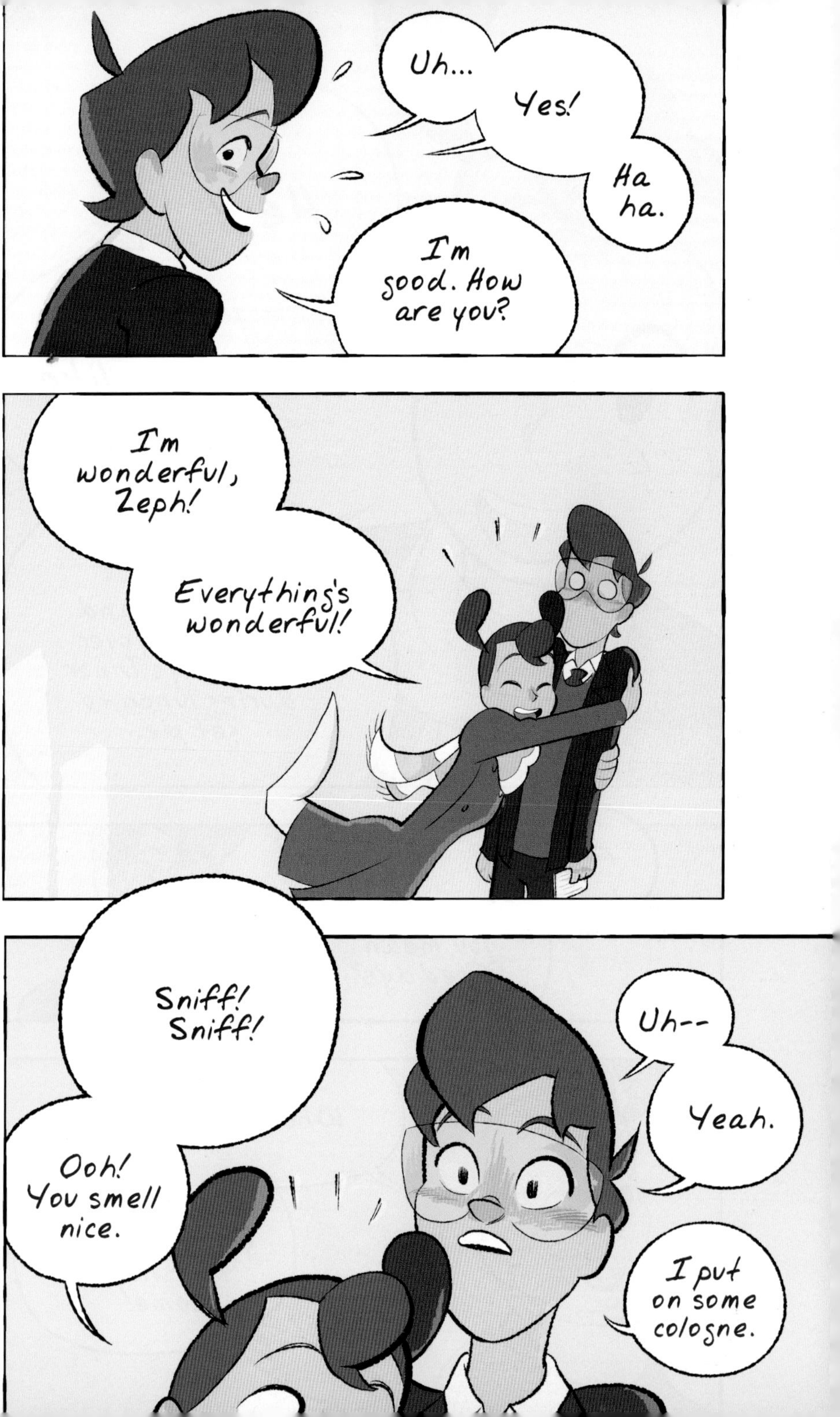
Uh...
Yes!
Ha ha.
I'm good. How are you?
I'm wonderful, Zeph!
Everything's wonderful!
Sniff! Sniff!
Uh--
Yeah.
Ooh! You smell nice.
I put on some cologne.

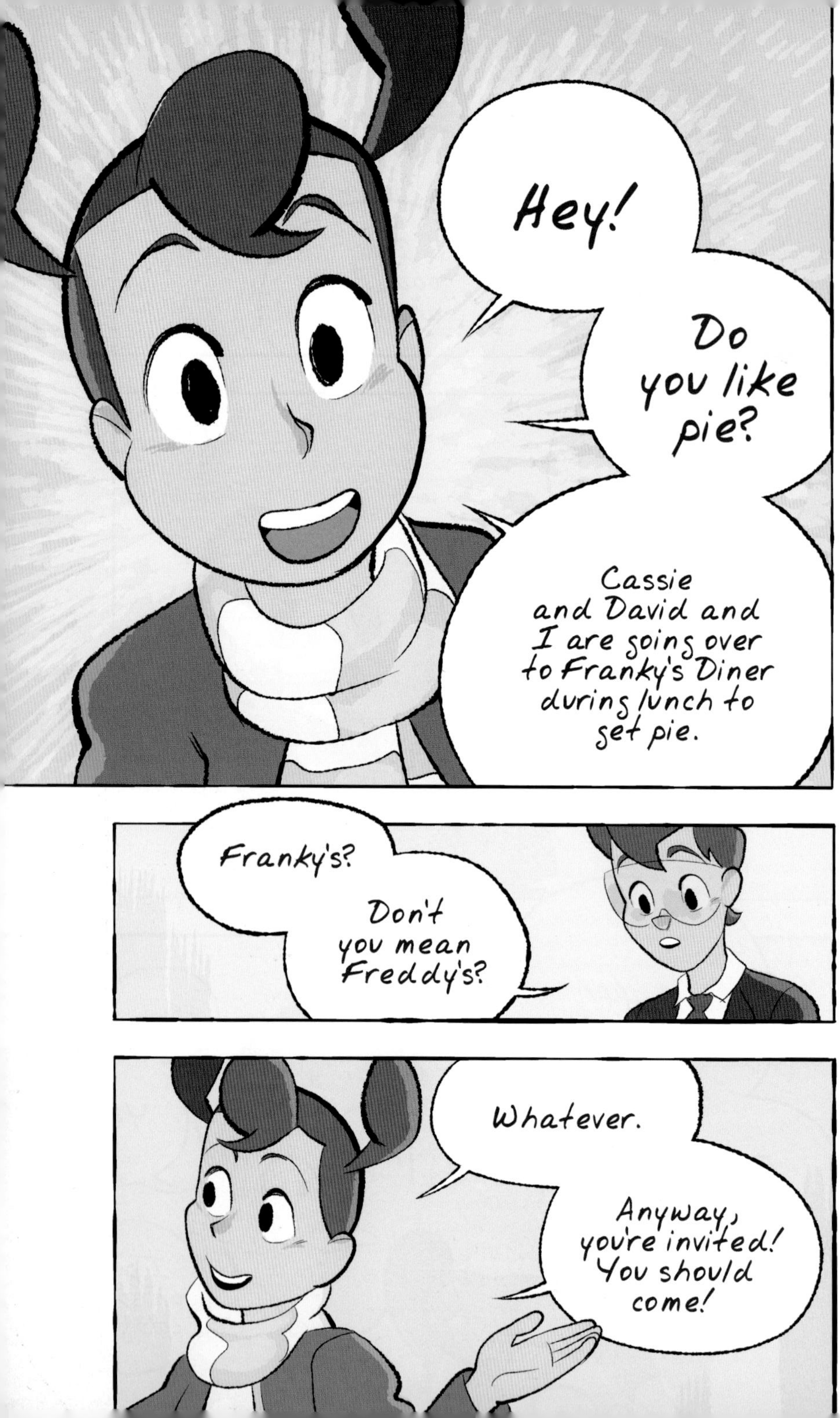
Hey!
Do you like pie?
Cassie and David and I are going over to Franky's Diner during lunch to get pie.
Franky's?
Don't you mean Freddy's?
Whatever.
Anyway, you're invited! You should come!

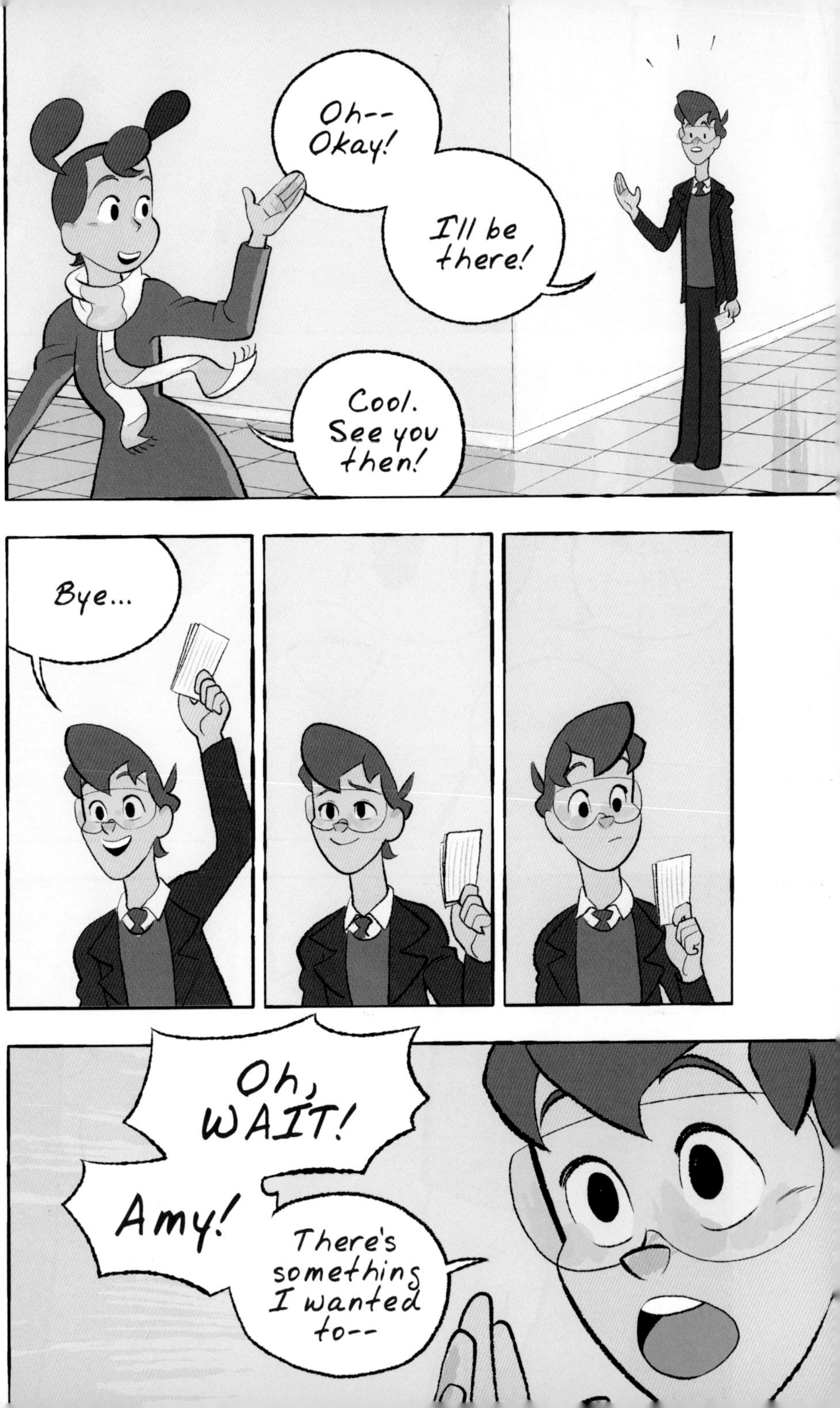
Oh--
Okay!
I'll be there!
Cool. See you then!
Bye...
Oh, WAIT!
Amy!
There's something I wanted to--

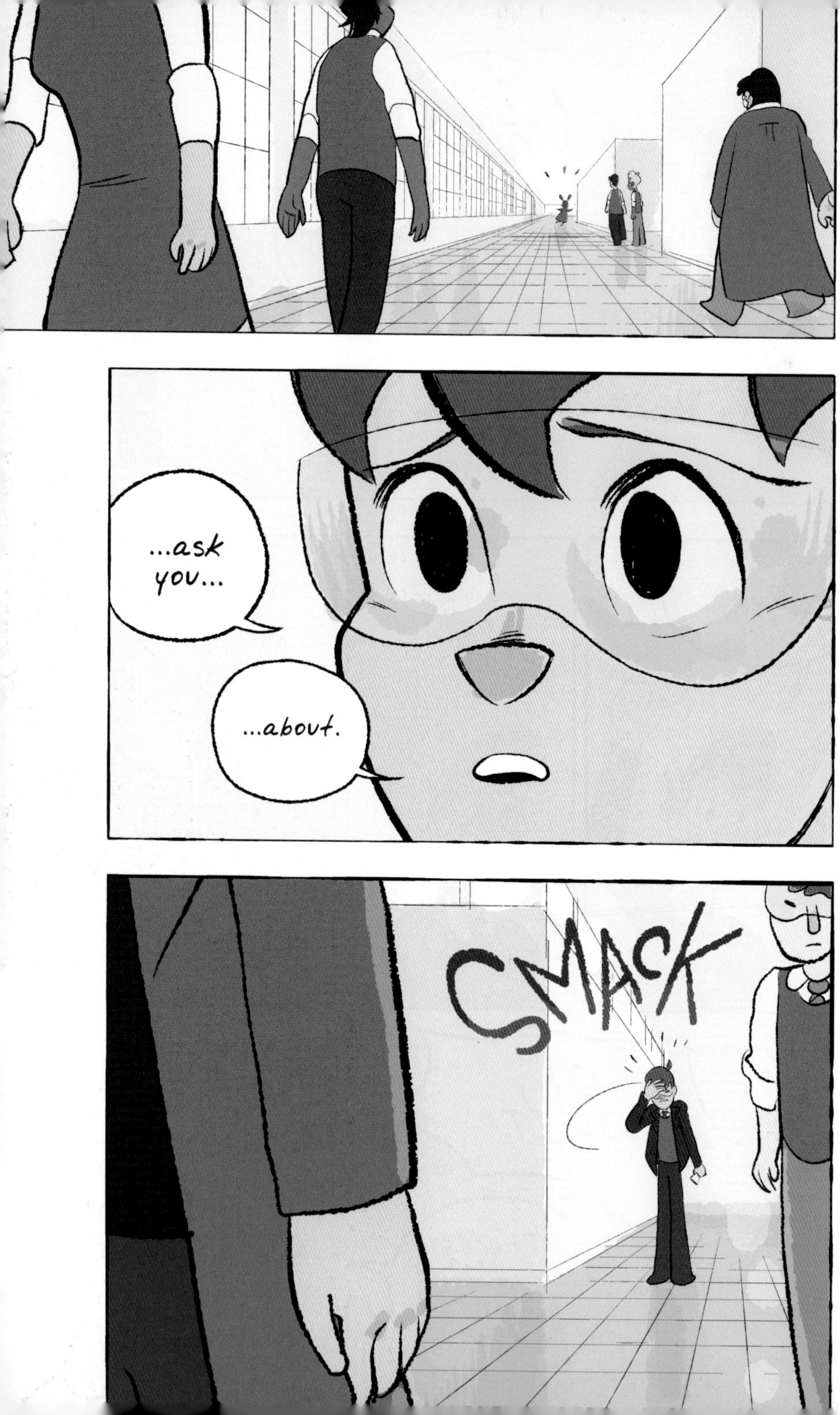
...ask you...
...about.
SMACK

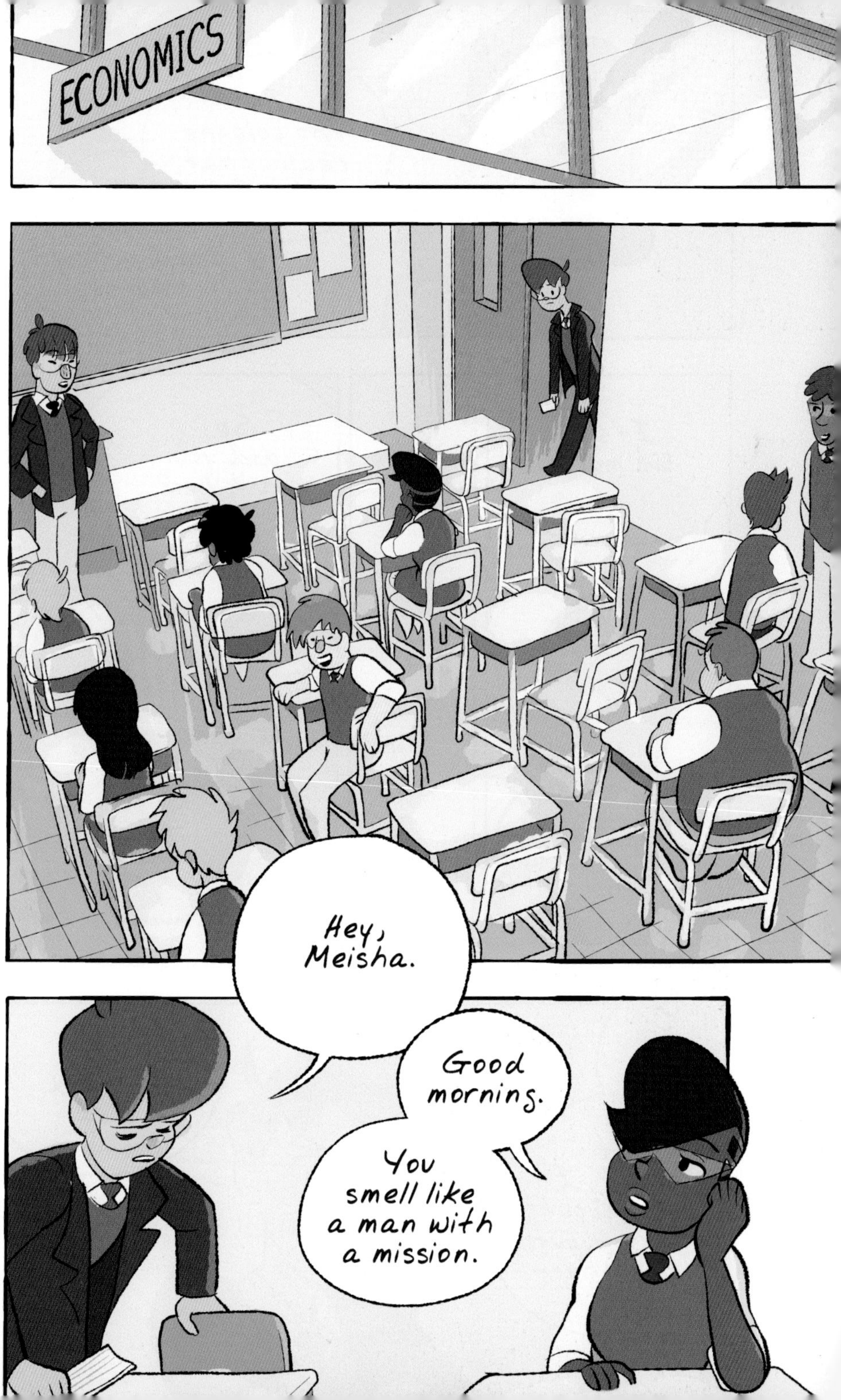
ECONOMICS
Hey, Meisha.
Good morning.
You smell like a man with a mission.

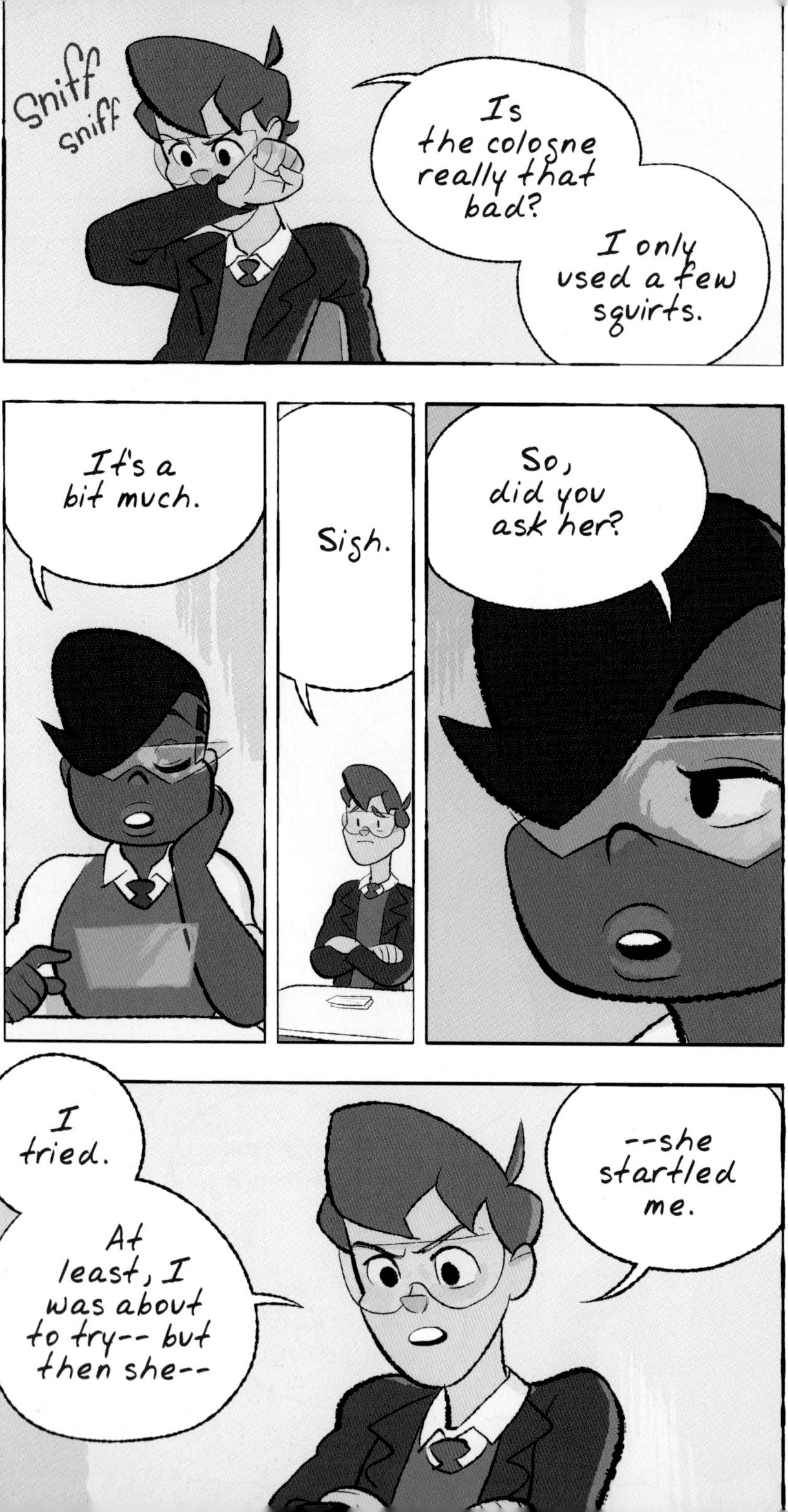
Sniff sniff
Is the cologne really that bad?
I only used a few squirts.
It's a bit much.
Sigh.
So, did you ask her?
I tried.
At least, I was about to try-- but then she--
--she startled me.

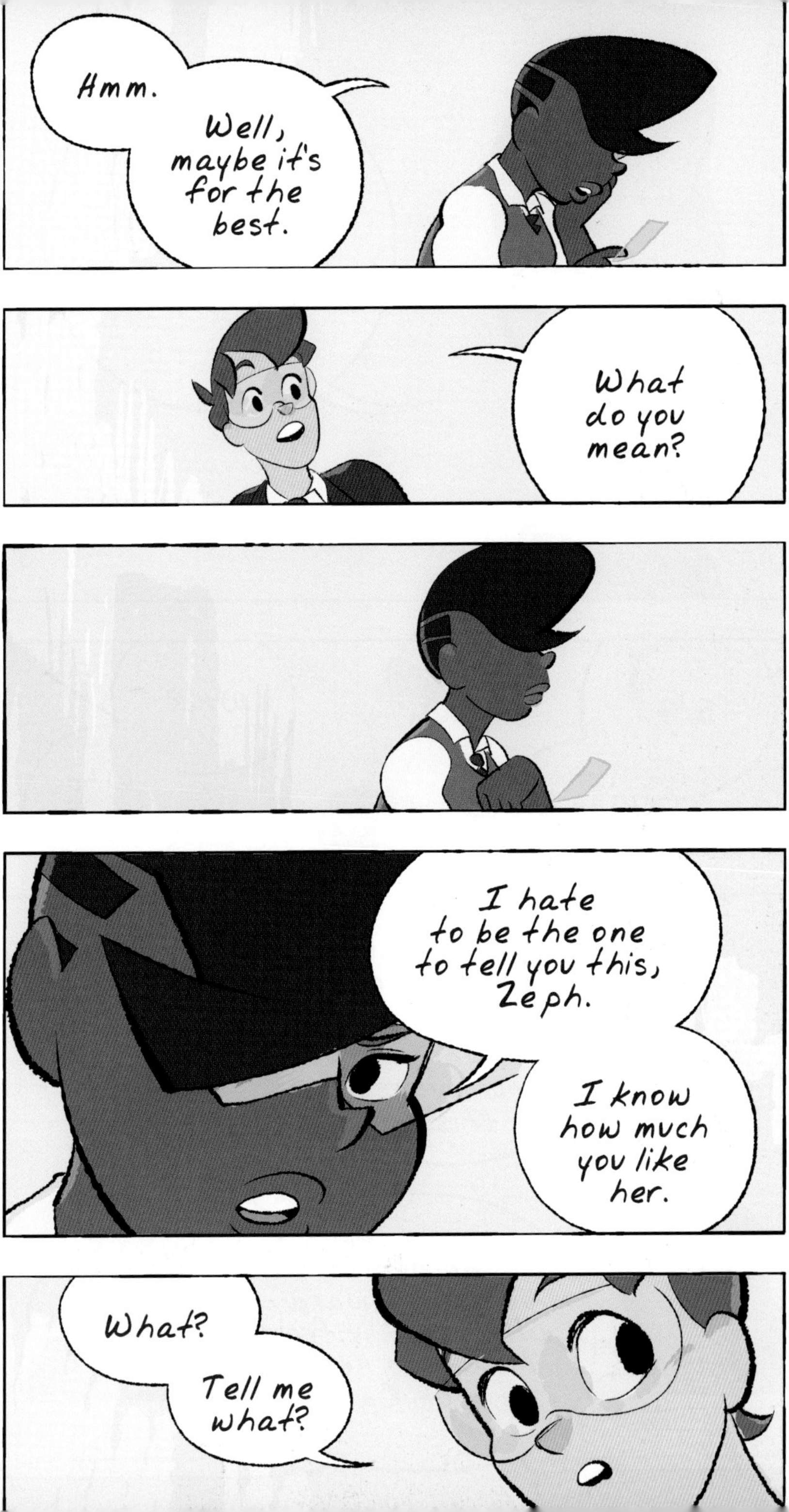
Hmm.
Well, maybe it's for the best.
What do you mean?
I hate to be the one to tell you this, Zeph.
I know how much you like her.
What?
Tell me what?

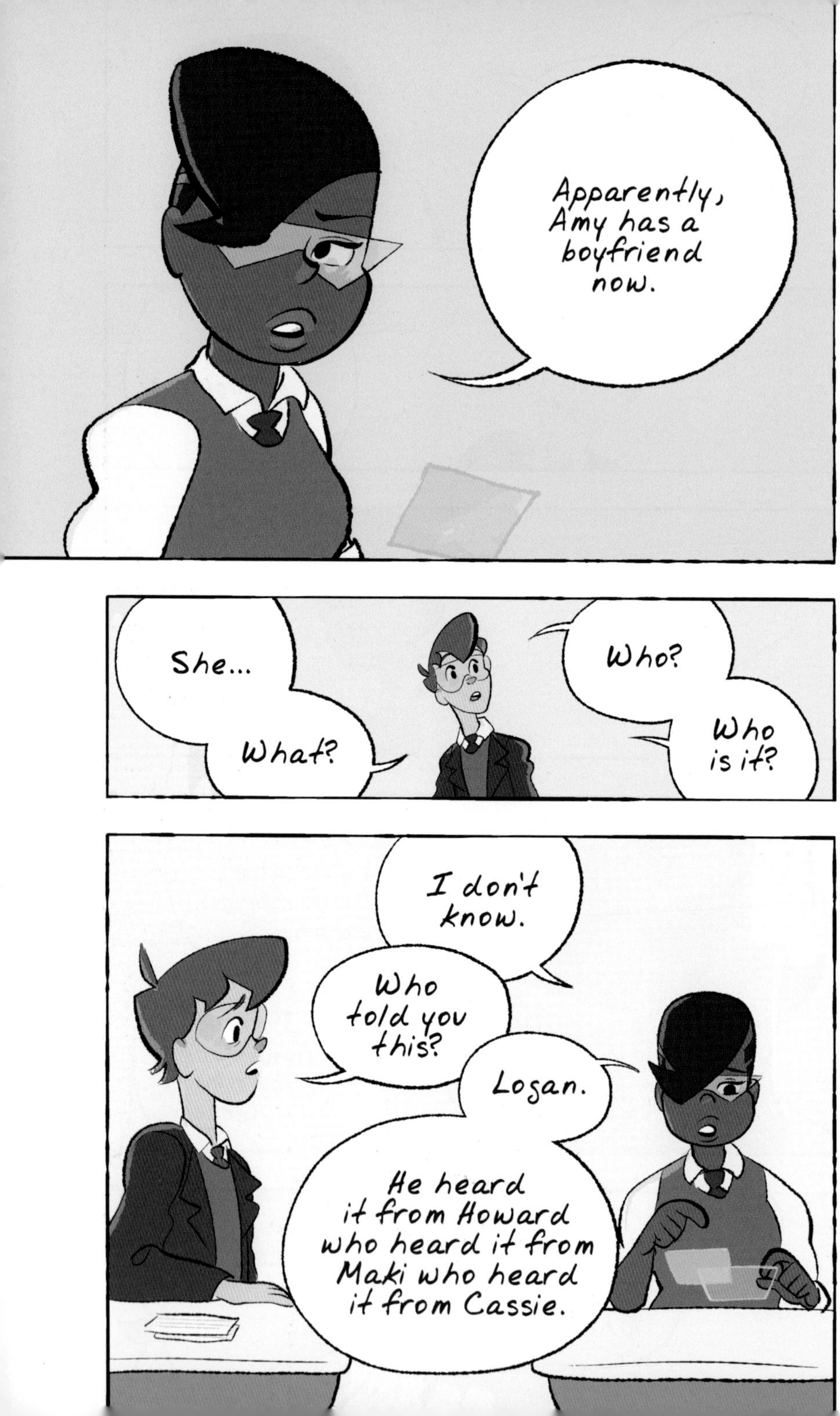
Apparently, Amy has a boyfriend now.
She...
What?
Who?
Who is it?
I don't know.
Who told you this?
Logan.
He heard it from Howard who heard it from Maki who heard it from Cassie.

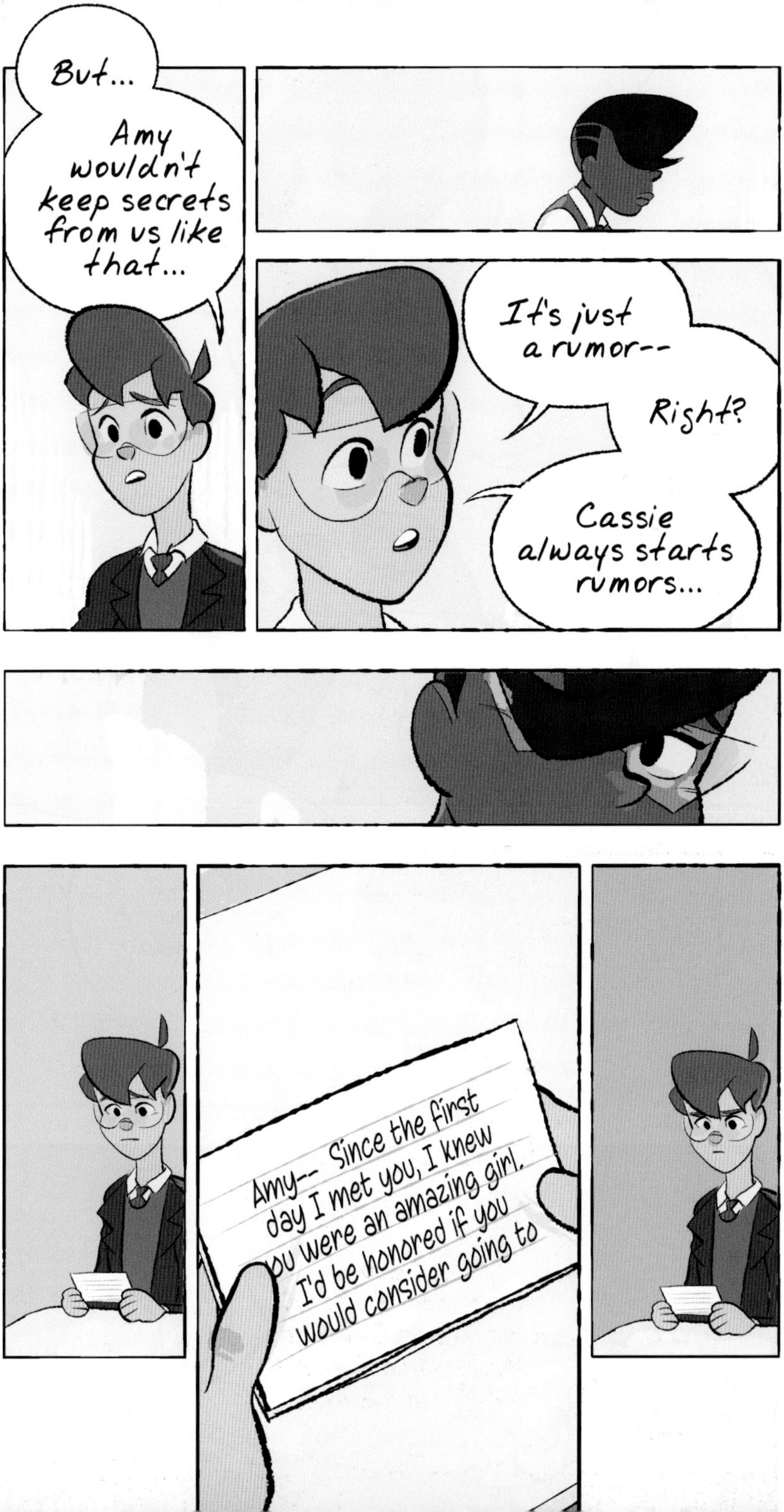
But...
Amy wouldn't keep secrets from us like that...
It's just a rumor--
Right?
Cassie always starts rumors...
Amy-- Since the first day I met you, I knew you were an amazing girl. I'd be honored if you would consider going to

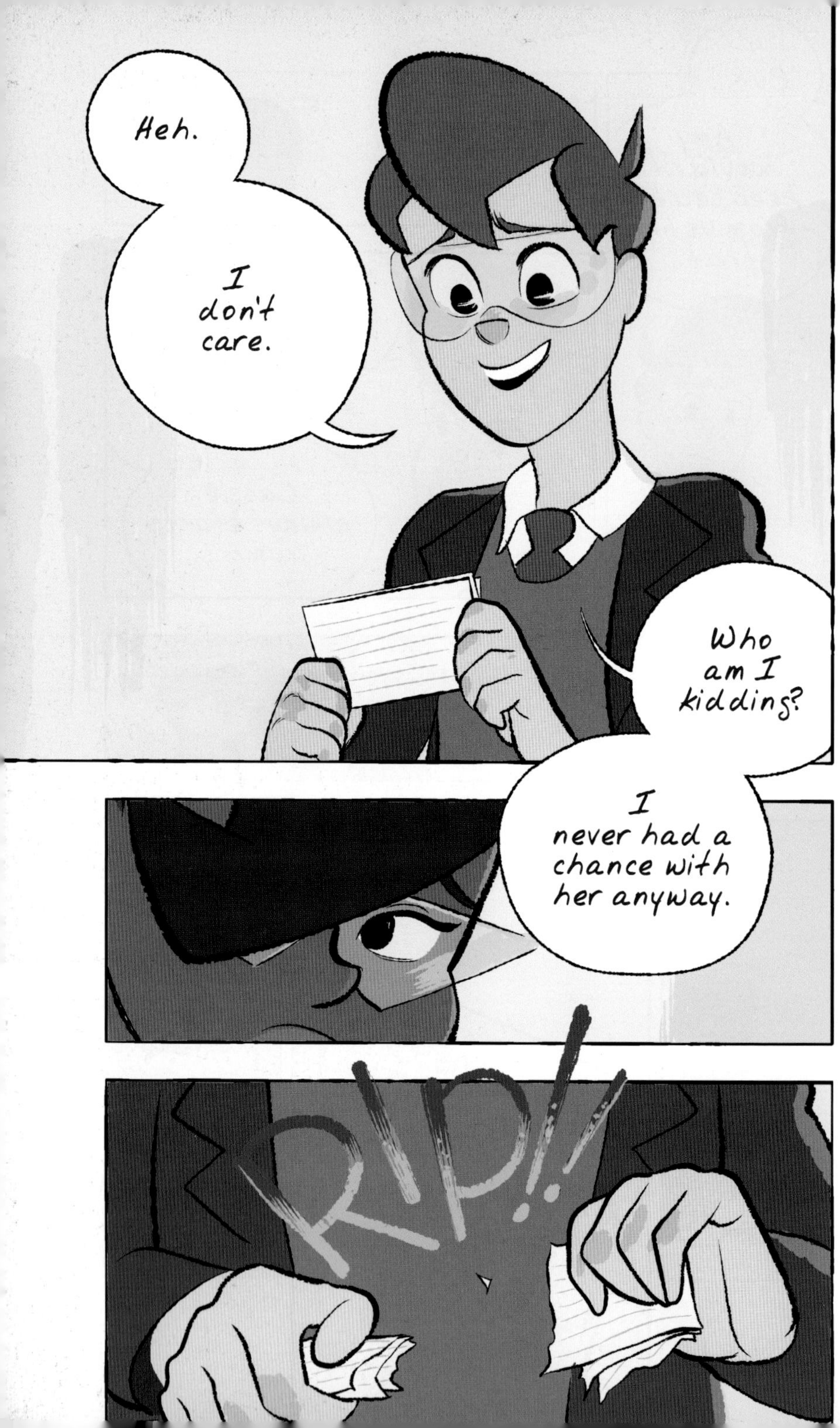
Heh.
I don't care.
Who am I kidding?
I never had a chance with her anyway.
RIP!!

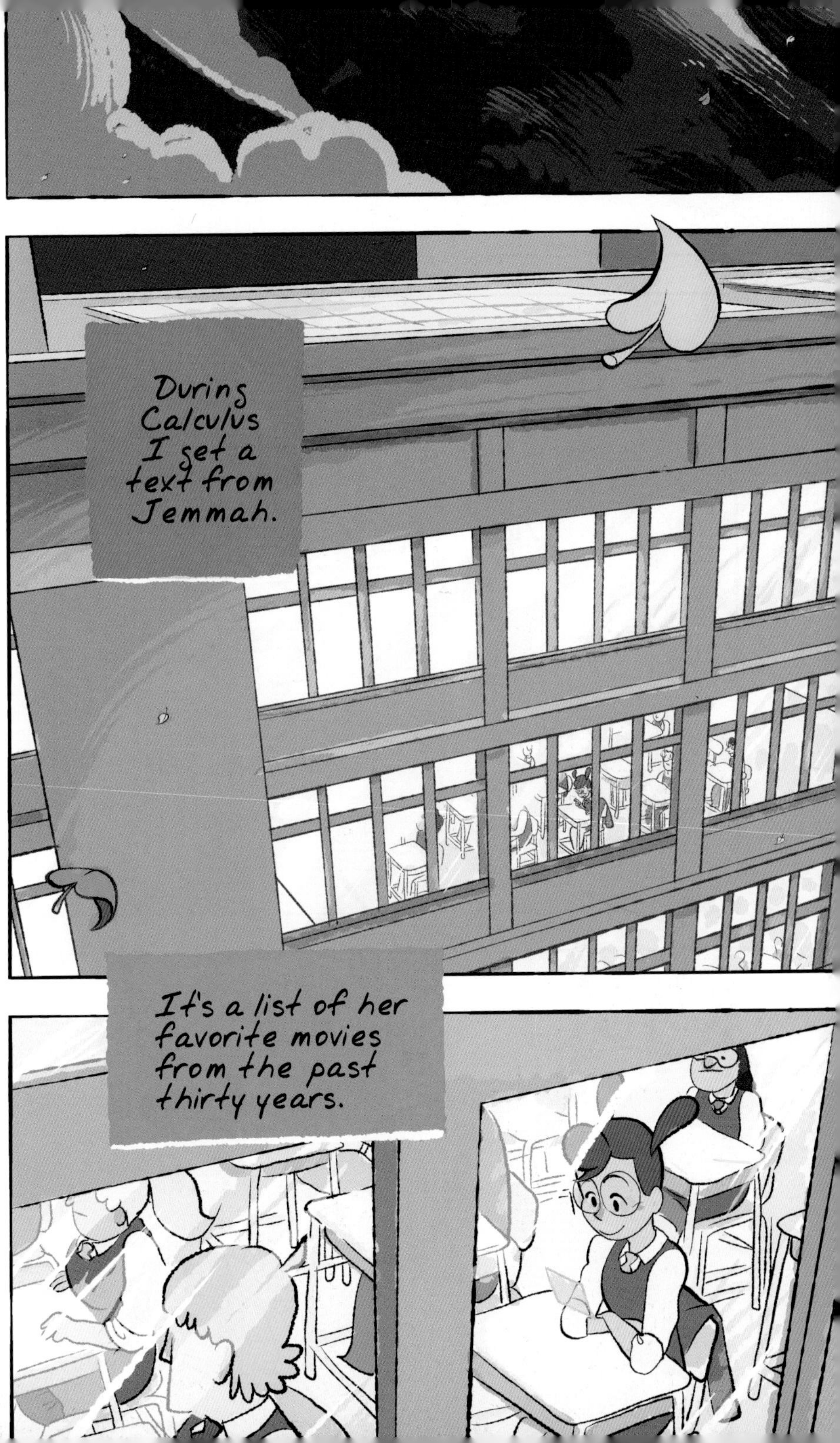
During Calculus I get a text from Jemmah.
It's a list of her favorite movies from the past thirty years.

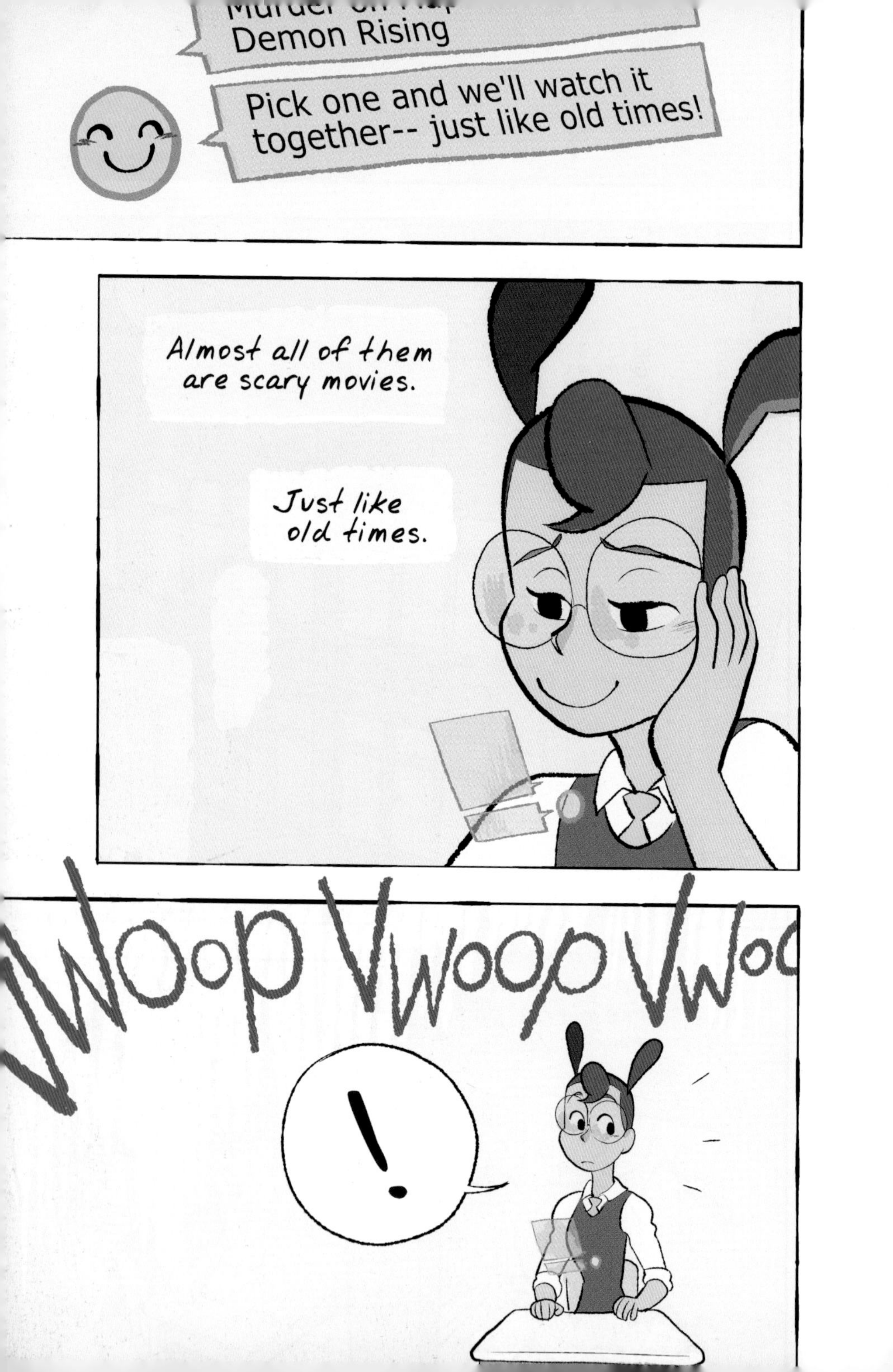
Demon Rising
Pick one and we'll watch it together-- just like old times!
Almost all of them are scary movies.
Just like old times.
Woop Woop Woo
!

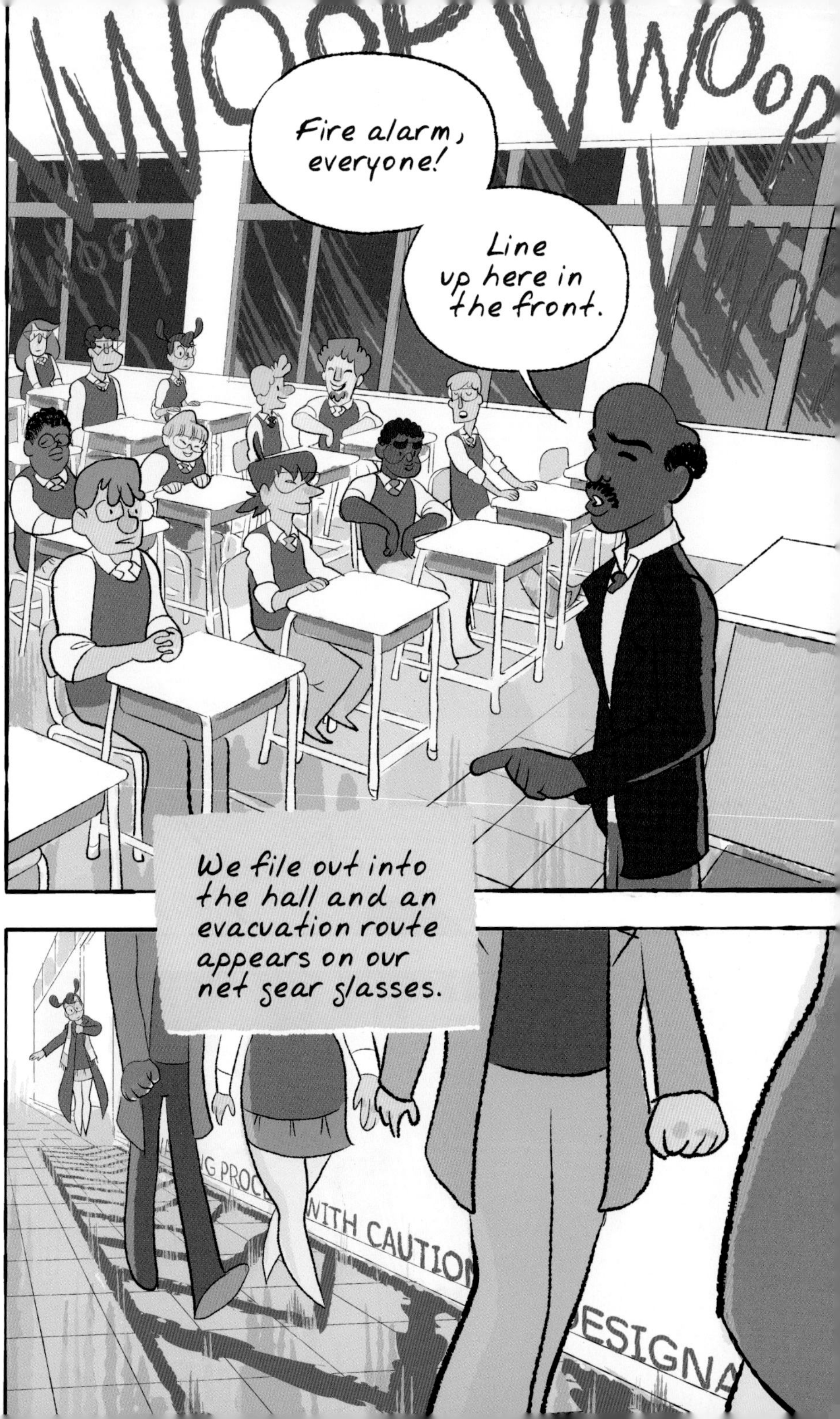
Fire alarm, everyone!
Line up here in the front.
We file out into the hall and an evacuation route appears on our net gear glasses.
WITH CAUTION

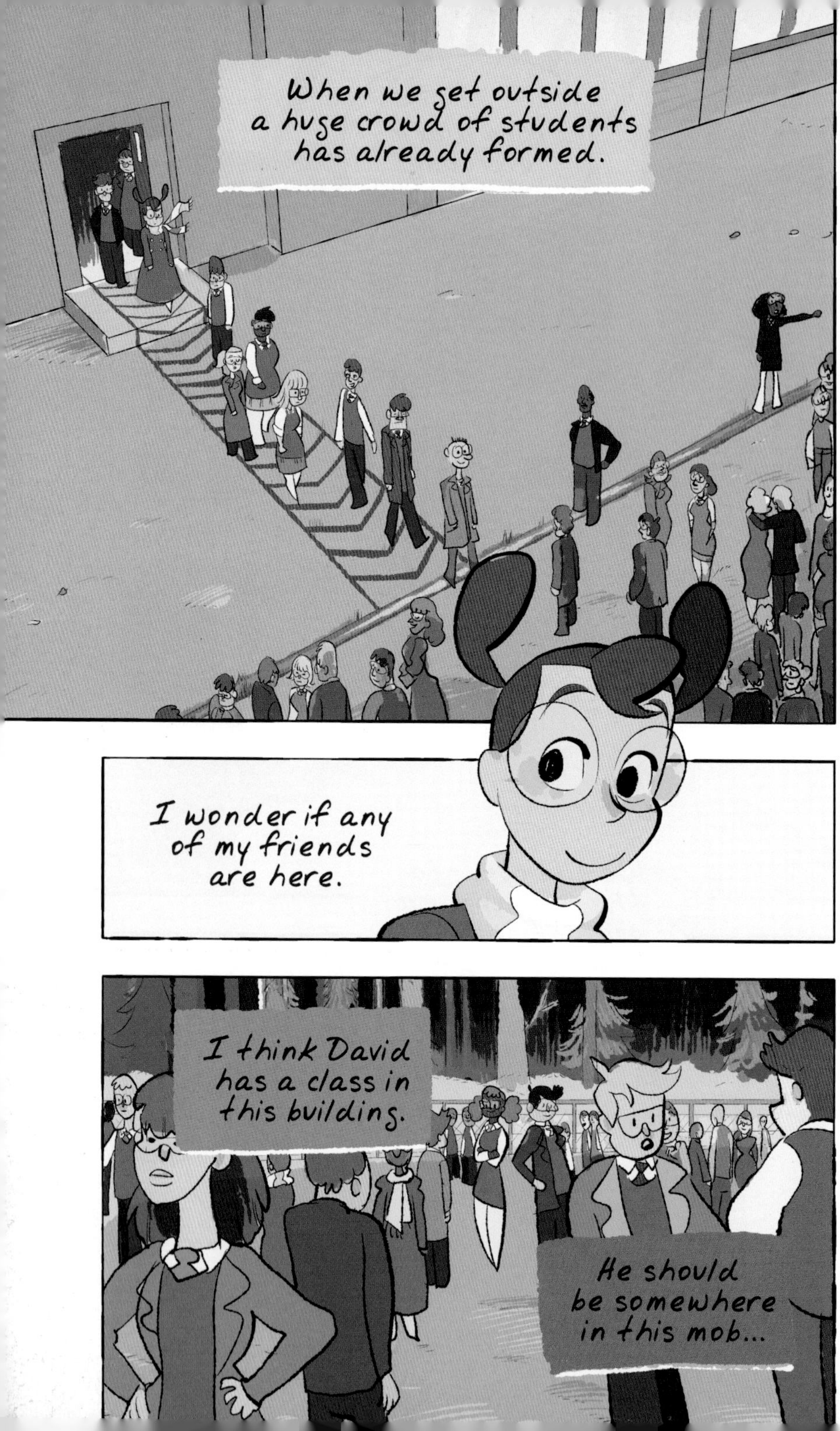
When we get outside a huge crowd of students has already formed.
I wonder if any of my friends are here.
I think David has a class in this building.
He should be somewhere in this mob...

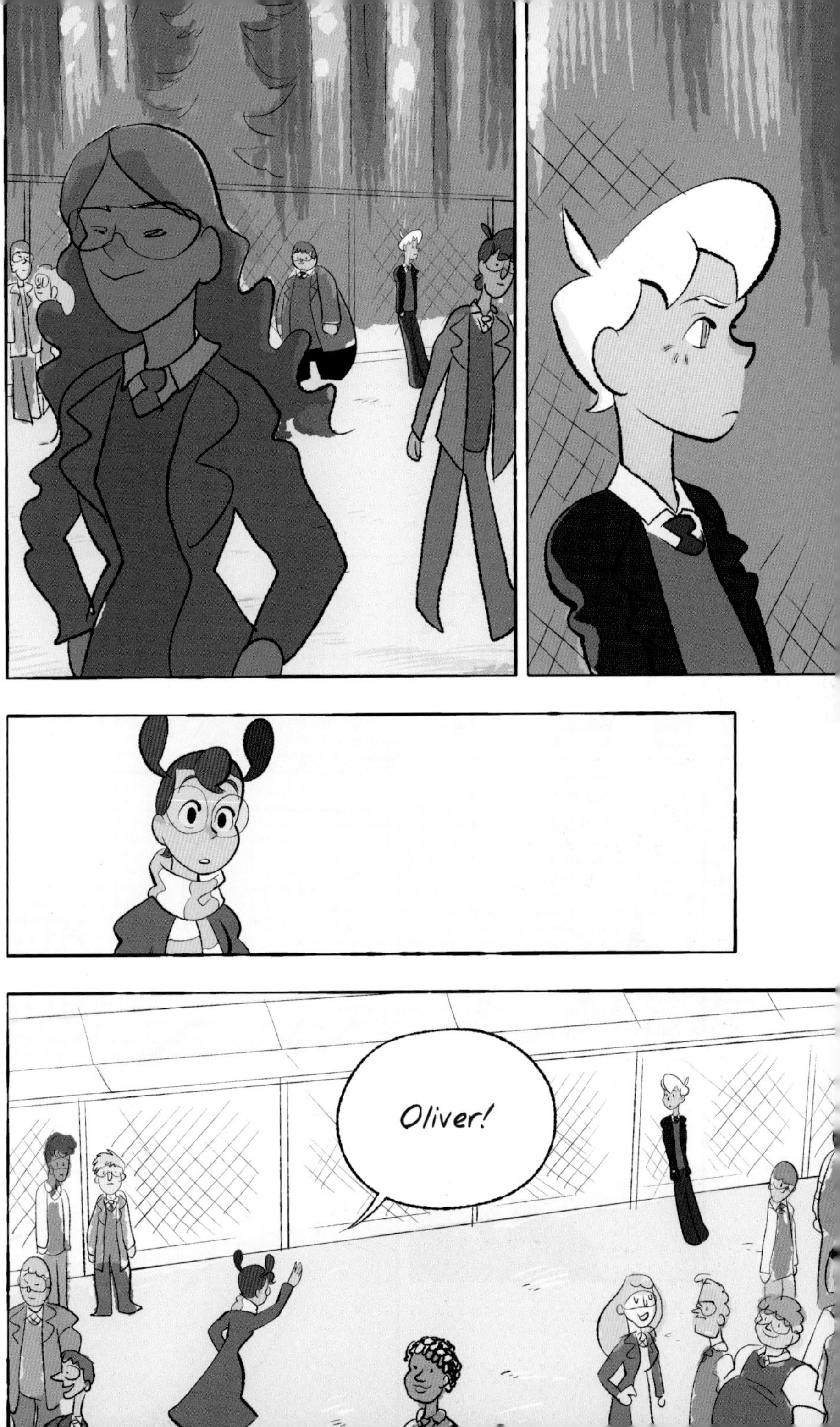
Oliver!

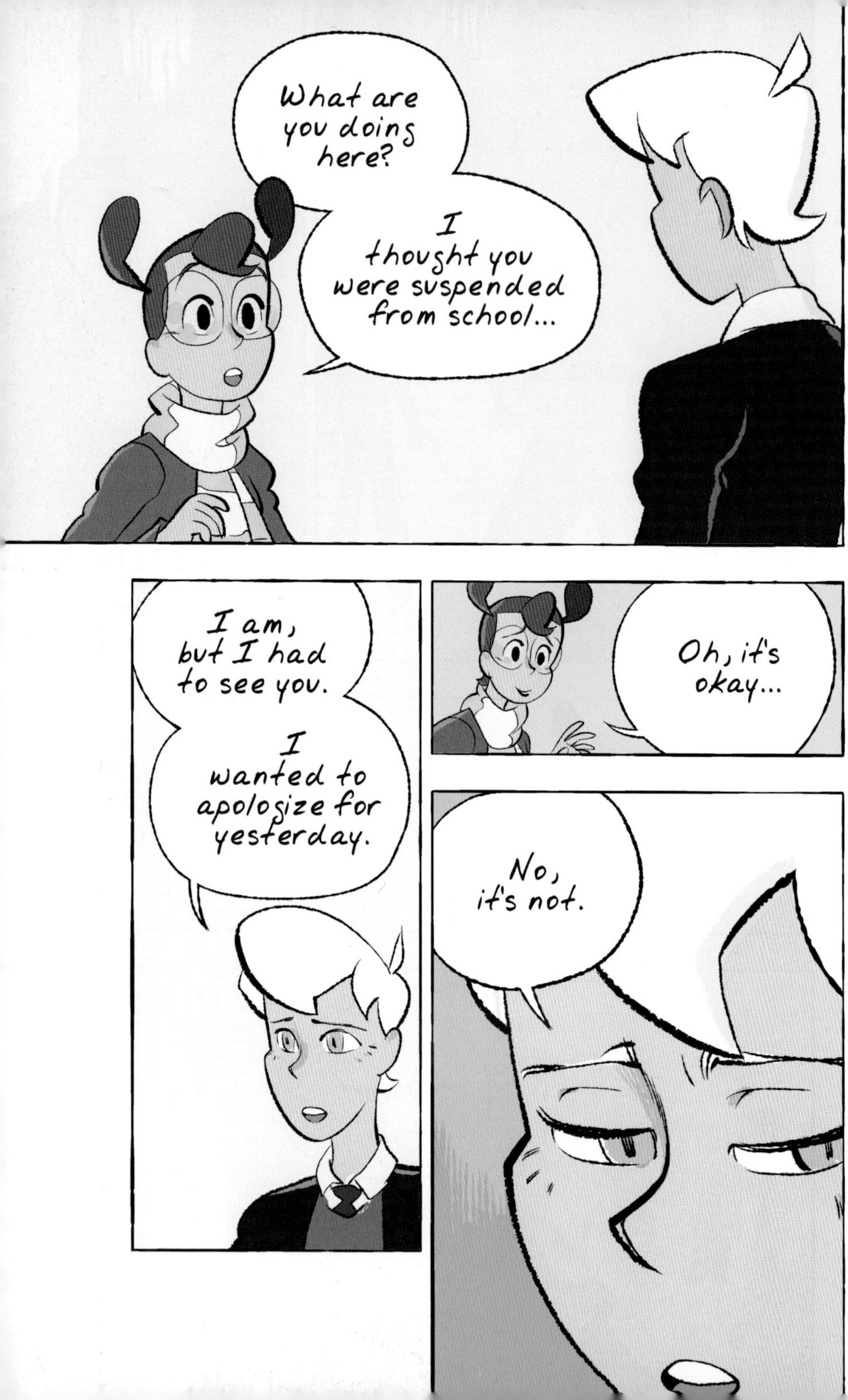
What are you doins here?
I thought you were suspended from school...
I am, but I had to see you.
I wanted to apologize for yesterday.
Oh, it's okay...
No, it's not.

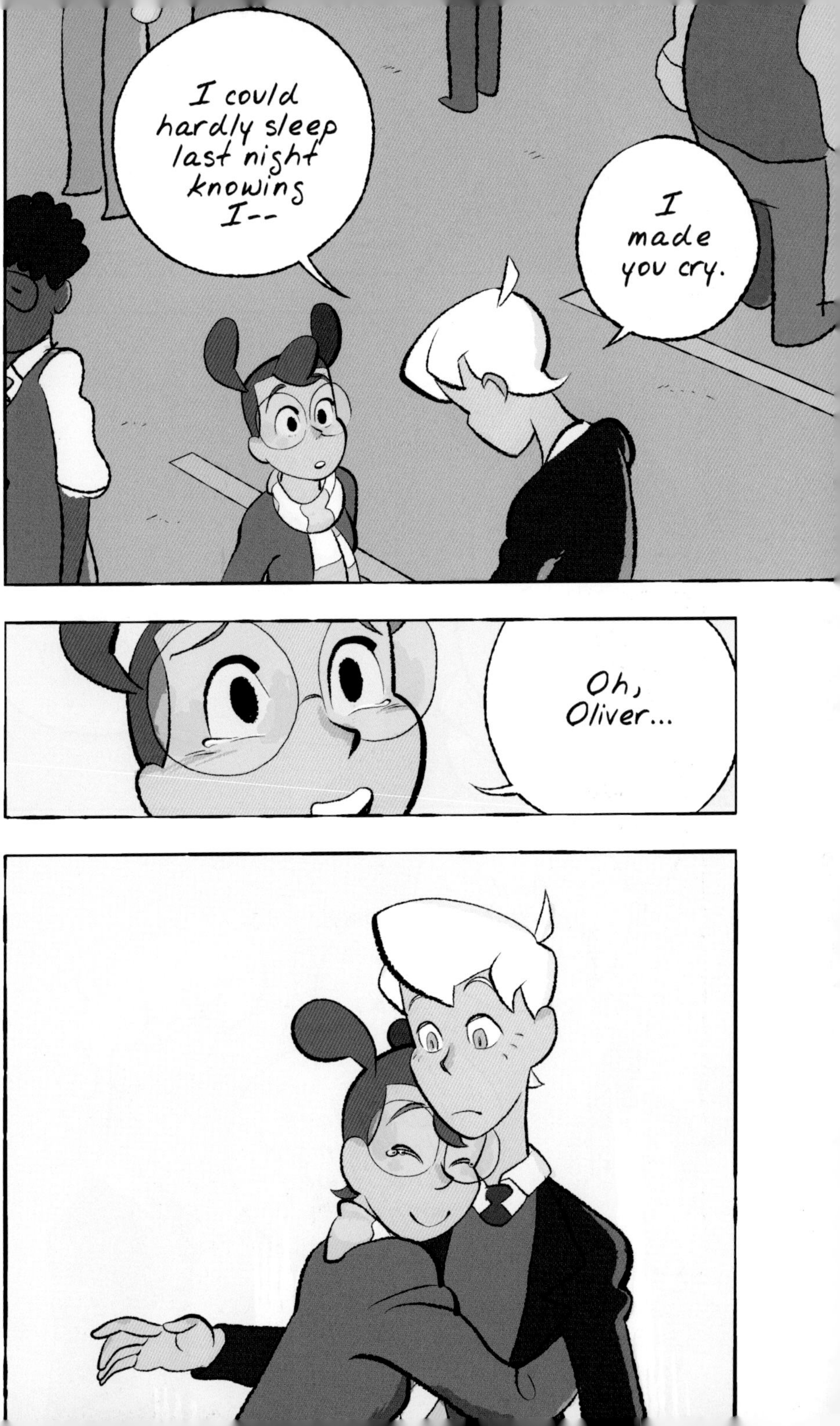
I could hardly sleep last night knowins I--
I made you cry.
Oh, Oliver...

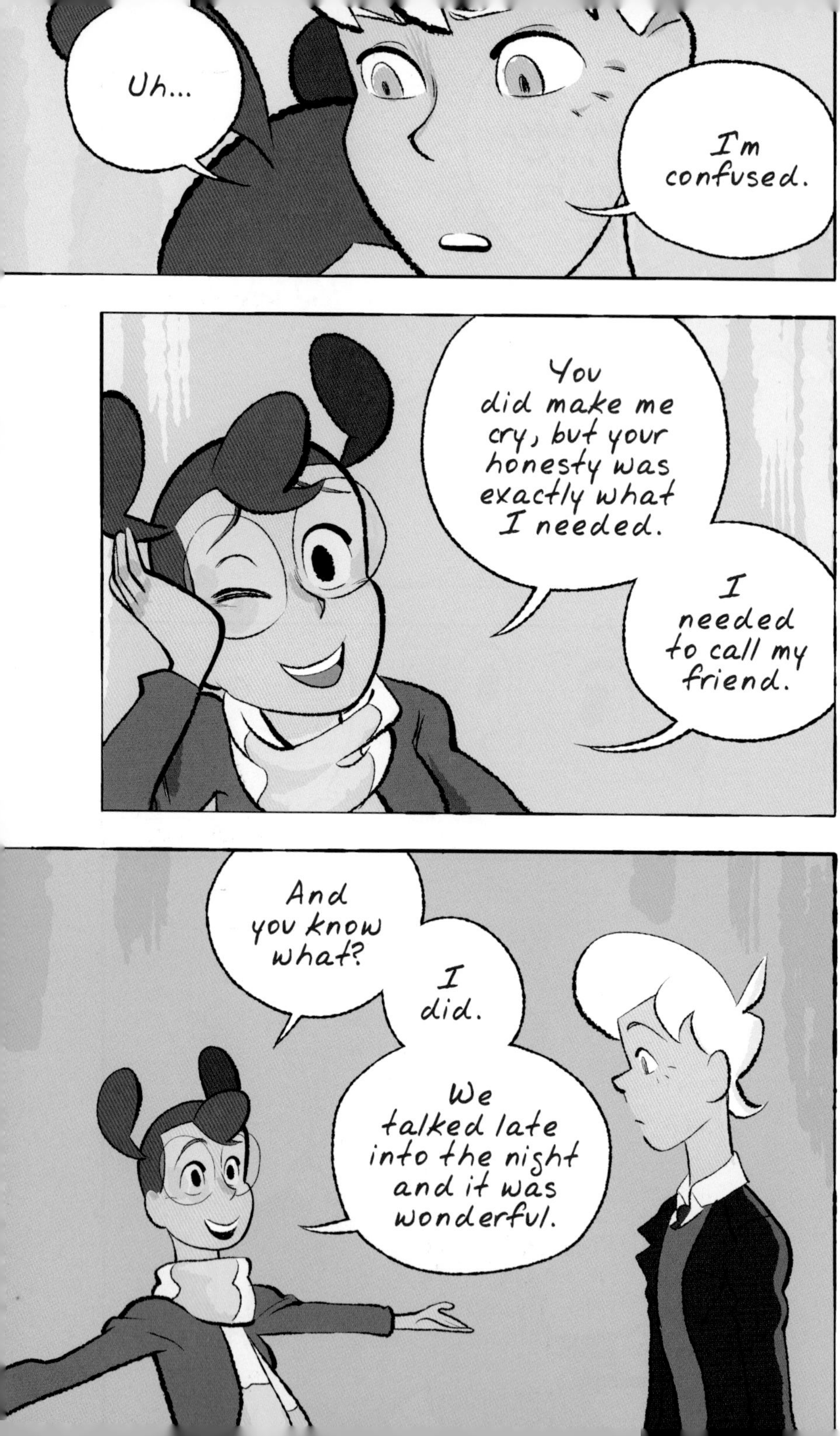
Uh...
I'm confused.
You did make me cry, but your honesty was exactly what I needed.
I needed to call my friend.
And you know what?
I did.
We talked late into the night and it was wonderful.

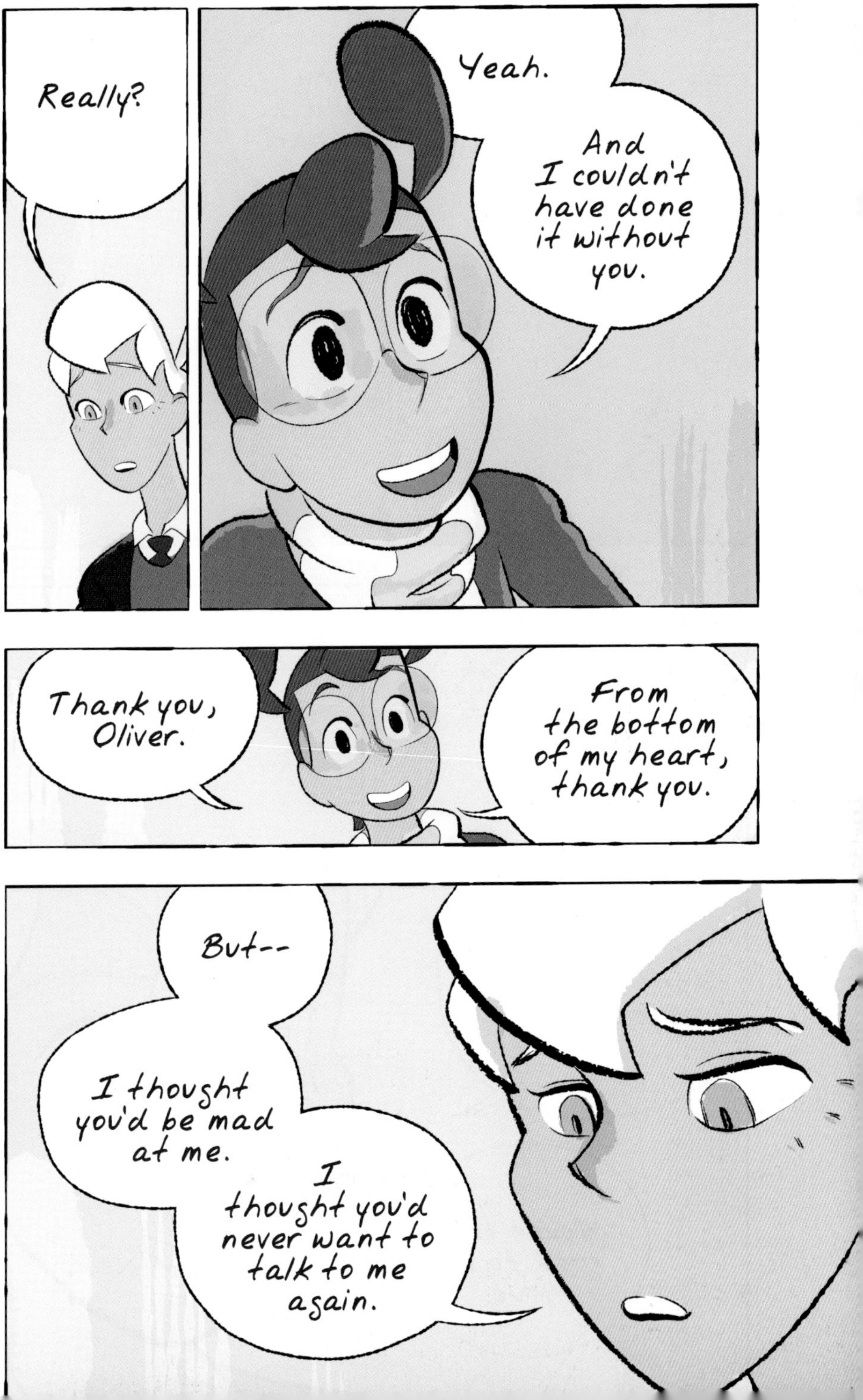
Really?
Yeah.
And I couldn't have done it without you.
Thank you, Oliver.
From the bottom of my heart, thank you.
But--
I thought you'd be mad at me.
I thought you'd never want to talk to me again.

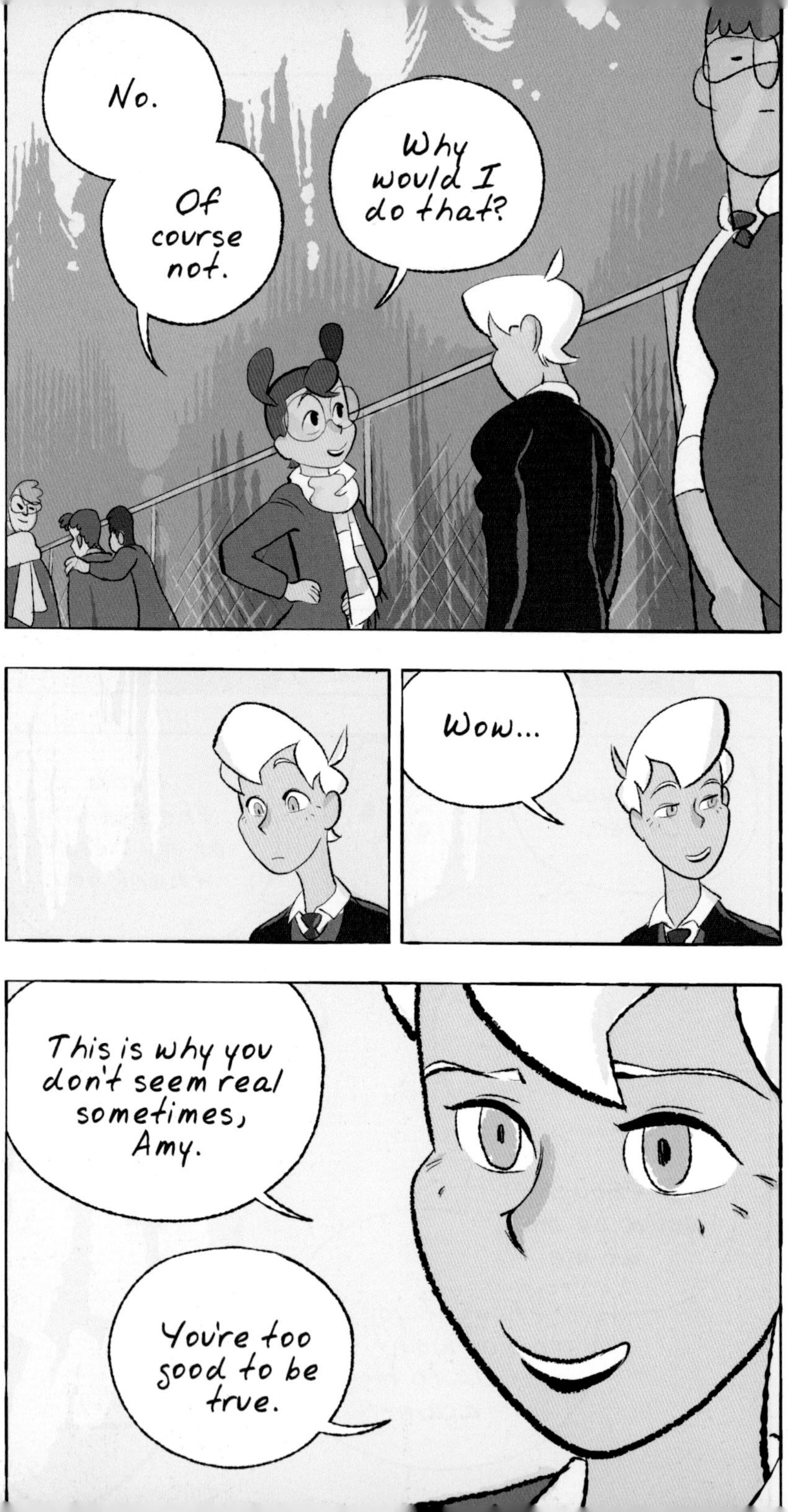
No.
Of course not.
Why would I do that?
Wow...
This is why you don't seem real sometimes, Amy.
You're too good to be true.

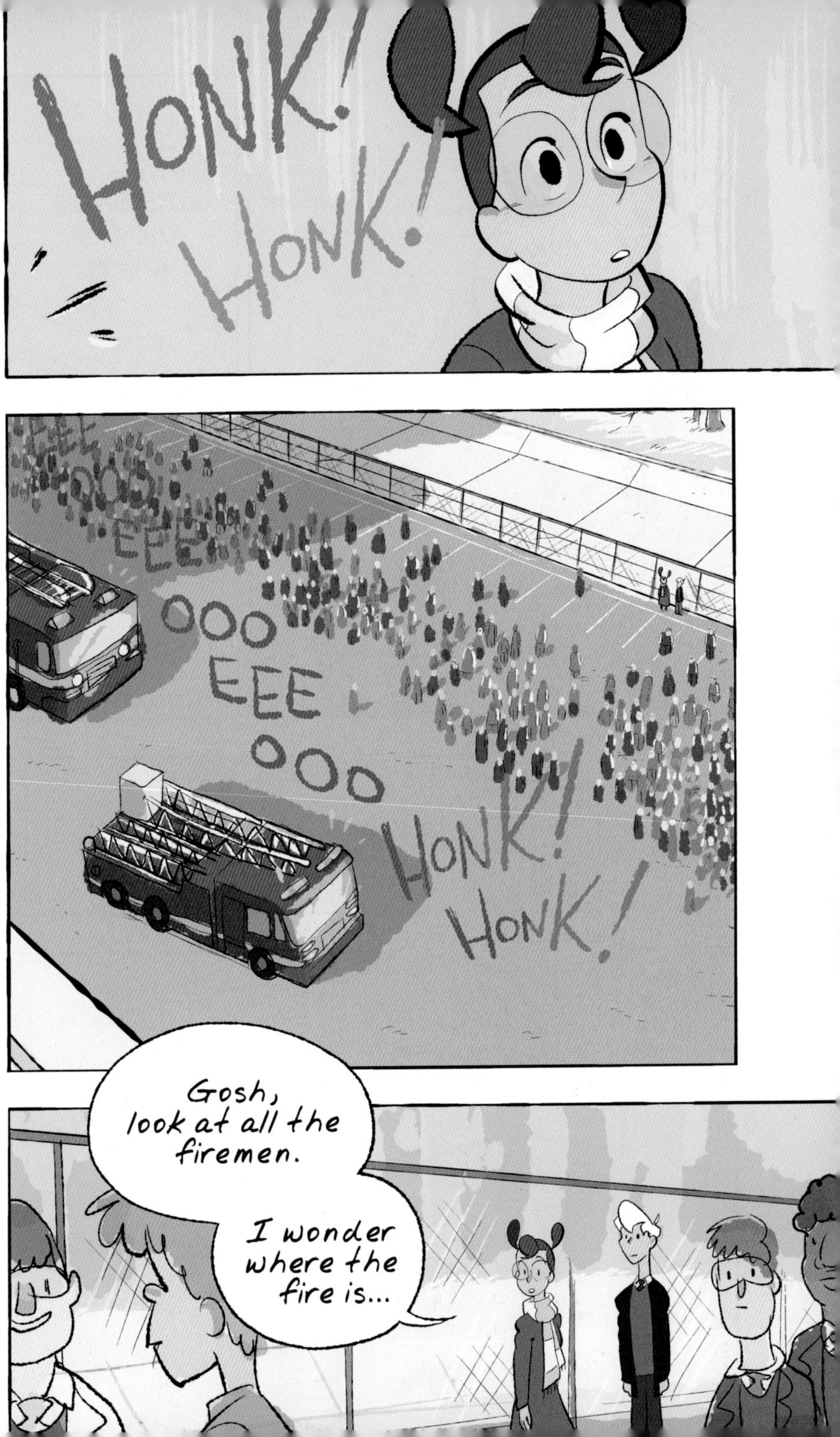
HONK! HONK!
EEE
OOO
EEE
OOO
EEE
OOO
HONK! HONK!
Gosh, look at all the firemen.
I wonder where the fire is...

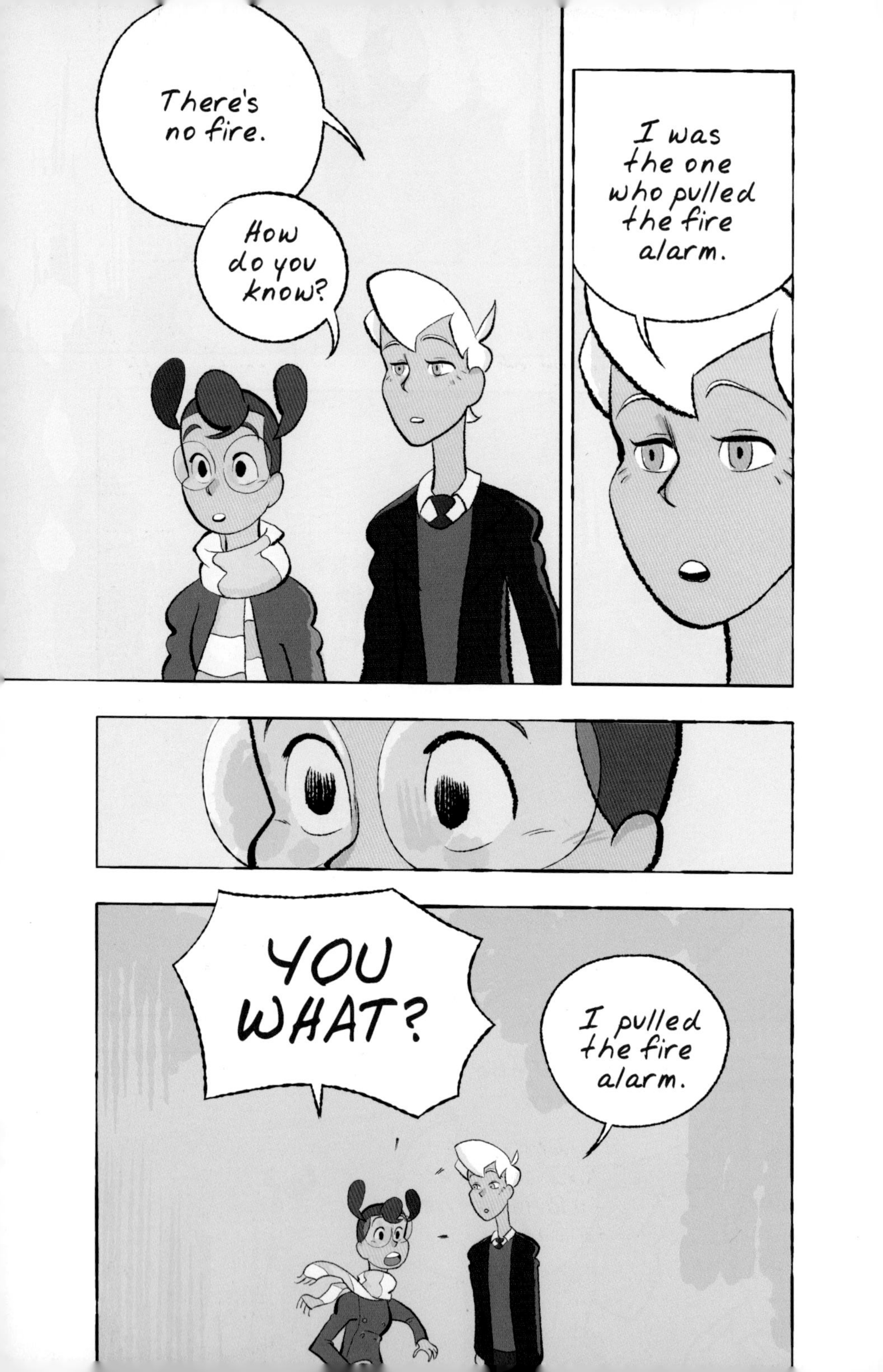
There's no fire.
How do you know?
I was the one who pulled the fire alarm.
YOU WHAT?
I pulled the fire alarm.

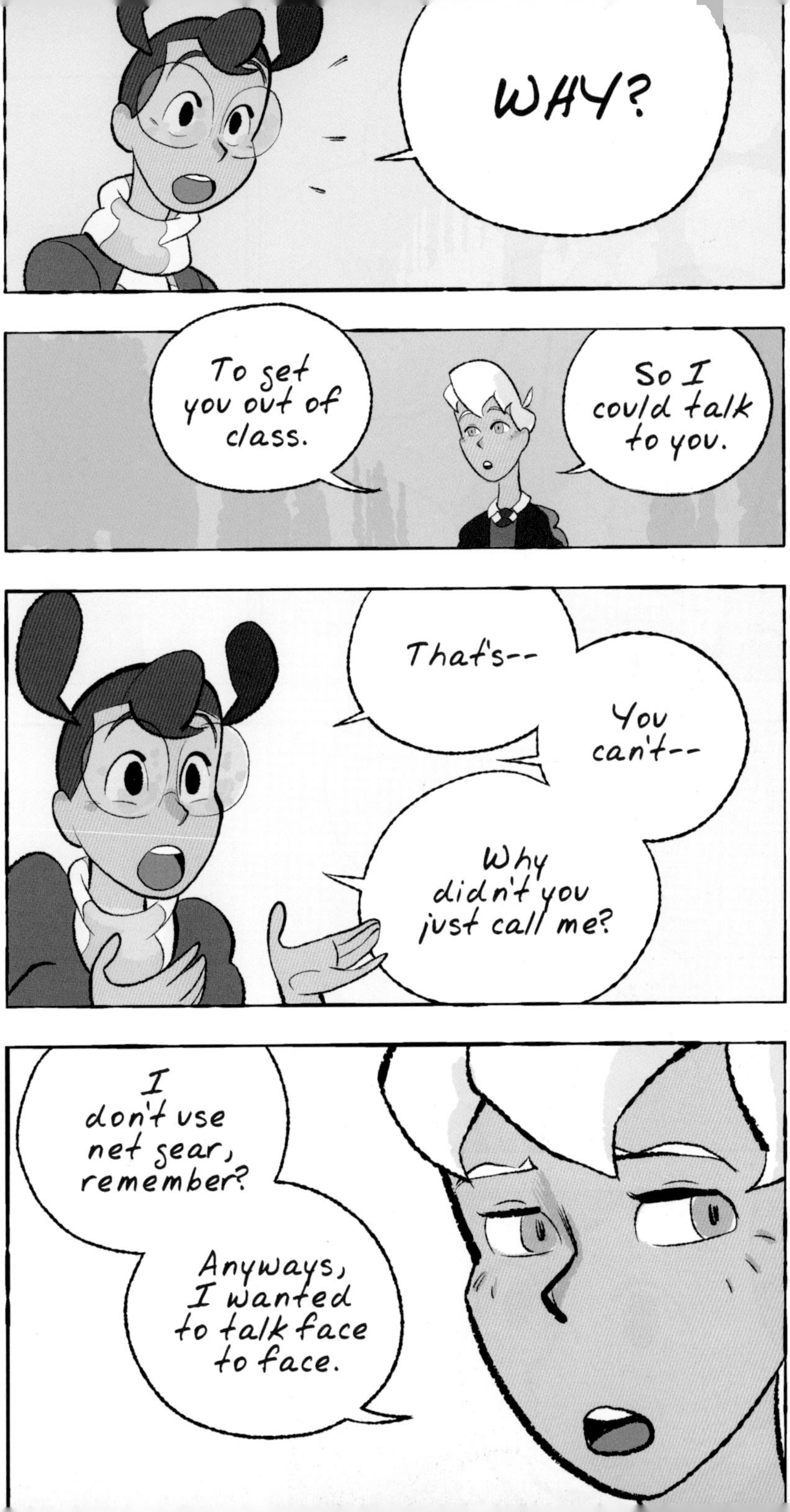
WHY?
To get you out of class.
So I could talk to you.
That's--
You can't--
Why didn't you just call me?
I don't use net gear, remember?
Anyways, I wanted to talk face to face.

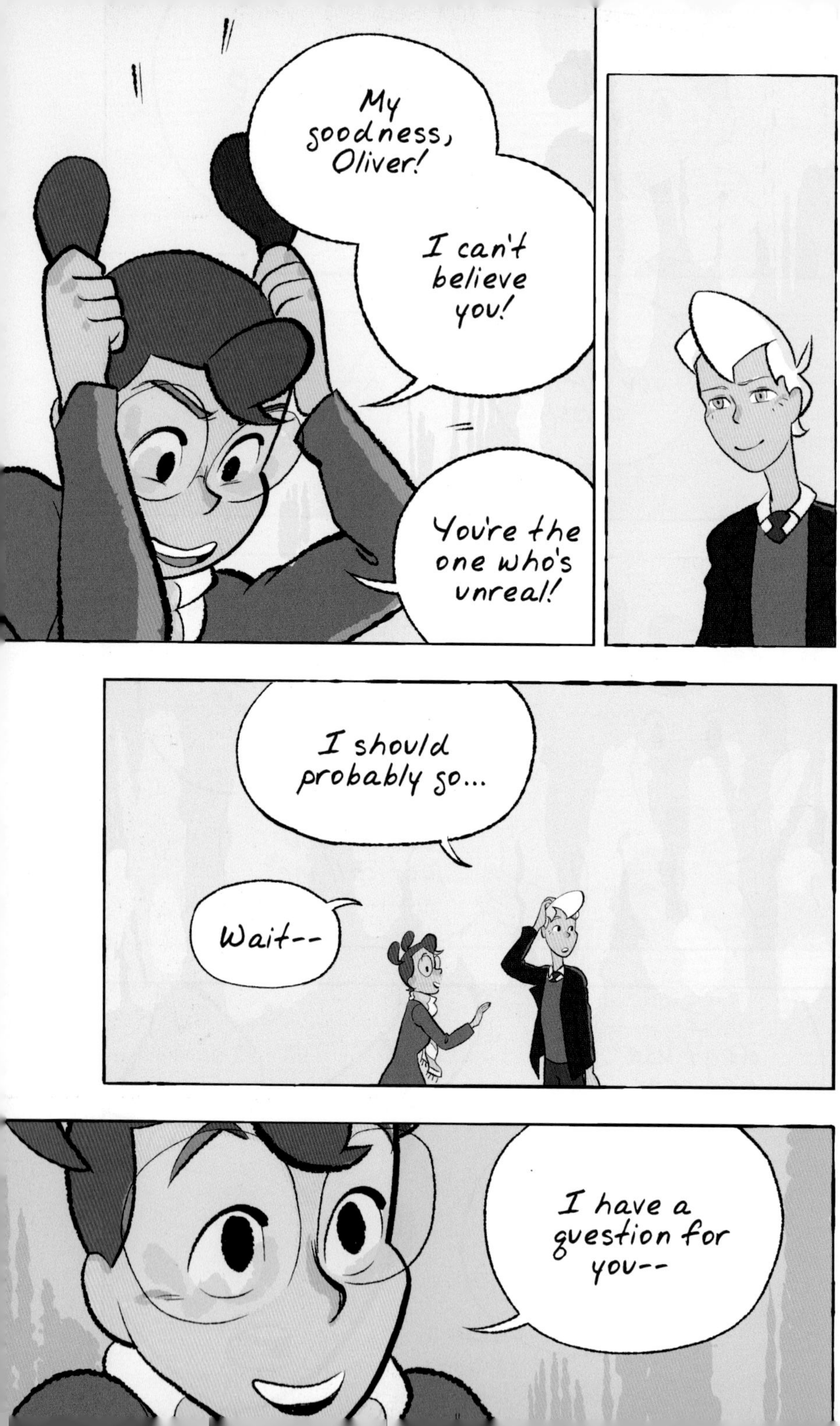
My goodness, Oliver!
I can't believe you!
You're the one who's unreal!
I should probably go...
Wait--
I have a question for you--

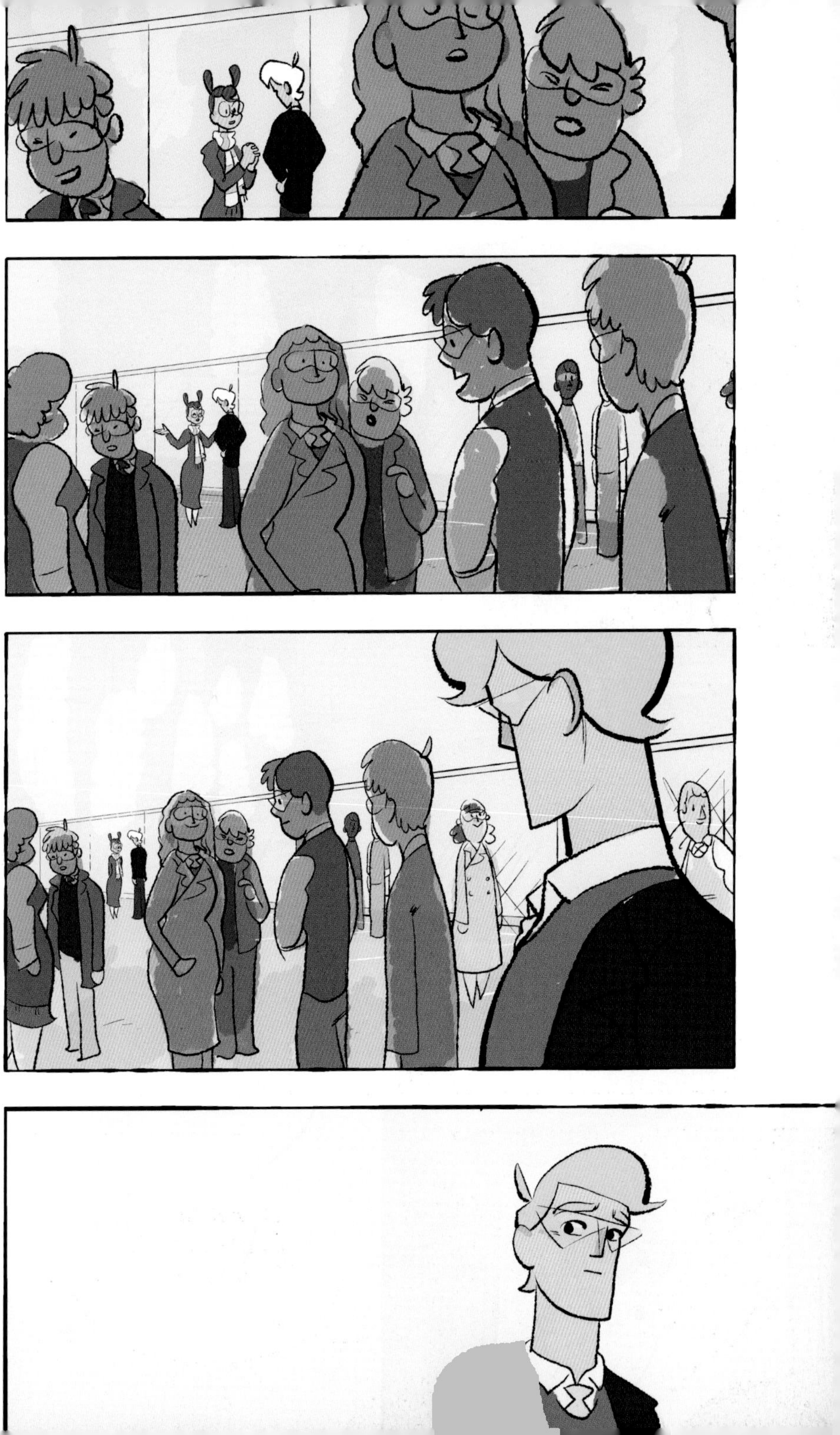

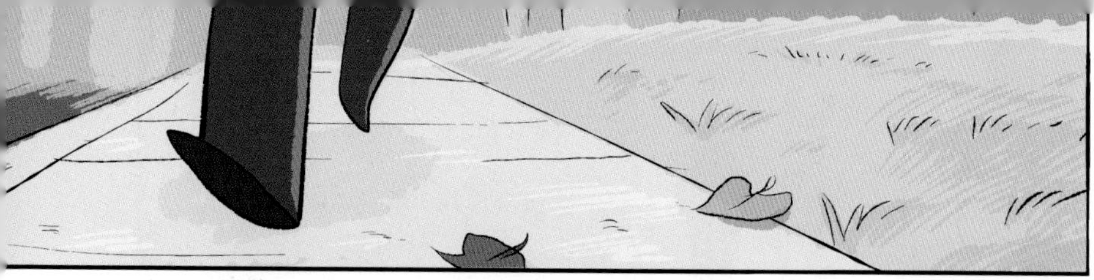

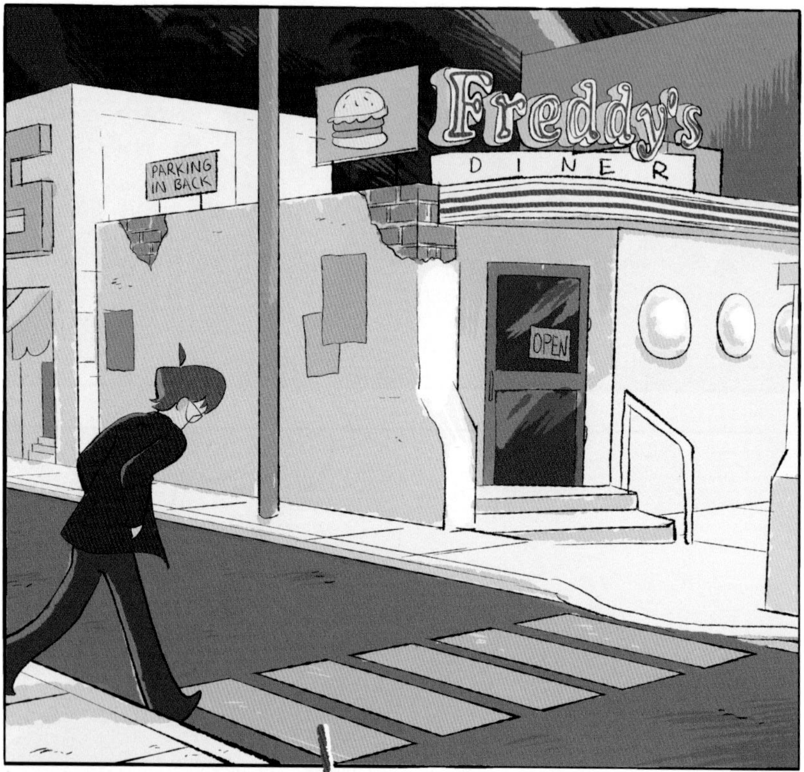
Freddy's
DINER
PARKING IN BACK
OPEN

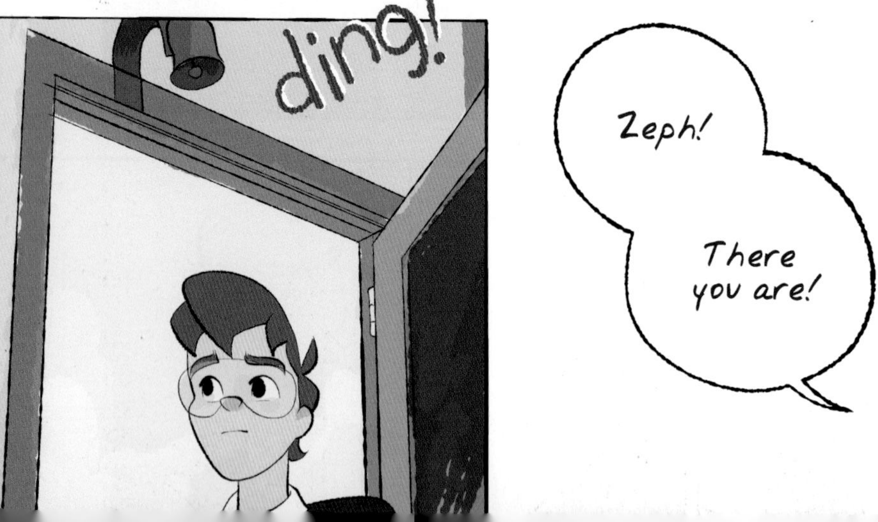
ding!
Zeph!
There you are!

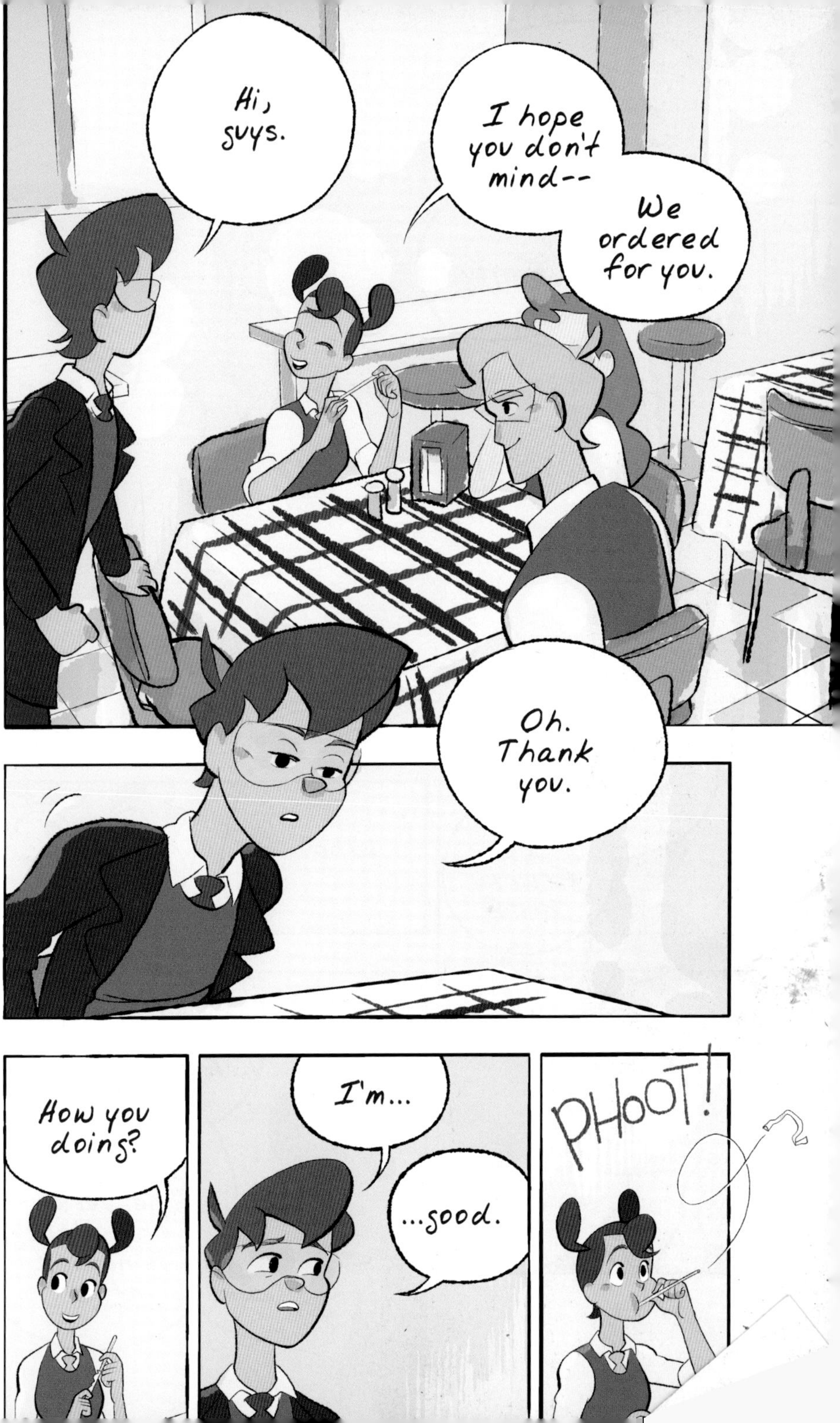
Hi, guys.
I hope you don't mind--
We ordered for you.
Oh. Thank you.
How you doing?
I'm...
...good.
PHOOT!

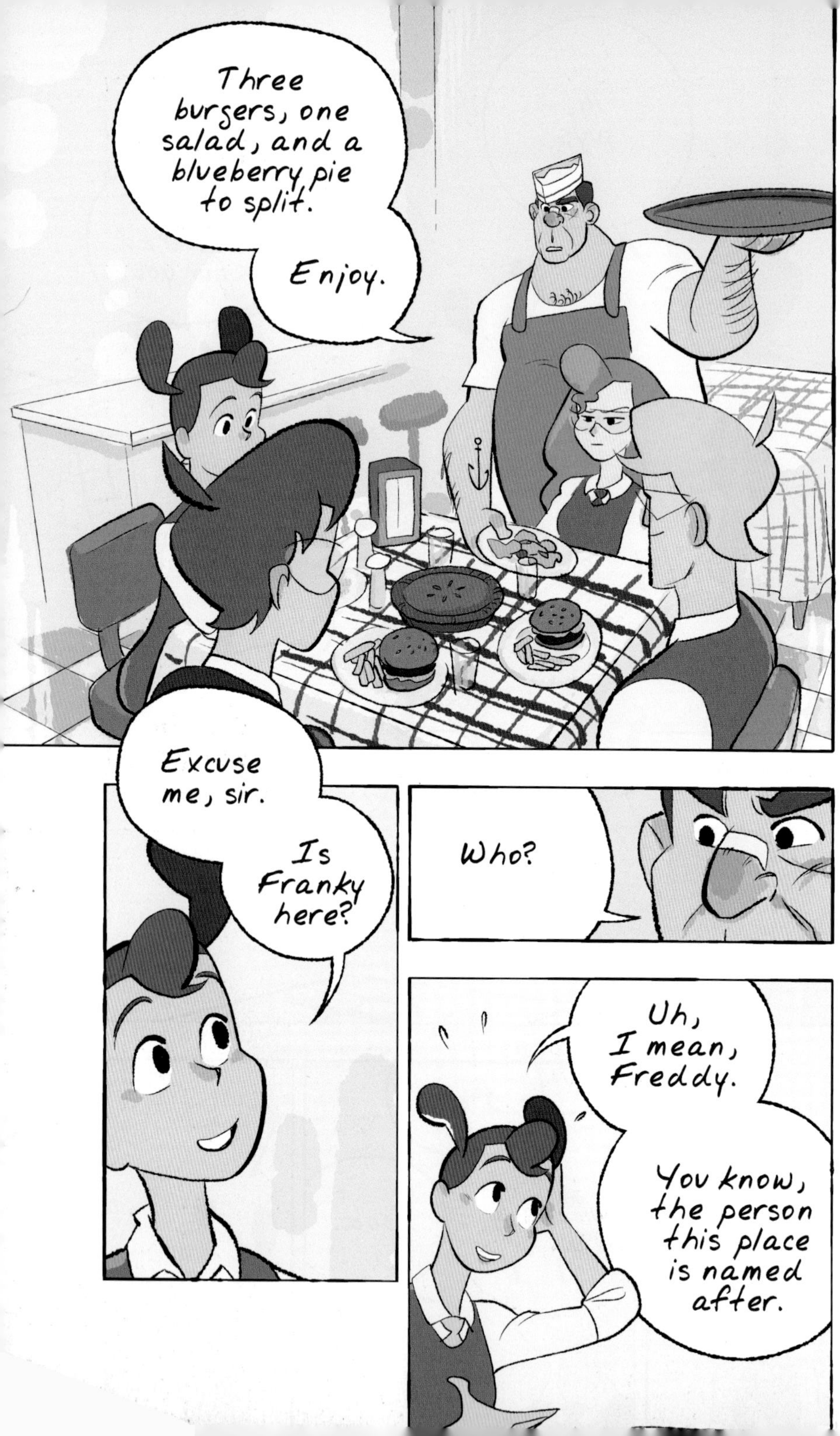
Three burgers, one salad, and a blueberry pie to split.
Enjoy.
Excuse me, sir.
Is Franky here?
Who?
Uh, I mean, Freddy.
You know, the person this place is named after.

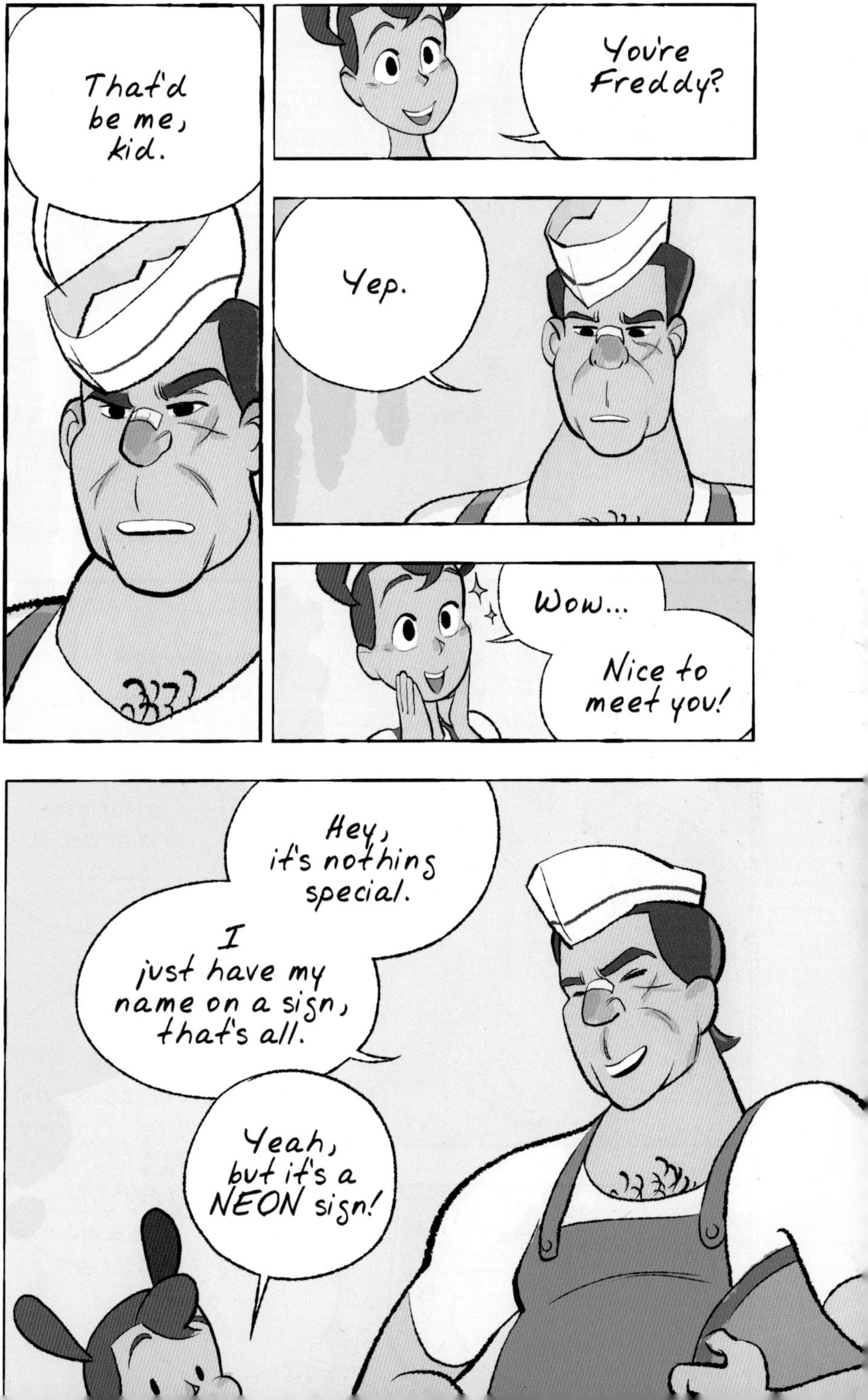
That'd be me, kid.
You're Freddy?
Yep.
Wow...
Nice to meet you!
Hey, it's nothing special.
I just have my name on a sign, that's all.
Yeah, but it's a NEON sign!

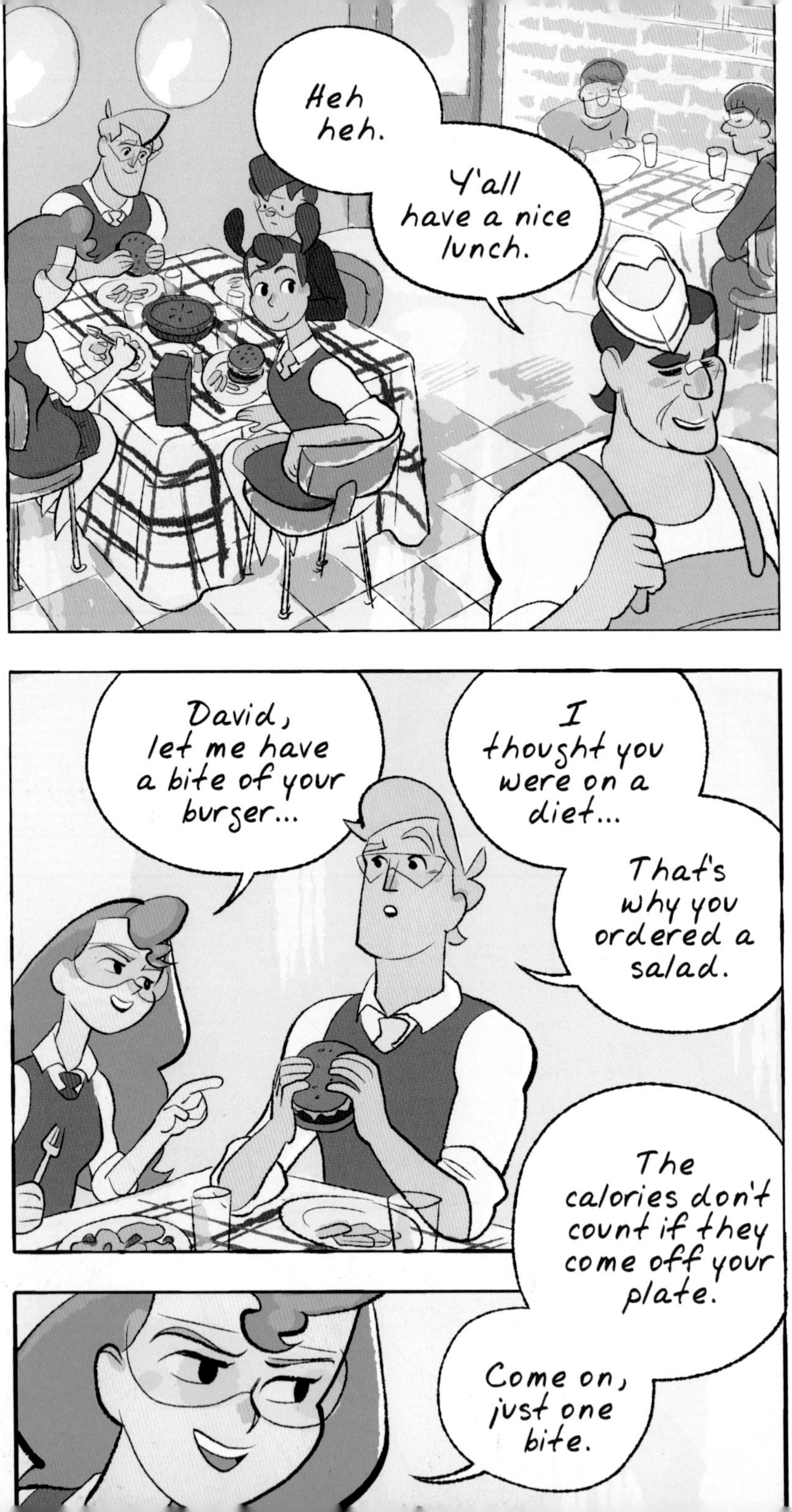
Heh heh.
Y'all have a nice lunch.
David, let me have a bite of your burger...
I thought you were on a diet...
That's why you ordered a salad.
The calories don't count if they come off your plate.
Come on, just one bite.

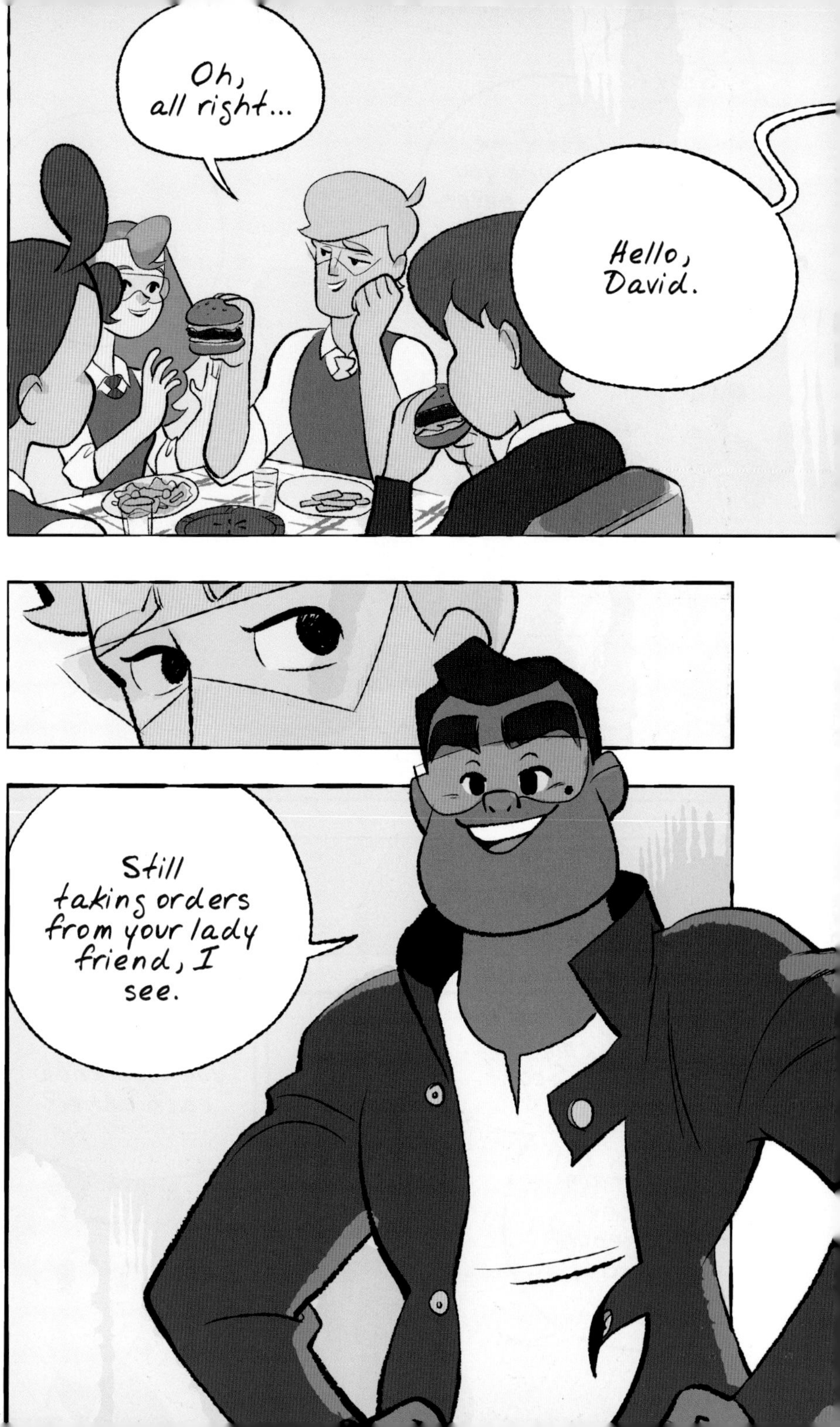
Oh, all right...
Hello, David.
Still taking orders from your lady friend, I see.

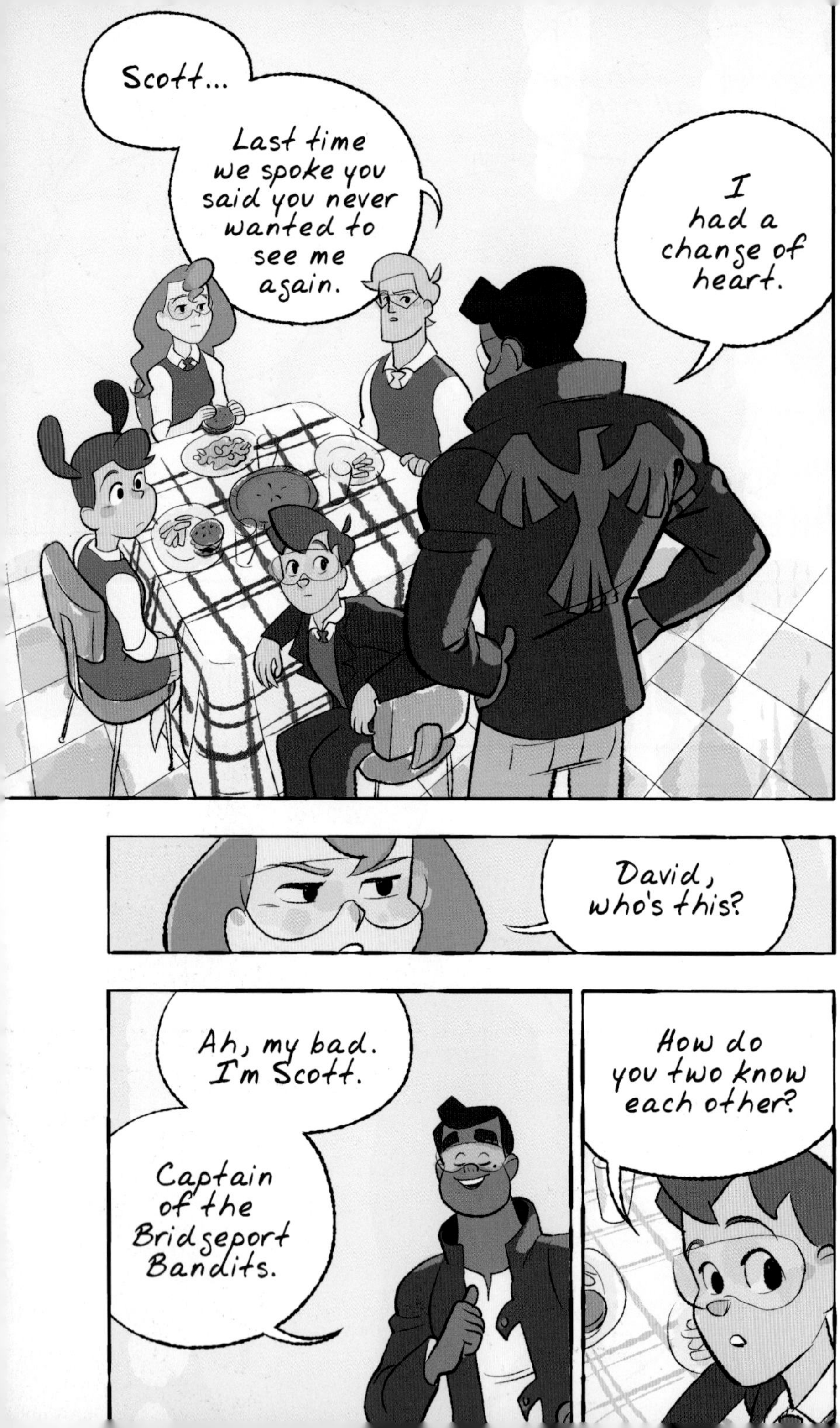
Scott...
Last time we spoke you said you never wanted to see me again.
I had a change of heart.
David, who's this?
Ah, my bad. I'm Scott.
Captain of the Bridgeport Bandits.
How do you two know each other?

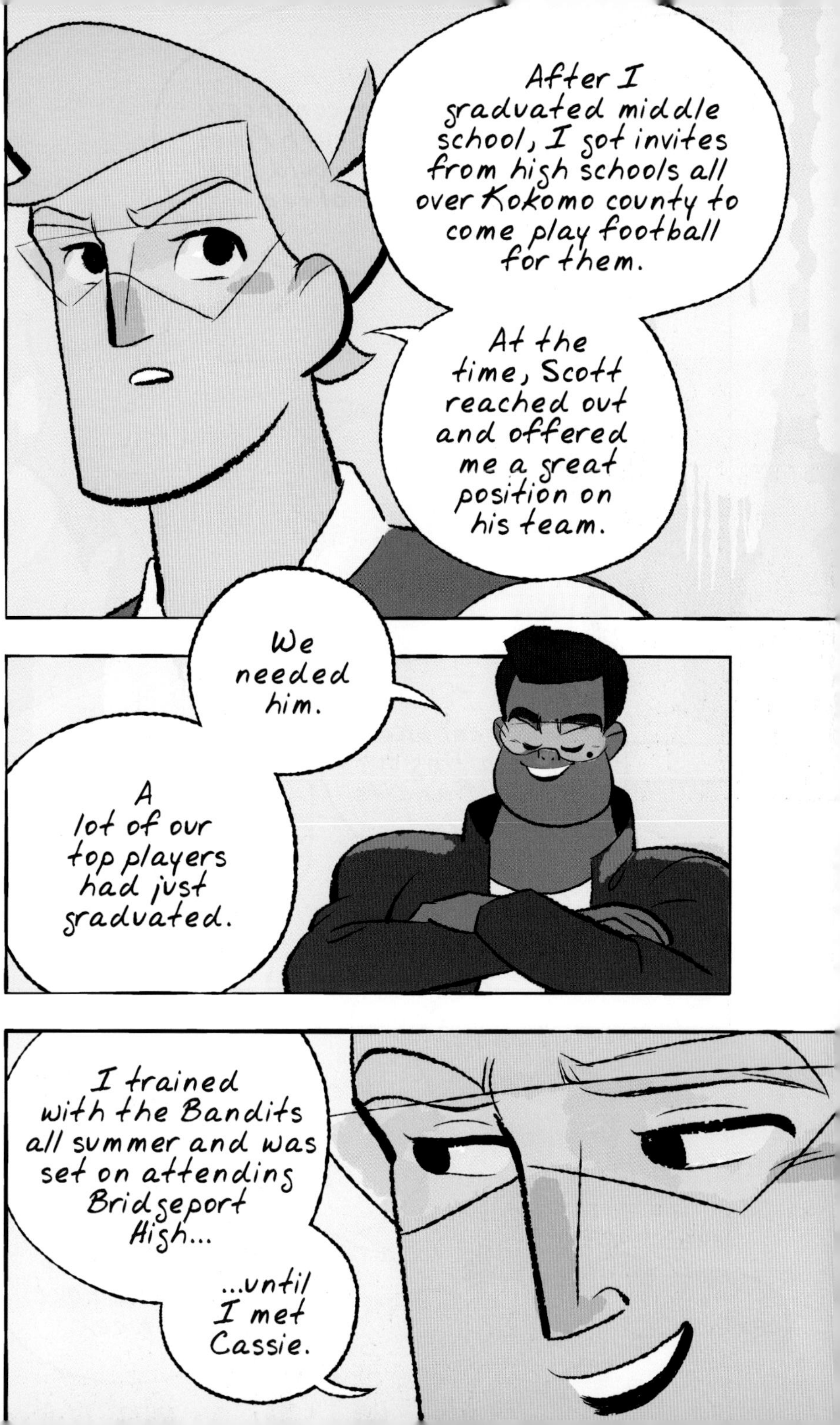
After I graduated middle school, I got invites from high schools all over Kokomo county to come play football for them.
At the time, Scott reached out and offered me a great position on his team.
We needed him.
A lot of our top players had just graduated.
I trained with the Bandits all summer and was set on attending Bridgeport High...
...until I met Cassie.

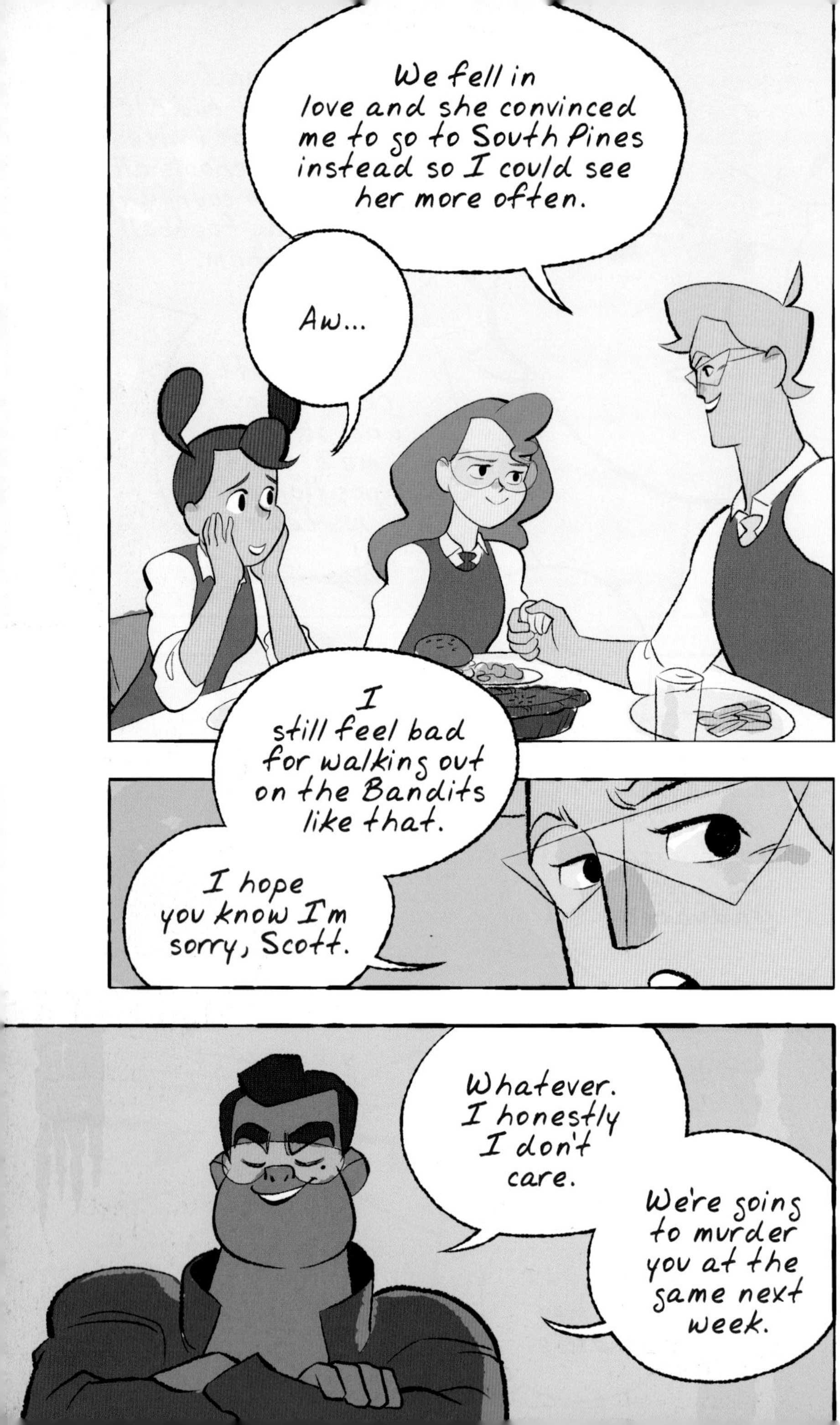
We fell in love and she convinced me to go to South Pines instead so I could see her more often.
Aw...
I still feel bad for walking out on the Bandits like that.
I hope you know I'm sorry, Scott.
Whatever. I honestly I don't care.
We're going to murder you at the same next week.

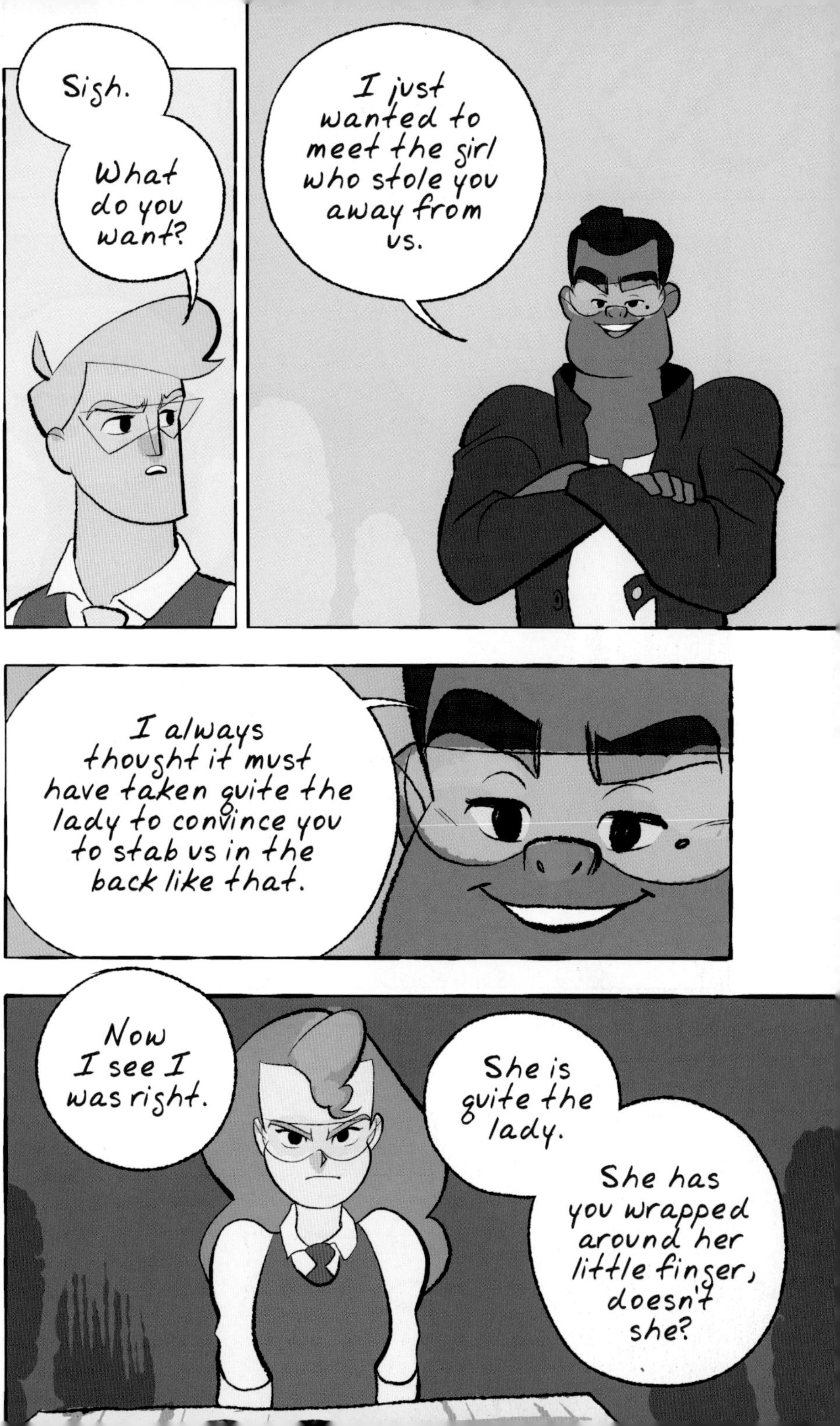
Sigh.
What do you want?
I just wanted to meet the girl who stole you away from us.
I always thought it must have taken quite the lady to convince you to stab us in the back like that.
Now I see I was right.
She is quite the lady.
She has you wrapped around her little finger, doesn't she?

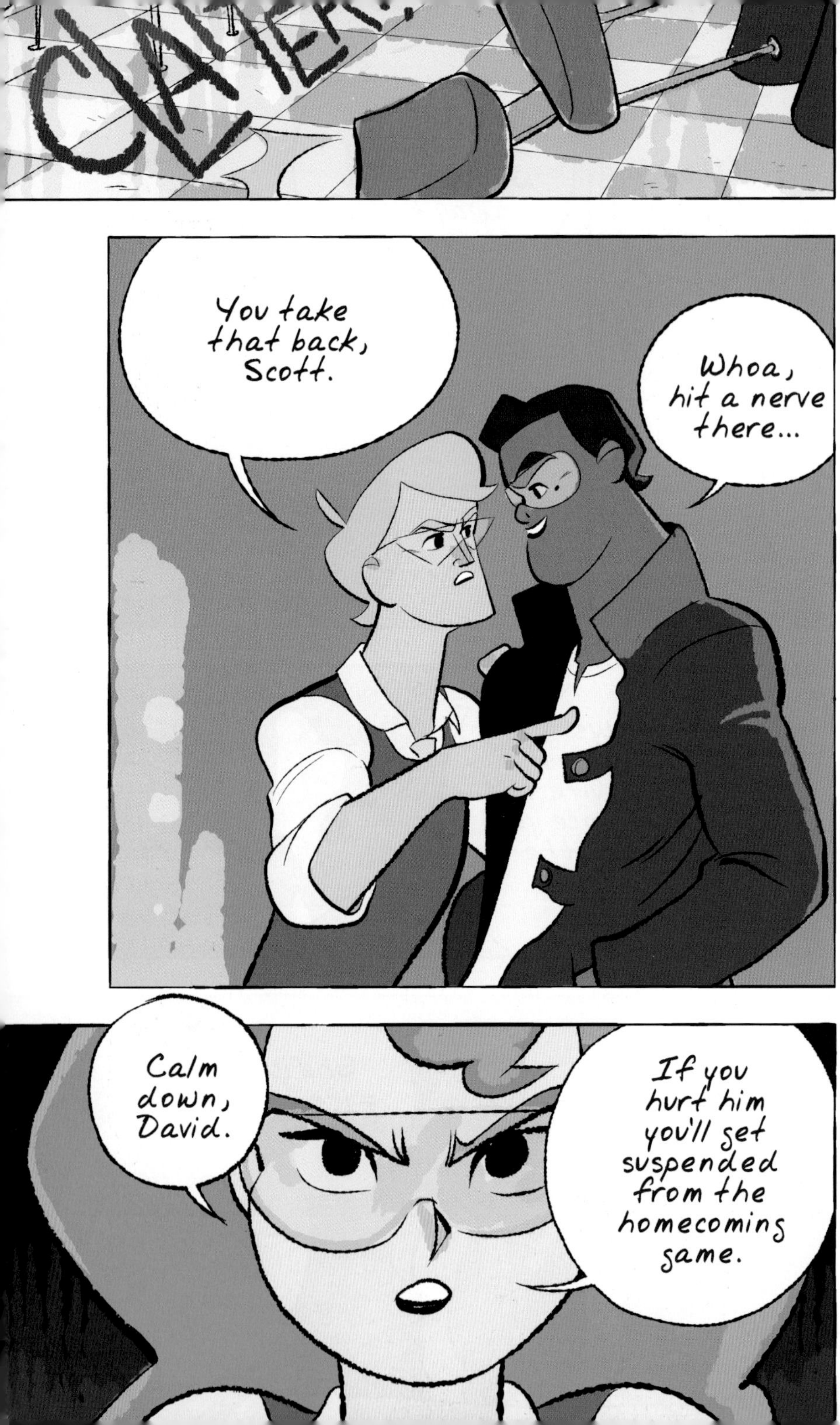
CLATTER!
You take that back, Scott.
Whoa, hit a nerve there...
Calm down, David.
If you hurt him you'll get suspended from the homecoming game.

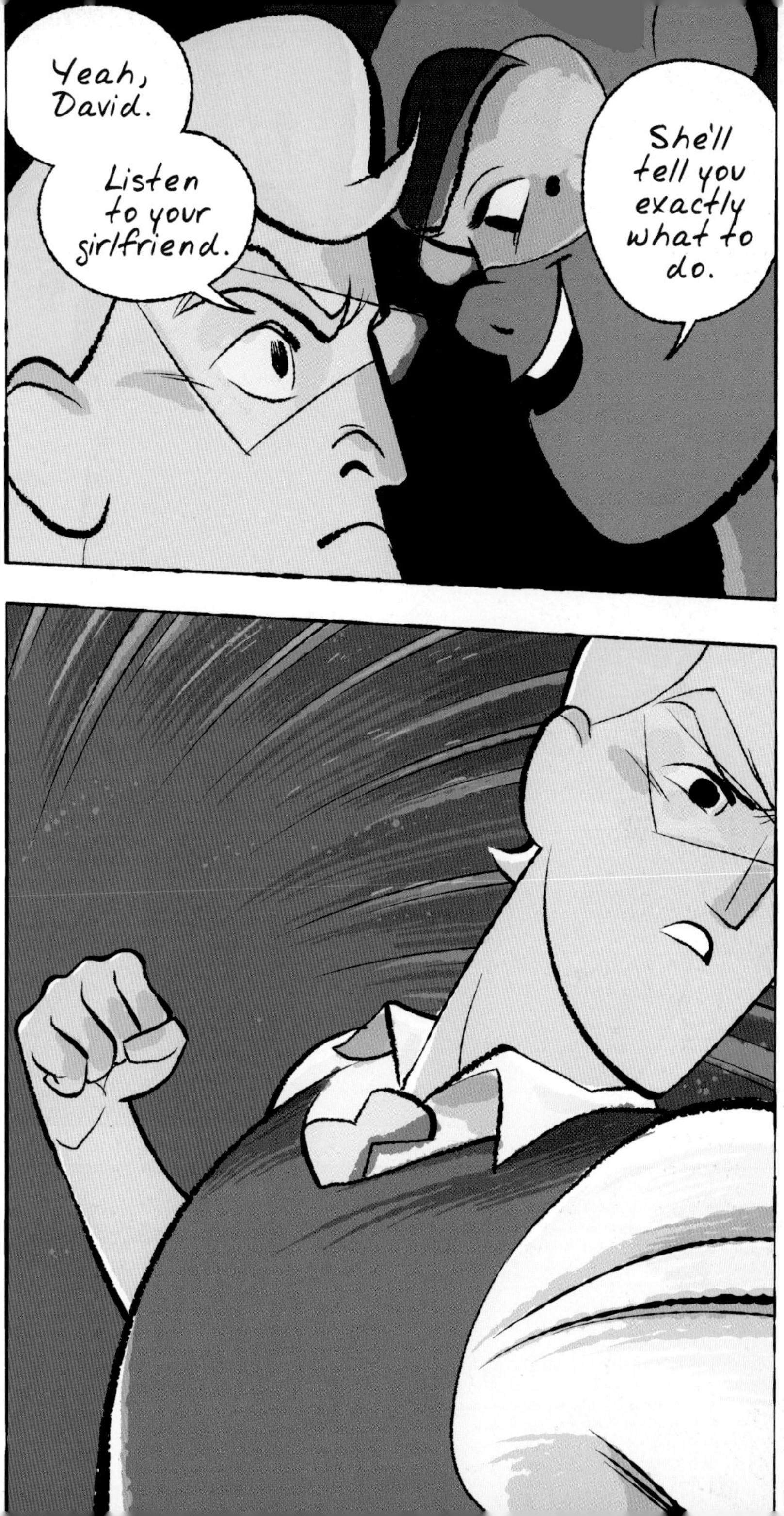
Yeah, David.
Listen to your girlfriend.
She'll tell you exactly what to do.

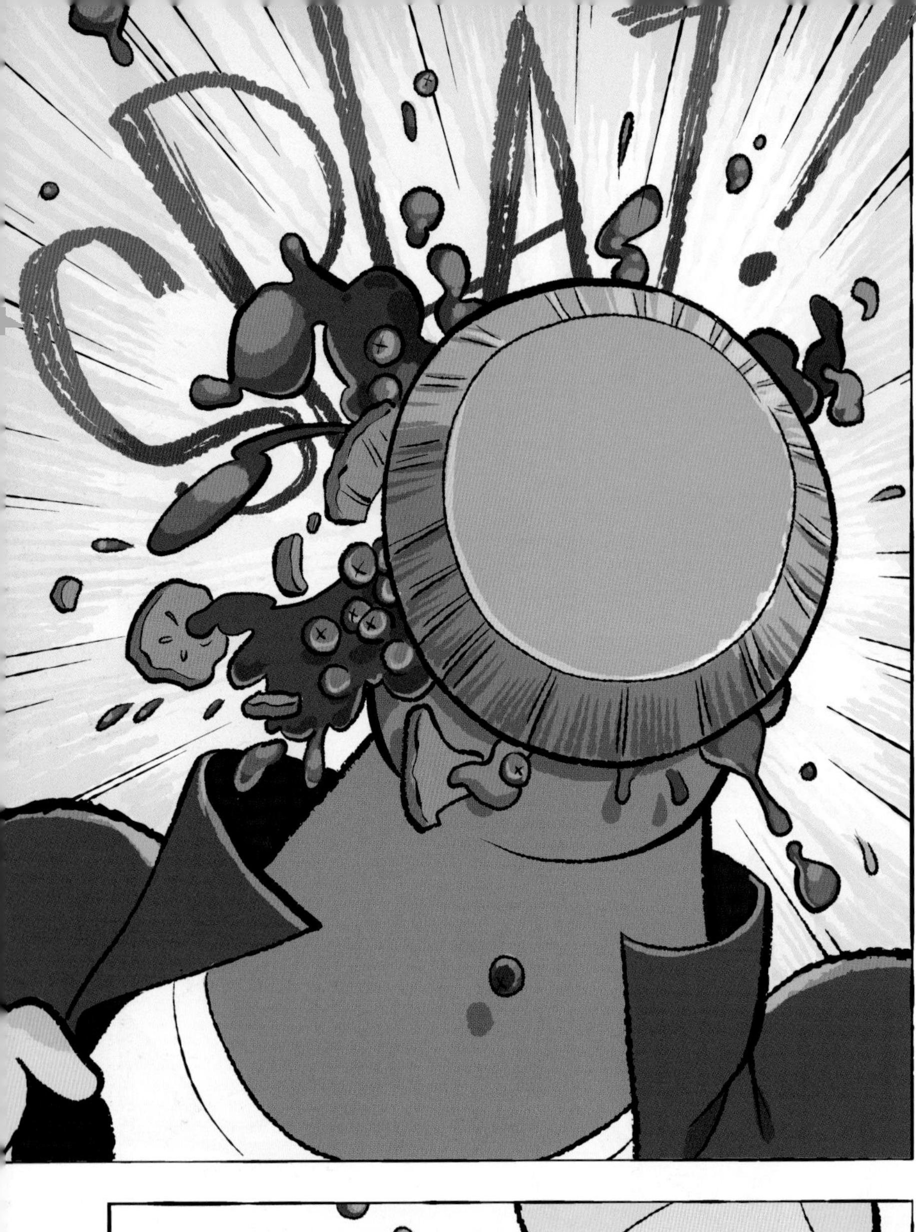
SPLAT!

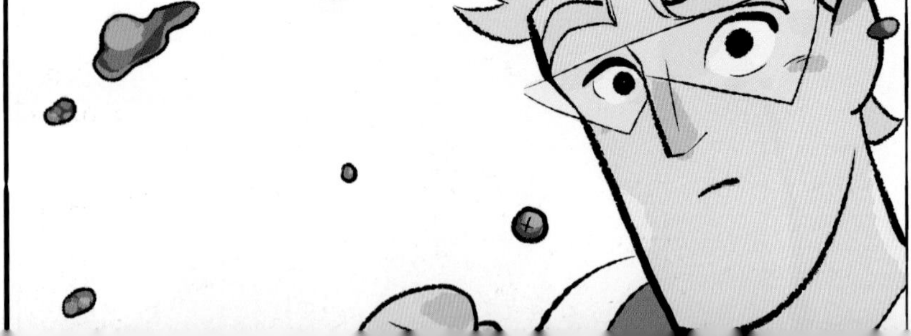

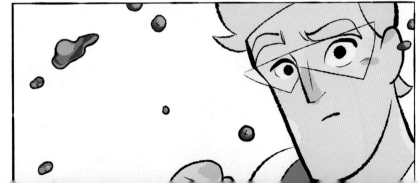

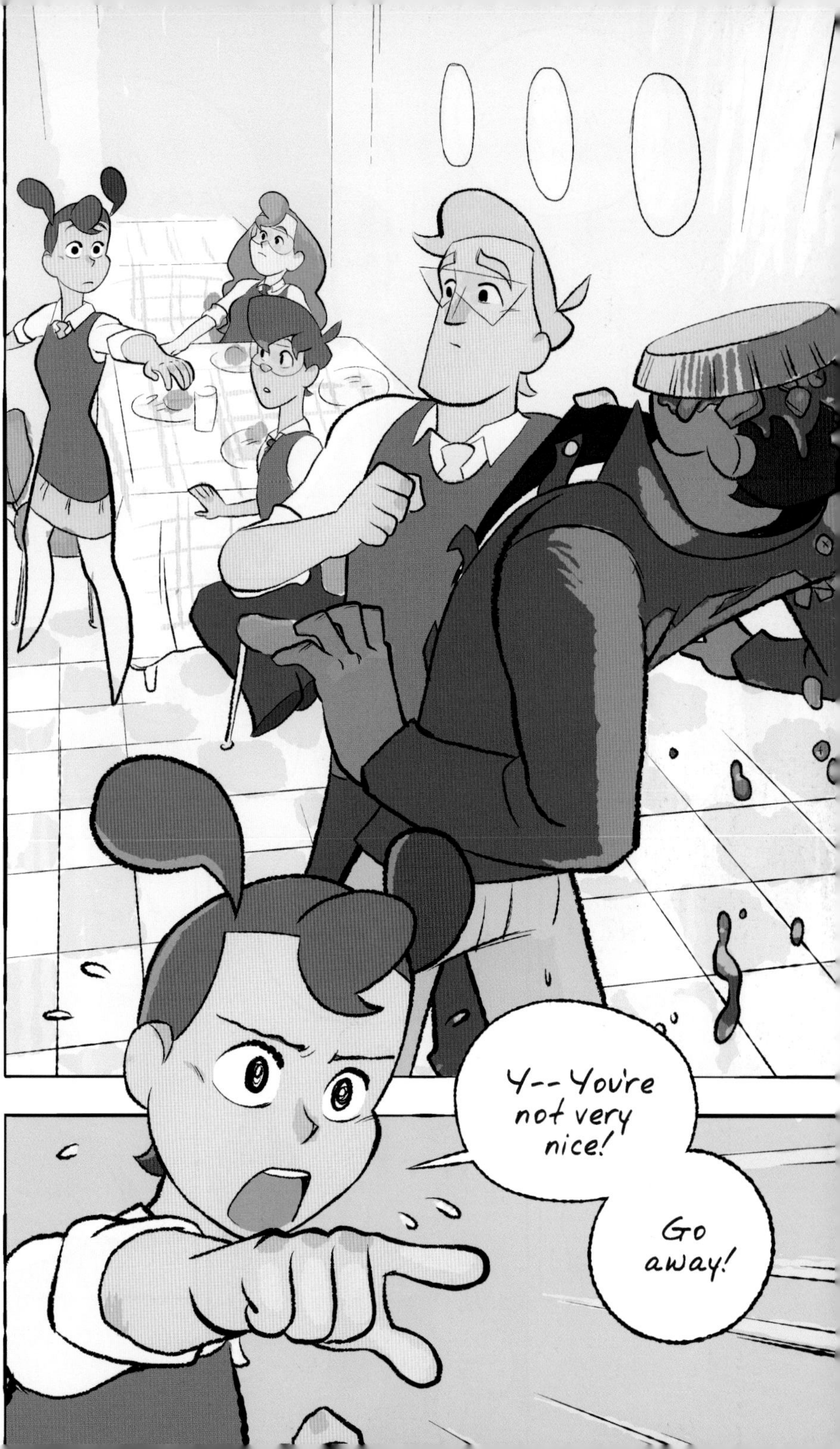
Y--You're not very nice!
Go away!

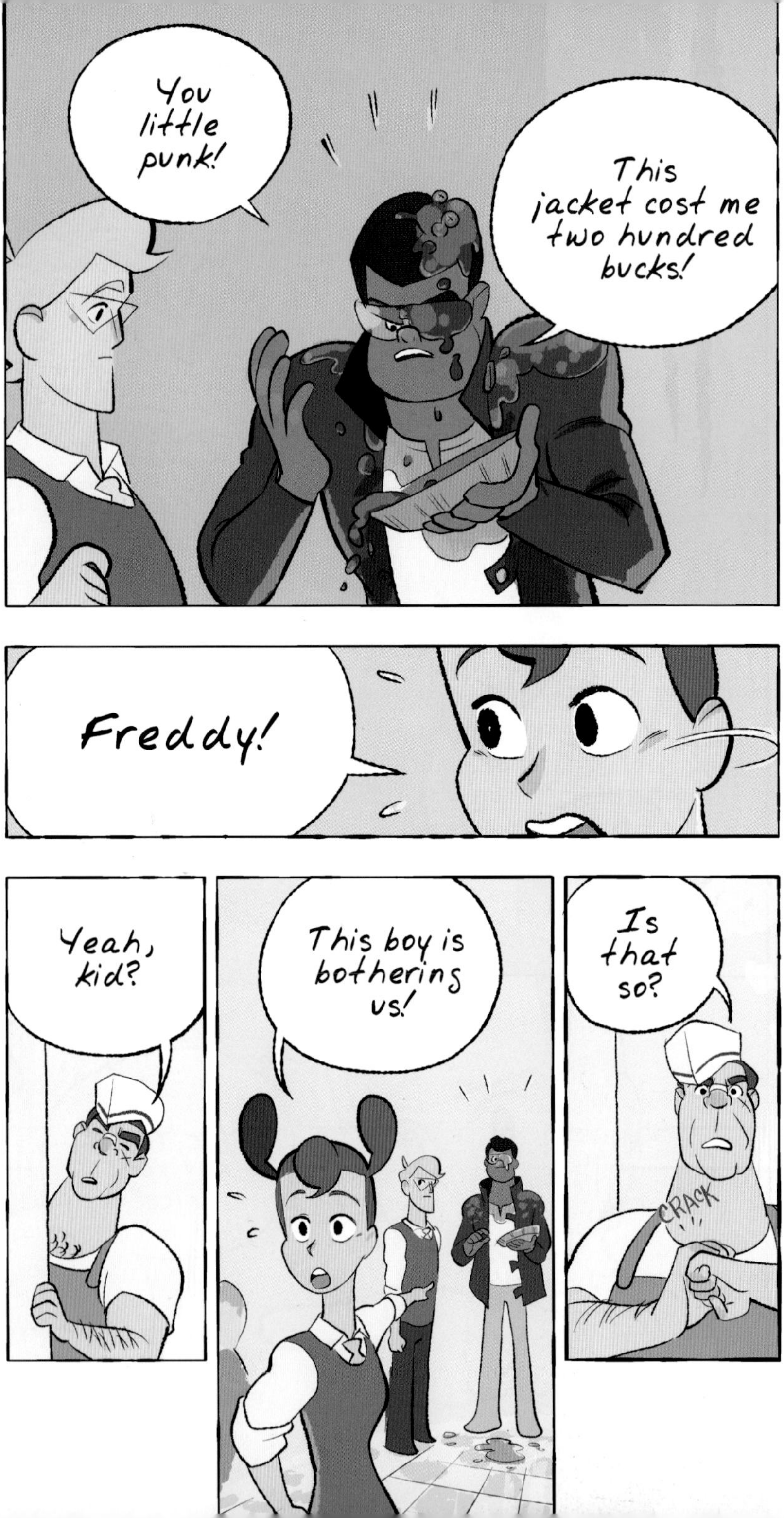
You little punk!
This jacket cost me two hundred bucks!
Freddy!
Yeah, kid?
This boy is bothering us!
Is that so?
CRACK

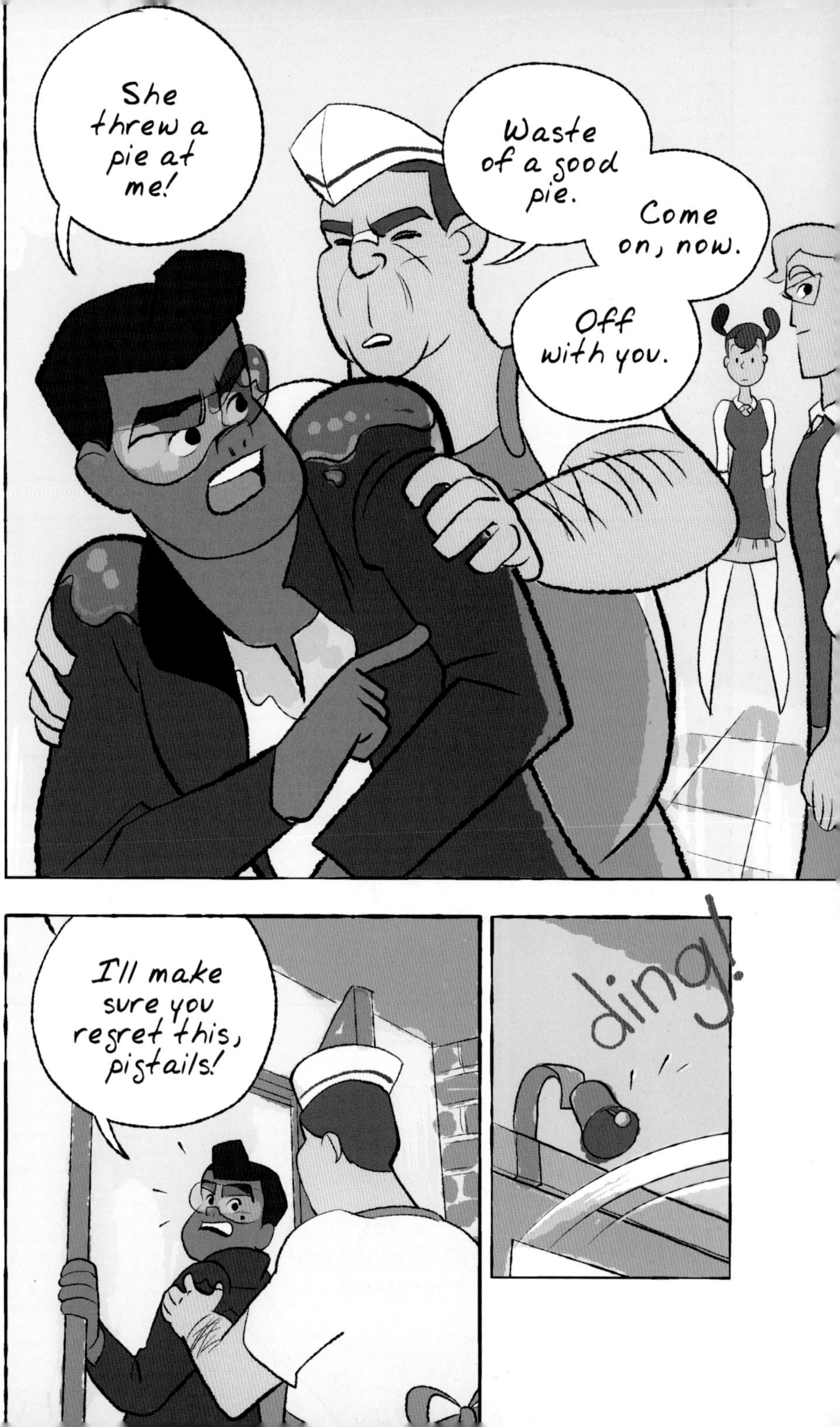
She threw a pie at me!
Waste of a good pie.
Come on, now.
Off with you.
I'll make sure you regret this, pigtails!
ding!

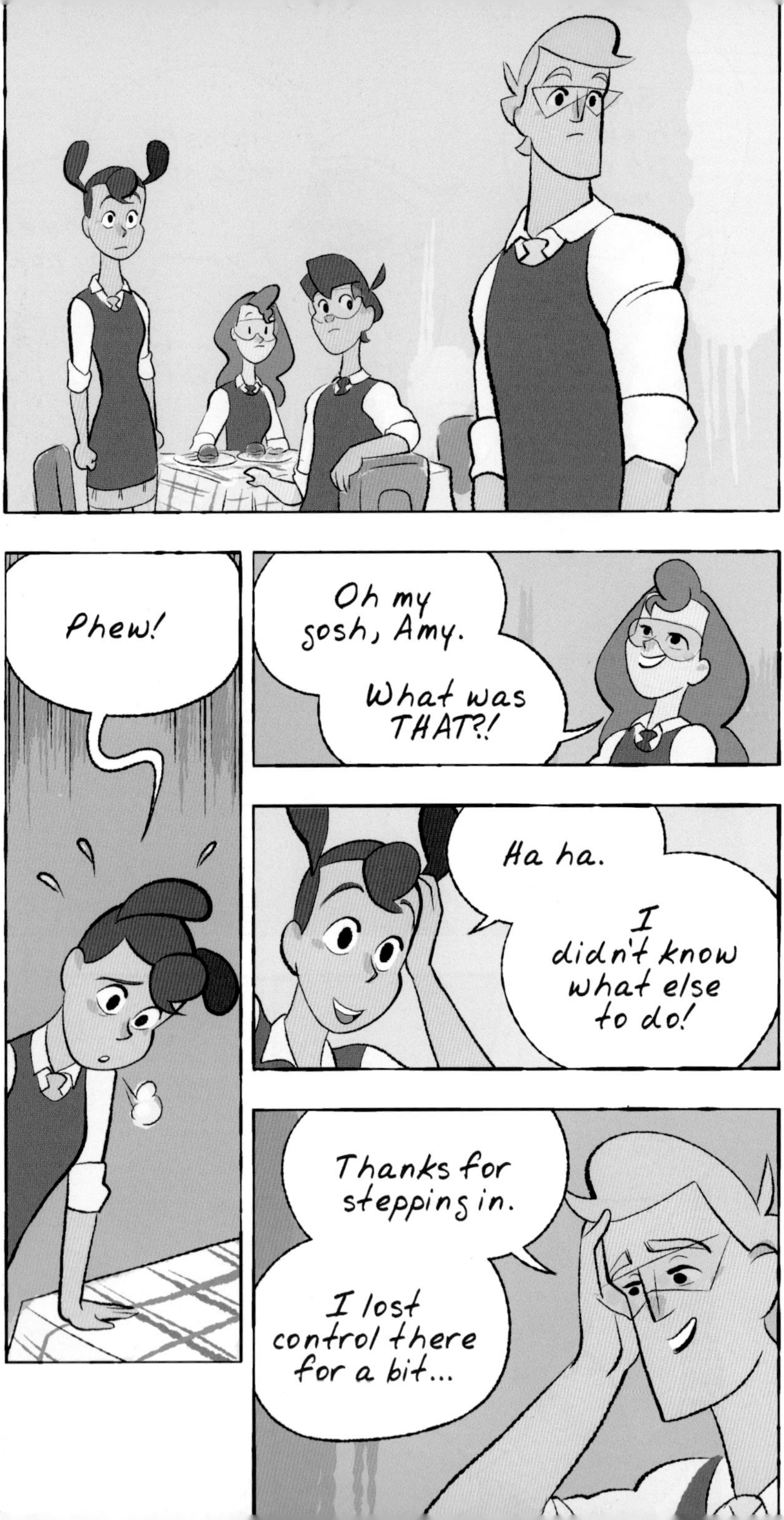
Phew!
Oh my gosh, Amy.
What was THAT?!
Ha ha.
I didn't know what else to do!
Thanks for stepping in.
I lost control there for a bit...

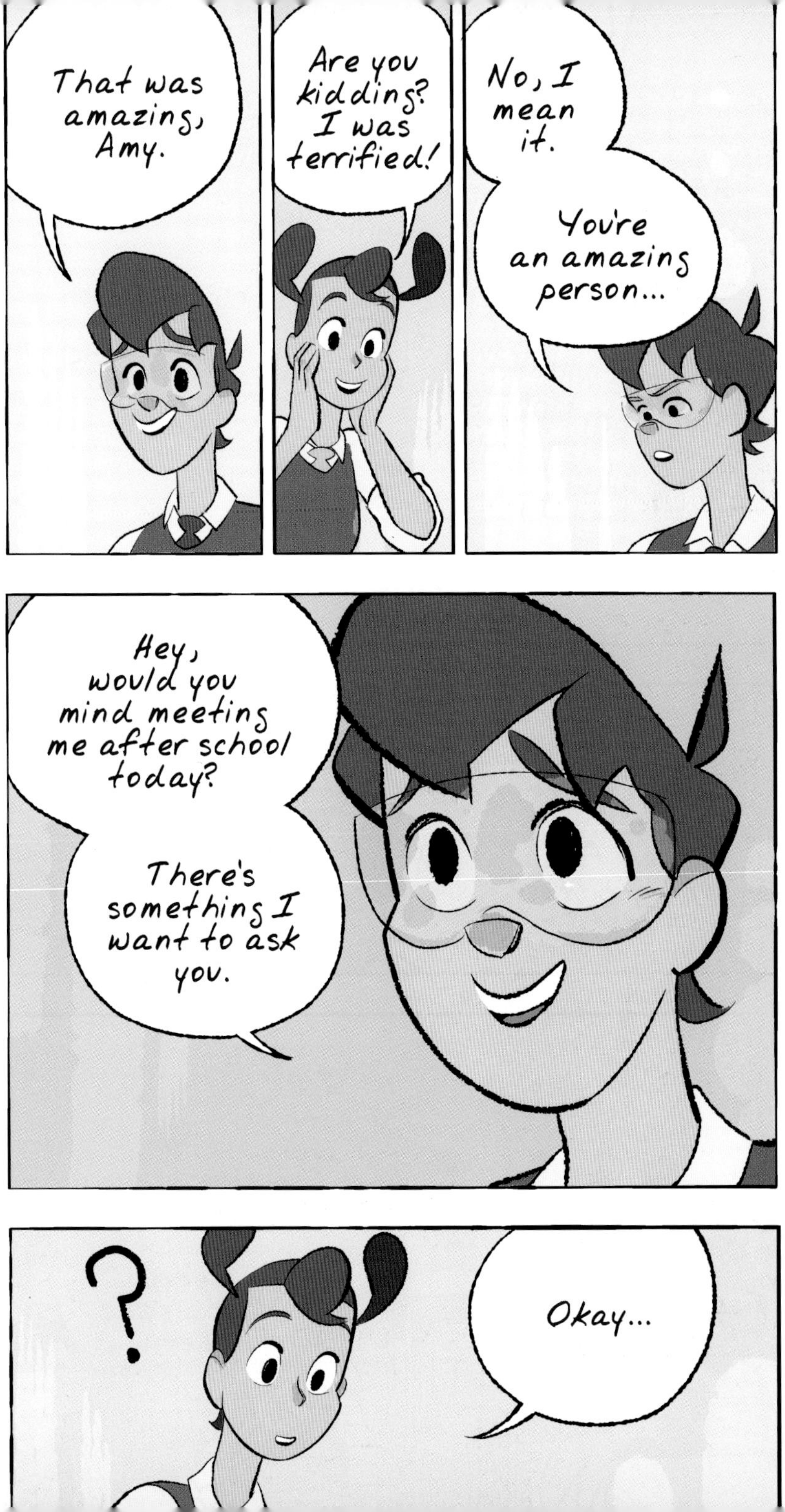
That was amazing, Amy.
Are you kidding? I was terrified!
No, I mean it.
You're an amazing person...
Hey, would you mind meeting me after school today?
There's something I want to ask you.
?
Okay...

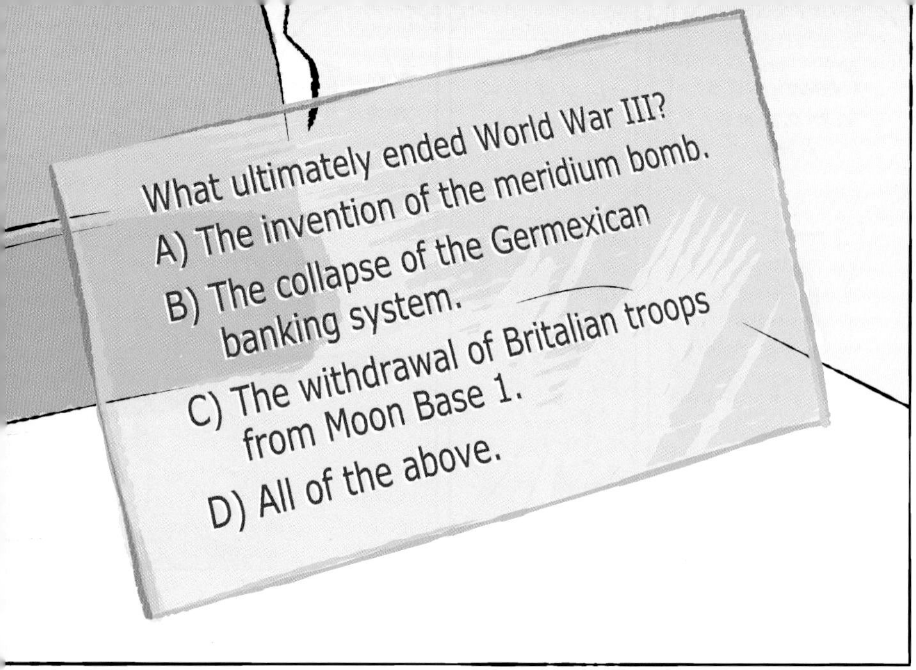
What ultimately ended World War III?
A) The invention of the meridium bomb.
B) The collapse of the Germexican banking system.
C) The withdrawal of Britalian troops from Moon Base 1.
D) All of the above.

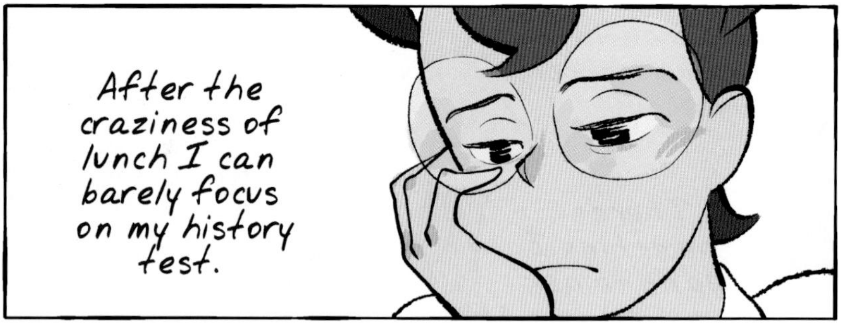
After the craziness of lunch I can barely focus on my history test.

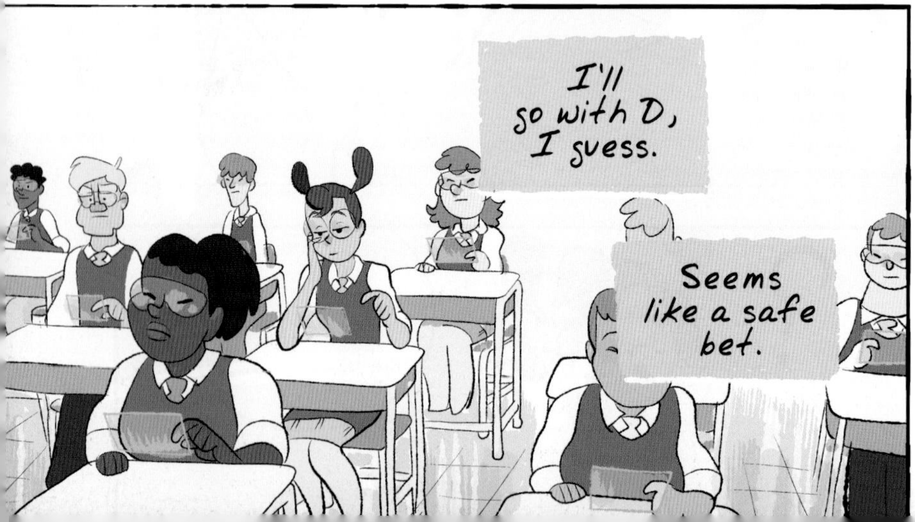
I'll go with D, I guess.
Seems like a safe bet.

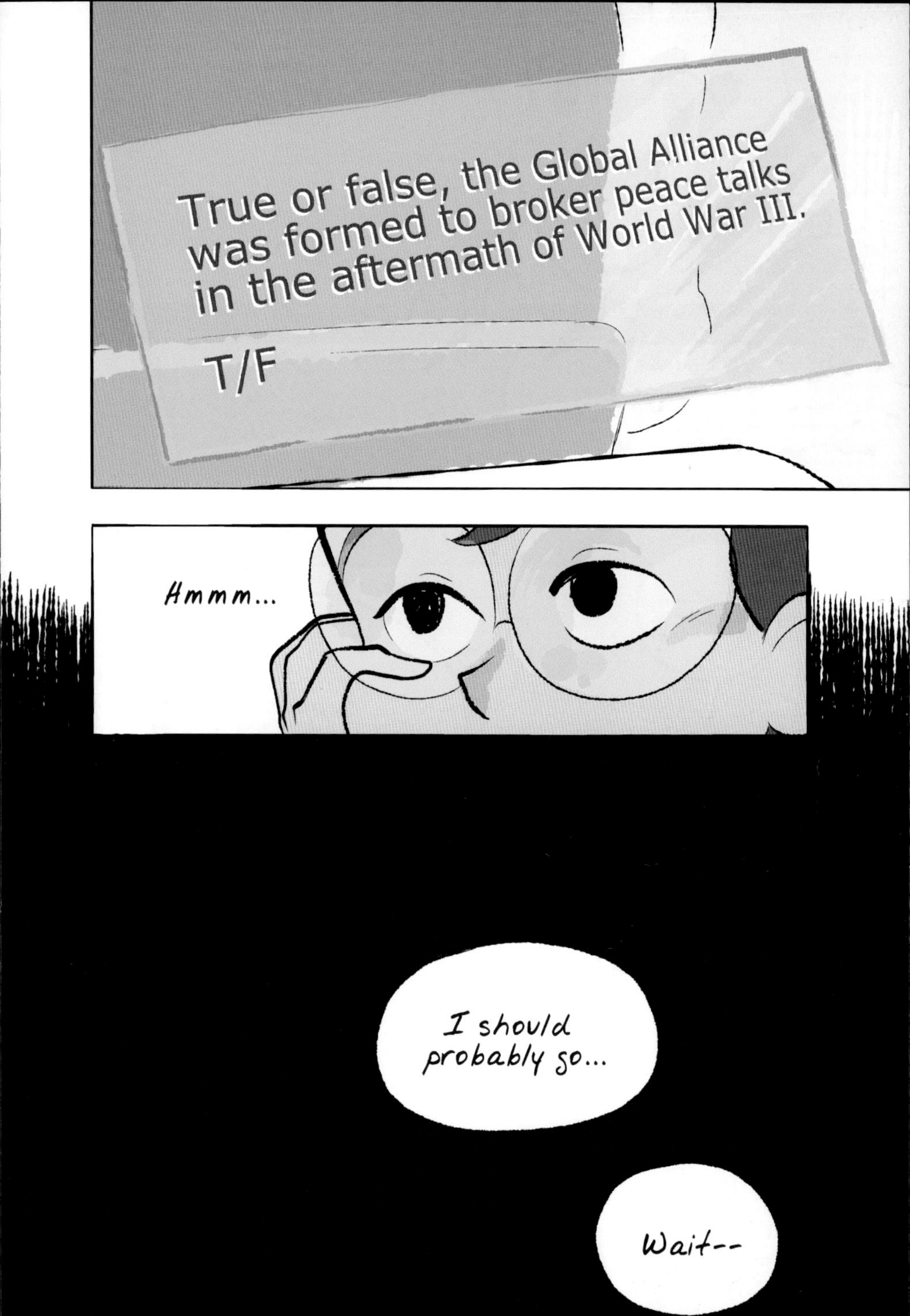
True or false, the Global Alliance was formed to broker peace talks in the aftermath of World War III.
T/F
Hmmm...
I should probably go...
Wait--

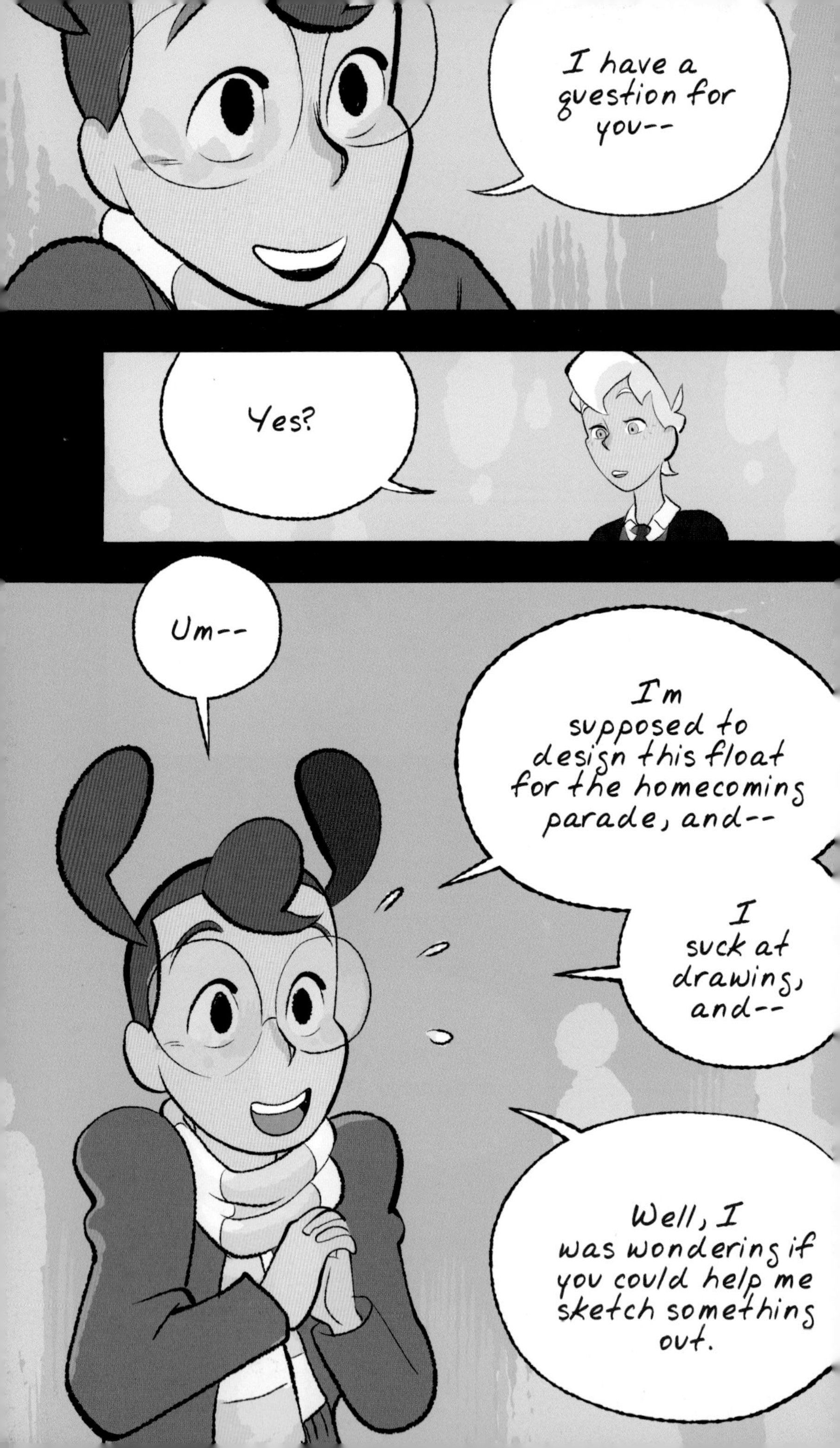
I have a question for you--
Yes?
Um--
I'm supposed to design this float for the homecoming parade, and--
I suck at drawing, and--
Well, I was wondering if you could help me sketch something out.

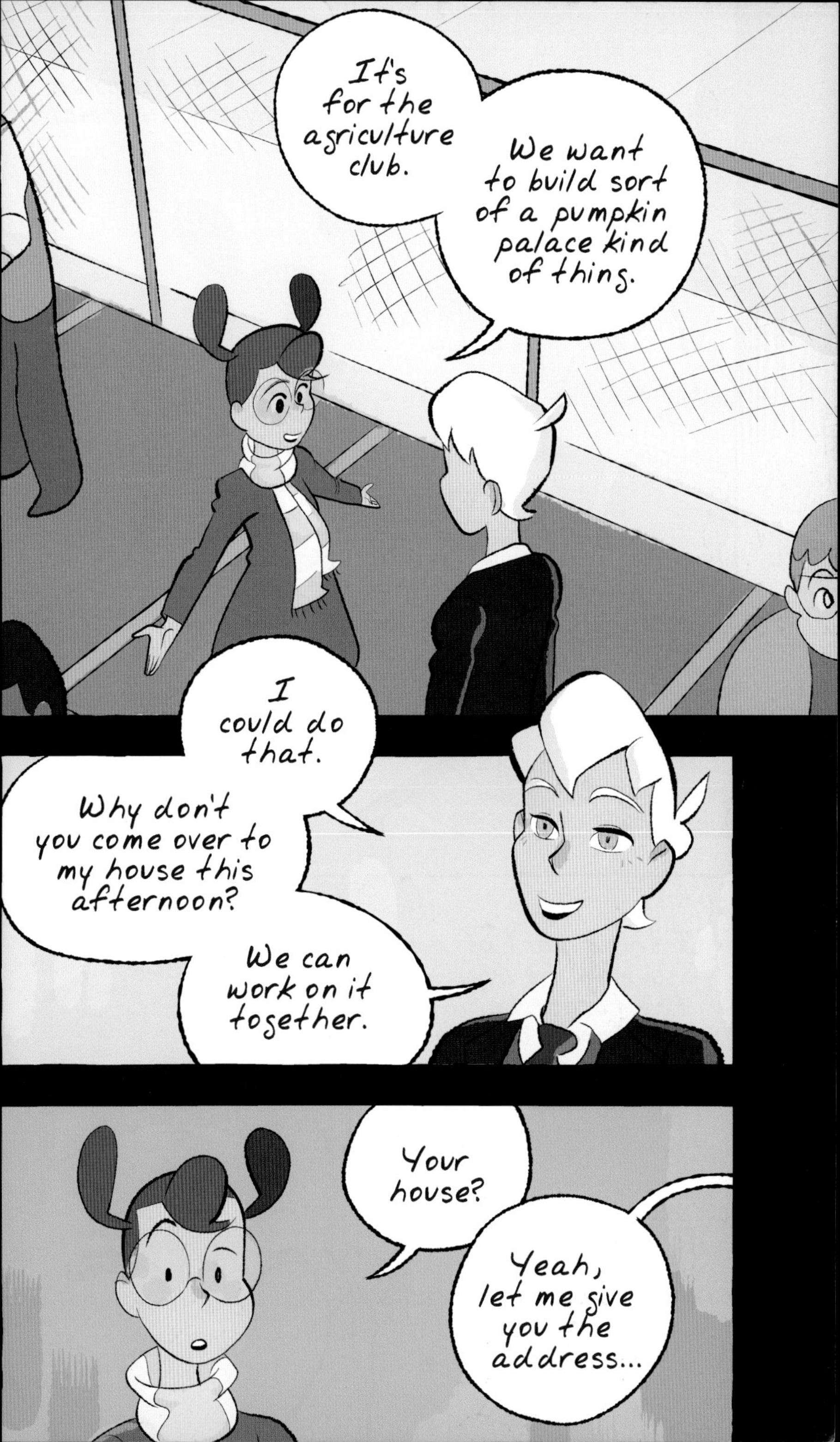
It's for the agriculture club.
We want to build sort of a pumpkin palace kind of thing.
I could do that.
Why don't you come over to my house this afternoon?
We can work on it together.
Your house?
Yeah, let me give you the address...

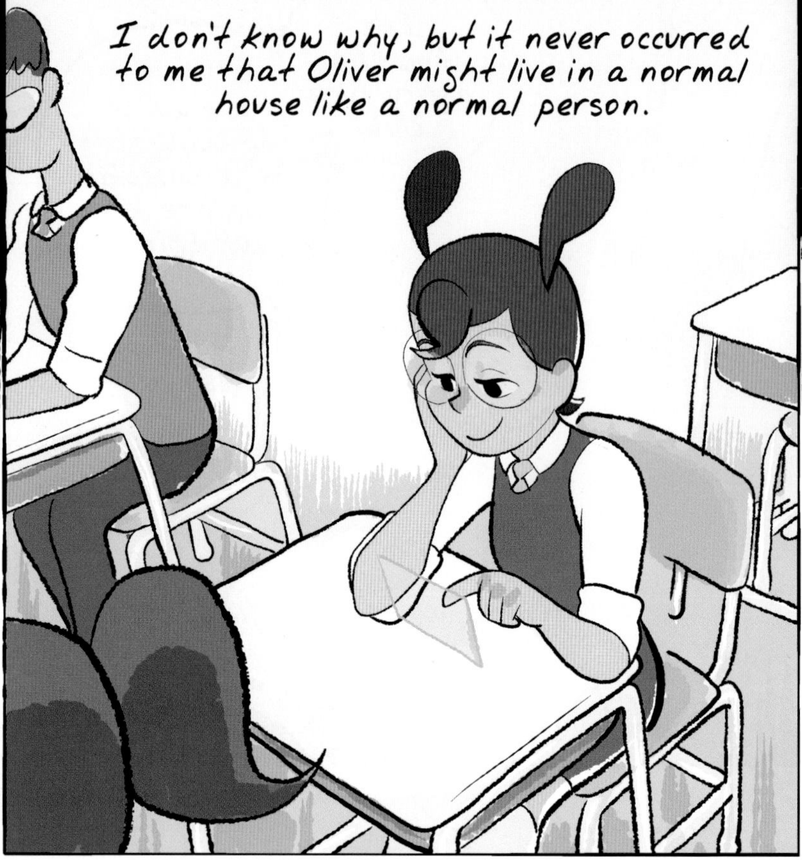
I don't know why, but it never occurred to me that Oliver might live in a normal house like a normal person.

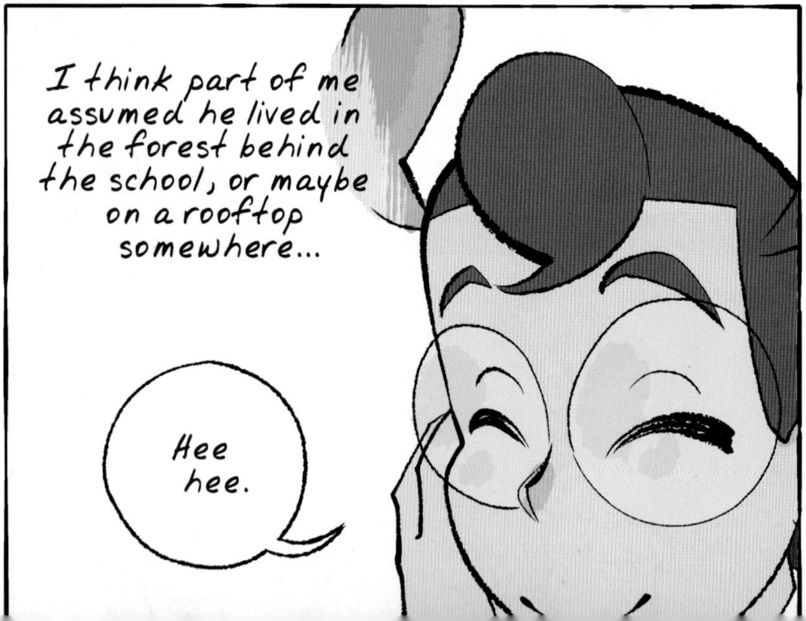
I think part of me assumed he lived in the forest behind the school, or maybe on a rooftop somewhere...
Hee hee.

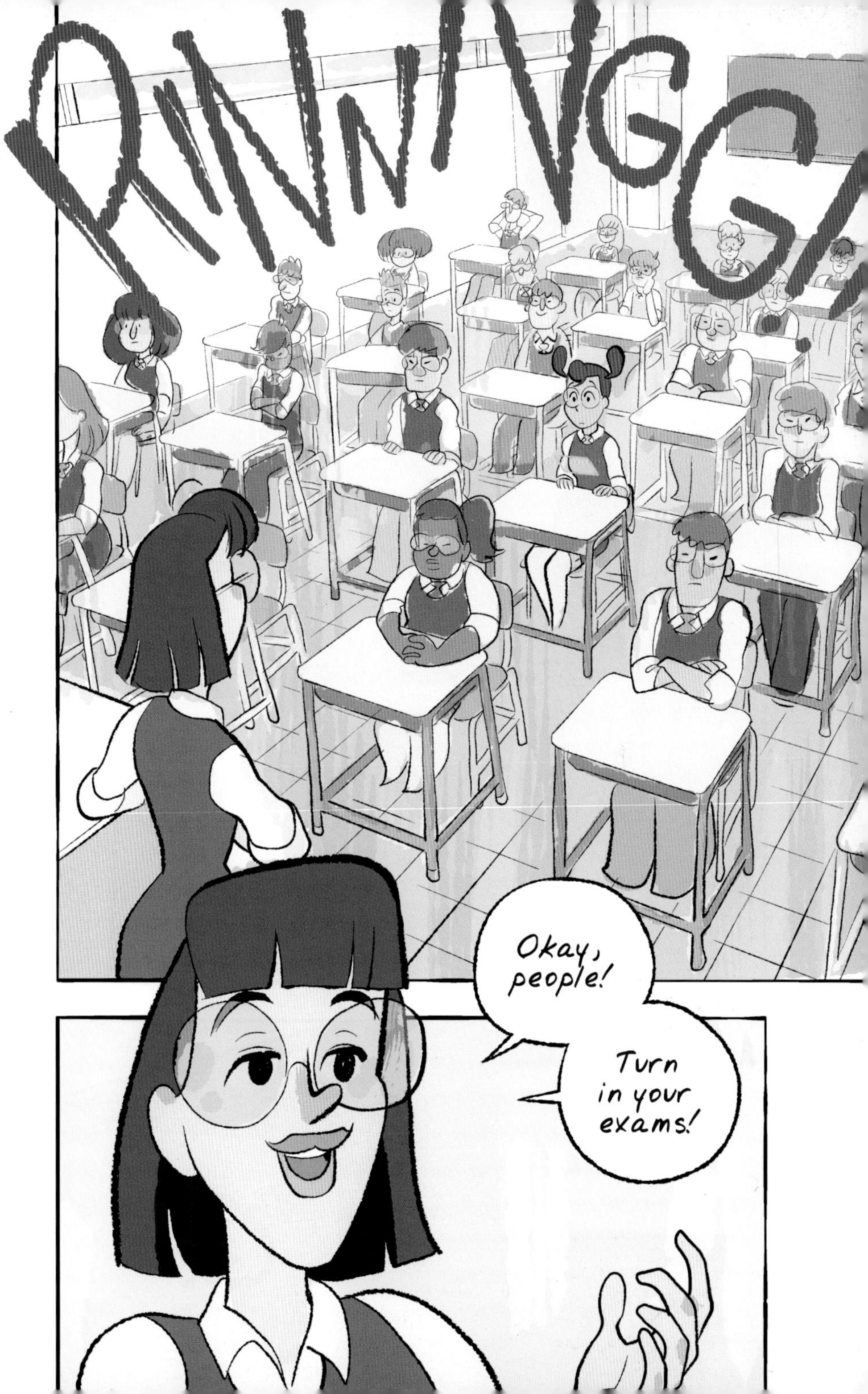
Okay, people!
Turn in your exams!

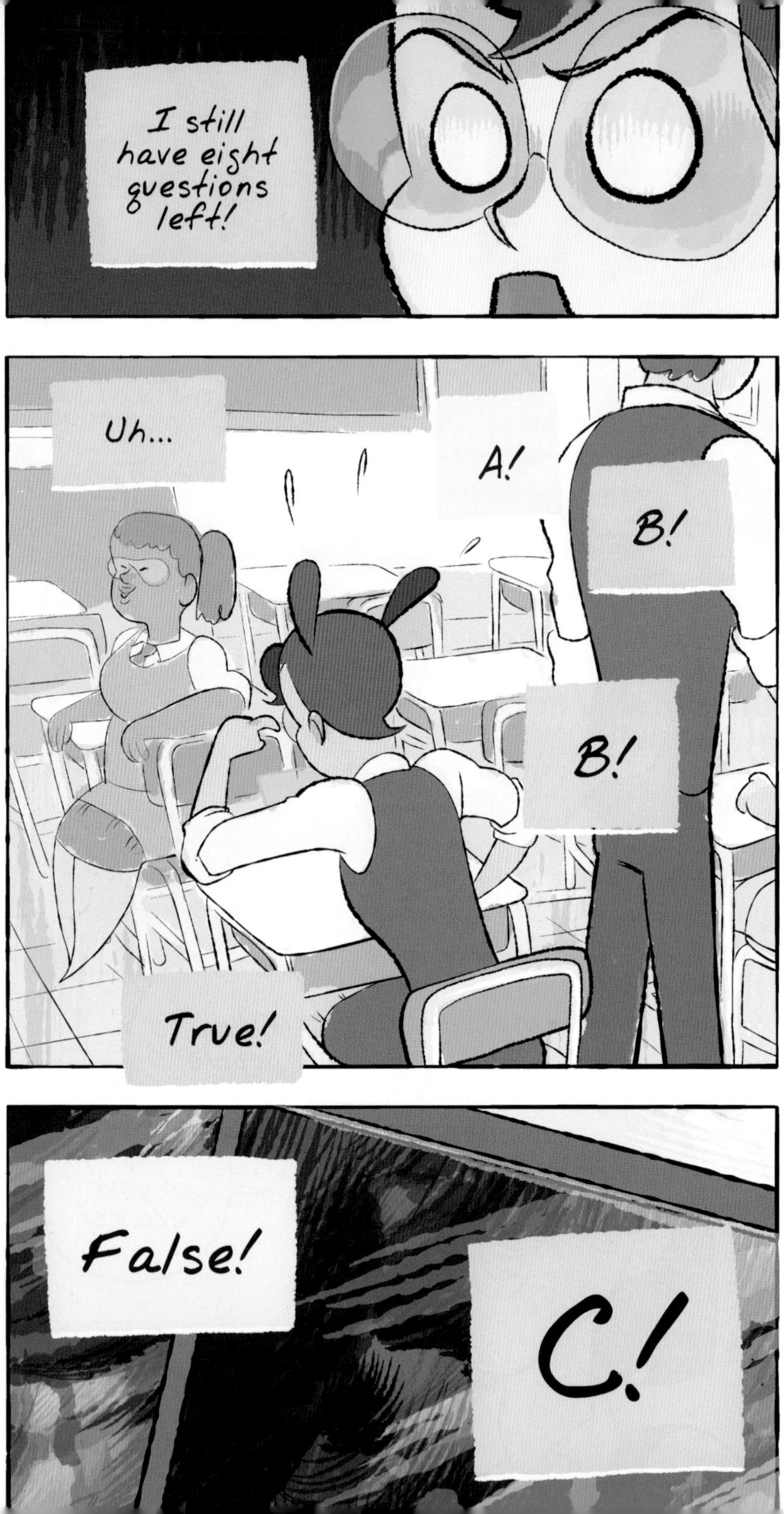
I still have eight questions left!
Uh...
A!
B!
B!
True!
False!
C!

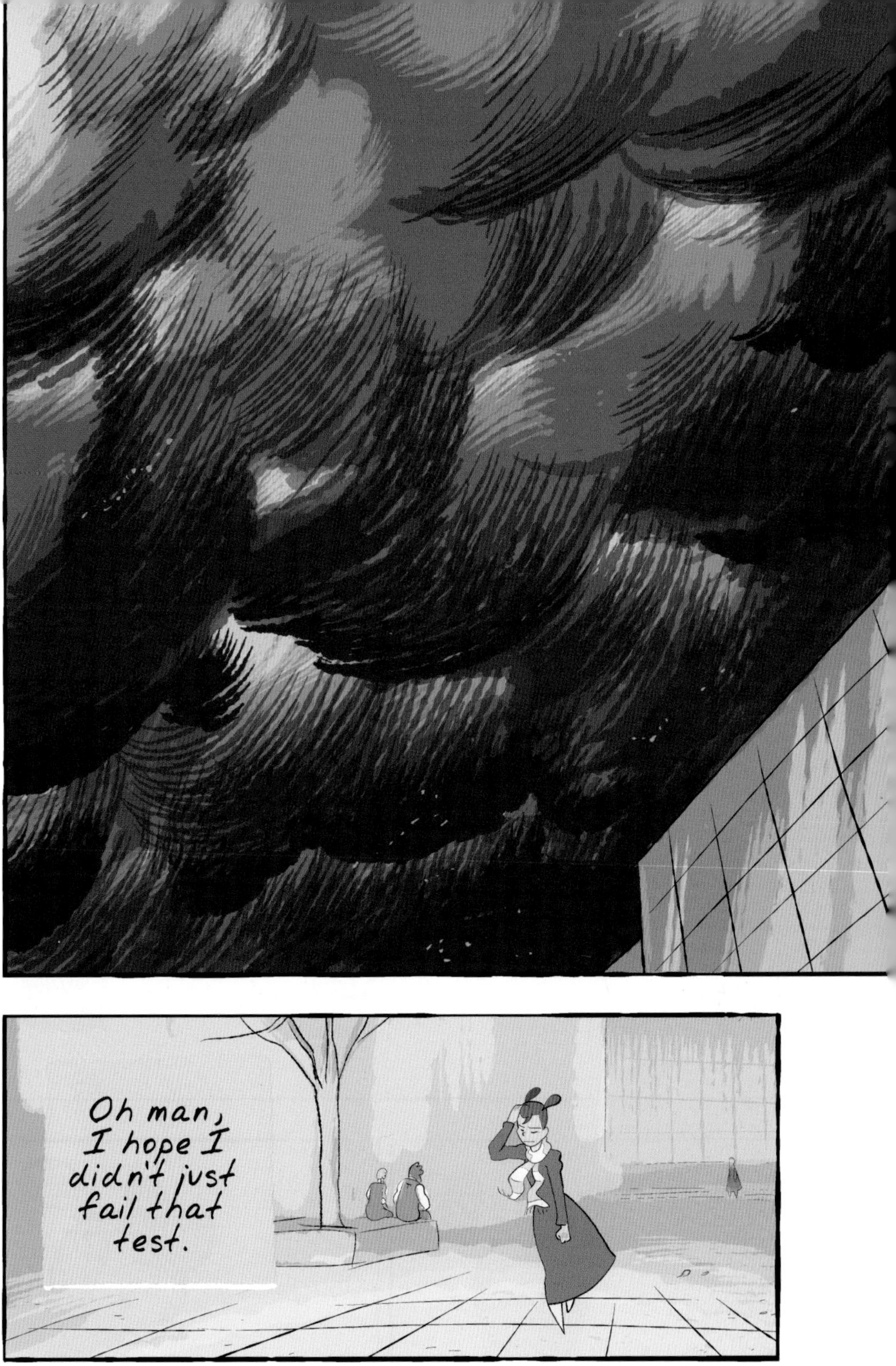
Oh man, I hope I didn't just fail that test.

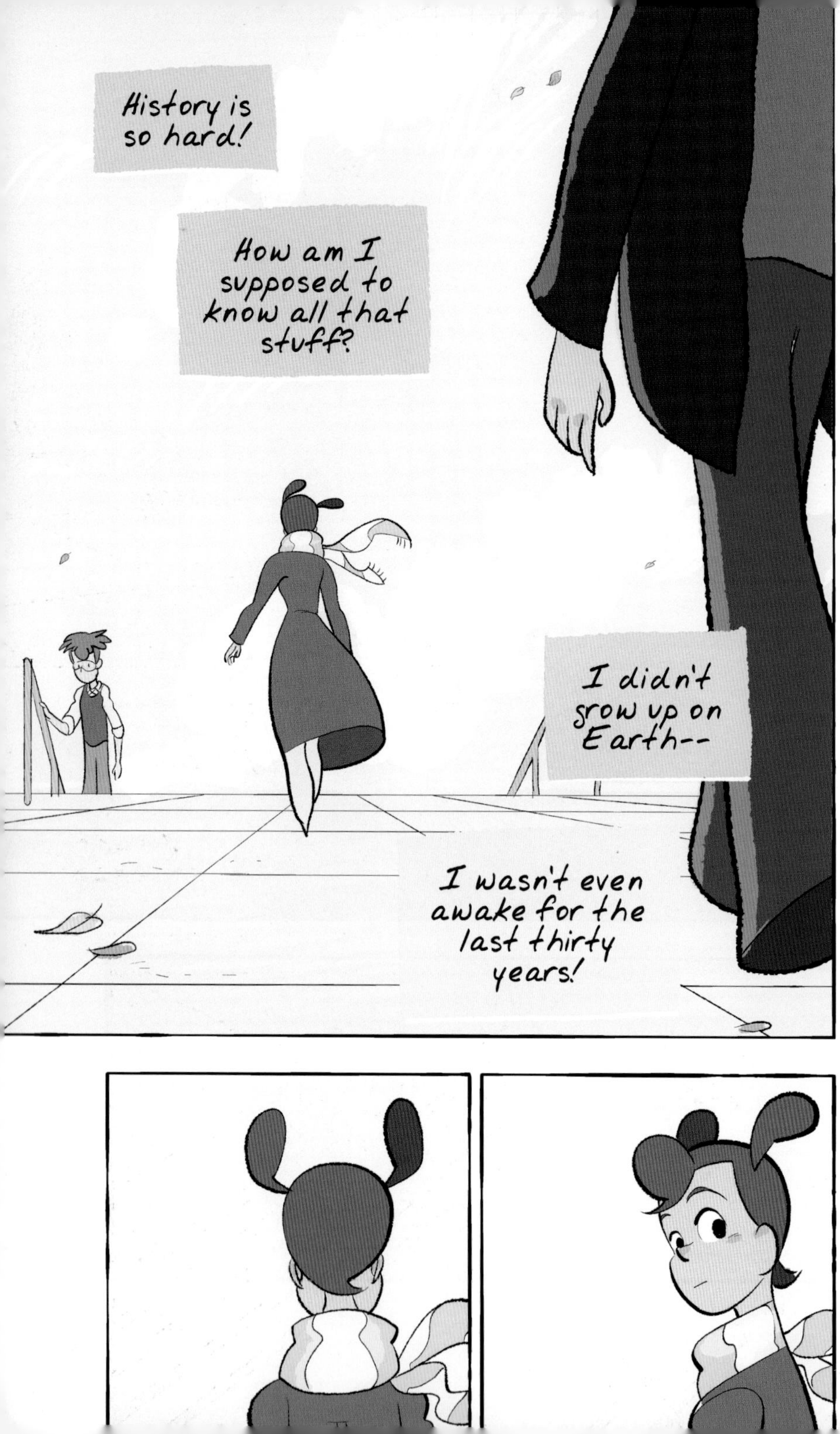
History is so hard!
How am I supposed to know all that stuff?
I didn't grow up on Earth--
I wasn't even awake for the last thirty years!

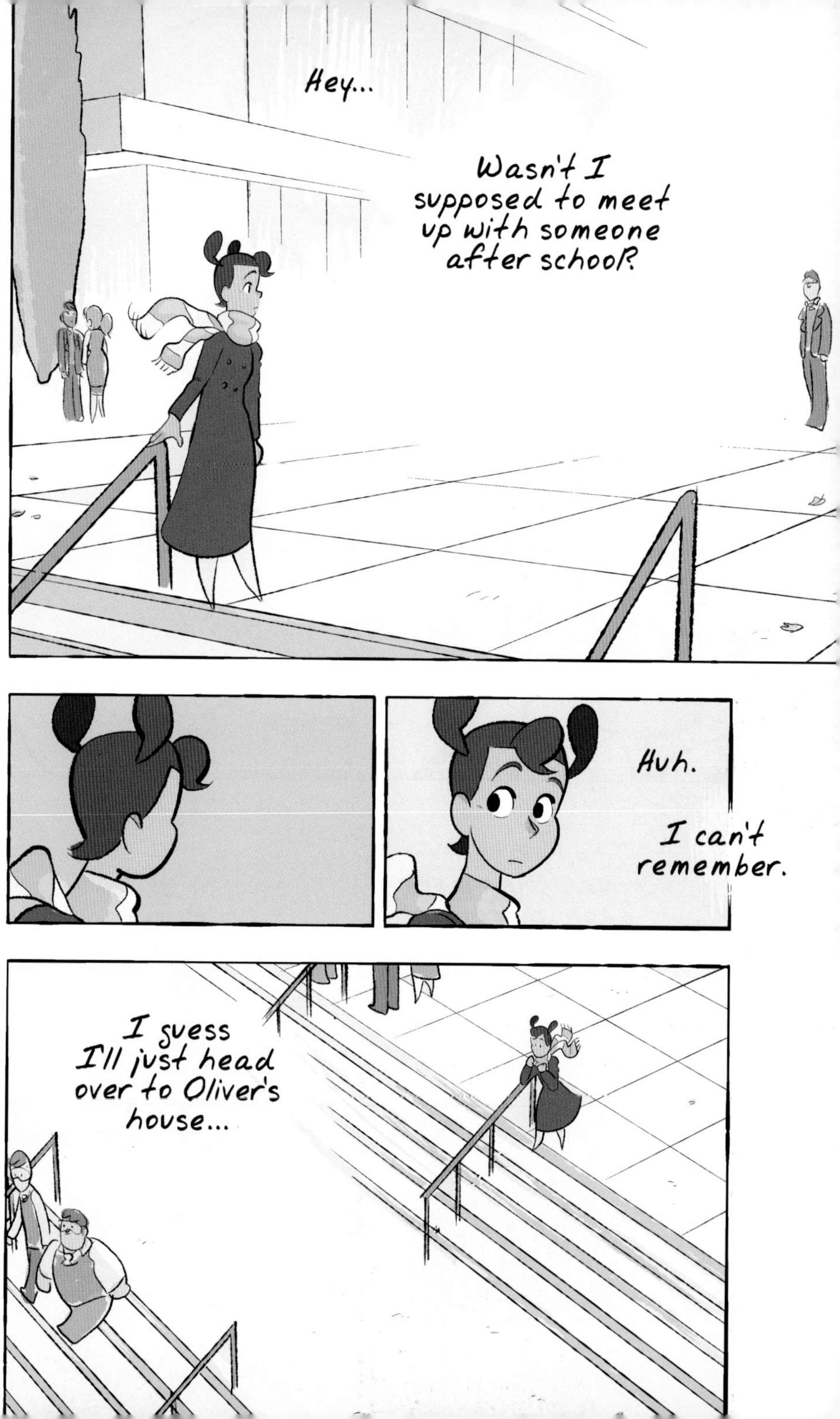
Hey...
Wasn't I supposed to meet up with someone after school?
Huh.
I can't remember.
I guess I'll just head over to Oliver's house...

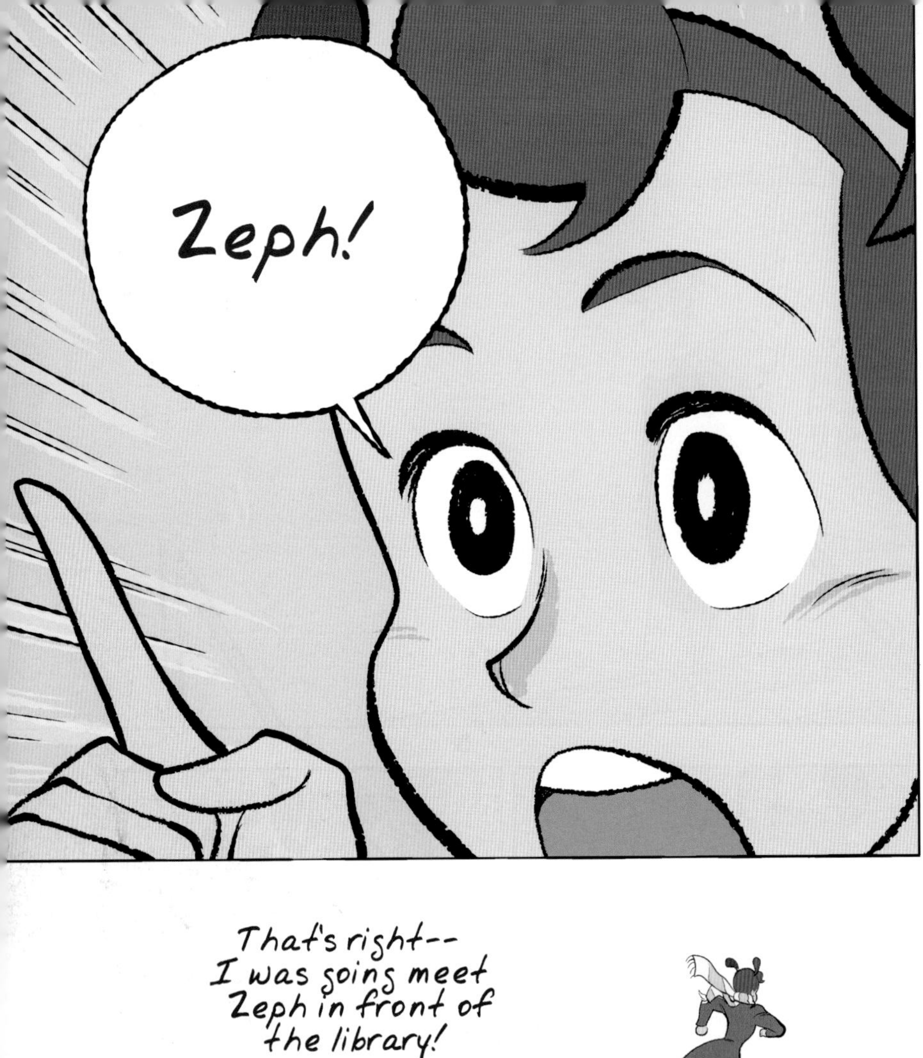
Zeph!

That's right--
I was going meet
Zeph in front of
the library!

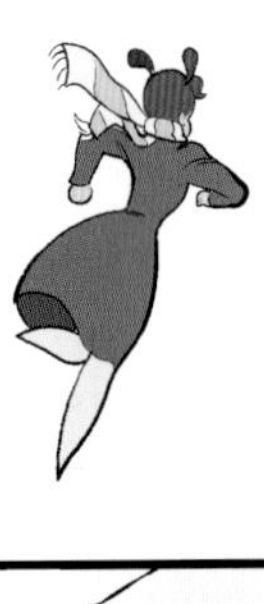

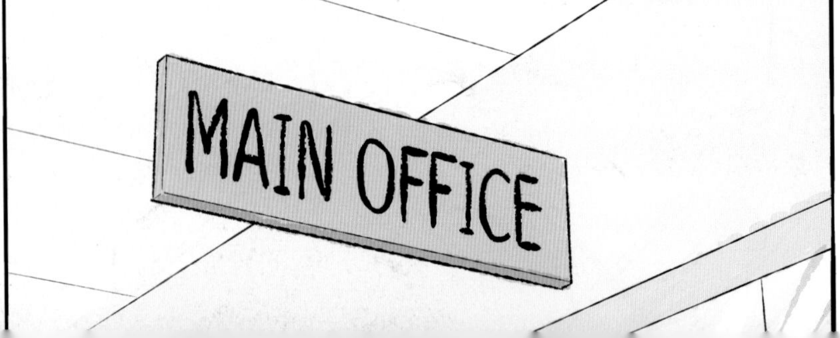
MAIN OFFICE

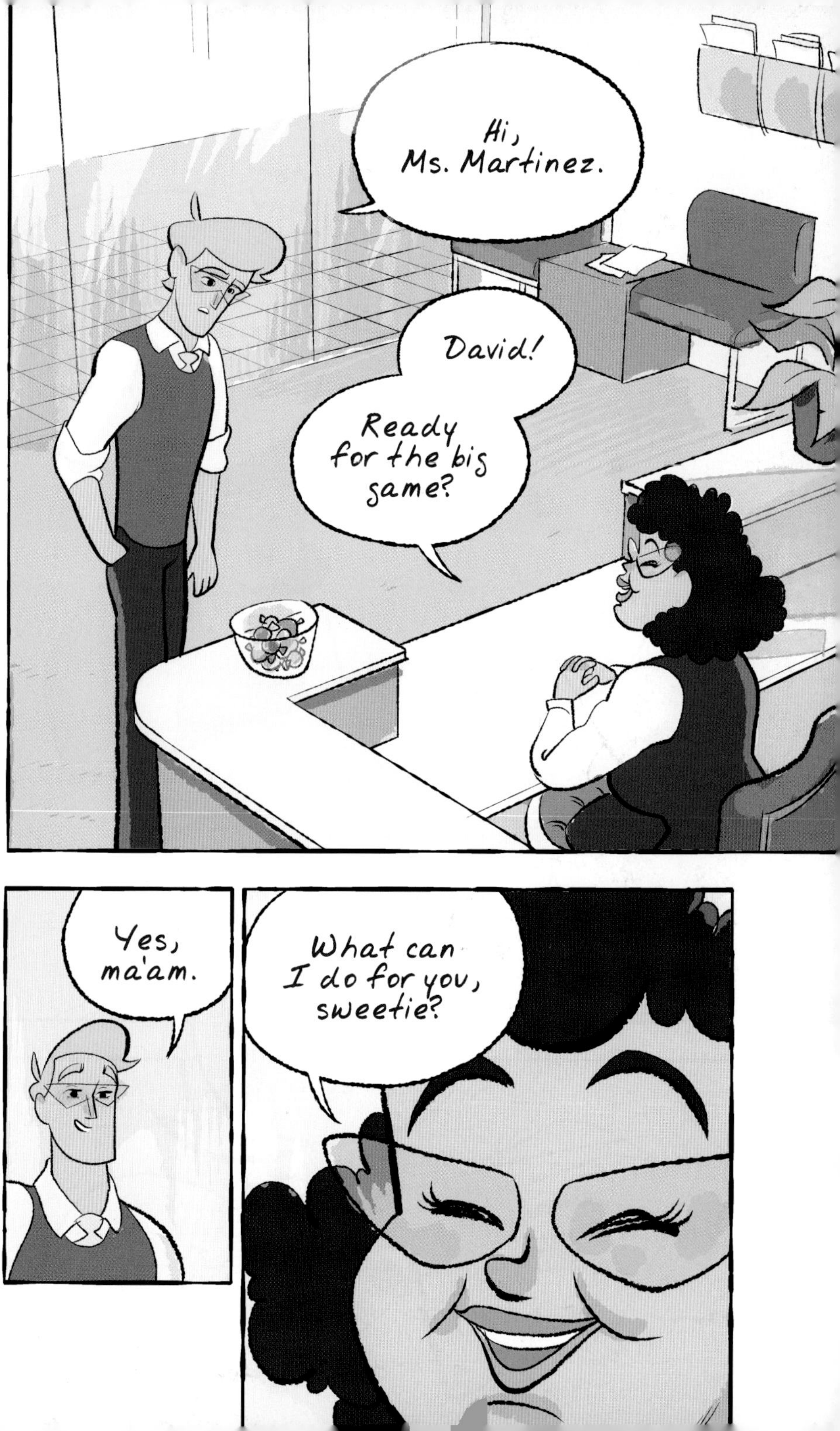
Hi, Ms. Martinez.
David!
Ready for the big game?
Yes, ma'am.
What can I do for you, sweetie?

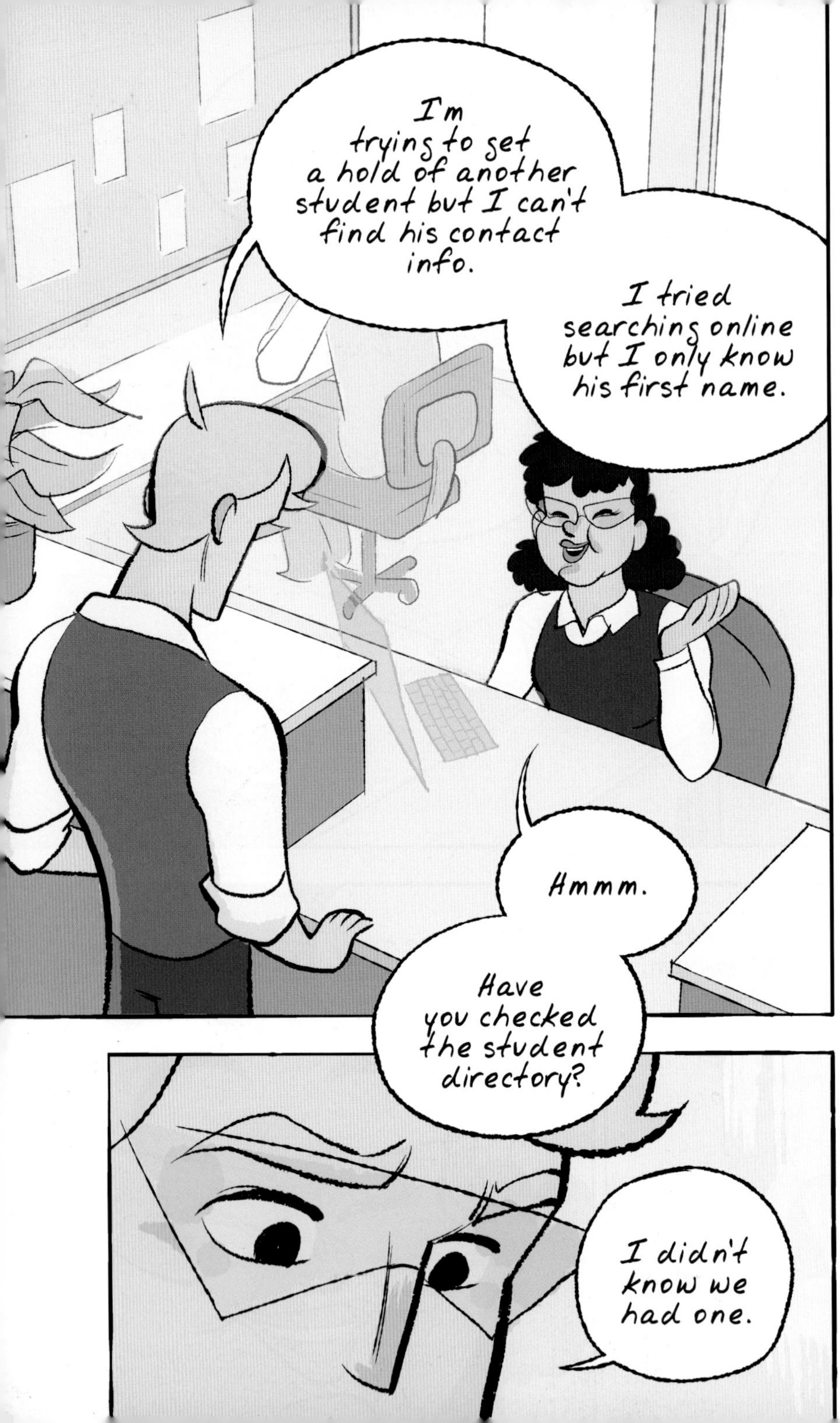
I'm trying to get a hold of another student but I can't find his contact info.
I tried searching online but I only know his first name.
Hmmm.
Have you checked the student directory?
I didn't know we had one.

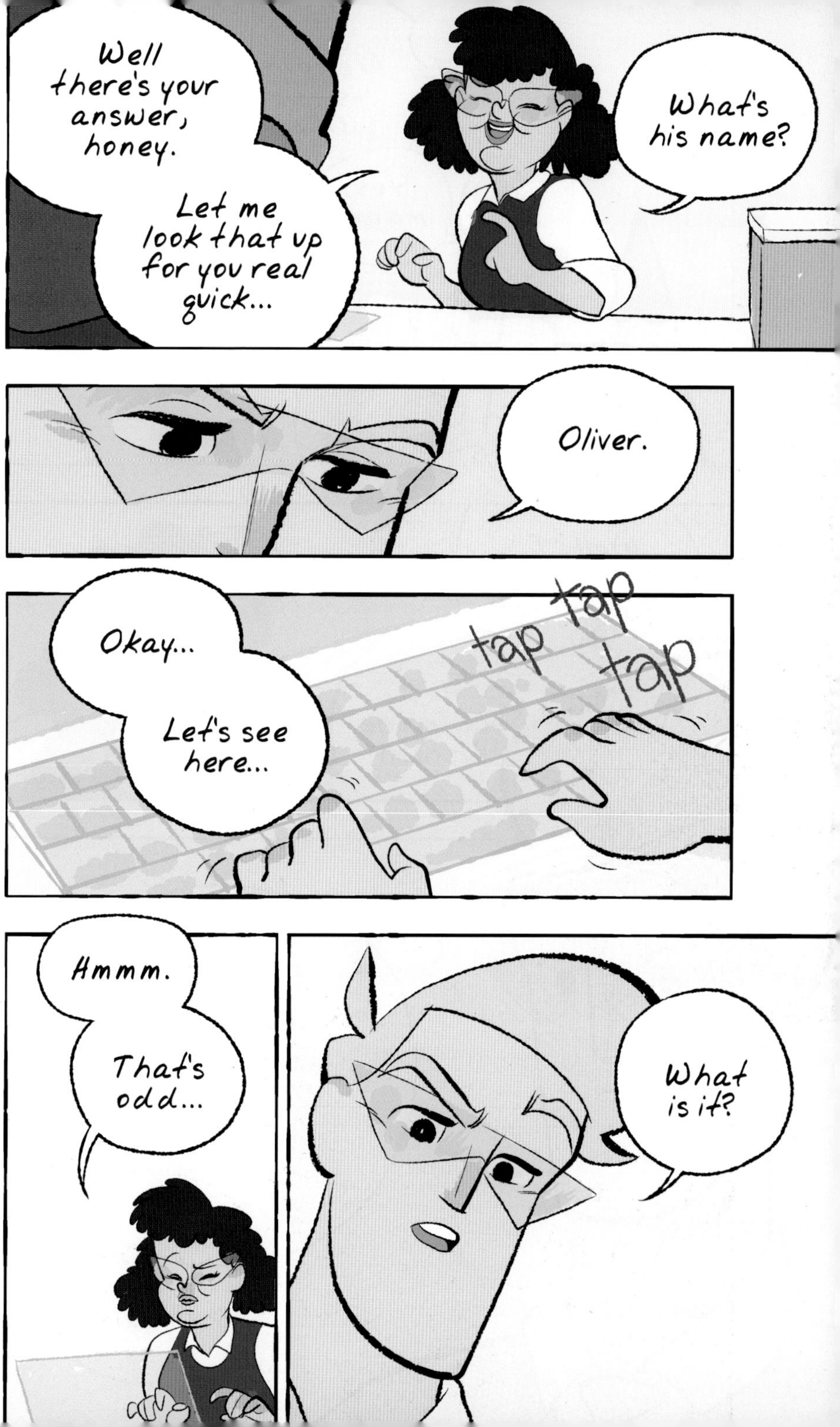
Well there's your answer, honey.
Let me look that up for you real quick...
What's his name?
Oliver.
Okay...
Let's see here...
tap tap tap
Hmmm.
That's odd...
What is it?

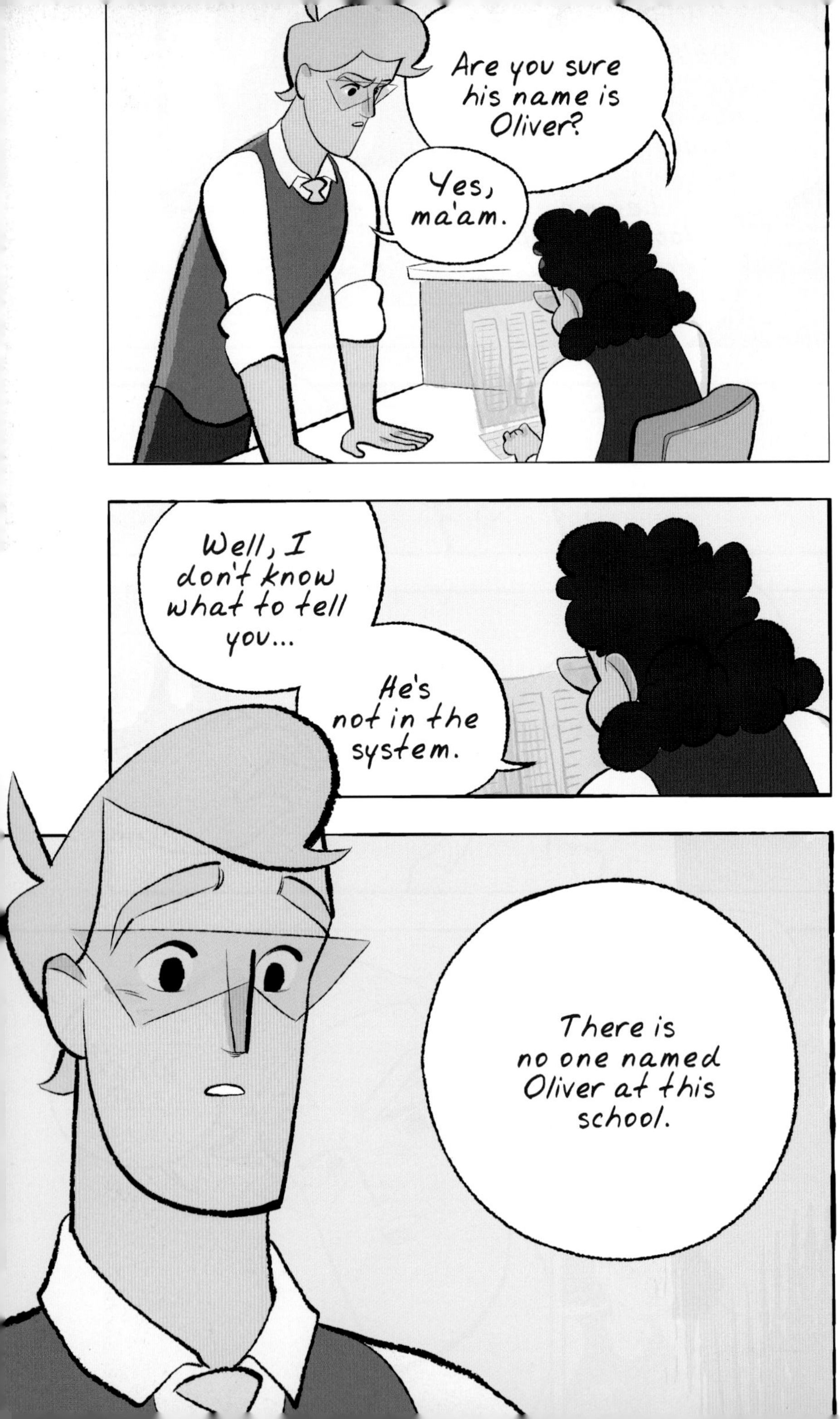
Are you sure his name is Oliver?
Yes, ma'am.
Well, I don't know what to tell you...
He's not in the system.
There is no one named Oliver at this school.

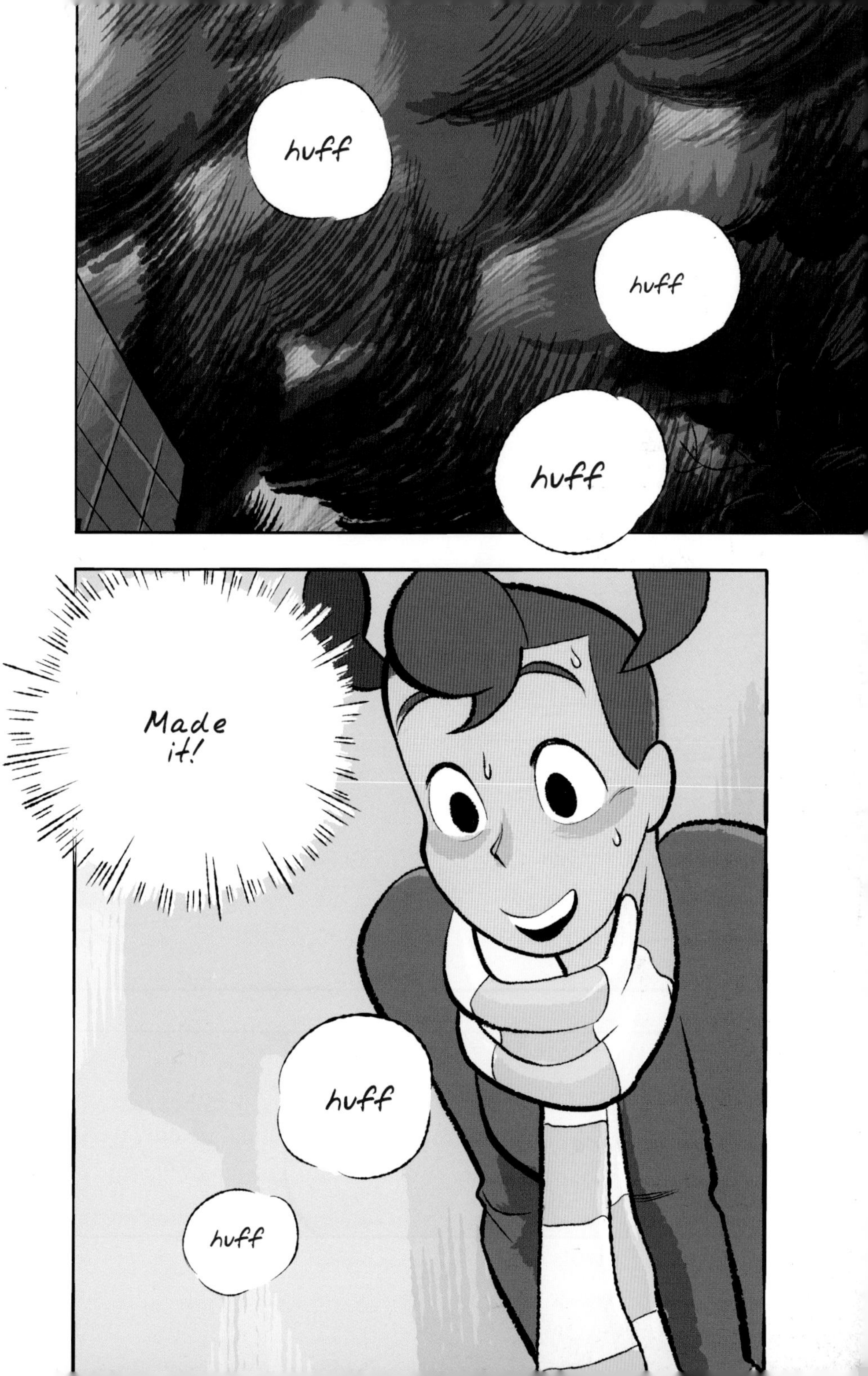
huff
huff
huff
Made it!
huff
huff

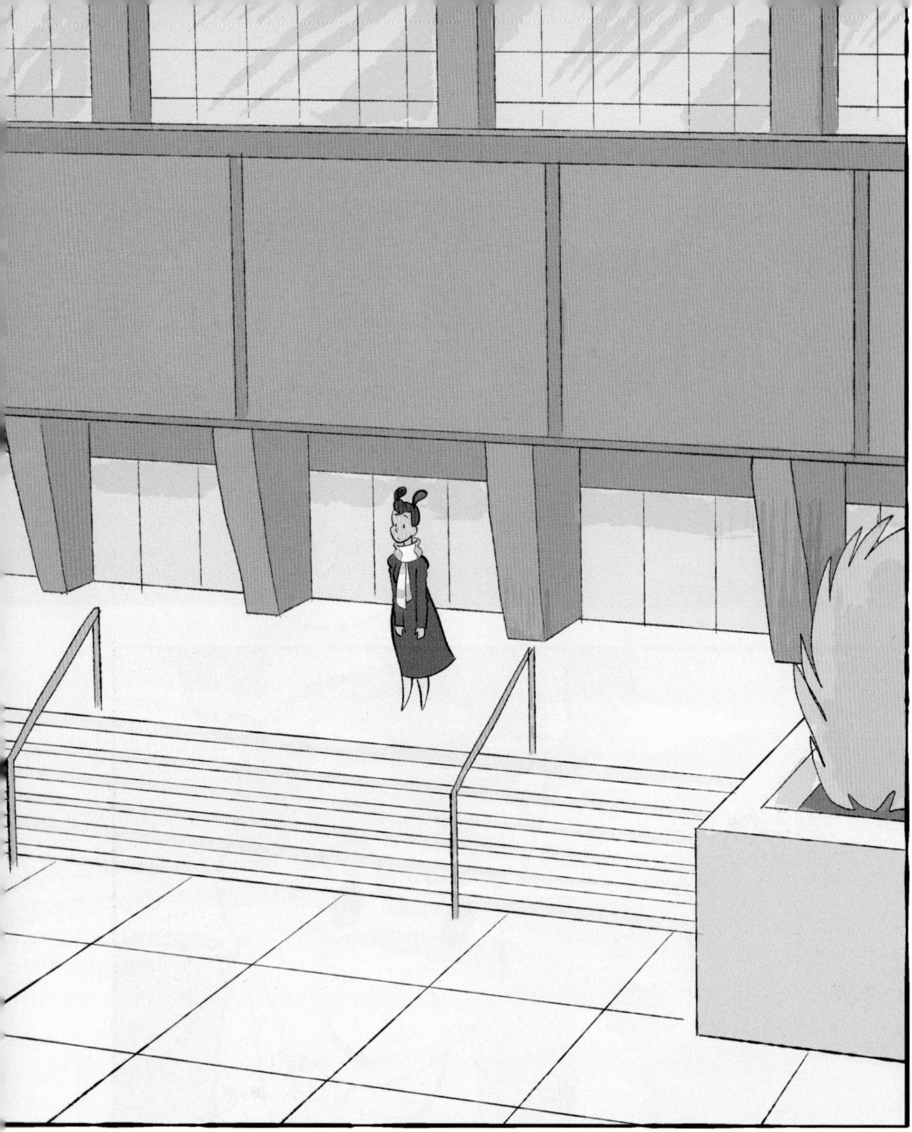

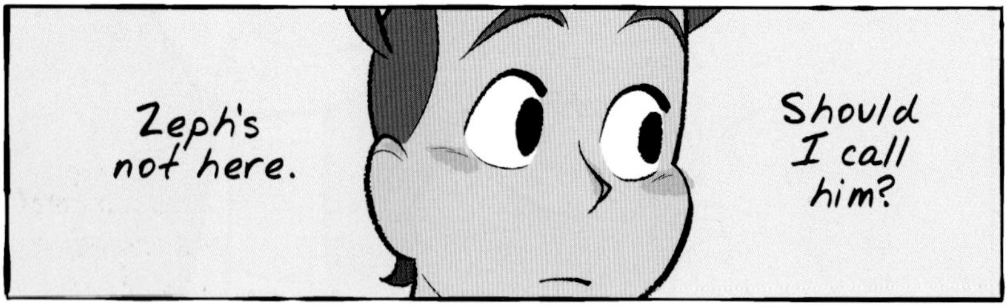
Zeph's not here.
Should I call him?

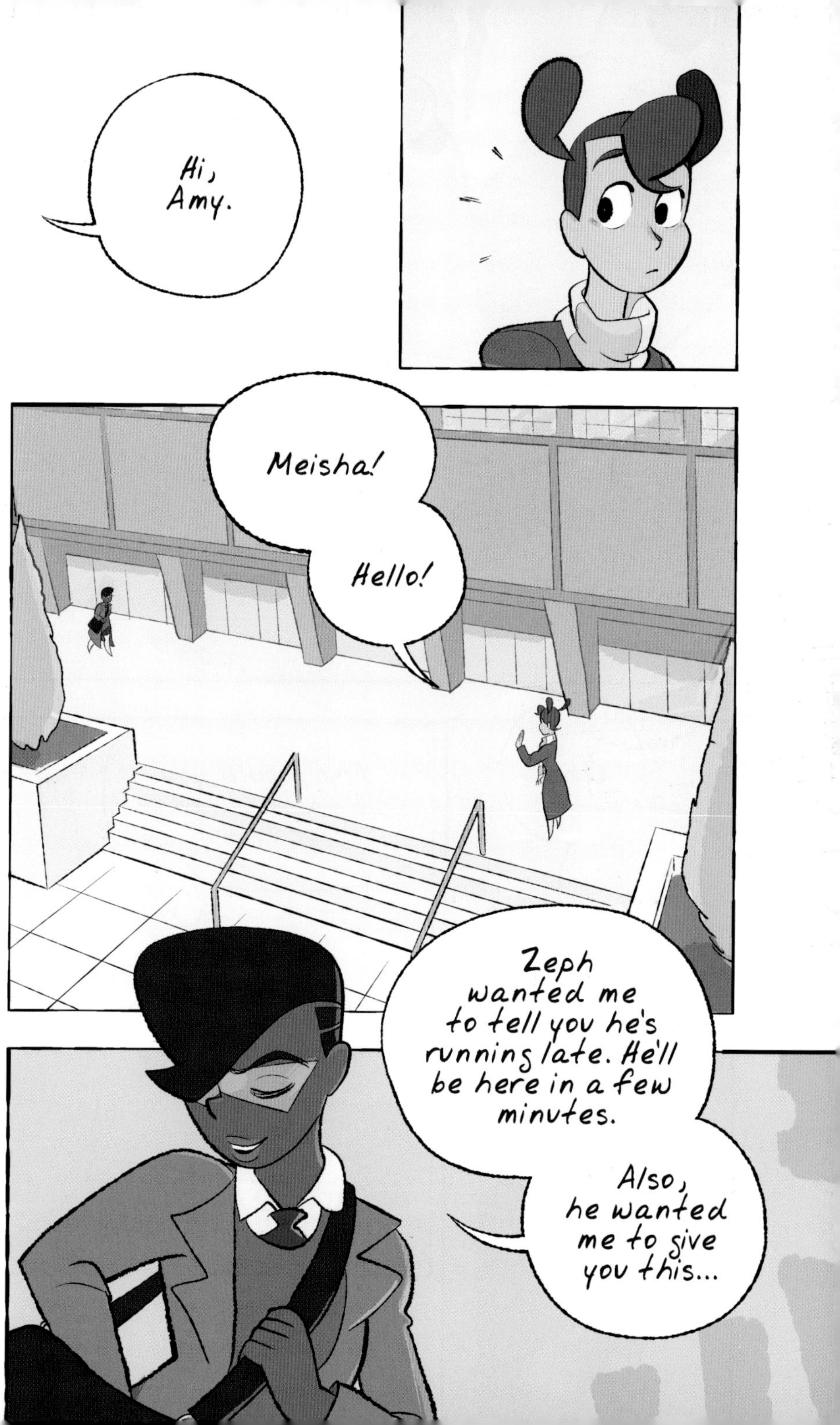
Hi, Amy.
Meisha!
Hello!
Zeph wanted me to tell you he's running late. He'll be here in a few minutes.
Also, he wanted me to give you this...

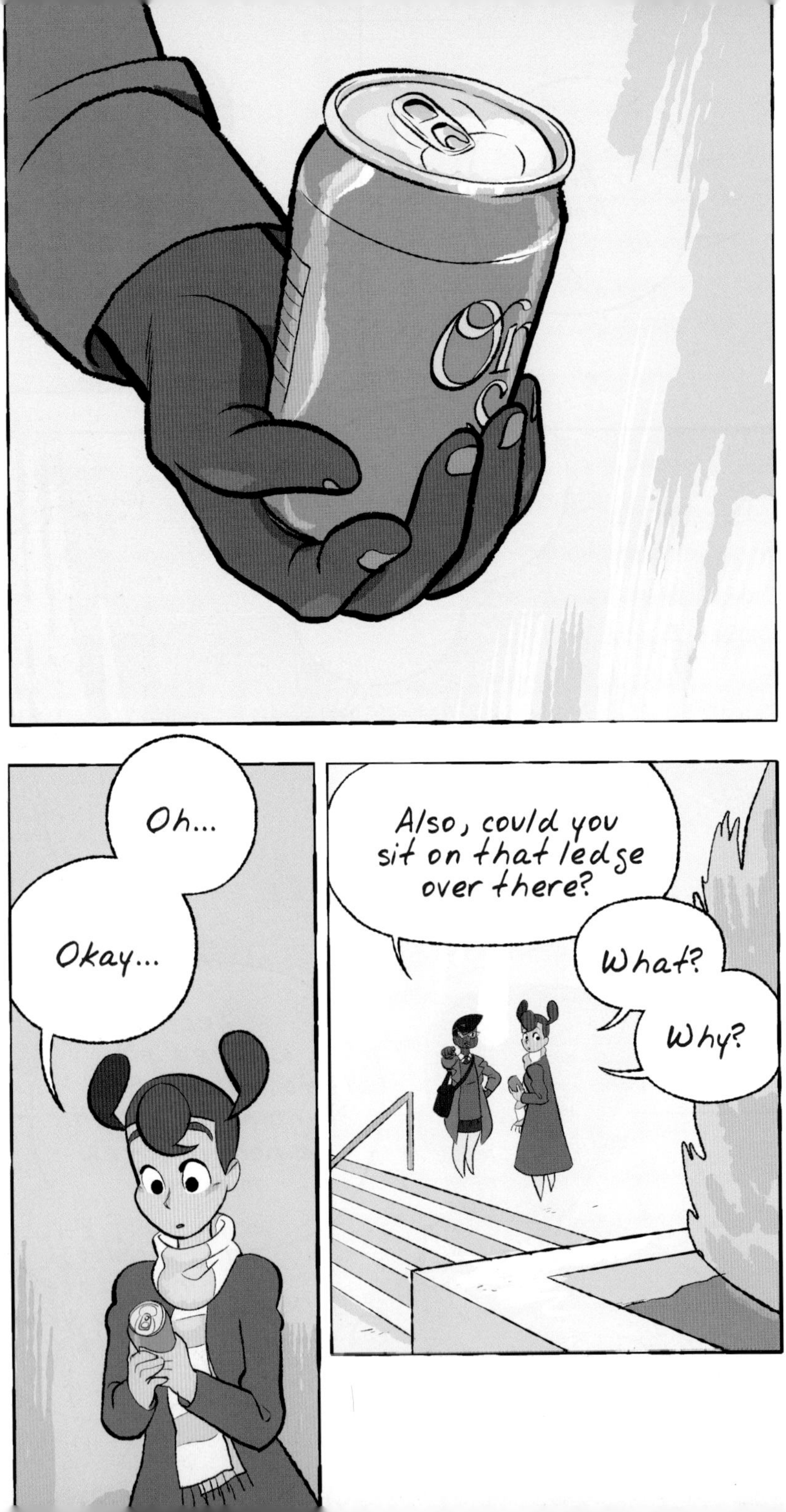
Oh...
Okay...
Also, could you sit on that ledge over there?
What?
Why?

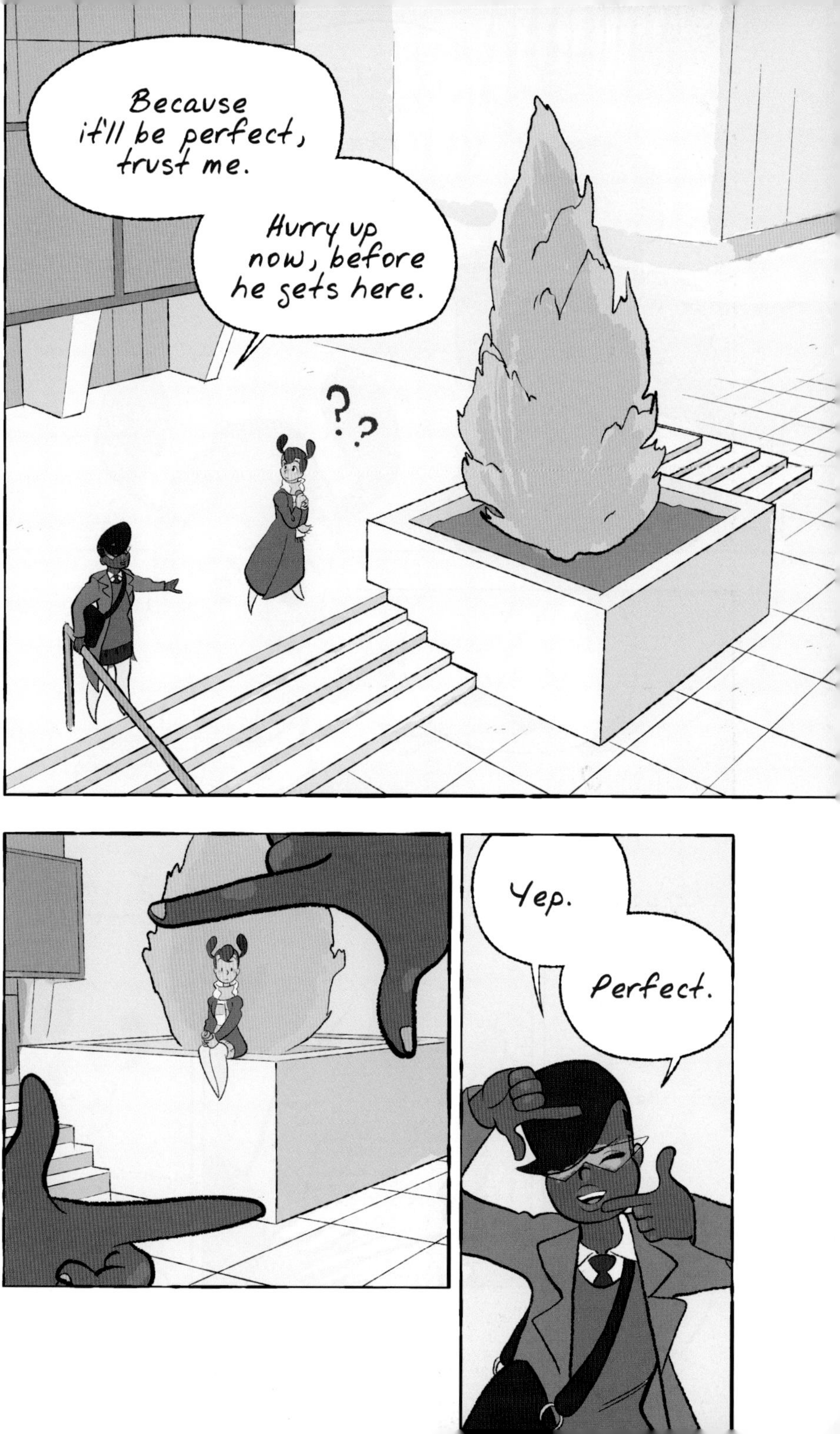
Because it'll be perfect, trust me.
Hurry up now, before he gets here.
??
Yep.
Perfect.

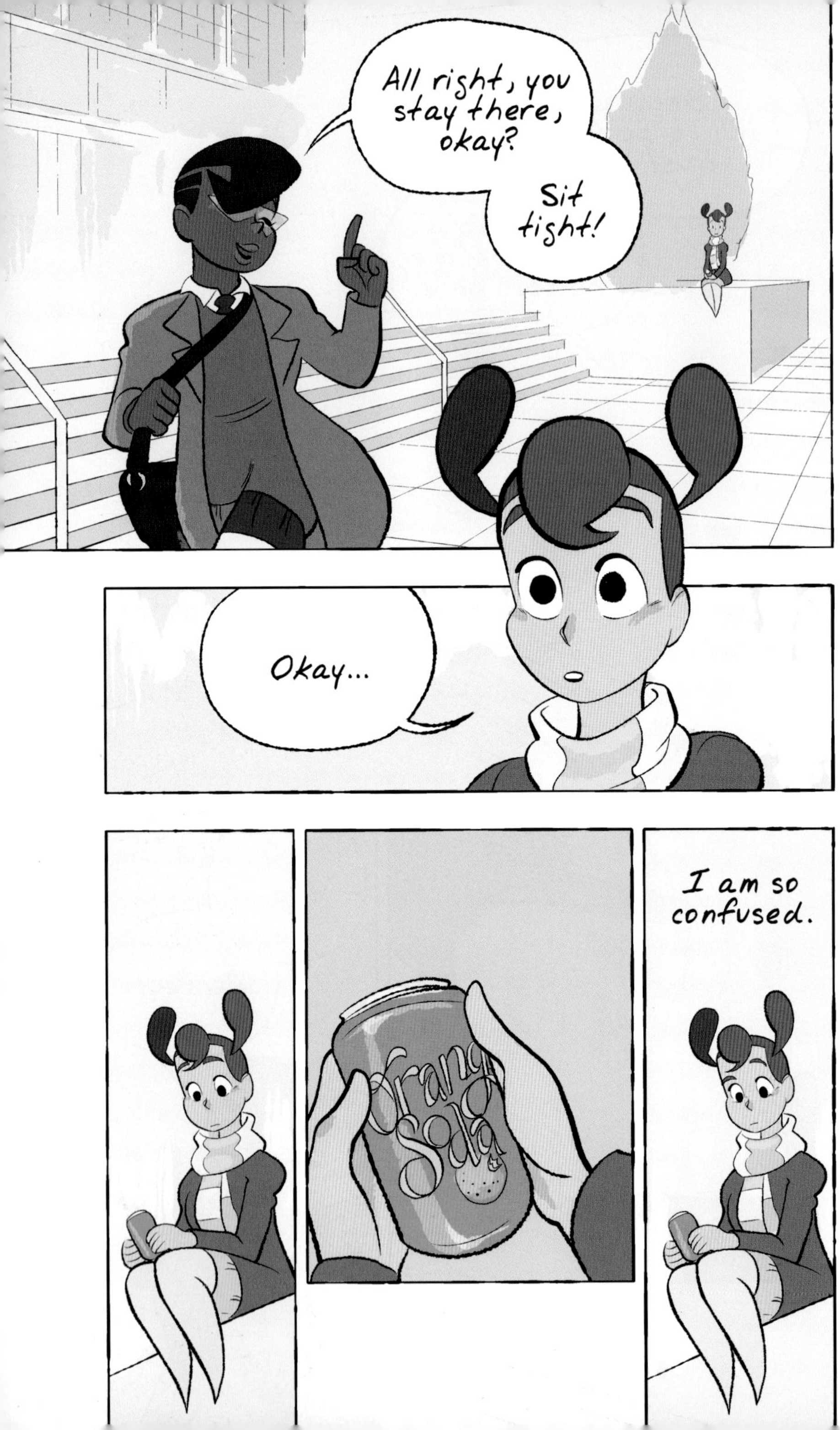
All right, you stay there, okay?
Sit tight!
Okay...
Orange Soda
I am so confused.

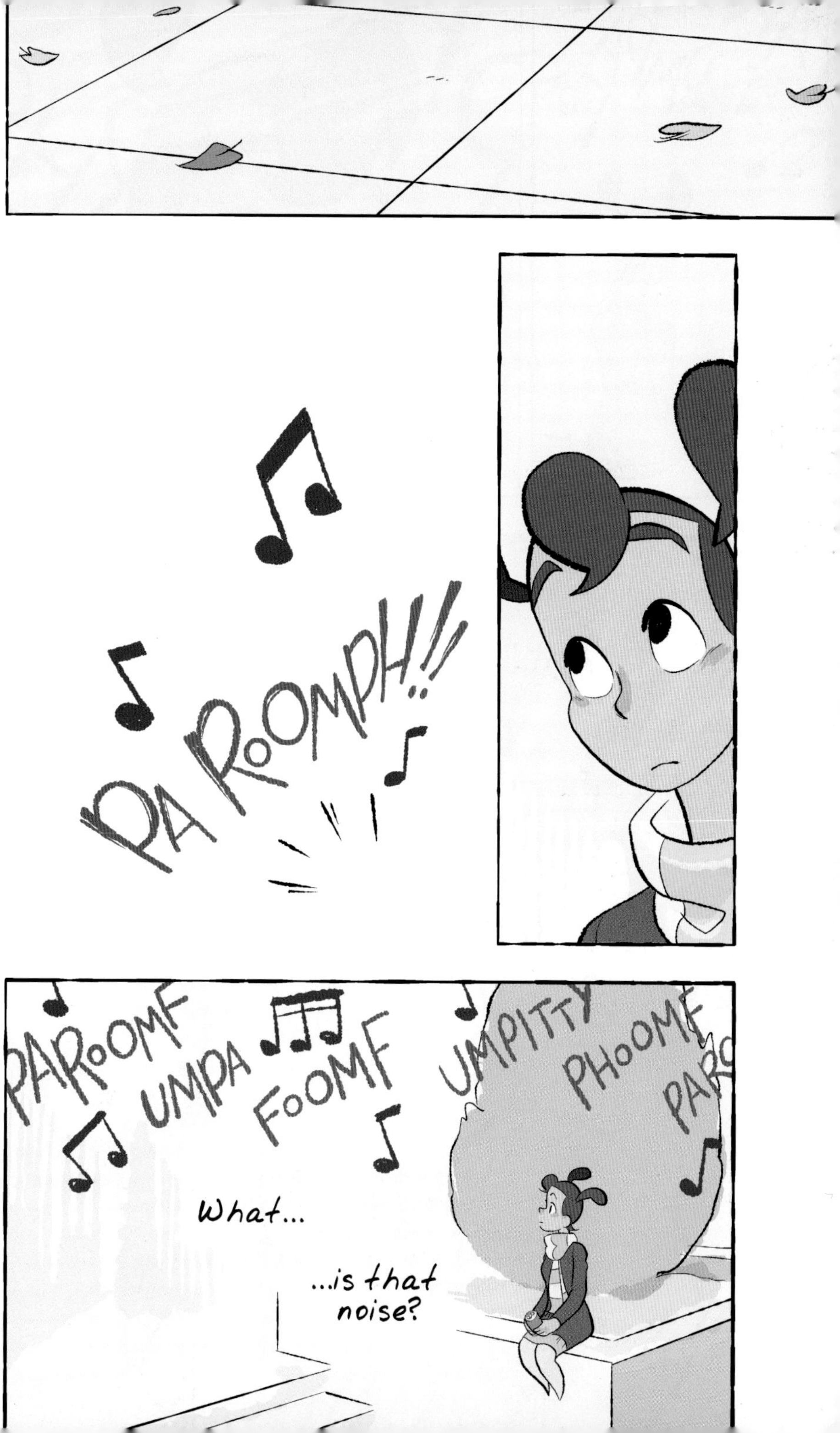
PAROOMPH!!
PAROOMF
UMPA
FOOMF
UMPITTY
PHOOMF
What...
...is that noise?

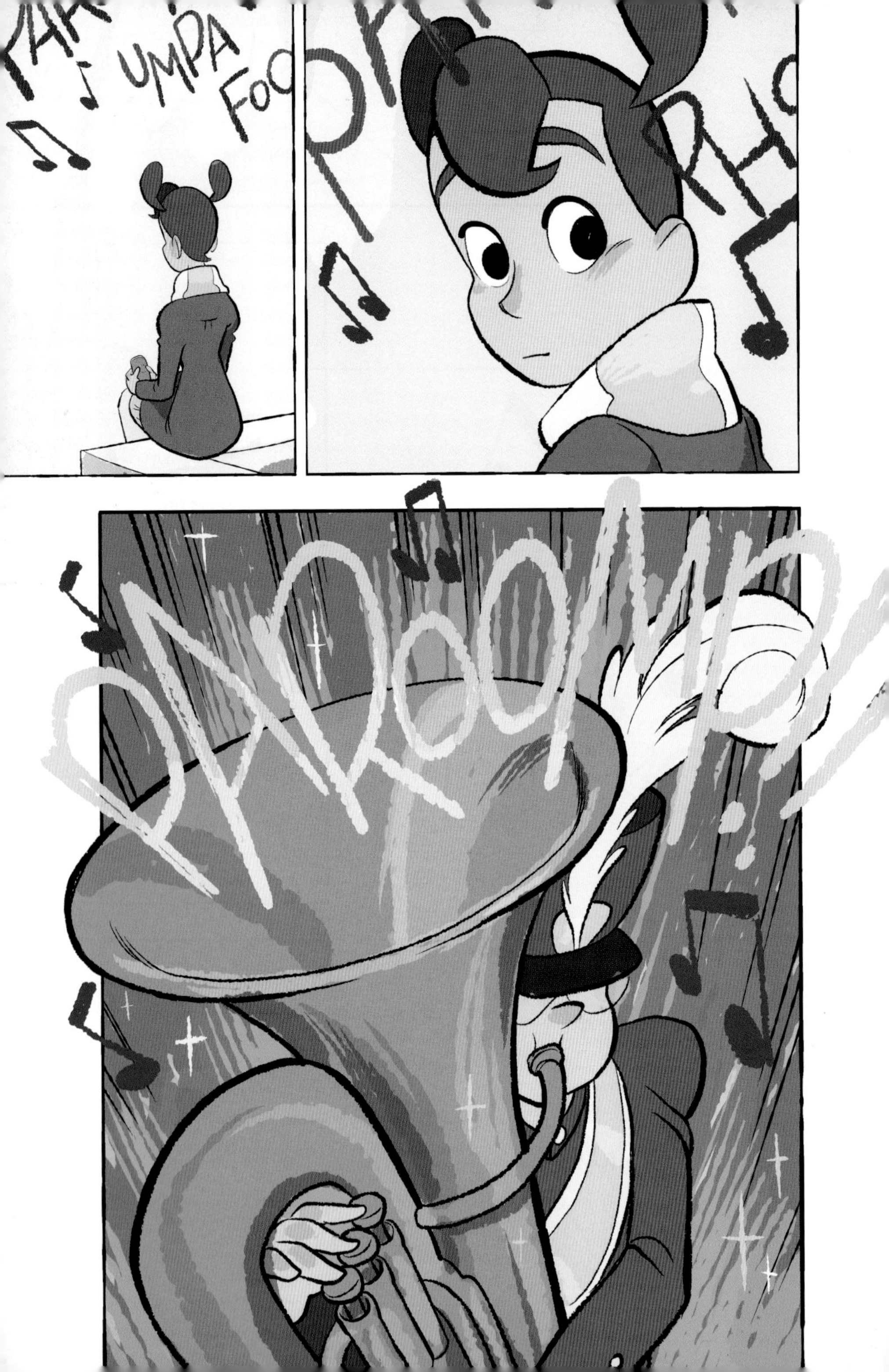
UMPA
PAROOMP!

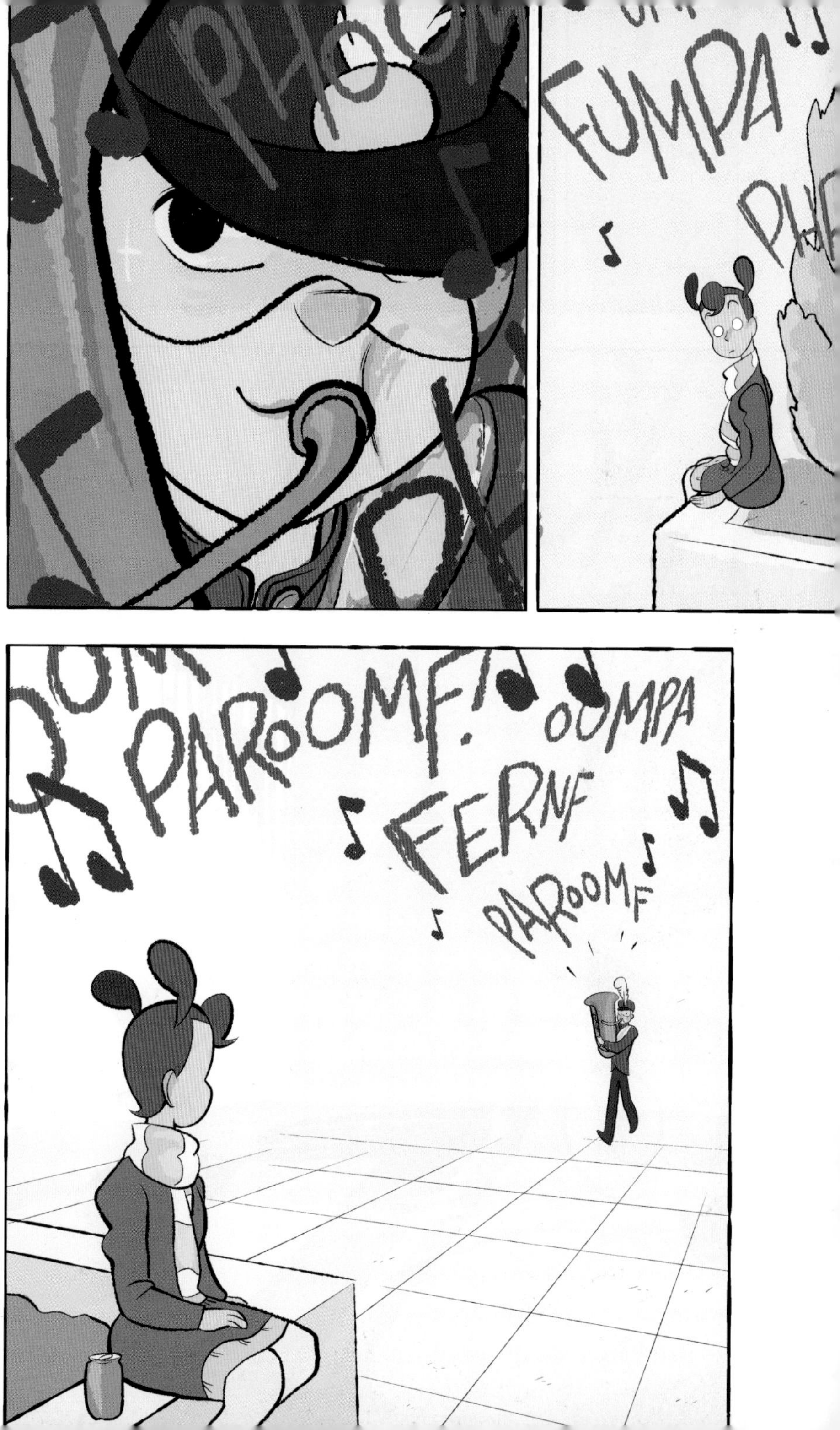
FUMPA
PAROOMF!
OOMPA
FERNF
PAROOMF

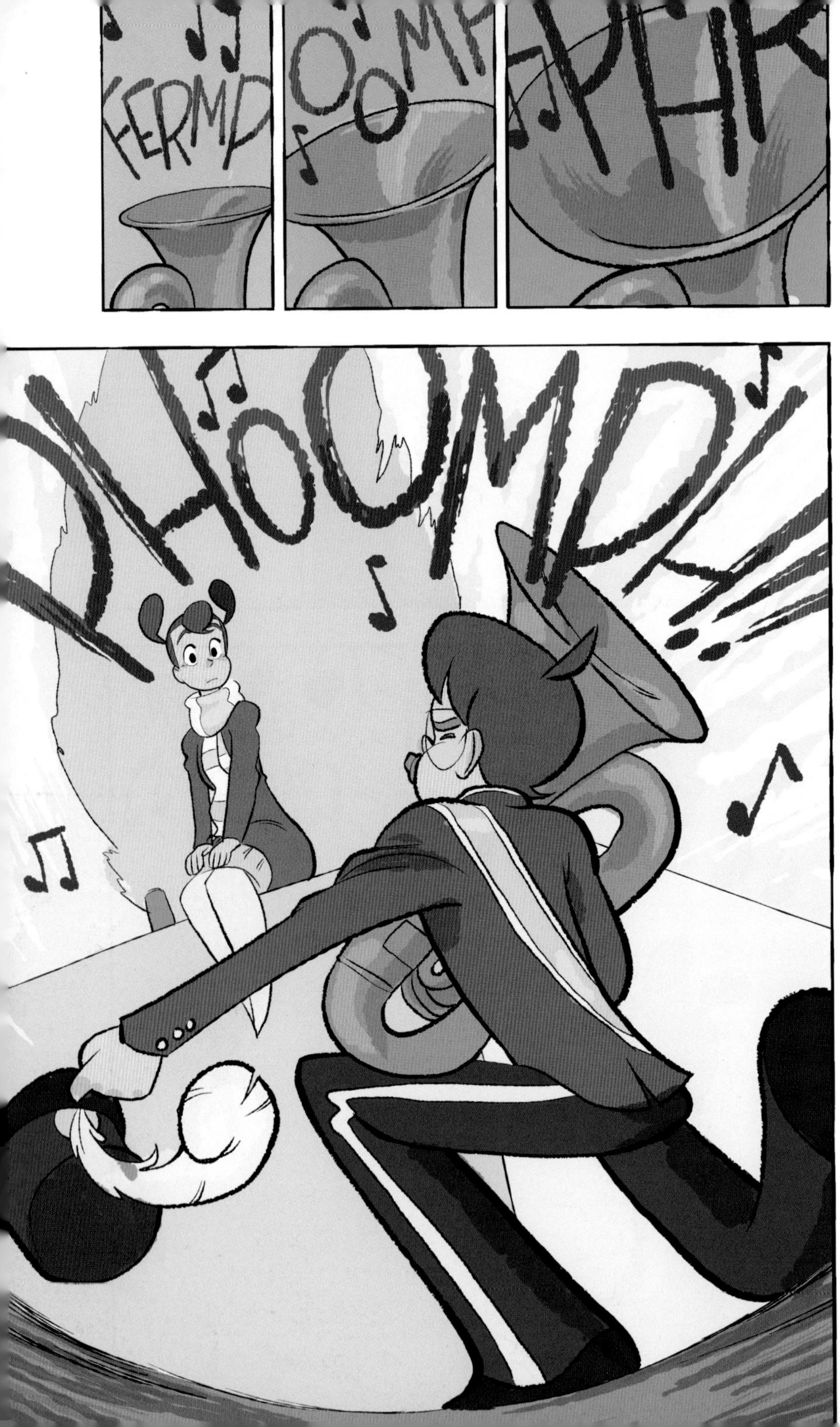
FERMP
OOMP
PHR
PHOOMPA!

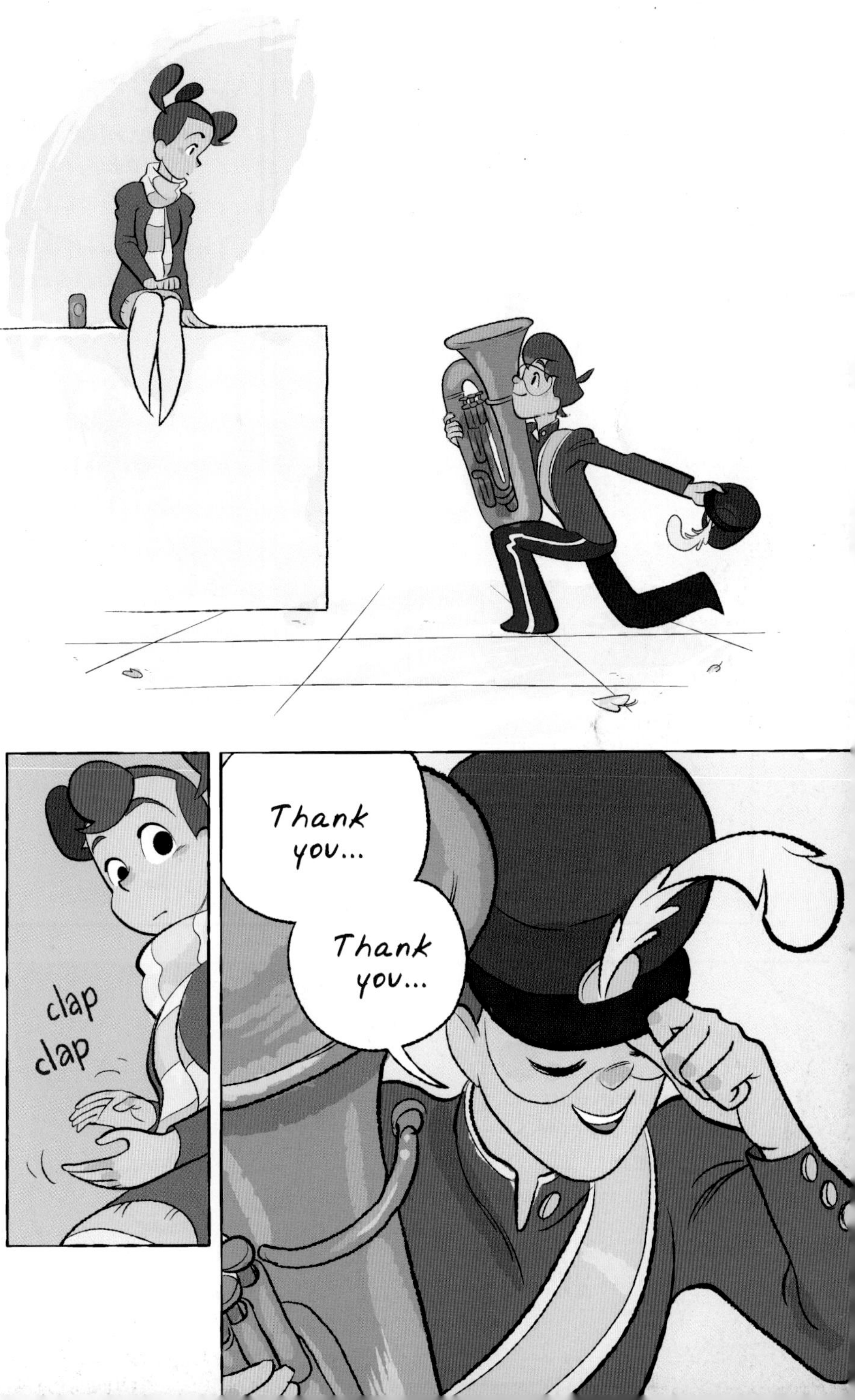
clap
clap
Thank you...
Thank you...

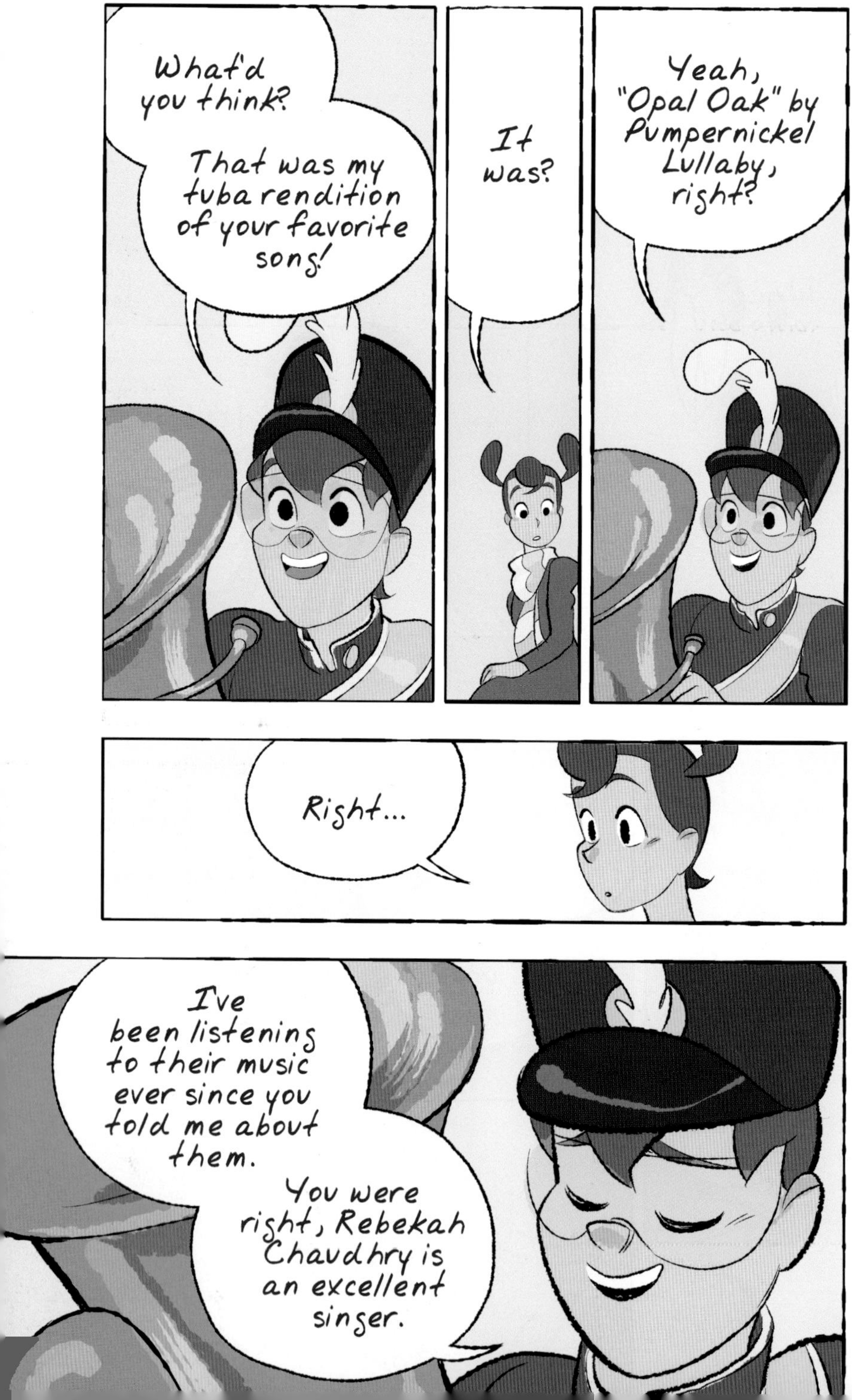
What'd you think?
That was my tuba rendition of your favorite song!
It was?
Yeah, "Opal Oak" by Pumpernickel Lullaby, right?
Right...
I've been listening to their music ever since you told me about them.
You were right, Rebekah Chaudhry is an excellent singer.

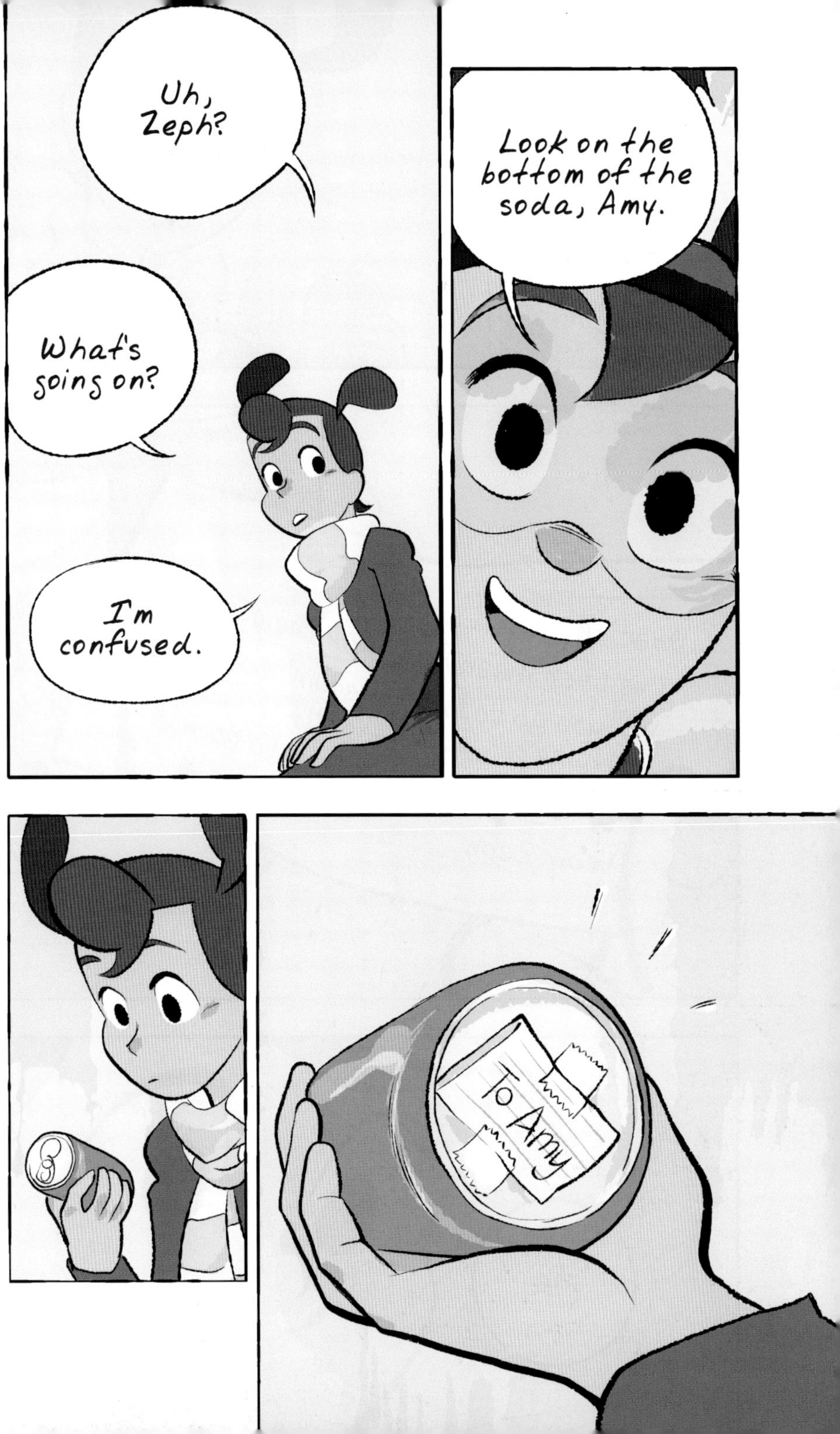
Uh, Zeph?
What's going on?
I'm confused.
Look on the bottom of the soda, Amy.
To Amy

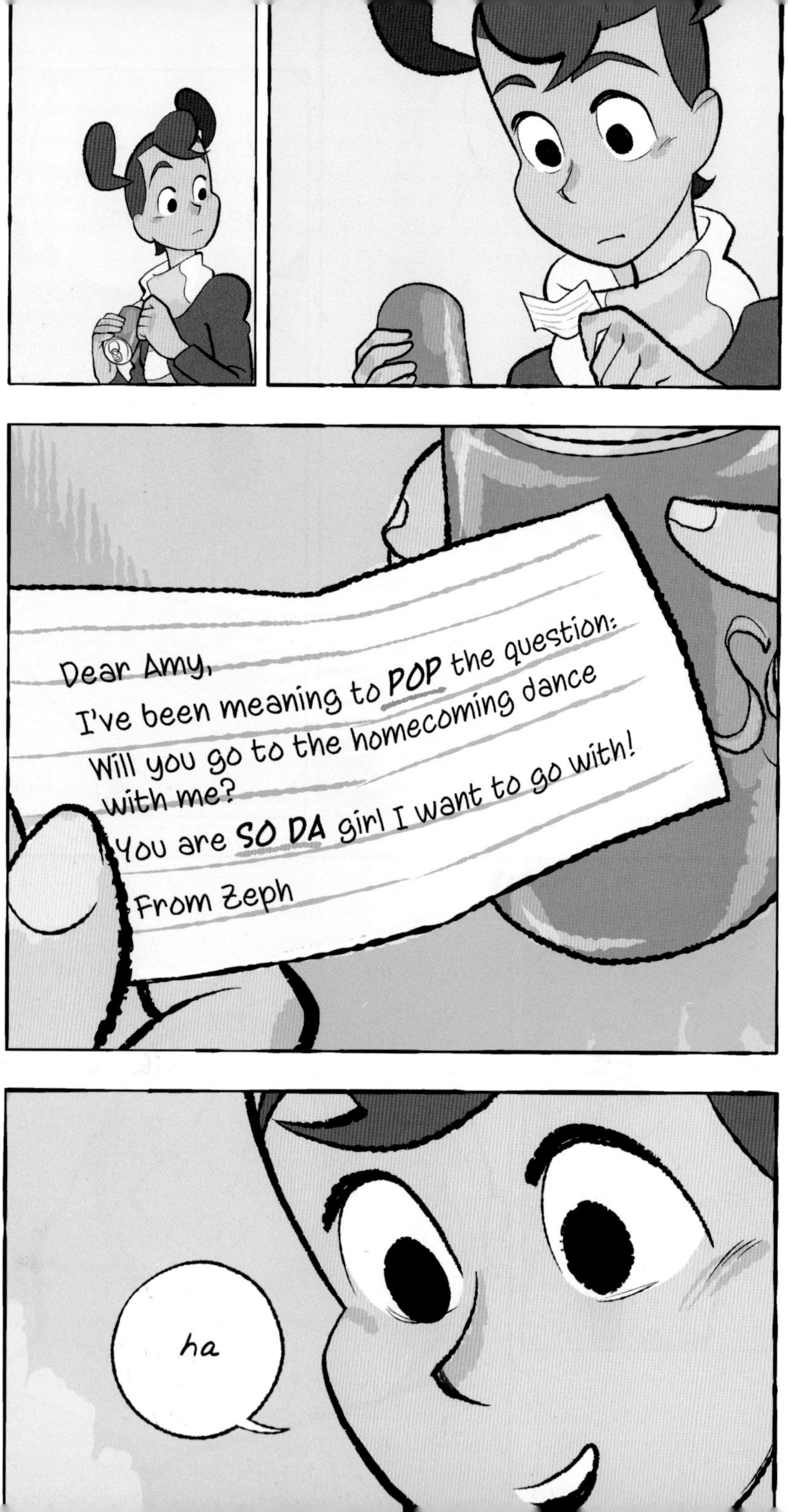
Dear Amy,
I've been meaning to POP the question:
Will you go to the homecoming dance with me?
You are SO DA girl I want to go with!
From Zeph
ha

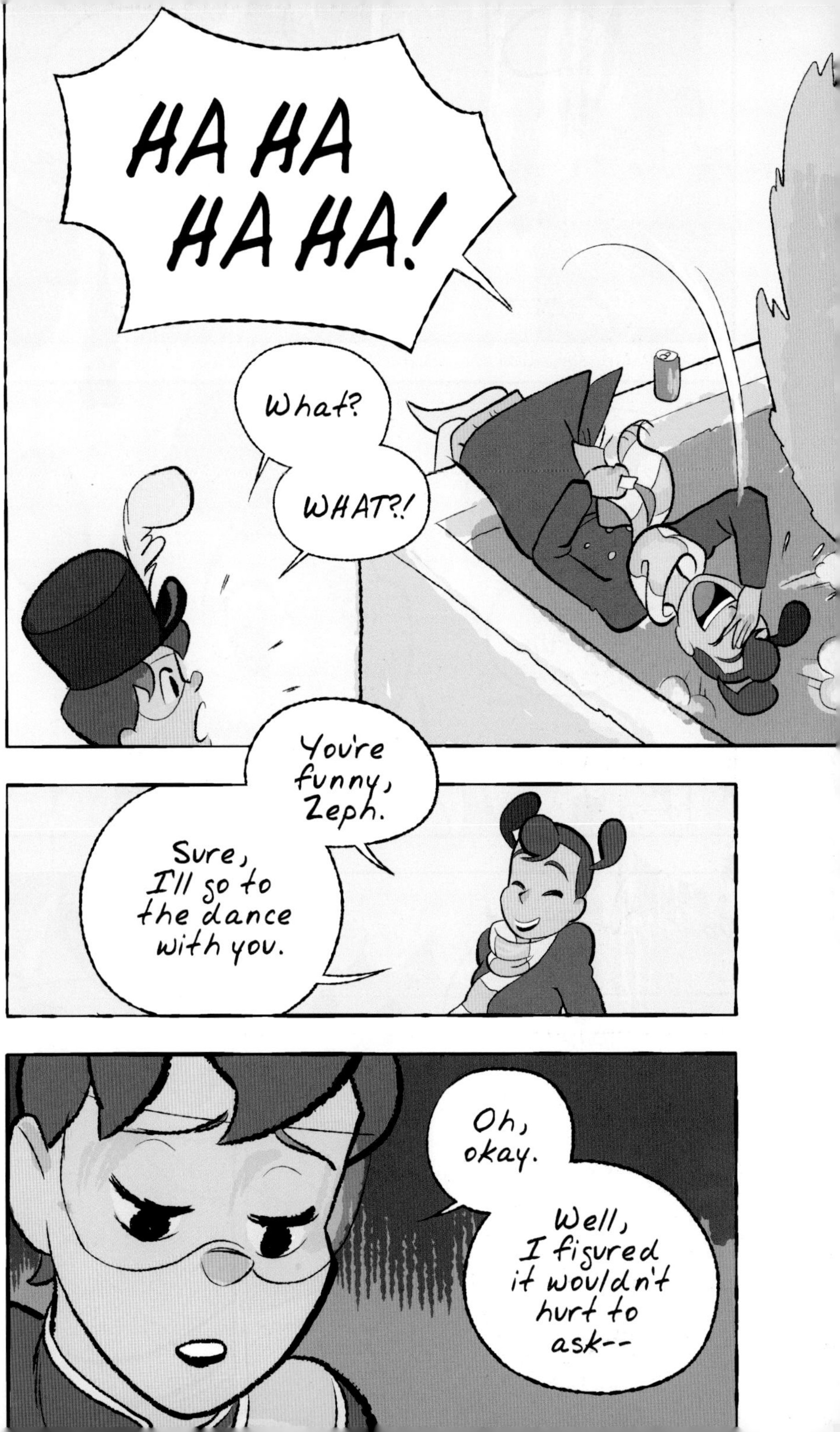
HA HA HA HA HA!
What?
WHAT?!
You're funny, Zeph.
Sure, I'll go to the dance with you.
Oh, okay.
Well, I figured it wouldn't hurt to ask--

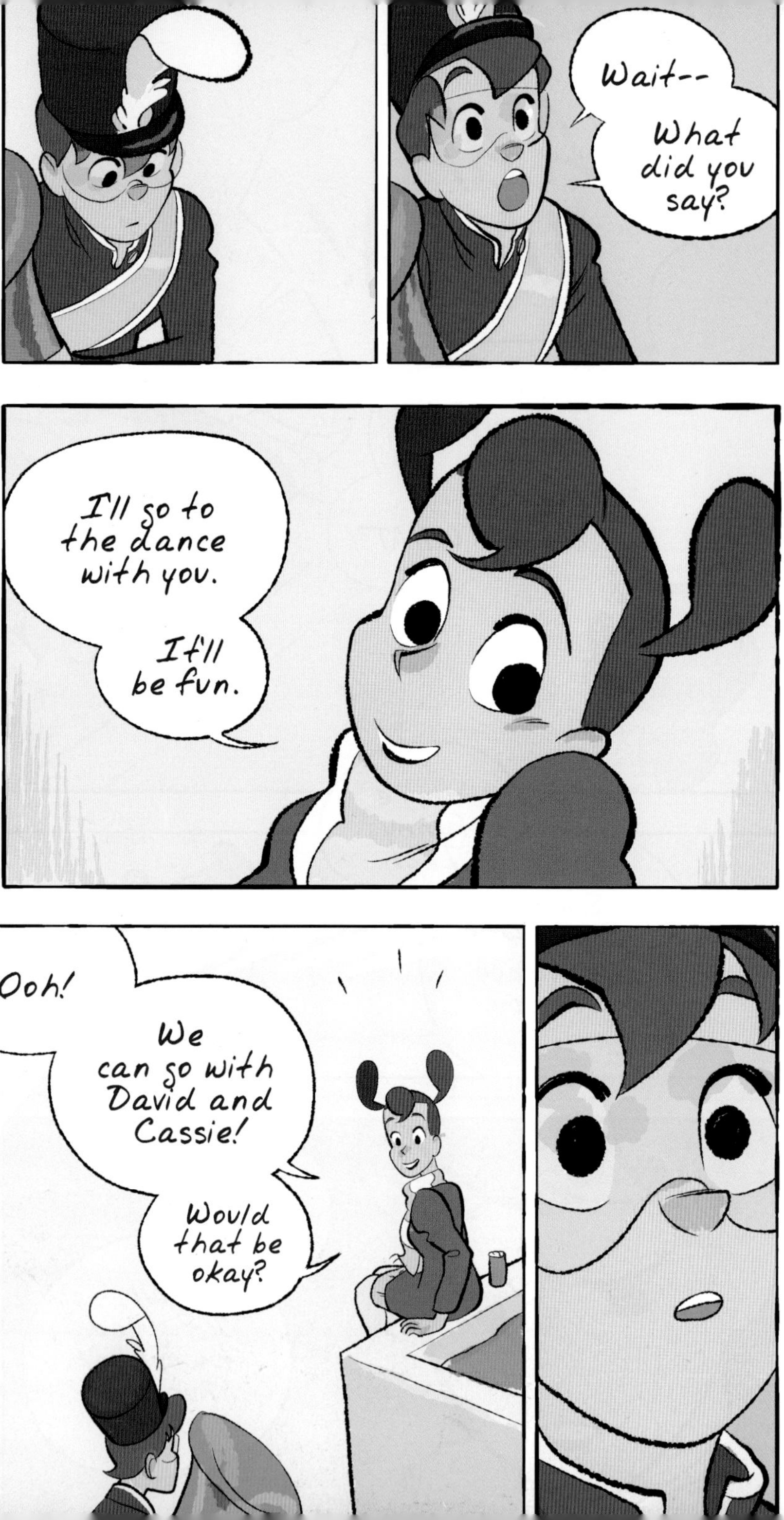
Wait--
What did you say?
I'll go to the dance with you.
It'll be fun.
Ooh!
We can go with David and Cassie!
Would that be okay?

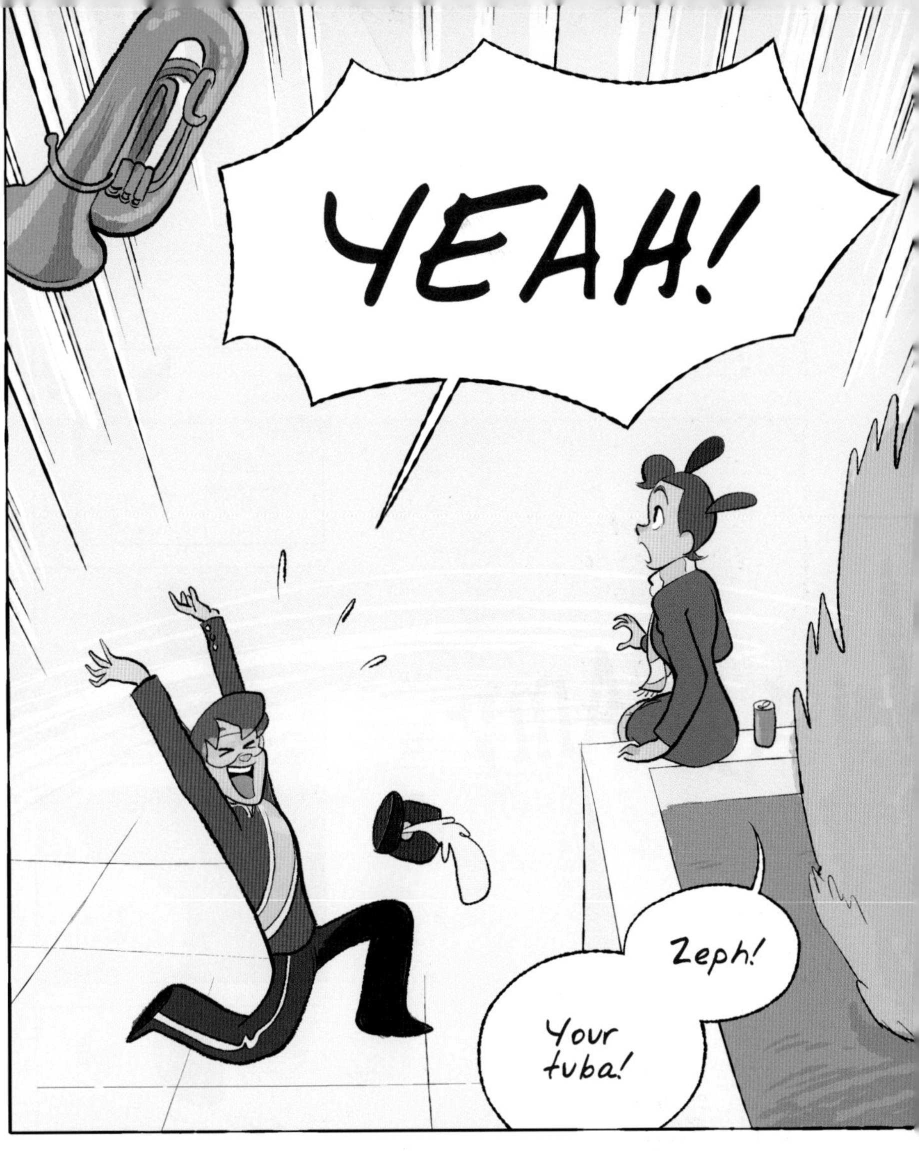
YEAH!
Zeph!
Your tuba!

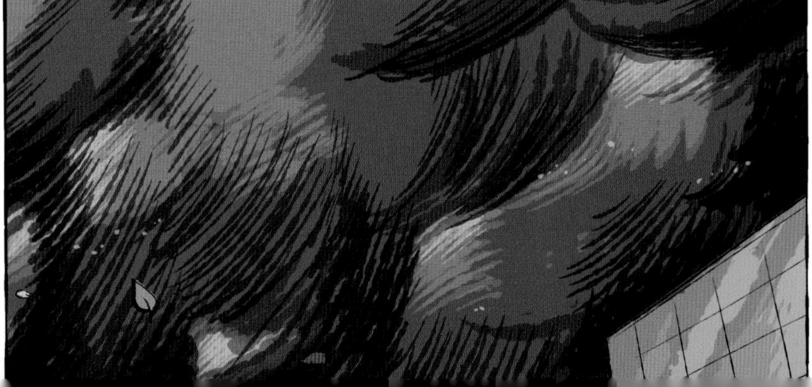

Li'l Amy

by
Stephen McCranie

My name's Amy.
I'm six years old.
This many.
I live out in deep space on a mining colony.
What do we mine, you might ask?
How should I know?
I'm only six years old!

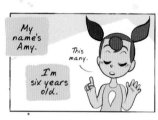

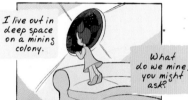

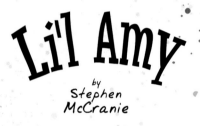

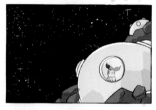

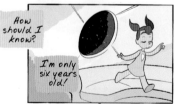

Mom, what do we mine on this mining colony anyway?
Meridium, sweetie.
Merry dee um.
Meridium.
Mary...
Meridium.
Mary had a little lamb!
Sigh...
Sweetie, stop bothering Mommy.
Why don't you go get ready for bed?
NO!
I DON'T WANNA GO TO BED!
wah!
wah!
The sooner you go to bed, the sooner you can wake up for your first day of school.
First day of school?
Amy, I've been telling you about this for like three weeks now.

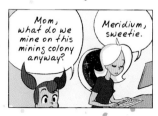

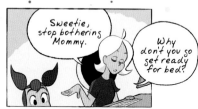

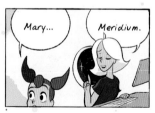

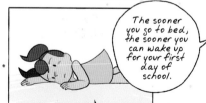

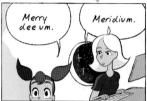

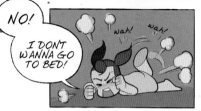

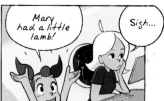

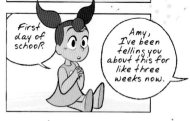

Yay!
First day of school!
First day of school!
OOF!
FOOMP!
First day of school!
Amy!
Go to bed!
The next day...
Do you want the blue dress or the pink one?
The yellow one!
Want me to curl your ponytails?
Yeah!
Wow!
I'm going to be the best dressed girl in my whole class!

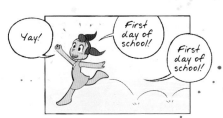

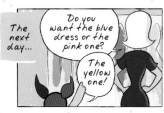

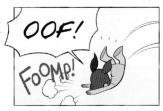

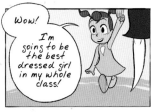

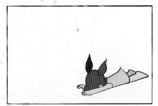

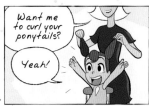

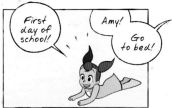

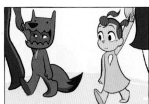

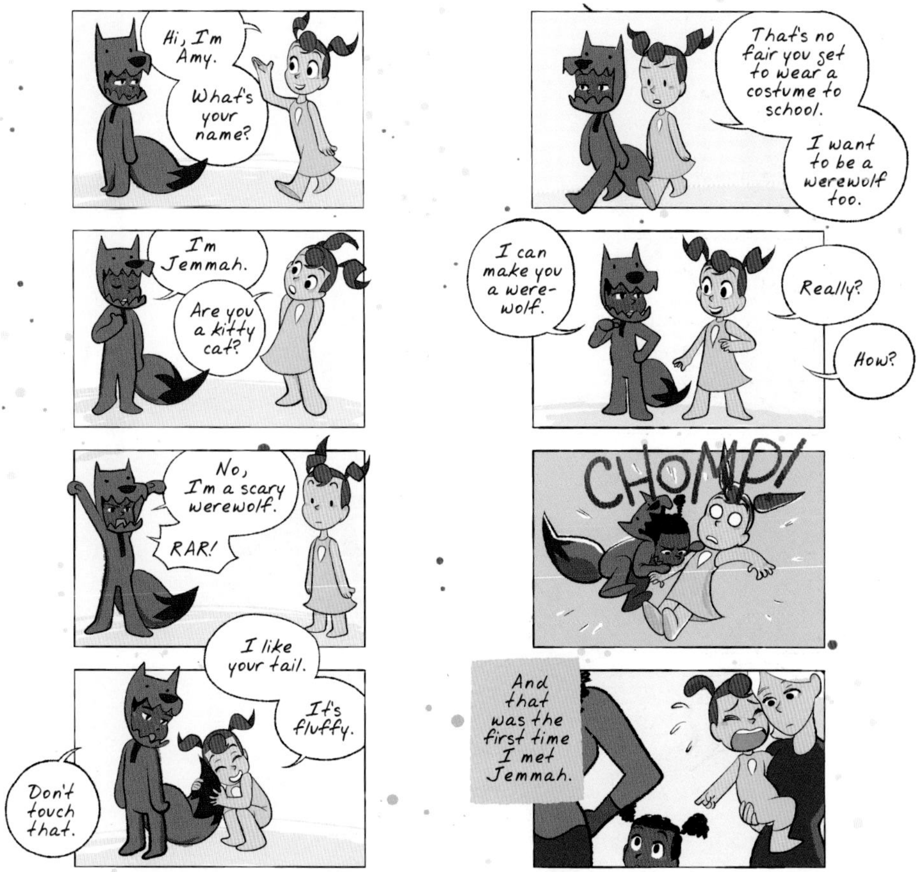
Hi, I'm Amy.
What's your name?
I'm Jemmah.
Are you a kitty cat?
No, I'm a scary werewolf.
RAR!
I like your tail.
It's fluffy.
Don't touch that.
That's no fair you get to wear a costume to school.
I want to be a werewolf too.
I can make you a were-wolf.
Really?
How?
CHOMP!
And that was the first time I met Jemmah.

MORE TITLES YOU MIGHT ENJOY

ALENA
Kim W. Andersson
Since arriving at a snobbish boarding school, Alena's been harassed every day by the lacrosse team. But Alena's best friend Josephine is not going to accept that anymore. If Alena does not fight back, then she will take matters into her own hands. There's just one problem . . . Josephine has been dead for a year.

$17.99 | ISBN 978-1-50670-215-5

ASTRID: CULT OF THE VOLCANIC MOON
Kim W. Andersson
Formerly the Galactic Coalition's top recruit, the now-disgraced Astrid is offered a special mission from her old commander. She'll prove herself worthy of another chance at becoming a Galactic Peacekeeper . . . if she can survive.

$19.99 | ISBN 978-1-61655-690-7

BANDETTE
Paul Tobin, Colleen Coover
A costumed teen burglar by the *nome d'arte* of Bandette and her group of street urchins find equal fun in both skirting and aiding the law, in this enchanting, Eisner-nominated series!

$14.99 each
Volume 1: Presto! | ISBN 978-1-61655-279-4
Volume 2: Stealers, Keepers! | ISBN 978-1-61655-668-6
Volume 3: The House of the Green Mask | ISBN 978-1-50670-219-3

BOUNTY
Kurtis Wiebe, Mindy Lee
The Gadflies were the most wanted criminals in the galaxy. Now, with a bounty to match their reputation, the Gadflies are forced to abandon banditry for a career as bounty hunters . . . 'cause if you can't beat 'em, join 'em—then rob 'em blind!

$14.99 | ISBN 978-1-50670-044-1

HEART IN A BOX
Kelly Thompson, Meredith McClaren
In a moment of post-heartbreak weakness, Emma wishes her heart away and a mysterious stranger obliges. But emptiness is even worse than grief, and Emma sets out to collect the pieces of her heart and face the cost of recapturing it.

$14.99 | ISBN 978-1-61655-694-5

HENCHGIRL
Kristen Gudsnuk
Mary Posa hates her job. She works long hours for little pay, no insurance, and worst of all, no respect. Her coworkers are jerks, and her boss doesn't appreciate her. He's also a supervillain. Cursed with a conscience, Mary would give anything to be something other than a henchgirl.

$17.99 | ISBN 978-1-50670-144-8

DARKHORSE.COM AVAILABLE AT YOUR LOCAL COMICS SHOP OR BOOKSTORE • TO FIND A COMICS SHOP IN YOUR AREA, VISIT COMICSHOPLOCATOR.COM
For more information or to order direct: •On the web: DarkHorse.com •Email: mailorder@darkhorse.com •Phone: 1-800-862-0052 Mon.–Fri. 9 AM to 5 PM Pacific Time.
Alena™, Astrid™ © Kim W. Andersson, by agreement with Grand Agency. Bandette™ © Paul Tobin and Colleen Coover. Bounty™ © Kurtis Wiebe and Mindy Lee. Heart in a Box™ © 1979 Semi-Finalist, Inc., and Meredith McClaren. Henchgirl™ © Kristen Gudsnuk. Dark Horse Books® and the Dark Horse logo are registered trademarks of Dark Horse Comics, Inc. All rights reserved. (BL 6041 P1)

THE SECRET LOVES OF GEEK GIRLS
Hope Nicholson, Margaret Atwood,
Mariko Tamaki, and more
The Secret Loves of Geek Girls is a nonfiction anthology mixing prose, comics, and illustrated stories on the lives and loves of an amazing cast of female creators.

$14.99 | ISBN 978-1-50670-099-1

THE SECRET LOVES OF GEEKS
Gerard Way, Dana Simpson, Hope Larson, and more
The follow-up to the smash hit *The Secret Loves of Geek Girls*, this brand new anthology features comic and prose stories from cartoonists and professional geeks about their most intimate, heartbreaking, and inspiring tales of love, sex, and dating. This volume includes creators of diverse genders, orientations, and cultural backgrounds.

$14.99 | ISBN 978-1-50670-473-9

MISFITS OF AVALON
Kel McDonald
Four misfit teens are reluctant recruits to save the mystical isle of Avalon. Magically empowered and directed by a talking dog, they must stop the rise of King Arthur. As they struggle to become a team, they're faced with the discovery that they may not be the good guys.

$14.99 each
Volume 1: The Queen of Air and Delinquency | ISBN 978-1-61655-538-2
Volume 2: The Ill-Made Guardian | ISBN 978-1-61655-748-5
Volume 3: The Future in the Wind | ISBN 978-1-61655-749-2

ZODIAC STARFORCE: BY THE POWER OF ASTRA
Kevin Panetta, Paulina Ganucheau
A group of teenage girls with magical powers have sworn to protect our planet against dark creatures. Known as the Zodiac Starforce, these high-school girls aren't just combating math tests—they're also battling monsters!

$12.99 | ISBN 978-1-61655-913-7

THE ADVENTURES OF SUPERHERO GIRL
Faith Erin Hicks
What if you can leap tall buildings and defeat alien monsters with your bare hands, but you buy your capes at secondhand stores and have a weakness for kittens? Faith Erin Hicks brings humor to the trials and tribulations of a young, female superhero, battling monsters both supernatural and mundane in an all-too-ordinary world.

$16.99 each | ISBN 978-1-61655-084-4
Expanded Edition | ISBN 978-1-50670-336-7

SPELL ON WHEELS
Kate Leth, Megan Levens, Marissa Louise
A road trip story. A magical revenge fantasy. A sisters-over-misters tale of three witches out to get back what was taken from them.

$14.99 | ISBN 978-1-50670-183-7

THE ONCE AND FUTURE QUEEN
Adam P. Knave, D.J. Kirkbride,
Nick Brokenshire, Frank Cvetkovic
It's out with the old myths and in with the new as a nineteen-year-old chess prodigy pulls Excalibur from the stone and becomes queen. Now, magic, romance, Fae, Merlin, and more await her!

$14.99 | ISBN 978-1-50670-250-6

DARKHORSE.COM AVAILABLE AT YOUR LOCAL COMICS SHOP OR BOOKSTORE • TO FIND A COMICS SHOP IN YOUR AREA, VISIT COMICSHOPLOCATOR.COM
For more information or to order direct: • On the web: DarkHorse.com • Email: mailorder@darkhorse.com • Phone: 1-800-862-0052 Mon.–Fri. 9 AM to 5 PM Pacific Time.

AXE COP
Malachai Nicolle, Ethan Nicolle
Bad guys, beware! Evil aliens, run for your lives! Axe Cop is here, and he's going to chop your head off! We live in a strange world, and our strange problems call for strange heroes. That's why Axe Cop is holding tryouts to build the greatest team of heroes ever assembled.

Volume 1	ISBN 978-1-59582-681-7	$14.99
Volume 2	ISBN 978-1-59582-825-5	$14.99
Volume 3	ISBN 978-1-59582-911-5	$14.99
Volume 4	ISBN 978-1-61655-057-8	$12.99
Volume 5	ISBN 978-1-61655-245-9	$14.99
Volume 6	ISBN 978-1-61655-424-8	$12.99

THE ADVENTURES OF DR. MCNINJA OMNIBUS
Christopher Hastings
He's a doctor! He's a ninja! And now, his earliest exploits are collected in one mighty omnibus volume! Featuring stories from the very beginnings of the Dr. McNinja web comic, this book offers a hefty dose of science, action, and outrageous comedy.
$24.99 | ISBN 978-1-61655-112-4

BREATH OF BONES: A TALE OF THE GOLEM
Steve Niles, Matt Santoro, Dave Wachter
A British plane crashes in a Jewish village, sparking a Nazi invasion. Using clay and mud from the river, the villagers bring to life a giant monster to battle for their freedom and future.
$14.99 | ISBN 978-1-61655-344-9

REBELS
Brian Wood, Andrea Mutti, Matthew Woodson, Ariela Kristantina, Tristan Jones
This is 1775. With the War for Independence playing out across the colonies, Seth and Mercy Abbott find their new marriage tested at every turn as the demands of the frontlines and the home front collide.

Volume 1: A Well-Regulated Militia
$24.99 | ISBN 978-1-61655-908-3

HOW TO TALK TO GIRLS AT PARTIES
Neil Gaiman, Gabriel Bá, Fábio Moon
Two teenage boys are in for a tremendous shock when they crash a party where the girls are far more than they appear!
$17.99 | ISBN 978-1-61655-955-7

NANJING: THE BURNING CITY
Ethan Young
After the bombs fell, the Imperial Japanese Army seized the Chinese capital of Nanjing. Two abandoned Chinese soldiers try to escape the city and what they'll encounter will haunt them. But in the face of horror, they'll learn that resistance and bravery cannot be destroyed.
$24.99 | ISBN 978-1-61655-752-2

THE BATTLES OF BRIDGET LEE: INVASION OF FARFALL
Ethan Young
There is no longer a generation that remembers a time before the Marauders invaded Earth. Bridget Lee, an ex–combat medic now residing at the outpost Farfall, may be the world's last hope. But Bridget will need to overcome her own fears before she can save her people.
$10.99 | ISBN 978-1-50670-012-0

DARKHORSE.COM AVAILABLE AT YOUR LOCAL COMICS SHOP OR BOOKSTORE | TO FIND A COMICS SHOP IN YOUR AREA, CALL 1-888-266-4226
For more information or to order direct: • On the web: DarkHorse.com • Email: mailorder@darkhorse.com • Phone: 1-800-862-0052 Mon.–Fri. 9 AM to 5 PM Pacific Time.

Axe Cop ™ © Ethan Nicolle and Malachai Nicolle. The Adventures of Dr. McNinja ™ © Chris Hastings. Breath of Bones ™ © Steve Niles, Matt Santoro, and Dave Wachter. How to Talk to Girls at Parties ™ © Neil Gaiman. Nanjing ™, The Battles of Bridget Lee ™ © Ethan Young. Rebels ™ © Brian Wood and Andrea Mutti. Dark Horse Books® and the Dark Horse logo are registered trademarks of Dark Horse Comics, Inc. All rights reserved. (BL 6051 P1)

HARROW COUNTY
Cullen Bunn, Tyler Crook
Emmy always knew that the woods surrounding her home crawled with ghosts and monsters. But on the eve of her eighteenth birthday, she learns that she is connected to these creatures—and to the land itself—in a way she never imagined.

$14.99 each
Volume 1: Countless Haints   ISBN 978-1-61655-780-5
Volume 2: Twice Told   ISBN 978-1-61655-900-7
Volume 3: Snake Doctor   ISBN 978-1-50670-071-7
Volume 4: Family Tree   ISBN 978-1-50670-141-7
Volume 5: Abandoned   ISBN 978-1-50670-190-5

SPACE-MULLET!
Daniel Warren Johnson
Ex–Space Marine Jonah and his copilot Alphius rove the galaxy, trying to get by. Drawn into one crazy adventure after another, they forge a crew of misfits into a family and face the darkest parts of the universe together.

$17.99 | ISBN 978-1-61655-912-0

EI8HT
Mike Johnson, Rafael Albuquerque
Welcome to the Meld, an inhospitable dimension in time where a chrononaut finds himself trapped. With no memory or feedback from the team of scientists that sent him, he can't count on anything but his heart and a stranger's voice to guide him to his destiny.

$17.99 | ISBN 978-1-61655-637-2

MUHAMMAD ALI
Sybille Titeux, Amazing Ameziane
Celebrating the life of the glorious athlete who metamorphosed from Cassius Clay to become a three-time heavyweight boxing legend, activist, and provocateur, Muhammad Ali is not only a titan in the world of sports but in the world itself, he dared to be different and to challenge and defy. Witness what made Ali different, what made him cool, what made him the Greatest.

$19.99 | ISBN 978-1-50670-318-3

THE FIFTH BEATLE: THE BRIAN EPSTEIN STORY
Vivek J. Tiwary, Andrew C. Robinson, Kyle Baker
The untold true story of Brian Epstein, the visionary manager who discovered and guided the Beatles to unprecedented international stardom. *The Fifth Beatle* is an uplifting, tragic, and ultimately inspirational human story about the struggle to overcome the odds..

$19.99 | ISBN 978-1-61655-256-5
Expanded Edition $14.99 | ISBN 978-1-61655-835-2

THE USAGI YOJIMBO SAGA
Stan Sakai
When a peace came upon Japan and samurai warriors found themselves suddenly unemployed and many of these ronin turned to banditry, found work, or traveled the musha shugyo to hone their spiritual and martial skills. Whether they took the honest road or the crooked path, the ronin were less than welcome. Such is the tale of Usagi Yojimbo.

$24.99 each
Volume 1   ISBN 978-1-61655-609-9
Volume 2   ISBN 978-1-61655-610-5
Volume 3   ISBN 978-1-61655-611-2
Volume 4   ISBN 978-1-61655-612-9

Volume 5   ISBN 978-1-61655-613-6
Volume 6   ISBN 978-1-61655-614-3
Volume 7   ISBN 978-1-61655-615-0
Legends   ISBN 978-1-50670-323-7

DARKHORSE.COM AVAILABLE AT YOUR LOCAL COMICS SHOP OR BOOKSTORE | TO FIND A COMICS SHOP IN YOUR AREA, CALL 1-888-266-4226
For more information or to order direct: • On the web: DarkHorse.com • Email: mailorder@darkhorse.com • Phone: 1-800-862-0052 Mon.–Fri. 9 AM to 5 PM Pacific Time.

DARK HORSE COMICS

EI8HT™ © Rafael Albuquerque and Mike Johnson. Harrow County™ © Cullen Bunn and Tyler Crook. Space-Mullet!™ © Daniel Warren Johnson. Muhammad Ali™ © ÉDITIONS DU LOMBARD (DARGAUD-LOMBARD S.A.). by Amazing Améziane, Sybille Titeux de la Croix. The Fifth Beatle™ © Tiwary Entertainment Group Ltd. Produced under license by M Press. Usagi Yojimbo™ © Stan Sakai. Dark Horse Books® and the Dark Horse logo are registered trademarks of Dark Horse Comics, Inc. All rights reserved. (BL 6051 P2)